P9-CDE-790

THE ESSENTIAL
Stephen King

**A RANKING OF
THE GREATEST NOVELS,
SHORT STORIES, MOVIES,
AND OTHER CREATIONS
OF THE WORLD'S MOST
POPULAR WRITER**

STEPHEN J. SPIGNESI

New Page Books
A Division of Career Press, Inc.
Franklin Lakes, NJ

The Essential Stephen King

Typeset by John J. O'Sullivan

Cover design by Lu Rossman/Digi Dog Design

Printed in the U.S.A. by Book-mart Press

To order this title, please call toll-free 1-800-CAREER-1 (NJ and Canada: 201-848-0310) to order using VISA or MasterCard, or for further information on books from Career Press.

The Career Press, Inc., 3 Tice Road, PO Box 687
Franklin Lakes, NJ 07417
www.careerpress.com
www.newpagebooks.com

Library of Congress Cataloging-in-Publication Data
Spignesi, Stephen J.
    The essential Stephen King : a ranking of the greatest novels, short stories, movies, and other creations of the world's most popular writer. / by Stephen J. Spignesi.
      p. cm.
    Includes bibliographical references and index.
    ISBN 1-56414-485-2 (hc.)
    1. King, Stephen, 1947—Criticism and interpretation. 2. Horror tales, American—
can—
    History and criticism. 3. Horror films—History and criticism. I. Title.

PS3561.I483 Z873 2001
    813'.54—dc21   2001030209

Dedication

This is in memory of
Dominick Spignesi.
I have not forgotten the face of my father.

Learn to do magic like me and we will drive to Princeton
in an old Ford with four retread skins and a loose
manifold that boils up the graphite stink of fresh-
cooked exhaust we will do hexes with Budweiser
pentagrams and old Diamond matchboxes

—from "The Hardcase Speaks"
A poem by Stephen King
December 1971

The place where you made your stand never really mattered
...only that you were there, and still on your feet.

—from *The Stand*

You can't be careful on a skateboard, man.

—from *It*

Acknowledgments

Special thanks, fond appreciation, and a big round of applause go out to the following kind souls, all of whom contributed in some way, either physically or psychically, to *The Essential Stephen King*...

Pam Spignesi

Stephen King

Charlie Fried

Jim Cole: (not only for his essay, but also for the Patrick Hockstetter tip).

John White

George Beahm

Tyson Blue

Bev Vincent

Dr. Michael Collings

Marsha DeFilippo

Mike Lewis

Ron Fry & everyone at Career Press/New Page Books

Stanley Wiater

Kevin Quigley & Charnel House

Dave Hinchberger & The Overlook Connection

Stu Tinker & Bettsbooks

Mick Garris

Frank Darabont

Michele Ballard

Justin Brooks

Paula Guran & the late, great *DarkEcho* Newsletter

Benoit Demois

Christopher Golden

Hank Wagner

Chris and Wanda Cavalier

Valerie Barnes

The SKEMERs

Lilja's Library

Noah Eisenhandler, Esq.

Andrew Rausch

Dr. Michael Luchini

Simon & Schuster & *simonsays.com*

Carter Spignesi

Lee & Frank Mandato

The University of New Haven & the UNH Library

www.stephenking.com

Anthony (The Antman!) Schwethelm

The fine folks at eBay

Victor & Rosalie Montequin

David B. Silva & *Hellnotes*

John Thornburn

Google.com

4Filmmakers.com

The Internet Movie Database (*imdb.com*)

Claire Gerus

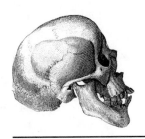

Contents

PRELUDE

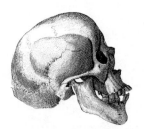

How Stephen King's Fans Feel About His Work

Please read this first (even though no one ever reads Introductions). In December 2000, the following question was posted on the Usenet Stephen King newsgroup *alt.books.stephen-king*:

What do you all read...the hardcovers or paperbacks?

Within minutes the following response was posted:

Stephen King = Hardcover

All others = Paperback

Before we get started, I might as well admit that I am probably the wrong guy to be writing this book. Why? Because I am a passionate Stephen King fan and, thus, you will not find much negative bias here regarding King's works.

In fact, the most difficult thing I have ever had to do in my career so far was pick 100—and only 100—Stephen King works for ranking and review. Until the day I turned this book in, I was rereading, rearranging, reconsidering, and rethinking my choices and where each work belonged on the list.

☠ 8 ☠

Now, I think I'm happy with the results ... I think.

Sometimes I would just move a story or novel up a notch because I appreciated it so much more after rereading it. Other times, I moved things down because they were not as impressive as I had remembered them to be.

In any case, I am finished with second-guessing. The list is the list. For better or worse. I'm sure you will not agree with all my choices. So be it. But do know that I tried to be fair and rational, but in the end, sometimes I just really liked a piece and promoted it for no other reason. Keep in mind what King told Bryant Gumbel on *The Early Show* in March 2001 when the interview shifted to King's thoughts on retiring: "I wouldn't publish stuff that I thought was substandard." Also keep in mind that you would be hard pressed to name another American writer about whom a book like this could be written. If a writer is as prolific as King, he or she may not be as talented. If a writer is profoundly talented, he or she may not be as prolific. One writer that does come to mind is Isaac Asimov. But the list of possibilities is darned small, thus emphasizing the special qualities of King's work.

> Most forms of human creativity have one aspect in common: the attempt to give some sense to the various impressions, emotions, experiences, and actions that fill our lives, and thereby to give some meaning and value to our existence.
>
> —Victor Weisskopf

The Essential Stephen King is a very important book.

No, not because I wrote it (wiseass), but because *Stephen King* is a very important American writer, and this book looks at what I consider to be his 100 greatest works from the past forty years. The earliest work reviewed in this book dates from 1960 ("The Thing at the Bottom of the Well"); the most recent, 2001 ("All That You Love Will Be Carried Away" and *Dreamcatcher*).

Counting my two *Stephen King Quiz Books*, this book—*The Essential Stephen King*—is my fifth, and probably the last, book I will write about the work of Stephen King.

Putting aside the two quiz books though, (which were fun spin-offs of my other books) the other two of my previous books about King's writings – *The Complete Stephen King Encyclopedia* and *The Lost Work of Stephen King*—required intensive research and enormous amounts of reading.

The Essential Stephen King required comparable amounts of study, but the book's primary objective also added *another* element to my workload: the comparative judgment of King's works. The premise of *The Essential Stephen King* is for me to rank Stephen King's one hundred greatest works, in order, from 1 to 100.

The idea of ranking King's writings came to me after completing my book *The Italian 100*, in which I ranked the most influential Italians and Italian-Americans in world history. It occurred to me that Stephen King's enormous body of work lent itself to this kind of evaluation, simply because not every artist hits a home run every time they come up to bat. And also because Stephen King's bedazzling prolificacy over the past quarter century has resulted in a catalog of works that are mostly hidden to his average fan.

Hidden?

"But Steve, How can that be?" I hear you asking. "King's books are all over the bookstores and the best-seller lists (and lately, the Internet), and the movie adaptations of his tales hit the cineplexes on a fairly regular basis."

All true.

Stephen King has *officially* published over three dozen novels, a score of novellas, and more than 100 short stories. He has also done two books of nonfiction, *Danse Macabre* (1981) and *On Writing* (2000) and a handful of oddities, like the comic book *Creepshow*, bound volumes of his screenplays, and the e-books *Riding the Bullet* and *The Plant*.

Yet the master pool of Stephen King writings from which I drew the top 100 consists of an astonishing 550 or so individual works, which included rare and unpublished works, as well. This treasure trove of creative output includes novels, novellas, short stories, screenplays, poetry, nonfiction essays, Introductions, Afterwords, album liner notes, letters to newspapers and magazines, recipes, and even crossword puzzle clues.

Like I said ... King's output bespeaks an astonishing level of creativity that is also, in many, many instances, literature of the highest order.

King is the Poe, Twain, Dickens, and Salinger of our time. Personally, I find King's work to be more accessible than Poe; more exciting than Twain; less long-winded than Dickens; and considerably more prolific than Salinger. A 2000 review on *Indigo.com* included the following trenchant praise:

> Two years ago, upon the release of King's *Bag of Bones*, people started to say that the guy could write. You know, really write—not like [John] Grisham or [Dean] Koontz, but like [John] Irving or [Don] DeLillo. Robert McCrum said in London's *The Observer* that King has "a well-focused literary sensibility. He is not only a much better writer than he's willing to admit, but his work anatomizes, with folksy charm, the social fabric of small-town American life. ... It also plumbs, with unnerving accuracy, the hopes and fears of an entire nation." Even Mordecai Richler went on record in a review of his own to say that King had been unfairly overlooked, "punished for being too accessible."

Even more intriguing is this September 2000 suggestion by *Citynet* writer Andrew Ervin in his essay "Nobel Oblige" that Stephen King be awarded a Nobel Prize for Literature (and he's serious):

> Because of his immense popularity, King has earned the ire of literary elitists the world over. While popularity doesn't necessarily equal greatness (see Crichton, Michael), one of the many wonders of democracy is that every once in a while, the masses get it right. King's genius can be found in many places, particularly in his ability to take the metaphorical and make it literal. It's a literary device that, in our time, only Franz Kafka and Dr. Seuss managed to pull off so well. ... Just this once, the Academy should bestow the award upon someone people actually read.

King is—at one time—a popular, paperback-at-the-beach writer; a writer respected by academia and studied at the high school and college levels; and a "collectible" writer whose works are also published in gorgeous, elaborately-designed limited editions often costing hundreds of dollars or more.

Stephen King is popular with the average reader looking for a few hours respite. He is highly regarded by the many professors of American literature and fellow writers who are all hard-wired to recognize fine writing. He is sought after by book collectors, some of who have collections valued in the six-figure range and who are often dubbed "supercollectors" for their penchant for completeness and their willingness to pay whatever it costs to add to their Stephen King collection.

If Stephen King were not as prolific as he has been for the past 25-plus years, a book like *The Essential Stephen King* would not be possible. There simply would not be enough works to choose from, and a book looking at less than one hundred works would not be commercially feasible. Perhaps a magazine or journal article could be written, but a book ranking 100 works (or people, as in the case of my *Italian 100*) requires an enormous bibliographic or historical landscape to use as a basis for evaluation. And Stephen King's body of work is extensive enough to warrant such a critical analysis and deconstruction.

But there is something perilous about presuming to know which of an artist's works are better than others. I know this, and it was with some trepidation that I decided to take on the task of ranking King's 100 greatest works. I knew that I would piss off some fans, frustrate others, and that my conclusions would be debated and contested for as long as the book is in print.

A fan's opinion is usually emotion-based. A fan will state with conviction that he or she "loves" a novel or short story or movie, yet if pushed to explain why, they will often fall back on emotional platitudes that do not really explain their passion for the work. "I just love it," is often the vague response to a request for an explanation.

But "favorite" doesn't always mean "best" and, as fragile, indefinable, and ethereal art is, the creation of art is a *craft* and thus, the materials and tools needed to produce a work of art can be identified, evaluated, and, yes, *ranked*.

I tried to use specific criteria to evaluate the work of Stephen King and, yes, even though the judgment of these criteria is mine and mine alone, these are still effective parameters with which to judge individual works.

My criteria included:

- An exciting, irresistible storyline.
- Memorable, intriguing, and above all, honest characters.
- The beauty, grace, and power of King's use of language.
- Pulse-pounding suspense and a palpable sense of fear.
- An engaging narrative voice.

☠ Humor and wit.

☠ The significance of the work's themes.

In addition to these basic guidelines, though, I also factored in whether or not I felt an intangible appeal emanating from the work; a visceral "something" that just made the work so much fun to read that I couldn't stop turning pages. This delicate, nameless, and compelling allure of the "essence" of a work allowed me some slack in judging the other elements of the piece in question.

Please do not misunderstand the purpose of this book: I will not provide detailed plot summaries of King's novels, short stories, and essays. No synopsis can do judgement to the vision — and the execution of that vision—that Stephen King had for each tale or piece. Rather, I will try to place each work in a context and highlight what is best about it and why it belongs where it does on my Top 100 list. But as with any attempt to quantify the unquantifiable, the opinions expressed in this book are mine and mine alone, are defiantly subjective, and may or may not jibe with your ideas about Stephen King's work. Sorry, but that's just the way it is.

That said, though, you will find that, paradoxically, I am a little more expansive when it comes to talking about some of the short stories and short essays than I am for the novels. The reason for this is simple: space. This book contains approximately 130,000 words. I allowed a thousand words or so for each of the "Top 100" essays and there is no way I could do justice to a novel's plot in that small a space. Short stories, on the other hand, lend themselves to a succinct summary and so I sometimes talk at length about a short story's plotline, while treating the novels differently. I hope you do not find this somewhat schizo appproach too jarring.

So with all that said, I will keep my concluding remarks short and sweet.

1. Stephen King: I'm a big fan. (But you probably figured that one out already.)
2. Stephen King is a far better writer than he is perceived to be by many elitist critics and academics.
3. Stephen King is one of the most important and influential writers of the 20th century.
4. The day is coming (it may even already be here) when literary elitists who delight in dismissing genre fiction as drek will realize that Stephen King may be known as a horror writer, but, in reality, has far more mainstream work than genre. Much of his work will stand the test of time. Ultimately, it will be viewed as terrific American Literature, which it most definitely is.

Now let's move on to the essential work of one of the true creative, literary giants of the 20th century. (And if reading through this book makes you want to go back and re-read some (or all) of King's works, don't say I didn't warn you!)

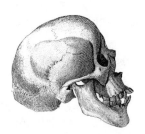

What You'll Find in Each Chapter

—Stephen J. Spignesi

January 2001

I followed a template while writing about each of the top 100 Stephen King works, and here is what I used as my blueprint, with a brief explanation of what to expect from each section. (**Note:** The 100 works reviewed in *The Essential Stephen King* cover a time span ranging from 1960, when King was 13 years old, through 2001, with King now 54 years old.)

- ☠ **Ranking:** This is where I believe the work ranks on the top 100 listing of Stephen King's works.
- ☠ **Title.**
- ☠ **Date:** This is the date of first publication, as well as the date of subsequent publication in a revised version. (For instance, *The Stand* has both dates listed, the original 1978 publication, and the unexpurgated edition in 1990. *The*

Plant has *five* dates listed; some short stories get the same treatment.)

- ✖ **Quote:** This is a brief, pithy extract from the work that I believe perfectly sets the stage for the story King goes on to tell.

- ✖ **Why it made the top 100:** In this section I discuss the work, including why the work made it into the top 100; notable instances in the work of writing excellence, and connections with other King works and/or King's life.

- ✖ **C. V.:** This heading ("C. V.") is an homage to Stephen King's use of this acronym (which stands for "Curriculum Vitae") in *On Writing*. I wanted to indicate that I would be providing a "C. V." of the work being discussed, i.e. a summary of the story's story, its history, etc.

- ✖ **Main characters:** The primary characters whose stories are told in the tale, as well as certain people King mentions in the work (even if they do not actually appear in the narrative).

- ✖ **Did you know?** Something unusual or little-known about the work being discussed.

- ✖ **The King speaks:** If King said something specific about the work, I tried to cite a remark or two that helps further illuminate the novel, story, or essay.

- ✖ **What I really liked about it:** A specific element or overall manifest appeal of the work that makes it memorable to me personally.

- ✖ **Film adaptations:** Movie versions of the work, with the occasional commentary.

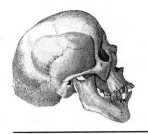

It
(1986)

The clown seized his arm.
And George saw the clown's face change.
What he saw then was terrible enough to make his worst imaginings of the thing in the cellar look like sweet dreams; what he saw destroyed his sanity in one clawing stroke.

Why *It* belongs in the number 1 spot:

It is more than just a novel.

I know, I know...that sounds like fan hyperbole, but truth be told, *It* is undeniably a contemporary literature *event*.

I remember finishing reading *It* and feeling the way I did when I turned the last page of Dickens's *Great Expectations*: unabashed awe at the storytelling talents of the author.

It is not only one of King's longest works (only the uncut *The Stand* is longer and then only by a few thousand words), but *It* is the book I and many other King researchers and fans consider to be his *magnum opus*. It is the greatest manifestation of his many narrative gifts, and the book that may very well be the definitive, quintessential "Stephen King" novel—if we make the questionable leap that such a thing can even be defined.

Pepperdine English professor and Stephen King authority Dr. Michael Collings feels that *It* and *The Stand* are interchangeable as holders of the number 1 spot on the list of King's top 100 works. He told me that he considers both novels "contemporary epics" (and, he specified, "in the true, literary sense of the term, not the facile commercial sense") and admitted to now and then surrendering to this belief and stating that *both* novels are his "top pick."

I decided to grant *It* the hallowed rank of number 1, however, because I believe wholeheartedly that the novel is a literary performance of the highest caliber; yes, even more accomplished than *The Stand*.

In his gargantuan epic, King juggles multiple characters, parallel and overlapping timelines, a ghoul's parade of monsters, plus several complex sociocultural themes. These include childhood and coming of age, child abuse, spousal abuse, homophobia, bigotry, the nature of existence, the eternal nature of good and evil, and the power of faith, trust, and love.

Longtime King fans (King calls them his "Constant Readers") can intuitively sense when Stephen King was in "the zone" (not the Dead Zone!) while writing a specific work. The story seems to emanate a narrative confidence and flow that seems to transcend the mere words with which it is being told. I have often described this experience as being pulled through the book; being dragged through the story at breakneck speed; the tale being absorbed by the brain almost by osmosis, seemingly without actually reading the words. This is a feeble way of describing a transcendent experience, but I think you Constant Readers have an understanding of this phenomenon. It happens with *The Stand*, *The Shining*, *'Salem's Lot*, *Misery*, *The Green Mile*, *Pet Sematary*, and many other works, but never more so than with *It*.

King was in the aforementioned zone when he wrote *It* (as I am sure J. R. R. Tolkien was likewise inspired when he wrote his *The Lord of the Rings* trilogy) and he has never been better. You want proof? In lieu of rereading the entire novel (which King fans have been known to do on a regular basis...likewise, *The Stand*), open *It* anywhere, and read an excerpt for a taste of just how good Stephen King can be.

The story told in *It* is truly epic. The haunted town of Derry, Maine has a dark soul. In 1958, seven friends—dubbed The Losers Club—fight an apocalyptic battle with It, a monster from "outside" who has been feeding on Derry's children in 27-year cycles for centuries. It is gravely wounded in the 1958 battle and returns to its subterranean pit beneath the town to heal. The Losers promise to return to Derry if It ever resurfaces and, in 1985, they must come together to honor their vow and try and defeat and destroy It for the final time.

King confidently interweaves the dual stories of all seven Losers, plus the stories of an array of myriad secondary characters, using only italic typeface to indicate flashbacks to 1958, all the while managing to keep everyone's story clear in the reader's mind at all times. It—*It*—is truly a virtuoso performance.

I do not recommend *It* to first-time King readers. The novel is daunting and may scare off readers who are not used to novels over 50,000 words, let alone 550,000 or so words. It requires effort and concentration, yet it pays off in amazing ways, and thus, *It* should be "prepared for," for lack of a better term. I usually suggest newcomers to King begin with something more accessible like *The Dead Zone* or *'Salem's Lot*; then move on to *The Shining* and *The Stand*; then to the stories in *Skeleton Crew*; and then, finally, to *It*. They can then go back and fill in the holes in their Stephen King reading list, but by that time they will have experienced a healthy, heaping dose of Stephen King's imaginative powers and storytelling genius.

Both scholars and fans now perceive *It* alike as the completion of the "monster" phase of King's career as a novelist. From *It* on, for the most part, King has focused on the "monster *within*" (as opposed to from the outside). Such works include *Misery*, *The Dark Half*, *Gerald's Game*, *Dolores Claiborne*, *Rose Madder*, and other diverse works; in addition to novels that ponder the existence of God and his involvement (or lack thereof) in human events, as in *Desperation*, *The Green Mile*, and others. The Mummy, the Werewolf, and the other classic denizens of the horror genre are of less interest to King in his post-*It* works. *It* may be his final word on childhood and its mythic hold on the adult. There will be child characters in later works, but *It* marks a turning point in King's treatment of childhood: We get the sense that the underlying message at the conclusion of *It* is that childhood can once again be remembered with nostalgia, rather than fear.

So there you have it: I consider *It* the best thing Stephen King has ever written. "So far."

☠ **C. V.** ☠

Main Characters

Bill Denbrough, Ben Hanscom, Eddie Kaspbrak, Beverly Marsh, Mike Hanlon, Richie Tozier, Stanley Uris, Pennywise the Clown.

Did You Know?

Stephen King's middle name is "Edwin," and in *It*, there is character named "Eddie King," described as "a bearded man whose spectacles were almost as fat as his gut." Eddie King was one of the guys who were playing poker in the Sleepy Silver Dollar the day Claude Heroux went nuts and killed everyone in the game. Eddie King's demise was particularly grisly. When Claude began his rampage, Eddie tried to flee but ended up falling out of his chair and landing flat on his back on the floor. Claude straddled King (who was screaming to Claude that he had just gotten married a month ago) and buried an axe in Eddie King's

The King Speaks

"Sometime in the summer of 1981 I realized that I had to write about the troll under the bridge or leave him—IT—forever. Part of me cried to let it go. But part of me cried for the chance; did more than cry; it *demanded*. I remember sitting on the porch, smoking, asking myself if I had really gotten old enough to be afraid to *try*, to just jump in and drive fast.

I got up off the porch, went into my study, cranked up some rock 'n' roll, and started to write the book. I knew it would be long, but I didn't know *how* long. I found myself remembering that part of *The Hobbit* where Bilbo Baggins marvels at how way may lead on to way; you may leave your front door and think you are only strolling down your front walk, but at the end of your walk is the street, and you may turn left or you may turn right, but either way there will be another street, another avenue, and roads, and highways, and a whole world." [Note: King was 34 when he started writing *It*; he was 38 when he finished it.]

—From "How *IT* Happened" (1986)

ample belly. Claude then wiggled the axe out, and swung again, this time putting an end to Eddie's screaming, and to Eddie. "Claude Heroux wasn't done with him, however; he began to chop King up like kindling-wood."

What I Really Liked About It

The flawless evocation of childhood summers, plus a slew of too-many-to-mention elements of the novel that I greatly enjoyed. There really isn't anything I did not like about *It*. In fact, like *The Lord of the Rings*, I actually wished it were longer! Perhaps we can hope for *It: The Second Millennium* one of these years?

Film Adaptations

Stephen King's It (TV-miniseries, 1990); starring Tim Curry, Richard Thomas, Annette O'Toole, John Ritter, Tim Reid, Harry Anderson, Dennis Christopher, Richard Masur, Olivia Hussey, Seth Green; directed by Tommy Lee Wallace; screenplay by Lawrence D. Cohen (Part 1) and Lawrence D. Cohen and Tommy Lee Wallace (Part 2). (Grade: B+.)

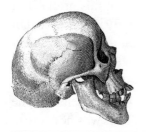

NUMBER 2

The Stand
(1978, 1990)

Randall Flagg, the dark man, strode south on US 51, listening to the nightsounds that pressed close on both sides of this narrow road that would take him sooner or later out of Idaho and into Nevada.

Why it made the top 10:

Even though I think *It* is a "better" book, *The Stand*—amazingly in both the original and unexpurgated versions—still retains its exalted status as the fans' favorite Stephen King novel.

The Stand holds a unique place in Stephen King's body of work: It is his *first epic*.

The Dark Tower and *The Talisman* and, I suppose, even *It*, would follow, but after *Carrie*, *'Salem's Lot*, and *The Shining*, all of an easily identified (and, unfortunately, pigeonholed) genre, King published the multigenre *The Stand* and turned fans' expectations for his work on its head. Here was a science fiction/horror/fantasy tale told in a voluminous 823 pages in hardcover (complete with the only official author photo of Stephen King holding a lit cigarette) that was as multifaceted in locale and character as *The Shining* was the exact opposite.

The story is now the stuff of legend: A superflu wipes out 99.4 percent of the world's population. The survivors (all of whom are somehow immune to the flu, known as Captain Trips) are psychically called to either the light (the centenarian Mother Abagail in Nebraska) or the dark (Randall Flagg in Las Vegas). There are fascinating characters galore in the novel and God has a cameo in the story's confrontational finale.

King has always been intrigued with the question of the existence/presence of an empirical evil in the affairs of mankind, and Randall Flagg (and many of his "RF" characters throughout King's entire canon) is the manifestation of this primal evil reality. In *The Stand*, we first meet Mr. Flagg and learn that not only is he legion, but that he is indestructible (as the coda to the uncut edition of *The Stand* unequivocally tells us).

King is at the peak of his creative powers in *The Stand*. Understanding how important *The Stand* is relative to King's complete body of work, it makes total sense that he would want his readers to experience his full vision of the story. This is why he chose to release the uncut version of the epic a dozen years after the expurgated edition was published.

☠ C. V. ☠

 ## Main Characters

Nick Andros, Nadine Cross, Tom Cullen, Mother Abagail Freemantle, Randall Flagg, Frannie Goldsmith, Lloyd Henreid, Harold Lauder, Stu Redman, Trashcan Man, Larry Underwood, The Kid.

 ## Did You Know?

When Stephen King completed writing *The Stand* in 1977, he did not have the power he does now. Today, King can publish two hardcovers at once (*Desperation* and *The Regulators*); six individual novellas in a row (*The Green Mile*); a novel and novella available only on the Internet (*Riding the Bullet* and *The Plant*), and everything sells. *Everything sells.* Publishers don't balk anymore or fear Stephen King overexposure. Back in 1977, it was a different story. King was required to cut almost 150,000 words from the manuscript of *The Stand* (bringing it down to around 400,000 words) before Doubleday would publish it. King reissued the novel with the cut material restored (plus some minor editorial changes) in 1990 as *The Stand: The Complete & Uncut Edition*. (See my *Complete Stephen King Encyclopedia* for details on the restored characters and scenes.)

The King Speaks

"I wrote 'A dark man with no face' and then glanced up and saw that grisly little motto again: 'Once in every generation a plague will fall among them.' And that was that. I spent the next two years writing an apparently endless book called *The Stand*. It got to the point where I began describing it to friends as my own little Vietnam, because I kept telling myself that in another hundred pages or so I would begin to see the light at the end of the tunnel."

—From an interview with Mel Allen
in the March 1979 issue of *Yankee* magazine

What I Really Liked About It

The epic, Tolkienesque quality to the narrative (set in an instantly recognizable American landscape); the characters of Mother Abagail and Frannie Goldsmith; the Lincoln Tunnel scene (of course).

Film Adaptations

Stephen King's The Stand (1994, ABC-TV miniseries), starring Gary Sinise, Molly Ringwald, Jamey Sheridan, Ruby Dee, Miguel Ferrer, Laura San Giacamo, Rob Lowe, Adam Storke, Matt Frewer, Corin Nemec, Ray Walston, Bill Fagerbakke, Ossie Davis, Shawnee Smith, Rick Aviles, Joe Bob Briggs, Michael Lookinland, Ed Harris, Kathy Bates, Kareem Abdul-Jabar, Stephen King, Sam Raimi; directed by Mick Garris, screenplay by Stephen King. (Grade: B+.)

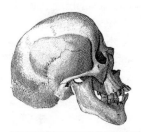

The Shining
(1977)

Jack Torrance thought: Officious little prick.
Ullman stood five-five, and when he moved, it was with the prissy speed that seems
to be the exclusive domain of all small plump men.

☠☠☠

A shaft of light coming from another room, the bathroom, harsh white light and a
word flickering on and off in the medicine cabinet mirror like a red eye, REDRUM,
REDRUM, REDRUM

Why it made the top 10:

The Shining is one of Stephen King's most literary novels.

His writing in this novel is superb and the book is structured as a five-part tragedy (it was originally conceptualized as a play), *Prefatory Matters, Closing Day, The Wasps' Nest, Snowbound,* and *Matters of Life and Death.*

Each section has several titled chapters and King pulls you through the story with amazing deftness and skill. Since *The Shining* is a brilliantly rendered, contemporary Gothic horror novel, it is one of the few Stephen King novels that professors of literature are not averse to teaching in class. *The Shining* is also one of the King works that most experts and fans believe will still be read 50 years from now.

The King Speaks

"When I was writing *The Shining* there was a scene I was terrified of having to face writing. Writing is a pretty intense act of visualization. I won't say it's magic, but it's pretty close to magic. There was this woman in the tub, dead and bloated for years, and she gets up and starts to come for the boy who can't get the door open ... The closer I got to having to write it, the more I worried about it. I didn't want to have to face that unspeakable thing in the tub, any more than the boy did. Two or three nights running, before I got to that section, I dreamed there was a nuclear explosion on the lake where we lived. The mushroom cloud turned into a huge red bird that was coming for me, but when I finished with the scene, it was gone."

—From a March 1979 interview with Mel Allen
in *Yankee* magazine

Jack Torrance, an alcoholic writer and disgraced teacher takes a caretaker's job at a huge hotel in the Colorado Mountains and moves his wife and son into the hotel for the winter. Jack and Wendy's son Danny has the gift of "the shining," the ability to see possible futures as well as the spirits of the dead. It turns out that the huge and ominous Overlook Hotel houses sentient, evil spirits who pursue Danny and his powers through the failings and weaknesses of his father. The Overlook uses Jack Torrance as a tool in its attempt to ultimately kill Wendy and take control of Danny. A chef at the hotel, Dick Hallorann, is also psychic and ultimately becomes Danny's ally in his battle against his father and the spirits of the Overlook. The Overlook pulls out all the stops in its malevolent quest, though, including bringing to life the huge animal topiary that sits on the grounds of the hotel and providing Jack with the opportunity to fall off the wagon—in a hotel that always removes all the adult beverages at the end of each season. As Jack descends into madness, Wendy and Danny find themselves in a battle for their lives—a battle that ends in a fiery inferno and the apparently inevitable death of Jack.

King's strong use of interior monologues for Jack Torrance reflects the claustrophobia of being locked up in a hulking, haunted hotel all winter. As Wendy and Danny are trapped in the Overlook, so are Jack and we (the reader) trapped in the nightmare landscape of Jack's mind. This is a very effective device and one that King uses for maximum shudders.

King's first two novels, *Carrie* and *'Salem's Lot*, were the books that served as the genesis of his spectacular, "brand name" mega-career. *The Shining* (King's first universally acknowledged *masterpiece*) elevated him to the perch he still sits in today, that of the world's King of Horror (although he is now becoming more vocal about his displeasure at being pigeonholed into such a niche).

The Shining is about as important as it gets. It is one of those rare books *about which* a book—*The Shining Reader* by Dr. Anthony Magistrale—has been written. The undeniable *gravitas* of the novel has also spawned some fairly serious literary critique, including such essays as "The Redrum of Time: A Meditation on Francisco Goya's 'Saturn Devouring His Children' and Stephen King's *The Shining*" by Greg Weller, and "The Red Death's Sway: Setting and Character in Poe's 'The Mask of the Red Death' and King's *The Shining*" by Leonard Mustazza.

In *The Shining*, King tackled his own personal feelings regarding occasional anger towards his children and he used the writing of the novel and the development of the Jack Torrance character as a means to try and understand those inexplicable outbursts of rage we all have felt towards our children from time to time. Born of frustration, impatience, and exhaustion (as well as, for some people—like Jack—liberal doses of alcohol), these episodes need to be handled so things don't get out of hand and result in a child getting hurt. In *The Shining*, Jack Torrance breaks his son's arm when he comes home and finds that Danny had made a mess of his papers. Jack was drunk at the time and when he pulled Danny up off the floor, he used just a wee bit too much strength and little Danny ended up in a cast. This was one of the primary catalysts for Jack to give up drinking.

As Jack explores the hotel's basement, King interweaves the history of the Overlook into the story, dramatically illustrating the hotel's sordid past and setting us up for Jack's complete surrender to the evil powers running the show.

King's use of "redrum" as a totemic portent sent to Danny by his alter ego Tony is clever and has become an oft-cited part of the culture.

The Shining was Stephen King's first bestseller and today, more than 20 years later, it is still in print and has been translated into dozens of languages.

☠ **C. V.** ☠

Main Characters

Jack Torrance, Danny Torrance, Wendy Torrance, Dick Hallorann, Delbert Grady, The Overlook Hotel.

Did You Know?

Stephen King finds inspiration everywhere. In the mid-1970s, King and his wife Tabitha checked into the Stanley Hotel in Estes Park, Colorado—exactly when the hotel was preparing to close for the season. King and his wife ended up essentially alone in the hotel (along with a skeleton crew—sorry) and since King's mind works the way it does, the story of the Torrances came to him and—lucky for us—he decided to write it down. Many of the elements of the novel—the fire hose, the long corridors, the ballroom, etc.—are derived from King's stay at the Stanley.

What I Really Liked About It

The Shining was the first Stephen King novel I ever read and it is the book that got me hooked. I had always enjoyed reading and there had been many books that thoroughly engaged me. However, *The Shining* was an entirely different experience for me: It was the first book I literally could not put down; could not stop turning the pages; and the first book that went beyond simply scaring me. *The Shining* terrified me in a way no book before ever had.

Film Adaptations

1. *The Shining* (1980), starring Jack Nicholson, Shelly Duvall, Danny Lloyd, Scatman Crothers; directed by Stanley Kubrick, screenplay by Stanley Kubrick and Diane Johnson. (Grade: A.) 2. *Stephen King's The Shining* (1997 ABC-TV miniseries), starring Steven Weber, Rebecca DeMornay; directed by Mick Garris; screenplay by Stephen King. (In his June 1983 *Playboy* interview, King said, "I'd like to remake *The Shining* someday, maybe even direct it myself if anybody will give me enough rope to hang myself with.") (Grade: B+.)

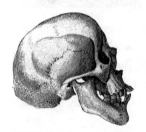

The Dead Zone (1979)

*She drew her breath in raggedly, her back straightening,
her eyes going wide and round. "Johnny...?"*

Why it made the top 10:

The way King's 1999 *Hearts in Atlantis* is a story of the 1960s; his *The Dead
Zone*—published 20 years before *Hearts*—is a story of the decade of the 1970s, and
was Stephen King's first *New York Times* number 1 bestseller.

King was in his early 30s when he published this amazing novel. *The Dead Zone*
appeared after a span of extraordinary creativity, the five-year period that included the
publication of *Carrie*, *'Salem's Lot*, *The Shining*, *The Stand*, plus the stories of *Night
Shift*. Any writer would be proud of even one of these volumes; King published them at
a rate of one a year.

The Dead Zone speaks to political vagaries; those fateful flukes of events that can
often change the path of history in this country. In the novel, Johnny Smith, King's American Everyman, awakens from a 55-month coma with an inoperable brain tumor and the
ability to see into the future. Cursed with a gift he never wanted, Johnny one days shakes

the hand of Greg Stillson, a third-party candidate for President, witnesses a nuclear Armageddon caused by Stillson, and realizes that he must sacrifice himself for the greater good. Fulfilling the mandate of the literary school of naturalism (fate rules man but we have the power to make moral decisions) often used by King, Johnny was given prescience by a twist of fate. He was given a turn of the Wheel of Fortune (a powerful symbol throughout the novel), but then makes the morally correct decision to do what is necessary for the many, instead of the one (my nod to Mr. Spock in *Star Trek; The Wrath of Khan*, of course).

King's writing in *The Dead Zone* is superb and powerful, and the novel contains elements of suspense while serving as both a political thriller and a poignant love story.

The Dead Zone is the novel to recommend to people who have never read King or those who proclaim, "I never read that horror stuff!"

☠ **C. V.** ☠

Main Characters

Johnny Smith, Greg Stillson, Sarah Bracknell, Frank Dodd, Vera Smith, Herb Smith.

Did You Know?

During the period when Johnny was in his coma, Sarah Bracknell lived in Veazie, Maine...on *Flagg* Street. (Hmmm.)

What I Really Liked About It

Everything...but especially the final scene in the graveyard. This scene ranks with King's absolute best.

Film Adaptations

The Dead Zone (1983), starring Christopher Walken, Brooke Adams, Tom Skerritt, Herbert Lom, Anthony Zerbe, Colleen Dewhurst; directed by David Cronenberg; screenplay by Jeffrey Boam. (This is by far one of the all-time best adaptations of a Stephen King work.) (Grade: A.)

The King Speaks

"What always happens for me—with a book—is that you frame the idea of the book or the 'what if.' And little by little, characters will take shape. Generally as a result of a secondary decision about the plot. ... In the case of *The Dead Zone*, it was simply what if a man was able to have this ability to see the future. What if you were to explore that idea in the book, if he was just an ordinary guy that could really do it? The secondary thing was the visualization of this guy taking a test paper from a student, and saying, 'You gotta go home right away. Your house is burning down.' That never actually appears in the book, but it set the thing of him as a teacher; there were some other decisions that were made, and then it was time to pick the book up and begin to go."

—From a July 1984 interview with David Sherman
in *Fangoria* magazine.

TV Adaptations

In January 2001, it was announced that Michael Piller (*Star Trek: Voyager*) was developing a series based on King's novel *The Dead Zone* for the UPN television network. The series was tentatively scheduled for UPN's 2001-2002 season.

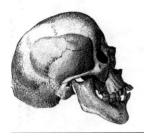

The Green Mile
(1996)

Consisting of 6 installments:

The Two Dead Girls; *The Mouse on the Mile*; *Coffey's Hands*; *The Bad Death of Eduard Delacroix*; *Night Journey*; *Coffey on the Mile*

This happened in 1932, when the state penitentiary was still at Cold Mountain. And the electric chair was there, too, of course.

Why it made the top 10:

The sheer excellence and overwhelming success of Frank Darabont's film adaptation of King's *The Green Mile* has somewhat overshadowed this novel. This tends to happen when a film version is so good that it becomes a presence unto itself and is the first thing people think of when they hear the title of the book. But the film would not have been as good as it is without Stephen King's superb source novel.

The Green Mile is in the top five of Stephen King's works because it is *Just That Good*. It compares with King's finest novels—*The Dead Zone*, *Misery*, *The Shining*, etc.—and it is King giving us what all those other tales likewise provided. Memorable characters, a thrilling story, elegant writing, and a theme that tackles the biggest issues of all: The existence (or nonexistence) of God, and an exploration of the possibility that Jesus Christ has been returning to our world repeatedly over the centuries—patiently waiting for the moment when we recognize him and embrace him...instead of killing him again and again.

The installment format seems to have galvanized King. He had to turn out a complete "chapter" (although each of the books was a hefty 25,000-30,000 words) in a very short time in order for his publisher to be able to get a new book out each month for six months in a row. Added to the deadline pressures, King also had to be sure that each installment concluded with a climax of sorts and he also had to clearly summarize the previous installments to refresh readers' memories. (Some readers did not like the installment program and "saved up" all six books to read at one sitting. I read them as they were published. Either way worked, since King's synopses were built into the first chapter of the new book and allowed narrator Paul Edgecombe to reminisce about what had gone before.)

The electric chair

Interestingly, the lack of an actual section called "Synopsis" apparently spurred Signet, King's publisher, to include capsule summaries of the previous books on the first page (opposite the inside cover) of each new installment.

The story is immediately engrossing: A giant black man named John Coffey ("J.C."...get it?) is found with the bodies of two dead white girls. A conclusion is leapt to, Coffey is convicted of the murders, and he is sentenced to death by electrocution. He is placed in the custody of Paul Edgecombe and his team on the Green Mile (death row) at Cold Mountain penitentiary. We are told Coffey's story decades later by Paul Edgecombe, writing from his retirement home. But there is much more to John Coffey than initially believed—including the miraculous power to heal with his touch—and Paul Edgecombe comes away from his time with Coffey a changed man. As are we, the readers of his profound story.

The Green Mile film turned a lot of people on to the (*written*) work of Stephen King (as did Darabont's previous King film *The Shawshank Redemption*). To many moviegoers, Stephen King was suddenly much more than just a horror writer.

☠ **C. V.** ☠

Main Characters

Paul Edgecombe, John Coffey, Brutus "Brutal" Howell, Warden Moores, Percy Wetmore, Billy "The Kid" Wharton, Eduard Delacroix...and Mr. Jingles

The King Speaks

"As far as *The Green Mile* (the movie) goes, I told Frank about the idea for the story before the first part was published and while I was still working on it. He was really excited by it and I told him I'd send him the parts. I told him that if he liked it could he do it. He was very cautious and said, 'Well, let me read it.' Well, he loves it and wants to do it. He jokes and says that he's now carving out the world's smallest film niche, which is a maker of Stephen King prison stories set in the 50s. There isn't a script yet and the negotiations are ongoing. As far as I'm concerned, it's Frank's for the doing and nobody else's."

—From a 1996 *World of Fandom* interview with Joseph Mauceri

Did You Know?

At one point there was a rumor going around that Tom Hanks was slated to play the John Coffey role in the film. Hanks explains this in an excerpt from Tyson Blue's book, *The Making of the Green Mile*:

> While rumors on the Internet and other sources had at least some rational basis, one went so far as to suggest that [Hanks] had even wanted to play John Coffey(!), the rationale being that he enjoyed taking roles which gave him a chance to expand the horizons of his acting. Hanks could easily understand how these rumors could begin. "That's the other thing that's really miraculous about this story is that they're all good roles," he said. "It's that kind of ensemble piece. You know, the only thing that makes me Number One on the call sheet is that Paul's the narrator! Other than that, all the guys have great parts. I certainly would have jumped at the chance to play, say, Wild Bill, or even Percy, although I'm not short enough to be Percy. It's such a key thing."

What I Really Liked About It

Everything...but especially the idea that Coffey was a manifestation of Jesus...and that he was just one of possibly many avatars of Christ that have been visiting us over the past two thousand years. (Oh, and I liked Mr. Jingles, of course.)

The King Speaks

"I wrote like a madman, trying to keep up with the crazy publishing schedule and at the same time trying to craft the book so that each part would have its own mini-climax, hoping that everything would fit, and knowing I'd be hung if it didn't."

—From the Introduction to the single-volume edition
of *The Green Mile*

Film Adaptations

The Green Mile (1999); starring Tom Hanks, David Morse, Bonnie Hunt, Michael Clarke Duncan, James Cromwell, Michael Jeter, Graham Greene, Doug Hutchison, Sam Rockwell, Barry Pepper, Jeffrey DeMunn, Patricia Clarkson, Harry Dean Stanton; directed by Frank Darabont; screenplay by Frank Darabont. (Grade: A.)

NUMBER 6

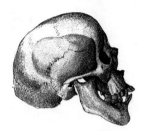

Bag of Bones
(1998)

I've lost my taste for spooks.

Why it made the top 10:

Stephen King has always liked British writers. His list of recommended books in the back of *On Writing* lists several Brits. In 1977, King even began writing a "Lord Peter Wimsey" novel (Wimsey is a detective character in series of mystery novels by British writer Dorothy Sayers) that he never published, but may have completed for his own gratification.

This penchant for British fiction directly influenced King's first novel for Scribner's, *Bag of Bones*, a masterful work that echoes Daphne du Maurier's 1938 classic, *Rebecca*, and which King describes as a "haunted love story." Add to that the references to British writer Thomas Hardy and King's literary influences (for this novel anyway) are blatant.

But *Bag of Bones* is not set in England, nor during the period in which *Rebecca* takes place. It is most assuredly an American novel, with American characters, set in 20th century America.

GEORGE BEAHM

At a signing at Betts Bookstore, Stephen King signs Bag of Bones *for a local reader who lives in nearby Orono. (Bookstore owner Stuart Tinker is in the background.)*

Bag of Bones was Stephen King's first authentic ghost story since *Pet Sematary*. It revisits Castle Rock and Derry (the setting of *It, Insomnia,* and *Dreamcatcher*), and centers on a best-selling writer's grief over his wife's death, a tragedy which is some-how related to some strange doings at their summer lakeside place, Sara Laughs, in western Maine.

Bag of Bones boasts an ancient curse, dazzling sequences of mind-boggling and horrifying paranormal activity, as well as a couple of the most memorable villains with which King has ever blessed us.

Again (as in *The Dark Half, Misery,* "Secret Window, Secret Garden," *Desperation, The Tommyknockers, The Shining,* etc.), King has as his main character a writer, this one a best-selling author of mysteries who has been a fixture on the best-seller list for years. Michael Noonan and his wife Jo had a wonderful life: His books made them wealthy, and their love fulfilled them in ways neither of them could have possibly ever dreamt was possible.

Then one day, while running across a shopping center parking lot to help an accident victim on the hottest day of the year, Jo Noonan suffers a brain aneurysm that kills her instantly, making Mike Noonan one of the youngest widowers in Maine.

Jo Noonan's death saddles Mike with one of the worst cases of writer's block imaginable. He has immediate and paralyzing panic attacks whenever he sits down to write following Jo's death. But this fixture on the best-seller list Mike Noonan is no fool: Even though he *published* one book a year, he *wrote* one-and-a-half books, resulting in a bank safe deposit box containing five unpublished novels, labeled simply, I, II, III, etc.

The King Speaks

"I hope *Bag of Bones* gave you at least one sleepless night. Sorry 'bout that; it's just the way I am. It gave me one or two, and ever since writing it I'm nervous about going down into the cellar—part of me keeps expecting the door to slam, the light to go out, and the knocking to start. But for me, at least, that's also part of the fun. If that makes me sick, hey, don't call the doctor."

—From King's May 1999 letter to reviewers of *Hearts in Atlantis*, included with review copies of the book

Out of necessity, Mike begins plundering his stash, providing his publisher—and his bottom-line fixated agent—with their one blockbuster a year, keeping his career alive temporarily, while trying to cope with being suddenly alone.

Michael Noonan decides to move to his lakefront house, Sara Laughs, and see if a change of scenery inspires him. As soon as he arrives in town, he meets a divorced young girl, Mattie Devore, and her three-year-old daughter, Ki. Mattie's wealthy father-in-law, William Devore (whose name should, as Dr. Michael Collings has so astutely noted, remind us of the verb "devour"), is conspiring to wrest custody of the little girl away from her mother. Michael Noonan is inexorably drawn into the struggle, during which he learns some dark secrets about the old man—and about the town and its past, a horror story that involves ferocious racism, rape, murder, and buried secrets.

According to King, "*Bag of Bones* contains everything I know about marriage, lust, and ghosts." The novel is King at the top of his game and the last 300 pages contain some of the best writing King has published.

In *The Stephen King Universe* by Stanley Wiater, Christopher Golden, and Hank Wagner, the authors write, "Simply stated, [*Bag of Bones*] ranks amongst the four or five best novels the author has written in his entire career." Okay, so Messrs. Wiater, Golden, and Wagner and I disagree on the ranking of this brilliant novel: I place it at number 6 in King's Top 10. This picayune difference does not, however, diminish our joint message: *Bag of Bones* is evidence of a master at the peak of his craft.

☠ **C. V.** ☠

George Beahm Speaks

"In *Bag of Bones*, King has, to my mind, deliberately written a mainstream novel that will appeal to a greater audience, perhaps gaining him part of the readership long denied him, as he attempts to shake off his reputation as America's best-loved boogeyman."

—From *Stephen King From A to Z*

Main Characters

Michael Noonan, Mattie Devore, Kyra "Ki" Devore, William Devore, Johanna Noonan, Rogette Whitmore, Sara Tidwell, Lance Devore, George Footman, Richard Osgood, John Storrow, The Red Tops.

Did You Know?

The title of the novel comes from something British author Thomas Hardy (a King favorite) reportedly once said: "Compared to the dullest human being actually walking about on the face of the earth and casting his shadow there, the most brilliantly drawn character in a novel is but a bag of bones." King's final reference to Hardy's remark (of several in the novel) occurs in the book's second to last paragraph when he writes, "Thomas Hardy, who supposedly said that the most brilliantly drawn character in a novel is but a bag of bones, stopped writing novels himself after finishing *Jude the Obscure* and while he was at the height of his narrative genius."

What I Really Liked About It

It's a page-turner, from the opening paragraph until the astonishing conclusion.

Film Adaptations

None.

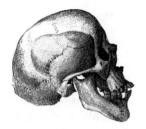

Misery
(1987)

"My name is Annie Wilkes. And I am —
"I know," he said. "You're my number-one fan."
"Yes," she said, smiling. "That's just what I am."

Why it made the top 10:

Some Stephen King fans perceived *Misery* as a Stephen King "Scream Heard 'Round the World"; a not-so-veiled purging of King's worst thoughts about his fans and the nature of celebrity and the mechanics of the writing process. The Dedication didn't help: "This is for Stephanie and Jim Leonard, who know why. Boy, *do* they." At the time *Misery* was published, Stephanie Leonard was editor of *Castle Rock: The Stephen King Newsletter* and dealt with Stephen King's fan mail on a daily basis. Thus, many fans believed that the Annie Wilkes character in the novel was Stephen King's spin on the worst elements of his multitude of fans. [See "Stephanie Leonard speaks" for more on the meaning of this dedication.]

Was this interpretation accurate?

Yes and no.

The King Speaks

"I wrote most of *Misery* by hand, sitting at Kipling's desk in Brown's Hotel in London...Then I found out he died at the desk. That spooked me, so I quit the hotel."

—From a 1998 interview with journalist Peter Conrad

Annie Wilkes *is* the worst manifestation of a "Number One Fan," but the scenario of a writer being held captive and forced to write a book "to order" is simply an imaginative writer asking "What if?" and then putting on paper the results of his speculative musings.

Misery was one of *five* books King published during a 14-month period of astonishing creativity. This span also included the publication of *It* (Chapter 1). Plus the second *Dark Tower* novel, *The Drawing of the Three* (Chapter 10), the fantasy *The Eyes of the Dragon* (Chapter 18) (which is connected in ways to the *Dark Tower* series), and the science fiction novel, *The Tommyknockers* (Chapter 72). Of this group, *It* was the most important book, but *Misery*—one of Stephen King's 10 best novels—was undoubtedly the most terrifying.

Paul Sheldon, a world-famous, best-selling author, completes the novel that kills off Misery Chastain, the heroine of his popular *Misery* series of romances. Sheldon has also written a contemporary novel called *Fast Cars* that he thinks might win him an American Book Award, and he is thrilled that he is finally free from writing books that made him a fortune, but which he hated writing. While on his way to the airport during a snowstorm, he goes off the road and is rescued by a psychotic nurse named Annie Wilkes who, he soon learns, happens to be his number one fan. Annie takes Paul to her isolated farmhouse where she nurses him back to health. Sheldon soon realizes that he is most assuredly *not* a guest, but instead a crippled captive. All hell breaks loose when Annie buys Paul's "Misery dies" novel and learns that her favorite character is no more.

Annie then forces Paul to write a novel in which he resurrects Misery Chastain and the tortured writer obliges—because his very life is the penalty if he does not satisfy his Number One Fan.

King deftly inserts Paul's actual *Misery* novel in typescript in *Misery,* and the overall effect is one of King's most frightening and well-written novels. If there is such a thing as a contemporary suspense classic, *Misery* is it.

☠ **C. V.** ☠

The King Speaks

Q: Have you had any bad experiences with a "Number One Fan" yourself?

SK: I haven't directly, but my wife has. There was a guy who broke into our house when she was home alone. It was about six o'clock in the morning, and she had just got up when she heard glass breaking downstairs.

Q: And she went down to investigate?

SK: Yes.

Q: What did he look like?

SK: He looked like Charles Manson with long hair, and he had a rucksack in his hands. He said that he was my biggest fan. Then he stopped suddenly and said he actually hated me because I'd stolen the novel *Misery* from his aunt. Then he held up the rucksack and said that he had a bomb and was going to blow her up.

Q: Jesus! What did your wife do?

SK: She ran out in her bare feet and nightgown, man! The police came round and he was still there. It turned out that all he had in the bag was a load of pencils and paperclips in a box.

Q: What was up with him, then?

SK: It turned out he was from Texas. His aunt was a nurse who'd been fired from some hospital, and he made a connection with the nurse in *Misery*.

—From a 1998 interview with journalist Ben Rawortit

Main Characters

Paul Sheldon, Annie Wilkes, Constant Reader, Misery Chastain, Charlie Merrill, assorted townsfolk and law enforcement personnel.

Did You Know?

Stephen King originally planned on publishing *Misery* as a "Richard Bachman" novel. He apparently felt it fit more neatly into old Dickey's body of work than into his own.

Stephanie Leonard Speaks

(In an interview in my *Complete Stephen King Encyclopedia*, I asked Stephanie, "What does the dedication mean?") Her response: "For some reason, maybe the way it was phrased, people assume there's a secret there, or an in-joke. What this means—*"Boy, do they [know]"*—is just that we've been party to his life for a long time and we've seen the fan mail and the people who hang around in front of his house snapping pictures, and the way the fame and the money has affected his life. Basically, we know all the little things that inspired *Misery*."

—From *The Complete Stephen King Encyclopedia*

What I Really Liked About It

The total immersion into Paul Sheldon's psyche; Annie's murderous backstory (revealed slowly); and the jaw-dropping climax (which is then amplified by Paul's experience of seeing Annie's ghost...or does he?)

Film Adaptations

Misery (1990), starring James Caan, Kathy Bates; directed by Rob Reiner; screenplay by William Goldman. Best Actress Academy Award to Kathy Bates. (This is one of the all-time best adaptations of a King novel to date. Bates won an Academy Award for her portrayal of psychonurse (and Constant Reader) Annie Wilkes.) (Grade: A.)

NUMBER 8

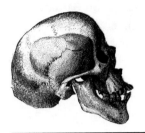

'Salem's Lot
(1975)

The house itself looked toward town. It was huge and rambling and sagging,
its windows haphazardly boarded shut, giving it that sinister look of
all old houses that have been empty for a long time.

Why it made the top 10:

The history of popular culture is replete with second-time failures: writers, actors, directors, musicians, etc., who have an enormous hit with their first effort, and then completely bomb with their sophomore project. Knowing this, then, the brilliance and success of Stephen King's second published book, *'Salem's Lot*, is all the more impressive. Granted, part of the reason for *'Salem's Lot* assured style and exemplary writing is that, even though it was Stephen King's second book, it wasn't *really* Stephen King's second book. It was his sixth. *Carrie* may have been King's first *published* novel; but he had written four complete novels prior to its publication, followed by book six, *'Salem's Lot*. There is no better experience than doing it, and by the time King published *'Salem's Lot*, he had paid his dues and passed the audition.

'Salem's Lot is one scary volcano of a book. Ben Mears returns to Jerusalem's Lot to write a book and discovers that "the town"—as the back jacket of the paperback tells us—"knew darkness." The novel is flawless in its depiction of small-town life in Maine,

The King Speaks

"The dinner conversation that night was a speculation on what might happen if Dracula returned today, not to London with its 'teeming millions' (as Stoker puts it with such purely Victorian complacency), but to rural America....I began to turn the idea over in my mind, and it began to coalesce into a possible novel. I thought it would make a good one, if I could create a fictional town with enough prosaic reality about it to offset the comic-book menace of a bunch of vampires."

—From "On Becoming a Brand Name"

with its isolation and guardedness, an atmosphere, King deftly illustrates, that could allow evil to take root and grow. This is a symbolic object lesson, of course (pedophiles, rapists, domestic abusers and other lowlifes thrive in a climate of secrecy), but King uses it as a tool to show how a card-carrying, bloodsucking, coffin-sleeping member of the undead could also set up shop and use such a place as his own Hometown Buffet.

'Salem's Lot is also noteworthy for being the first Stephen King novel with a writer as its protagonist. As Constant Readers know, writer characters are abundant in King's body of work, but *'Salem's Lot*'s Ben Mears deserves special recognition as King's first.

'Salem's Lot is one of King's most accessible novels, is easily teachable, and, when read in conjunction with Bram Stoker's *Dracula*, could actually make high school Contemporary American Literature classes a pleasure to attend!

☠ **C. V.** ☠

Main Characters

Ben Mears, Mark Petrie, Kurt Barlow, Susan Norton, Danny Glick, Richard Throckett Straker.

Did You Know?

King once gave serious though to writing a sequel to *'Salem's Lot*. In a 1982 interview with *Fangoria* magazine, King actually revealed how such a sequel would begin: "I think about a sequel a lot. I even know who would be in it and how it would launch...it's

Somebody Else Speaks

"'*Salem's Lot* stands today as one of the finest treatments of the traditional vampire since Bram Stoker's *Dracula* (1897) and one of the last serious treatments of the mythos surrounding the vampire that had developed over the course of the preceding century."

—From George Beahm's
The Stephen King Companion (revised edition)

Father Callahan. I know where he is....He went to New York City and from New York he drifted across the country and he landed in Detroit. He's in the inner city and he's running a soup kitchen for alcoholics...and he's been attacked a couple of times and...people think he's crazy. He doesn't wear the turned-around collar anymore, but he's...trying to get right with God. So one day this guy comes in. He's dying and he says, 'I have to talk to you, Father Callahan.' And Callahan says, 'I'm not a Father anymore and how did you know that?' [As the guy dies], the last thing he says as he grabs Callahan by the shirt and pulls him down into this mist of beer and whiskey and puke...is, 'It's not over in the Lot, yet.' Then he drops dead."

What I Really Liked About It

As one of King's most viscerally frightening works, *'Salem's Lot* is perhaps even more engrossing when reread.

Film Adaptations

Salem's Lot (TV-miniseries, 1979); starring David Soul, James Mason, Lance Kerwin, Bonnie Bedelia, Lew Ayres, Julie Cobb, Elisha Cook Jr., George Dzundza, Ed Flanders, Clarissa Kaye-Mason, Geoffrey Lewis, Barney McFadden, Kenneth McMillan, Fred Willard, Marie Windsor; directed by Tobe Hooper; screenplay by Paul Monash. (This film, in various cut and uncut versions was also known as *Blood Thirst*, *Salem's Lot: The Miniseries*, and *Salem's Lot: The Movie*.) (Grade: B-.)

Number 9

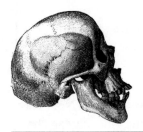

Pet Sematary
(1983)

"These are secret things, Louis...the soil of a man's heart is stonier...like the soil up in the old Micmac burying ground. A man grows what he can...and he tends it."

Why it made the top 10:

The death of a child.

To a parent, it is the ultimate horror. I have heard countless parents say—immediately and with absolutely *no* qualms—that if they were faced with the choice of their child dying or themselves dying, they would selflessly sacrifice themselves to save the life of their child. But what happens if the parent is *not* given that choice, and the child is simply taken from them, by illness or accident? If that was the case, and the parent had a way of reversing tragedy; of bringing their child back...what would mom or dad do? And what would be the consequences?

This horror is the subject of *Pet Sematary*.

Even the bare bones plot of *Pet Sematary*, spoken plainly, has not-so-subtle intimations of dread: A grieving father buries his son in a graveyard that can resurrect the dead...except that when the dead come back, they're *changed*.

Louis Creed and his wife Rachel (the Biblical names are not accidental) have two children, Ellie and Gage. Ellie's cat Church (again, the religious reference is significant) is killed by a truck on the road in front of their home. (This incident was based on the similar death of King's daughter Naomi's cat, Smucky.) The death of Church is so traumatizing to Ellie that her father decides to use the secret information given him by his neighbor, Jud Crandall. There is a Micmac burial ground off in the woods where anything that's buried comes back to life. But this power comes with a price: The resurrected are not the way they were in life.

Louis Creed is willing to do anything to ease Ellie's pain, and so he buries Church there, and the cat does, indeed, come back. Except that he's a mean, vicious hellcat instead of the lovable kitty Ellie had cherished.

Does this teach Louis a lesson? Of course not. And when his son Gage is killed on the same road, he buries his boy in the same ground and he too comes back. A demonic child-monster, he first kills Jud, and then his mother. By this time Louis is completely insane and, yes, also buries his dead wife in the unholy place. The novel concludes with Rachel coming back to visit her hubby...who is, by now, as doomed as doomed can be.

Pet Sematary is one of King's powerful works and is unquestionably one of his finest literary achievements.

☠ **C. V.** ☠

Main Characters

Louis Creed, Jud Crandall, Rachel Creed, Victor Pascow, Irwin Goldman, Gage Creed, Ellie Creed, Missy Dandridge, Marcy Charlton, Steve Masterton, Dory Goldman, Zelda Goldman, Church.

Did You Know?

Pet Sematary is the novel Stephen King felt was too horrific to publish. In fact, when he finished it in 1979, he put it in a drawer and refused to offer it for publication. As fulfillment of a contract with Doubleday, though, King eventually relented and allowed publication in 1983, but he refused to participate in the promotion of the book. (The jacket flap copy of the Doubleday hardcover edition of *Pet Sematary* began, "Can Stephen King scare even *himself*? Has the author of *Carrie*, *The Shining*, *Cujo*, and *Christine* ever conceived a story so horrifying that he was for a time unwilling to finish writing it? Yes. *This* is it.")

The King Speaks

"When ideas come, they don't arrive with trumpets. They are quiet—there is no drama involved. I can remember crossing the road, and thinking that the cat had been killed in the road...and [I thought], what if a kid died in that road? And we had had this experience with Owen running toward the road, where I had just grabbed him and pulled him back. And the two things just came together—on one side of this two-lane highway was the idea of what if the cat came back, and on the other side of the highway was what if the kid came back—so that when I reached the other side, I had been galvanized by the idea, but not in any melodramatic way. I knew immediately that it was a novel."

—From an interview with Douglas E. Winter,
from *Stephen King: The Art of Darkness*

What I Really Liked About It

I suppose it is kind of twisted to admit actually "liking" anything about a book so dark, so pessimistic, so *sad*...but I still think *Pet Sematary*—King's aversion to it even to this day notwithstanding—is a masterful horror story. It is superbly written, and, yes, I "enjoyed" reading it. The novel looks death—and our ways of dealing with it—straight in the face. I personally try not to look away while I'm reading it.

Film Adaptations

Pet Sematary (1989); starring Dale Midkiff, Fred Gwynne, Denise Crosby, Brad Greenquist, Michael Lombard, Miko Hughes, Blaze Berdahl, Susan Blommaert, Mara Clark, Kavi Raz, Mary Louise Wilson, Andrew Hubatsek, Liz Davies, Kara Dalke, Matthew August Ferrell; directed by Mary Lambert; screenplay by Stephen King. (Grade: B-.)

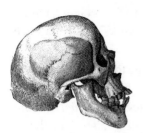

The Dark Tower Epic (1982, 1987, 1991, 1997, 2002[?])

*Guess this ain't Lord's Prayer country.
You're a gunslinger. That right?*

Why it made the top 10:

Before we begin, I'd like to make a statement which I think speaks volumes (pun intended) about Stephen King, and it is this:

For countless other writers past and present, *The Dark Tower* epic *alone* would be *a life's work.*

I thought long and hard about how to rank King's *Dark Tower* stories in *The Essential Stephen King*. I even consulted a number of King authorities (many of whose names you would immediately recognize) for opinions on whether the individual novels should be ranked as separate books/stories, or as part of an overall, inclusive ranking that considered *The Dark Tower* epic a single work.

The cohorts and colleagues I palavered with had varying opinions on what I should do.

Many believed *The Dark Tower* books should be ranked and reviewed individually.

☠ A screenwriter who has adapted King told me, "I think each book is too distinctive and unique to be lumped together as one collection...especially since that 'collection' is not yet complete. I know this means more work for you, but, hey, you wanted my opinion!"

☠ A well-known writer who has written several books about King advised, "If these were all fairly short books, such as *The Gunslinger*, I'd say rank them as a single work. But since the later volumes have been huge, and since each stands alone as a unit, and (partially due to their having been issued at such widely-spaced intervals) also reflect different stages of King's career, I think they would more properly be considered as individual works, particularly the last three. I'd go with individuality."

☠ An indefatigable King bibliographer and friend of mine told me, "Definitely rank them all separately. I believe that they all have a distinctive feel, especially *The Gunslinger*....*The Gunslinger* has a dark feel to it, *The Drawing of the Three* has a weird '80s America' feel to it, *The Waste Lands* has a dark fantasy feel, and *Wizard and Glass* has a kind of western/romance/fantasy feel. My point is, they should be ranked separately, because they all have their own distinct sensibility."

But then there were those who made strong arguments not to treat the books as separate entities.

☠ A well-known King dealer wrote, "They *are* individual novels...which is why you ask the question...but I believe they shouldn't be split up. They are part of 'one picture' and in one vein. I say keep them together."

☠ A well-respected King supercollector wrote, "I believe you should treat it the same way you would treat Tolkien's *Lord of the Rings* trilogy and for much the same reasons. I vote for one series. I am sure you are treating *The Green Mile* as one story. *The Dark Tower* is one story told in many large parts over a long time frame but it *is* one long story."

☠ A writer and acknowledged King expert wrote, "Are you treating *The Green Mile* as six books or one? I think you should follow your lead by how you treat *The Green Mile*. If someone was discussing Tolkien, I don't think that anyone would rank the three component releases of *The Lord of the Rings* trilogy separately. Or would they? I wouldn't at least. So, bottom line, my decision is to treat *The Dark Tower* as a single entity, which, ironically, is still quite *incomplete* as of this writing. However, I wish there was a way to treat *The Gunslinger* separate from the others because it's my favorite of the four!"

I decided to go with a single ranking for the complete *Dark Tower* epic.

I do acknowledge the individuality of each book, however, by looking at each one separately, in chronological order, but without ranking them within the context of *The Dark Tower* epic. Like Tolkien's oft-compared-to *Lord of the Rings* trilogy, *The Dark Tower* is one story. You may like *The Fellowship of the Ring* better than the *The Two Towers* (or vice versa, etc.), but they are each still part of one big tale. That rule also applies to *The Dark Tower*, and, truth be told, King's completed *Dark Tower* series will probably become as important and beloved as Tolkien's *Lord of the Rings* trilogy. It would not surprise me if, like *The Lord of the Rings*, King's series survives in boxed sets, single-volume editions, commemorative editions, etc. And don't dismiss the possibility of a one-volume edition of this enormous series. Think of those gigantic, oversized *Complete Works of William Shakespeare* editions. That format is what I think could be used quite effectively for *The Dark Tower* series.

King has projected the complete series at seven or eight volumes. The most recent (as of this writing) installment, *Wizard and Glass*, runs approximately 300,000 words. Extrapolating from this (and this is, of course, pure speculation) we're talking about a complete series in excess of 2 million words, but easily fit into a single (albeit huge) volume. (And you thought the gorgeous boxed edition of the *Uncut Stand* was the ultimate King edition!)

The Dark Tower epic is a multi-layered, multi-timeline, multi-character, multi-genre saga that, for all its complexity, is really about only one person, Roland Deschain of Gilead and his sacred quest to find the Dark Tower. Since it would be impossible to adequately summarize the complex narrative events of the four books currently comprising *The Dark Tower* series in the very limited space available here, I will be succinct when talking about each volume and not attempt a *"Cliff's Notes* for *The Dark Tower* Series." No such summation could do justice to the brilliance of King's vision. (It would be like asking someone to briefly summarize *The Lord of the Rings*. "Well, there was this Hobbit...")

(**Note:** I do not include *The Dark Tower* story "The Little Sisters of Eluria" in this overall *"Dark Tower* Epic" chapter. I ranked and reviewed it separately. As we Constant Readers know, *The Dark Tower* mythos is intertwined in many of Stephen King's works. I decided that only books released specifically as part of *The Dark Tower* series belonged in this chapter. Thus, "Little Sisters," *Insomnia, Hearts in Atlantis*, and even "Paranoid: A Chant," all of which are part of Roland's story, were not included under the "Epic" umbrella.)

The Dark Tower: The Gunslinger (1982)

This is a collection of five independently published short stories, all of which are episodic, somewhat prefatory contributions to *The Dark Tower* mythos. These stories are now perceived as five long chapters of the first *Dark Tower* novel. They are:

1. "The Gunslinger"
2. "The Way Station"
3. "The Oracle and the Mountains"
4. "The Slow Mutants"
5. "The Gunslinger and the Dark Man"

The Gunslinger referred to, or introduced us to, several key characters in the epic, including Roland of Gilead, Jake Chambers, Walter the Man in Black, Susan, Maerlyn/

Marten/Flagg, Sylvia Pittston, Roland's mother Gabrielle, Roland's father Steven (also at times referred to as Roland), Cort, and Cuthbert.

"The Gunslinger" begins with a line that fits Stephen King's own description of an opener that *works*: it's a *great hooker*. (See King's nonfiction essay "Great Hookers I Have Known" in his collection *Secret Windows* for more on what makes a killer opening sentence.) "The Gunslinger" begins, "The man in black fled across the desert, and the gunslinger followed."

The man in black is Walter; the gunslinger is Roland of Gilead. We soon learn that Roland is on a quest to find the Dark Tower, the nexus of all existence, and he knows that Walter will play a key role in his journey. At this point in the story, Roland is not sure why the Tower calls him, but find it, he must. It is his *ka*, his fate.

During his journey, Roland arrives at Tull, where Walter had previously visited and resurrected a dead man. Walter has planted a trap for Roland, putting into the minds of the townsfolk the suggestion that the gunslinger that would soon visit was a demon, an antichrist, and when Roland is subsequently attacked, he slaughters everyone in town— 58 men, women, and children—before moving on.

At a way station in the desert, Roland meets Jake Chambers, a young boy from 20th century New York, who, he will soon learn, is also a key player in Roland's quest for the Tower. Jake and Roland continue pursuing the Man in Black, at one point confronting hideous creatures known as Slow Mutants. Jake is ultimately sacrificed for Roland's quest for the Tower (embracing his own death, Jake tells Roland, "Go then. There are other worlds than these.") and the gunslinger meets up with the Man in Black on a beach where Roland's fortune is told and the set up for Book II, *The Drawing of the Three* is established.

 Main Characters

Roland of Gilead, Jake Chambers, Walter the Man in Black, Susan, Maerlyn/Marten/ Flagg, Sylvia Pittston, Roland's mother Gabrielle, Roland's father Steven (also at times referred to as Roland the Elder), Cort, Cuthbert.

The Dark Tower II: The Drawing of the Three (1987)

The Drawing of the Three may have been one of the most eagerly awaited Stephen King novels of his prolific career. Fans were excited: King's legendary *Dark Tower* series would continue, and with a full-blown novel, not just a series of connected short stories.

The Drawing of the Three begins where *The Gunslinger* left off, on the beach with Roland, who is now 10 years older.

Roland is continuing his quest for the Tower (the nexus of all creation), and while walking north on a beach, he is attacked and injured by a lobstrosity. A giant lobster who bites off two of his fingers and a toe, including his right index finger, his trigger finger, and infects him with a strange poison.

Further up the beach Roland comes upon three freestanding doors labeled The Prisoner, The Lady of Shadows, and The Pusher. These doors open onto other worlds and deliver Eddie Dean, Odetta Holmes, and Detta Walker to Roland—the drawing of the foretold three.

Ultimately Detta and Odetta merge into a single personality—Susannah Dean. This installment concludes with Roland affirming to the others his pledge to find the Dark Tower—no matter what it takes.

 ## Main Characters

Roland, Eddie Dean, Odetta Holmes, Detta Walker, Susannah Dean, Jake Chambers, The Man in Black, Jack Mort, Flagg.

The Dark Tower III: The Waste Lands (1991)

The Waste Lands (the title is a reference to T. S. Eliot's seminal poem "The Waste Land") is a complex and layered novel. In it, King deftly utilizes multiple time frames, multiple narrative viewpoints, false histories, premonitions, and also introduces exotic new characters like Gasher, Oy the Billy-Bumbler, the Tick-Tock Man, and Blaine the sentient and insane train that promises to kill the Three unless they can solve his riddles.

The intricately plotted story sets up threads that will be expanded on in future volumes (including the appearance of the Turtle), and also offers some of King's most intense scenes of the series. Scenes such as Eddie and Susannah's walk down the Street of the Turtle in the city of Lud, following the Path of the Beam. In this scene, there are countless corpses hanging from speaker poles—most of them mummies, but some still in the putrefying stages of decay. Ugh.

Another interesting element of the story is the fact that in Lud the two warring factions are the Pubes and the Grays. Is it significant that the infectious, marauding aliens in *Dreamcatcher* are called "Grayboys" and that the alien that possesses Jonesy is identified as "Mr. Gray"? And how does this all connect to The Turtle and the Dark Tower itself? Obviously, there are many connections between *The Dark Tower* story and the stories told in other King works and there may be a great deal yet to be learned about the origins of many of the beings and peoples in the series.

The Waste Lands is yet another chapter—another step forward—in what is clearly one of King's most important (and transcendent) works.

 ## Main Characters

Roland, Eddie Dean, Susannah Dean, Oy, Little Blaine, Richard Fannin, Tick-Tock Man, Shardik, The Guardians, Cuthbert, Alain, The Pubes, The Grays.

The Dark Tower IV: Wizard and Glass (1997)

This installment—the fourth of *The Dark Tower* epic—tells of Roland's desperate proposal to the insane Blaine the Mono of a bargain and its consequences. Following their escape from Blaine, Roland's *ka-tet*—Roland, Susannah, Eddie, Jake, Oy—lose their way and must recover the path to the Dark Tower.

King also reveals to his readers something he had not yet written about until this volume: Roland's past and his tragic, absolutely *Shakespearean* act that explains a great deal about Roland's state of mind throughout his quest. (Some other reviews have revealed this critical event involving Roland's mother, but I think it best for the reader to come upon it in his or her own good time. If you've read *Wizard and Glass*, then you know; if you haven't read it yet, then "no spoilers here.")

The one and only Randall Flagg makes an appearance in this chapter of the epic and his presence further establishes the connections not only among the different worlds that co-exist as Roland travels the Path of the Beam, but also of the myriad connections between many of King's works. A newspaper article that the group sees shortly after fleeing Blaine makes even more concrete and blatant a specific connection with another King epic.

We also learn of Roland's relationship as a younger man with his one true love, Susan Delgado. King takes great pains to tell their story, to emphasize Roland's love for Susan, and, following yet another horrific tragedy, lead the reader to even more conclusions regarding Roland's psyche.

King deftly uses *Wizard of Oz* elements and references (many from the movie version) to establish a metaphorical subtext in this volume. Also, it is learned that Susannah is pregnant with the child of either Eddie or a demon that raped her. Will her baby be human or demon? Stay tuned.

We also learn what Thinnies are (which explains a lot) and we are introduced to the character of Sheemie who could be considered a foreshadowing of the character with Down's syndrome, Duddits, in King's 2001 novel *Dreamcatcher*.

'Salem's Lot rears its head here. It seems as though *The Stand* (Captain Trips is mentioned), *The Eyes of The Dragon, Insomnia* (The Crimson King is referred to), J. R. R. Tolkien's *Lord of the Rings* trilogy, and *The Wizard of Oz* all seem to be a part of the increasingly *epic* and engrossing *Dark Tower* epic.

King uses the phrase "essential weirdness" to describe the writing of *The Dark Tower* series and also admits that Roland's story is his "Jupiter"—his biggest story in a universe of imagination. Volume 5 and the Dark Tower are now closer.

 Main Characters

Roland Deschain, Eddie Dean, Susannah Dean, Jake Chambers, Oy, Blaine, Little Blaine, Steven Deschain, Susan Delgado, Cuthbert Allgood, Alain Johns, Rhea of the Coos, Eldred Jonas, Sheemie, John Farson, Walter.

The Dark Tower V: The Crawling Shadow (2002[?])

King has revealed that the working title for this fifth *Dark Tower* installment is, in fact, *The Crawling Shadow*, but he also said (during a September 19, 2000 AOL chat) that the title will "probably change, as that's sort of corny." (Personally, I kind of like it...it has kind of a "Sauron" feel to it, don't you think?)

There was talk that this installment (still unpublished (and unstarted?) as of spring 2001) was originally to be called *The Dark Tower V: Thunderclap*, referring to the dark place where, King tells us, Father Callahan from *'Salem's Lot*, now resides.

11

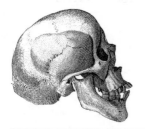

Insomnia
(1994)

Complete the circle, Ralph and Lois.
Don't be afraid. All is well.

Why it made the top 100:

After studying the world of Stephen King and talking to a great many fans, I have concluded that there are three levels of Stephen King fan: the *Casual*, the *Serious*, and the *Fanatic*.

Insomnia is not for the Casual fan. I know many Casuals who put the enormous novel down about a third of the way into it because it simply was not the "Stephen King book" they were expecting. *Insomnia* is for the Serious or Fanatic fan. It is a dense read, laden with subtext that references mythology, religion, and King's *Dark Tower* mythos. This syntactical complexity makes it somewhat less accessible than straight-on narratives like, say, *The Green Mile* or *The Shining*, but this does not detract from the importance of this book in the King canon, nor of its contribution to the ongoing *Dark Tower* epic.

Insomnia starts off slowly, with a stately and measured narrative voice, giving us a depiction of the life and times of widowed senior citizen and Derry resident Ralph Roberts and his ever-troubling insomnia. As his insomnia worsens, he begins to see auras around people and, one sleepless night, he catches his first glimpse of the "bald doctors," who will play such an important role in the story, and in Ralph and his lady friend Lois's life.

The bald doctors are from a dimension beyond ours and act as harbingers of death, as well as serving as the actual executioners of humans. The doctors cut the (usually invisible) cord that connects humans' souls to existence on this level and Ralph has been selected to be one of the few who can see the doctors, as well as his fellow humans' auras.

Why have Ralph (and Lois) been so chosen? They have been selected for an important task—to save the life of a young boy who will one day save the Dark Tower. Yes, *Insomnia* is a *Dark Tower* novel, even though it is not actually part of the *Dark Tower* series. But the novel could have easily been called *The Dark Tower: Insomnia*, even though Roland only makes a brief appearance, and the story is actually more about Ralph and Lois than Roland and company.

Insomnia also marks the "debut," so to speak, of the Crimson King who is, quite possibly, Roland's ultimate nemesis. One of the more chilling scenes in the novel is when the Crimson King appears to Ralph as his mother.

Insomnia has an apocalyptic explosion scene (when kamikaze Ed Deepneau blows up the Derry Civic Center), as in *It*, and the novel also introduces us to the concept of the Four Constants of Existence: Life, Death, the Random, and the Purpose. Who serves the constants is also revealed in a conversation between Atropos and Clotho and Ralph and Lois.

The *Dark Tower* story is advanced in *Insomnia*, perhaps more so than in some of the *Dark Tower* narratives, simply because King takes time to explain the meaning of Roland's quest and how the different levels of existence co-exist and interact. His discussion of Long-timers, Short-timers, and All-timers and their varying powers and limitations is one of the more fascinating sequences in the novel.

Insomnia is a difficult novel, yet one well worth the effort. King fans who have put it down would do well to try again, especially if they are fans of the ongoing *Dark Tower* epic.

☠ **C. V.** ☠

 Main Characters

Ralph Roberts, Lois Chasse, Lachesis, Ed Deepneau, Patrick Danville, Susan Edwina Day, Helen Deepneau, Bill McGovern, Dorrance Martstellar, the Crimson King, the Green Man.

Did You Know?

Insomnia is dedicated to King's wife Tabby, and also to musician Al Kooper. Kooper was one of the professional "ringers" who toured with King's band The Rock Bottom Remainders and who participated in their band-written book *Mid-Life Confidential*.

What I Really Liked About It

I love *Insomnia*'s slowly revealed connections to *It*, *The Stand*, the *Dark Tower* epic, the *Eyes of the Dragon* and, referentially, the *Lord of the Rings* trilogy. But the moment that always gets me (and which has always made fans cry) is Ralph's death scene at the end of the novel, and specifically, Clotho's generous gift to Lois: "She was in a dark place filled with the sweet smells of hay and cows...." Clotho's gift brought Lois a glorious peace that greatly comforted her as she lost her beloved Ralph. (The short, one-paragraph scene in which the Derry Civic Center explodes is also quite noteworthy for the punch it packs in its brevity.)

Film Adaptations

None.

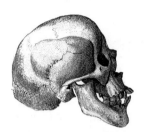

The Talisman
(with Peter Straub)
(1984)

*Long seconds before Jack opened his eyes, he knew from the
richness and clarity of the smells about him
that he had flipped into the Territories.*

Why it made the top 100:

In 1989, introducing my chapter on *The Talisman* in my *Complete Stephen King Encyclopedia*, I wrote:

The Talisman is a weird one among King fans. I've found that most of King's readers fall into one of three categories when it comes to *The Talisman*: "I hate it," "I love it," or "I haven't read it" (or, "I couldn't get through it").

Back then, I fell into Category 2; today, I still do. And adding an element of anticipation and excitement is the fact that, now, right at this moment, in the final days of 2000 and the early days of 2001, Stephen King and Peter Straub are collaborating on *Black House: The Talisman II*, the sequel to their 1984 cowritten epic. (Reportedly it was King's wife Tabitha who came up with the title for the sequel.)

Dedicated to their mothers, Ruth King and Elvena Straub, *The Talisman* is a masterful quest epic in the tradition of J. R. R. Tolkien and, yes, Mark Twain. (Jack *Sawyer* is not an

The King Speaks

"We both agreed that it would be nice to make the book seamless—it shouldn't seem like a game to readers to try to figure out who wrote what ... When I worked on my half of the copy editing, I went through large chunks of the manuscript unsure myself who had written what..."

—From an interview with Douglas E. Winter in
Stephen King: The Art of Darkness

accident.) In fact, the authors acknowledge as much in the chapter "Richard at Thayer" when they write, "...the conversation to come might be easier if the books on the desk were *The Lord of the Rings* and *Watership Down* instead of *Organic Chemistry* and *Mathematical Puzzles*." Also, at one point in the story, Jack takes Wolf to see Ralph Bakshi's odd animated/live action *Lord of the Rings* film at a theater in Muncie, Indiana.

The Talisman begins with Young Jack Sawyer setting out on a cross-country quest to find a cure for the cancer that is slowly killing his mother Lily. Jack has been told of his mission by Speedy Parker, who gives him the magical potion that will allow Jack to "flip" back and forth between our world and the parallel world, the Territories. Jack learns that many of us here have a Twinner in the Territories and that Lily's Twinner is Queen Laura DeLoessian, suffering from a mysterious and possibly fatal sleeping sickness. The magical Talisman will cure Jack's mother and her Twinner the Queen, and it is Jack's mission to find it and bring it back to the Alhambra Hotel in New Hampshire where Lily lays dying.

Jack "lights out" and faces mind-boggling challenges and terrors as he seeks to save his mother's life and also defeat their bitterest enemy, Morgan Sloat, the evil business partner of Jack's late father. In the end, Jack finds the Talisman and the epic novel concludes with Lily being cured and the Queen opening her eyes in her bedroom in the Territories.

Of course, no such synopsis can do justice to the breathtaking stories told in *The Talisman*; a unique achievement for King and Straub, a work which contains some of their finest work, and which makes us all the more eager for the sequel currently being written.

☠ **C. V.** ☠

Main Characters

Jack Sawyer, Lily Cavanaugh Sawyer, Reverend Sunlight Gardener, Richard Sloat, Morgan Sloat, Wolf, and assorted Twinners of these characters.

Did You Know?

Stephen King's enormous popularity and worldwide fame was not allowed to overshadow the fact that *The Talisman* was a *collaborative* project and that its two authors each contributed to the book on an equal basis. The title page lists the two authors in alphabetical order; the copyright does likewise. The most blatant indication of the deliberate insistence that the two authors receive equal billing, though, is on the front and rear covers of the hardcover. The front of the book jacket has Stephen King on the top and Peter Straub on the bottom; the rear of the jacket has Peter Straub on the top and Stephen King on the bottom.

What I Really Liked About It

As a big *Lord of the Rings* fan (I have read the Trilogy over a dozen times since its publication), *The Talisman*, to me, was the best of Tolkien melded with the best of King. Thus, I found it irresistible.

Film Adaptations

The Talisman (ABC miniseries); production begins in 2001; screenplay by Richard LaGravenese.

NUMBER 13

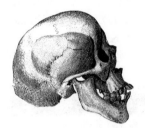

Desperation
(1996)

David put his head back against the seat,
closed his eyes, and began to pray.

Why it made the top 100:

In the four-year period from 1996 through 2000, Stephen King published the serial novel *The Green Mile*, the two-book set consisting of *Desperation* and *The Regulators,* the fourth *Dark Tower* novel *Wizard and Glass*, and *Bag of Bones*. Additionally, he published the elegantly crafted collection *Hearts in Atlantis*, the unexpected "surprise" novel *The Girl Who Loved Tom Gordon*, and the wonderful nonfiction memoir, *On Writing*. Finally, he published the groundbreaking e-books, *Riding the Bullet* and *The Plant*.

We should keep in mind that this creative output was from a man who earns millions of dollars a year in royalties and film rights *without* writing a word. And that a measure of this body of work was produced while recovering from a near-fatal accident that left him crippled and wracked with "near-apocalyptic" pain.

Does the phrase "work ethic" spring to mind?

Desperation, the second publication of this four-year run, was very well received by King fans upon its publication; its companion book *The Regulators* left many with a crinkled brow. (See the chapter on Richard Bachman's *The Regulators*.)

Desperation is what has come to be known as "classic King" (or "Klassic King," as some way-too-clever journalists might suggest); the Stephen King of *The Stand* and *The Shining* and *'Salem's Lot*, and even *It*. It is a sprawling tale of a band of ... pilgrims? ... who come face to face with a minion of a possibly eternal evil and who must depend on the wisdom and God-centeredness of a young boy who just may have a direct line to the Big Guy himself.

Tellingly, one of the final exchanges of dialogue in *Desperation* refers to a Biblical passage, specifically, I John 4:8:

He that loveth not, knoweth not God; for God is love.

Desperation begins ominously (and disturbingly if you're a cat lover).

Peter and Mary Jackson see a dead cat nailed to a speed limit sign on the outskirts of Desperation, Nevada. Shortly thereafter they are stopped for speeding by a cop named Collie Entragian who just might be not of our (humans, that is) species.

The Jacksons, the Carvers, a writer named Johnny, and several others all end up captives of Entragian and their fate ultimately lies in the hands—and prayers—of young David Carver.

Desperation is a page-turner that is also well-written and has some of King's most memorable scenes—David's escape from a jail cell using Irish Spring soap is just one of them.

Some critics saw the dual publication of *Desperation* and *The Regulators* as a marketing gimmick to sell two books at once, and this somewhat colored the reviews. The merits (or faults) of *The Regulators* aside, *Desperation* is one of King's best and deserves a review on its own virtues. Using that criterion, it's a keeper.

☠ **C. V.** ☠

Main Characters

David Carver, Johnny Marinville, Peter Jackson, Mary Jackson, Ralph Carver, Ellen Carver, Kirsten Carver, Steve Ames, Cynthia Smith, Brian Ross, Cary Ripton, Brad Josephson, Allen Symes, Tom Billingsley, Collie Entragian, Tak.

Did You Know?

Considering the spiritual/metaphysical bent to some of King's more thoughtful recent works (including *The Green Mile*, *Desperation*, and *The Girl Who Loved Tom Gordon* from the list cited above), his comments on religion in his March 5, 1999 letter to

The King Speaks

"Above all else, I'm interested in good and evil. And I'm interested in the question about whether or not there are powers of good and powers of evil that exist outside ourselves. I think that the concept of evil is something that's in the human heart. The goodness in the human heart is probably more interesting, psychologically, but in terms of myth, the idea that there are forces of evil and forces of good outside, and because I was raised in a fairly strict religious home, not hard-shelled Baptist or anything like that, I tend to coalesce those concepts around God symbols and devil symbols, and I put them in my work."

—From a November 17, 1988 interview with Janet Beaulieu

reviewers that was included with review copies of *The Girl Who Loved Tom Gordon* are especially interesting. "I have been writing about God—the possibility of God and the consequences for humans if God does exist—for 20 years now, ever since *The Stand*. I have no interest in preaching or in organized religion, and no patience with zealots who claim to have the one true pipeline to the Big Guy..."

What I Really Liked About It

Stephen King giving us one of the things he does best: a tale depicting an Armageddon-like battle between the force of evil—Tak—and the powers of good (and God)—11-year-old David Carver.

Film Adaptations

A film adaptation was in development as of the summer of 2000, but it had not yet been greenlighted. Mick Garris is slated to direct.

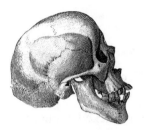

Hearts in Atlantis
(1999)

Bad eyes and bad blood-pressure were one thing;
bad ideas, bad dreams, and bad ends were another.

Why it made the top 100:

When I was working on this book, a trusted colleague of mine (a fellow King expert) and I were discussing how I should treat *Hearts In Atlantis*.

- Is it a novel?
- Is it a novella collection like *Four Past Midnight* or *Different Seasons*?
- Is it a short story collection like *Night Shift* or *Skeleton Crew*?
- Or is it a weird hybrid of all of the above and, thus, each work within its covers should be evaluated individually for inclusion in the top 100 list?

My friend described it as "a loose collection" but did agree with me that I should treat the book as a *novel*. Especially since, the formats of its individual works notwithstanding, the fact that every tale in the book is connected to the others by character, place, and events, mandates treating it as a single unit. (My friend also made the valid point that Scribner's, King's current publisher, would disagree with this decision since they were currently marketing 2001's *Dreamcatcher* as King's "first novel" since *Bag of Bones*. Upon reflection, I decided that publishing industry semantics will be disregarded for the purpose of this specific ranking.)

Hearts in Atlantis consists of five interconnected tales, all of which feature the same characters at varying stages of their lives (but not every character appears in every work in the collection).

The five individual works in the book are:

- *Low Men in Yellow Coats* (a novel).
- *Hearts in Atlantis* (a novella).
- "Blind Willie" (a short story).
- "Why We're in Vietnam" (a short story).
- "Heavenly Shades of Night Are Falling" (a short story).

Hearts in Atlantis is a landmark book for Stephen King and it contains some of his finest writing.

The "stars" of the book are Bobby Garfield, whose life path is tracked throughout the five tales and whose karmic wheel is touched by "other worlds than these," specifically the world of the Dark Tower and the Crimson King; and Bobby's girlfriend Carol Gerber.

The first story in the book, *Low Men in Yellow Coats* is a *Dark Tower* story. (And this revelation, when it came, was a genuine surprise).

When Bobby is 11 years old, a man named Ted Brautigan moves into the boarding house where Bobby lives with his widowed mother. Bobby and Ted soon establish a friendship and a bond and Bobby eventually learns that Ted is on the lam. Not from the cops, however, but from the low men in yellow coats, minions of the Crimson King, whom we already know from the *Dark Tower* series and *Insomnia*. Why do the low men want Ted? Because he is a "breaker," a being who can break the Beams that lead to the Dark Tower and the Crimson King wants to use him (against his will) to destroy the Beams and, thus, make the Dark Tower fall and destroy all of space and time. [See Chapter 74, "Everything's Eventual."] Ted is captured, however, due, in part, to Bobby's rejection ("chickening out") of him. Bobby's guilt sets him on the wrong path for many years of his life, until he receives an envelope from Ted, (who has apparently escaped the Crimson King) filled with rose petals, a resonant and recognizable image to readers familiar with the *Dark Tower* narrative.

The collection then moves to its title piece, *Hearts in Atlantis*, which tells the story of University of Maine freshman Pete Riley who gets caught up in a dangerous obsession with the card game Hearts. (And this obsession was *literally* dangerous—the hellhole of Vietnam awaited flunked-out college students.) Pete also gets romantically involved with none other than Carol Gerber, now an antiwar activist who was once rescued by Bobby when they were young and who will tragically die (or will she?) in a fire.

The third story, "Blind Willie," connects the first two by the character of Willie Shearman, who was one of the kids who violently assaulted Carol Gerber in *Low Men in Yellow Coats* and who has never been able to emotionally atone for his sins.

The fourth story, "Why We're in Vietnam," is about John "Sully-John" Sullivan, a friend of Bobby's from *Low Men*, and a Vietnam vet whose life was saved by the previous story's Willie Shearman. This tale boasts one of the most powerful scenes in the book, a terrifying sequence in which things fall from the sky onto the highway where Sully-John sits in traffic. This scene is really a depiction of Sullivan's death that ends on an exquisitely poignant and undeniably supernatural moment involving, of all things, a baseball glove—and another message from Ted Brautigan.

The book concludes with the brief story "Heavenly Shades of Night Are Falling" in which Bobby learns a truth about Carol Gerber, *and* Ted Brautigan, and ultimately himself. This story makes yet another *Dark Tower* connection when we learn that a certain Raymond Fiegler, the leader of the group that did the bombing in which Carol was killed, taught Carol a trick. He taught her how to become *dim* (an *Eyes of the Dragon* reference), which means that Fiegler, another "RF" character, is probably yet another manifestation of our old friend Randall Flagg.

With *Hearts in Atlantis*, Stephen King achieves a triad of monumental literary feats. He vividly portrays a generation and an era with a visceral reality, he tells the interwoven stories of a group of friends who live through times of trials and joys, and he adds yet another chapter to Roland's tale and the history of the Dark Tower.

☠ **C. V.** ☠

Main Characters

Bobby Garfield, Carol Gerber, John Sullivan, Ted Brautigan, Liz Garfield, Pete Riley, Skip Kirk, Nate Hoppenstand, Stokely Jones, Raymond Fiegler, Willie Shearman, The Crimson King, The Low Men.

Did You Know?

A section of the short story "Why We're in Vietnam" was originally published by King's Philtrum Press as a chapbook called "The New Lieutenant's Rap," which was given to party guests at an April 6, 1999 celebration in New York City marking King's 25th year in publishing. This segment was heavily revised for its eventual appearance in *Hearts in Atlantis*.

The King Speaks

"Although it is difficult to believe, the 60s are not fictional; they actually happened. ... I have tried to remain true to the spirit of the age. Is that really possible? I don't know, but I have tried."

— From "Author's Note" in *Hearts in Atlantis.*

What I Really Liked About It

I like very much the way King interweaves the various characters' lives throughout the collection, which, for me, is greatly enhanced by the fact that the book leads off with a *Dark Tower* connection.

Film Adaptations

Hearts in Atlantis (2002?); as of fall 2000 this was in development, with a screenplay by William Goldman.

NUMBER **15**

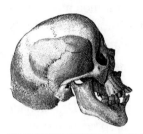

Dolores Claiborne
(1993)

One thing I found out on the day of the eclipse: if you live on an island and you try to kill someone, you better do a good job. If you don't, there's nowhere to run and nowhere to hide.

Why it made the top 100:

Which of Stephen King's "women's" novels will, in the end, be considered his finest? *Gerald's Game? Rose Madder? Dolores Claiborne?* (And a case can be made for also including *The Girl Who Loved Tom Gordon* in this "category.")

Dolores Claiborne, told entirely in the first person voice of Dolores Claiborne St. George (described in the novel's jacket copy as "an old Yankee bitch" with a "foul temper, foul mouth [and] foul life") is a Stephen King *tour de force*.

The novel opens with Dolores beginning her "purt-near a dozen of those tiny little tapes" narrative after being arrested for the murder of her employer, Vera Donovan. Vera fell down a flight of stairs and was discovered by Sammy Marchant, the mailman who placed Dolores at the scene of the crime and made it pretty clear that he thought Dolores was the one who had pushed her boss down the stairs.

Dolores uses the opportunity of her subsequent deposition to deny any culpability in the death of Vera Donovan ... but to admit murdering her husband Joe in 1963. And with that setup, we're off and running.

We eventually learn that Dolores murdered Joe by tricking him into falling down a well and then bashing his head in when he attempted to climb out. Dolores murdered Joe because she had had enough. Joe was a lazy, out-of-work drunk who took sadistic delight in what he called "home correction": physically, viciously abusing Dolores, including slamming her across her lower back with a piece of firewood. After Dolores threatens to kill Joe with an axe, he stops abusing her, but becomes impotent and then begins sexually molesting their young daughter Selena. That was enough for Dolores and thus, she set in motion the plan that would result in Joe ending up in the well.

Dolores is eventually cleared of any involvement in Vera Donovan's death ... and Joe and Vera are still dead.

Dolores Claiborne is a unique achievement by Stephen King. In fact, Dr. Michael Collings, with whom I consulted on my rankings for this book, went so far as to suggest that the novel could justifiably be placed in King's top 10. He told me, "Perhaps the only change I would make [in your top 10] would be to include *Dolores Claiborne*, if only because of its *tour de force* narrative—a single, unbroken monologue without chapter breaks or rests, driving the reader inexorably to discovery."

I did not rank *Dolores Claiborne* in the top 10, but Dr. Collings' point is well taken and emphasizes the unique nature of this novel in Stephen King's canon.

☠ **C. V.** ☠

 Main Characters

Dolores Claiborne, Joe St. George, Selena St. George, Vera Donovan, Andy Bissette, Dr. John McAuliffe.

 Did You Know?

Dolores Claiborne and *Gerald's Game* were written "in tandem," so to speak, and were intended to be a two-volume set called *In the Path of the Eclipse*. How are they connected? As Dolores, on Little Tall Island, is waiting for Joe to die during the July 20, 1963 eclipse, she experiences a psychic bond with young Jessie Burlingame of *Gerald's Game*, as Jessie's father is sexually molesting her. King does not fully explain the connection but it obviously has something to do with the fact that Dolores's daughter Selena was similarly abused by her father, Joe. (In a December 27, 1992 review of the novel in the *New York Times* by Bill Kent, Kent described this psychic link as "a gimmicky plot

The King Speaks

"Don't say that I'm stretching my range or that I've left horror behind. I'm just trying to find things I haven't done, to stay alive creatively."

—From a December 1992 interview with *USA Today* to promote *Dolores Claiborne*

twist" and decreed that "Mr. King also unconvincingly implies the existence of a psychic sisterhood of abused women.")

What I Really Liked About It

The sequence during which Dolores gives an account of Joe's plunge into the well, subsequent escape attempt, and eventual death is remarkable for its sense of visceral reality. By this point in the novel, we know Dolores (and by extension, Joe) so well that we can completely identify with both Dolores's exquisite tension and Joe's dawning comprehension of his doom, even as he tries desperately to escape. This segment is King at his most powerful.

Film Adaptations

Dolores Claiborne (1995); starring Kathy Bates, Jennifer Jason Leigh, Judy Parfitt, Christopher Plummer, David Strathairn, Eric Bogosian, John C. Reilly, Eileen Muth, Bob Gunton; directed by Taylor Hackford; screenplay by Tony Gilroy. (Grade: B+.)

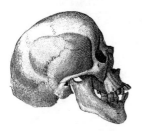

Cujo
(1981)

Monsters stay out of this room!
You have no business here.

☠ ☠ ☠

The monster never dies.

Why it made the top 100:

In Stephen King's *On Writing*, his 2000 autobiography-cum-writing manual, he admits, "At the end of my adventures I was drinking a case of 16-ounce tallboys a night, and there's one novel, *Cujo*, that I barely remember writing at all. I don't say that with pride or shame, only with a vague sense of sorrow and loss. I like that book. I wish I could remember enjoying the good parts as I put them down on the page."

Indeed. And there are plenty of "good parts" to enjoy in this dark and unsettling novel—even though "good," when used to describe a bleak book like *Cujo*, is a contradiction in terms. Not that there are *not* "good parts"—exciting, scary, well-written episodes that keep us turning the pages as fast as we can read them. It's just that *Cujo* is a relentlessly pessimistic book ... proof being that King had originally thought it should be a Richard Bachman novel.

In *The Stephen King Universe*, authors Stanley Wiater, Christopher Golden, and Hank Wagner tell us that the most frightening themes espoused in *Cujo* are the grim realities that "A single mistake can trash an entire career. Marriages can be bent or ruined. Spousal abuse and alcoholism can destroy families from within....Simply stated misery, unhappiness and shattered dreams know no age or social barriers. We live in a dangerous world, a world where even beloved pets can go mad and turn on their masters." Again, indeed.

As King always does in his most insightful works, in *Cujo* he again shows us the darkness hidden beneath the light. Castle Rock, Maine is, at first glance, an idyllic rural town. But its pretty face is a mask, behind which hides spousal abuse, rape, alcoholism, poverty—a whole slew of ugly dysfunctions.

The Trentons' marriage is falling apart; Vic Trenton's business is on life support; Tad Trenton senses a monster in his closet that might be the specter of Frank Dodd, the Castle Rock rapist from *The Dead Zone*; Donna is having an affair that goes bad. The list goes on. As if a manifestation of the nightmares the family (and especially Tad) are living through, Donna and Tad end up trapped by a murderous, rabid dog ... and, as King has often remarked regarding the ending of this sad story, sometimes, in real life, the kid dies.

King may not have conscious recollection of writing *Cujo*, but the writer in him knew what he was doing. Fast-paced and chilling, *Cujo* is insidious in its ability to terrorize us with the vagaries of everyday life. The unremarkable ordinariness of its characters makes their fates all the more real—and all the more frightening. After all, if it can happen to an innocent little kid, it can happen to us, right?

Right. And therein lies the true power of this novel.

 ☠ **C. V.** ☠

Main Characters

Cujo, Tad Trenton, Frank Dodd, Donna Trenton, Vic Trenton, Joe Camber, Charity Camber, Brett Camber, Steve Kemp, Roger Breakstone, Sheriff Bannerman.

Did You Know?

At one point in the novel, Donna Trenton recalls that "Cujo" was the name of one of the members of the radical terrorist group the Symbionese Liberation Army, the organization that kidnapped Patty Hearst. King has, from time to time, talked about a novel he began writing in 1974 called *The House on Value Street*, which was about the SLA's kidnapping of Patty Hearst. That novel metamorphosed into *The Stand*.

What I Really Liked About It

I completely agree with *Saturday Review* magazine when they describe *Cujo* as "grisly as *Carrie*, as ominous as *The Shining* [and] as eerie and absorbing as *The Dead Zone*." Who could ask for anything more?

The King Speaks

"I took the bike out there, and I just barely made it. And this huge Saint Bernard came out of the barn, growling. Then this guy came out and, I mean, he *was* Joe Camber—he looked like one of those guys out of *Deliverance*. And I was retreating, and wishing that I was not on my motorcycle, when the guy said, 'Don't worry. He don't bite.' And so I reached out to pet him, and the dog started to go for me. And the guy walked over and said, 'Down Gonzo,' or whatever the dog's name was, and gave him this huge whack on the rump, and the dog yelped and sat down. ... The guy said, 'Gonzo never done that before. I guess he don't like your face.'"

—From a 1982 interview with Douglas E. Winter
in *Stephen King: The Art of Darkness*

Film Adaptations

Cujo (1983); starring Dee Wallace, Danny Pintauro, Daniel Hugh-Kelly, Christopher Stone, Ed Lauter; directed by Lewis Teague; screenplay by Don Carlos Dunaway, Lauren Currier (Barbara Turner). (Grade: A-.)

NUMBER 17

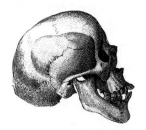

Rose Madder
(1995)

How can I hear crickets or smell grass?

Why it made the top 100:

There is a dark paradox manifested in the type of man that would hit a woman.

Abusers seem to believe that striking a wife or a girlfriend is a quintessential male prerogative, pure *machismo*, and a way to assert not only their masculinity but also their control over females, something they consider entitlement by virtue of their gender. Yet the truth is that a real man—an adult male who is mature enough and who knows himself well enough to stay in charge of his emotions—can keep his hands to himself, control his anger, and never strike another person out of rage.

In *Rose Madder*, Stephen King introduces us to a horrific example of the former in the character of Norman Daniels, an abusive cop who thinks nothing of beating and torturing not only his criminal suspects, but also his meekly subservient wife, Rosie. In *The Stephen King Universe*, King authorities Stanley Wiater, Christopher Golden, and Hank Wagner state with certainty that "*Rose Madder* stands as King's most unflinching look at abuse."

Norman Daniels, one of the most loathsome creatures King has ever created, might be the single King character that is the easiest to hate. And yet *Rose Madder* is not Norman's story, it is his wife Rosie's, a beset-upon woman who achieves a spiritual and psychic transformation thanks to the help of a female being named Rose Madder. Rose Madder parallels Rosie's *anima* and allows her to escape—and ultimately destroy her demon-husband, a monster whose parallel is the mythological bull Erinyes.

After a single drop of blood on a clean sheet provides the catalyst for Rose to flee Norman, she travels to a new place to live while also traveling to a new state of mind. One in which she recognizes her true value and is allowed a glimpse into other worlds than this.

Rose Madder is one of King's three books told from a woman's point of view—*Gerald's Game* and *Dolores Claiborne* are the other two. It is one of his most intricately plotted and symbolically rich works and stands as one of his finest novels.

☠ **C. V.** ☠

Main Characters

Rose McClendon Daniels, Norman Daniels, Rose Madder, Wendy Yarrow/Dorcas, Bill Steiner, Pamela Gertrude Steiner, Anna Stevenson, Robbie Lefferts, Erinyes.

Did You Know?

The character of Wendy Yarrow, who is reincarnated into the world of Rosie's painting as Dorcas and who acts as a mentor to Rosie, may be an *hommage* to King's wife Tabitha. Check out Chapter 9, verse 36 of *Acts of the Apostles* in *The Bible*: "Now there was at Joppa a certain disciple named Tabitha, which by interpretation is called Dorcas: this woman was full of good works and almsdeeds which she did."

What I Really Liked About It

I like everything about *Rose Madder*—the powerful characterization, the connections to the *Dark Tower* series, the flawless evocation and high drama of an abusive relationship, the mythological subtext, and even the behind-the-scenes detail about making recorded books. But I especially liked the scene when Rosie wakes up in her apartment and the "Rose Madder" painting has magically grown to the size of an entire wall and is now a portal to the place seen in the picture. Way cool. Who needs a holodeck when an old painting traded for a CZ ring can serve the same purpose, eh?

Publishers Weekly Speaks

"Relentlessly paced and brilliantly orchestrated, this cat-and-mouse game of a novel is one of King's most engrossing and topical horror stories...Crowded with character and incident, the novel builds to a nearly apocalyptic conclusion that combines the best of King's long novels—the breadth and vision of *The Stand*, for example—with the focused plot and careful psychological portraiture of *Dolores Claiborne*."

—From a May 1995 starred review in *Publishers Weekly*

 Film Adaptations

None so far. (There has been talk, though.)

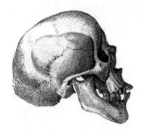

The Eyes of the Dragon (1984, 1987)

Peter was tried, found guilty of regicide, and ordered imprisoned for life in the cold two rooms at the top of the Needle.

Why it made the top 100:

When Stephen and Tabitha King's daughter Naomi was 12 or 13 years old, she did not like reading about vampires, haunted cars, pyrokinetic teens, Gypsy curses, or reanimated zombies (still dripping graveyard dirt). As a result, she had not found much in her father's work that appealed to her, as did the writings of Piers Anthony, John Steinbeck, Tanith Lee, and William Shakespeare.

So what's a dad to do (especially a dad who is the world's most popular writer) but write something made to order, something that *would* appeal to his grue-averse daughter?

And so he did. Stephen King wrote his epic fantasy novel *The Eyes of the Dragon* specifically for Naomi, hoping she'd read it and love it, and she did and she did.

This charming novel is dedicated to Naomi and also to King's "great friend" Ben Straub, King's *Talisman* series co-author Peter Straub's son.

The kingdom of Delain is ruled by King Roland, who has two sons, Peter and Thomas. Roland's Queen, the beloved Sasha, dies in childbirth. Roland dies soon thereafter and, as a result of the evil machinations of the magician Flagg (the same Flagg who appears in *The Stand* and the *Dark Tower* series), Peter, the rightful heir to Roland's throne, is imprisoned. The crown is then given to Thomas, who ends up becoming Flagg's lackey.

The story of whether or not Peter will escape from the Needle and regain the throne is one of intrigue, magic, deception, betrayal and, of course (this is a fairy tale, after all), a dragon.

The Eyes of the Dragon is a children's story, but it is also much more than that. It is one of those tales intended for a younger audience that ends up becoming a favorite of adults (usually the adult who read it aloud to the child!) and as beloved as the Oz stories, the Narnia stories, Tolkien's *The Hobbit*, and other wondrous fantasies.

The Eyes of the Dragon also connects to the ongoing epic quest King is recounting in the *Dark Tower* series, which now also includes alliances to the works *Insomnia*, *The Talisman*, *Rose Madder* and, tangentially, *Desperation*, *The Regulators*, and *It*. (Plus, *Eyes* has a little mouse.)

The Eyes of the Dragon is yet another of those King works you can offer to friends who insist they don't like "that horror stuff."

☠ **C. V.** ☠

Main Characters

Peter, Thomas, Roland the Good, Sasha, Flagg.

Did You Know?

In *The Eyes of the Dragon*, our friend Flagg owns a paperweight made of obsidian, which, at the time, was the hardest rock known. This is revealing, since obsidian, which is really natural glass with a hardness of only five (diamond, the hardest gem, is a 10), is only formed in areas of volcanic activity and is actually volcanic lava that cooled too quickly. This means that it is possible that at some point there had to have

The King Speaks

"I respected my daughter enough then—and now—to try and give her my best ... and that includes a refusal to 'talk down.' Or put another way, I did her the courtesy of writing for myself as well as for her."

—from the dust jacket flap copy of the trade hardcover edition
of *The Eyes of the Dragon*

been volcanoes in or near Delain (or that Flagg had traveled in areas with volcanic activity), and also that opal, peridot, onyx, aquamarine, emerald, topaz, cat's eye, ruby, sapphire, and, of course, diamond (all of which have hardness ratings higher than five) had not yet been discovered.

What I Really Liked About It

Stephen King writing in a fantasy/J. R. R. Tolkien mode? What's not to love? (Not to mention Flagg's ability to become "dim," the closest he could get to being completely invisible. Now *that's* a superpower I wouldn't mind having!)

Film Adaptations

An animated adaptation, with a $45 million budget, was scheduled for completion in early 2001 and release in late 2001 or early 2002.

NUMBER 19

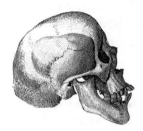

Firestarter
(1980)

"She's only a little girl, Wanless, after all. She can light fires, yes. Pyrokinesis, we call it. But you're making it sound like armageddon."

Why it made the top 100:

Firestarter is Stephen King at his most paranoid, and the novel can be thematically linked with King's 1985 poem, "Paranoid: A Chant" (see Chapter 99), in which a narrator believes he is being surveilled for some horrible, nefarious reason.

In *Firestarter*, the clandestine government agency The Shop performs ostensibly innocent experiments on college students, telling them that they are testing low-grade hallucinogenics for psychological study. The Shop was actually trying to stimulate paranormal abilities (better psychic powers through chemistry) for covert use and it did not have a contingency plan for what would happen if two of the test subjects married and had a child.

Two of the test subjects—Andy McGee and Vicky Tomlinson—*did* marry and have a child, Charlene Roberta—Charlie—and Charlie was born with pyrokinetic abilities. She was a firestarter.

The Shop inhumanly decides that all of the "Lot Six" (the drug used in the test) experiment subjects must be eliminated and *Firestarter* is the story of the organization's pursuit of Andy and Charlie, and Charlie's ultimate victory over the powers of bureaucratic evil.

Compelling characters abound in *Firestarter*. In addition to Charlie, there is the evil Native American operative John Rainbird whose specialty is efficient assassination. Cap Hollister is the man in charge of the Shop's "elimination" program, and Irv and Norma Manders, the elderly couple who conceal Andy and Charlie, defending them against The Shop, with Irv even taking a bullet for his efforts. (Interestingly, actor Martin Sheen played bad guys in two Stephen King film adaptations: The aforementioned Shop honcho Cap Hollister in *Firestarter*, and presidential candidate Greg Stillson in *The Dead Zone*).

Firestarter is a superior thriller with fully realized characters, an exciting chase scenario, an evil government agency, and a soupçon of "wild talents" (a la *Carrie*) making it truly one of King's strongest efforts, and the reason why it is ranked in *The Essential Stephen King*'s top 20.

☠ **C. V.** ☠

Main Characters

Charlie (Charlene Roberta) McGee, Andy McGee, Vicky McGee, John Rainbird, Dr. Joseph Wanless, Cap Hollister.

Did You Know?

In *Firestarter*, one of The Shop's clinical psychologists/psychotherapists is named Dr. Patrick Hockstetter. In King's 1986 novel *It*, we are told that a Derry resident named Patrick Hockstetter disappeared in 1958. (Eddie Kaspbrak does dream that he sees Hockstetter's decomposing body, but it is only a dream and by novel's end, Hockstetter is still missing) I suspect that these two Hockstetters are the same character. If this theory is correct, Patrick Hockstetter vanished from Derry in 1958 when he was approximately 11 years old and surfaced 20 or so years later as a Shop doctor, and King used *It* to reveal Hockstetter's back story, powerfully linking the two tales.

What I Really Liked About It

Firestarter contains elements of horror, as well as the gruesome scenes often depicted in horror novels (Herman Pynchot's suicide by sticking his arm down a garbage disposal

The King Speaks

"To me, the most horrifying scene in the book is the outright terrorism that goes on in a lunchroom when The Shop is looking for Andy and Charlie; this Shop agent terrorizes first a waitress and then a short-order cook—it's an awful piece of work. To suggest that there aren't guys like that who are actually getting their salaries from the taxpayers is to claim that there aren't guys like Gordon Liddy who ever worked for the CIA. And they love their work, man. They love their fucking work."

—From an interview with Douglas E. Winter
in *Stephen King: The Art of Darkness*

comes immediately to mind), and yet *Firestarter* is not a horror novel. It is a suspense thriller that can stand with (and in many cases, best) the best of Dean Koontz or Michael Crichton or Colin Forbes or Tom Clancy or Robert Ludlum or Nelson DeMille or James Patterson or even Ian Fleming. *Firestarter* is one of King's fastest-paced novels.

Film Adaptations

Firestarter (1984); starring David Keith, Drew Barrymore, Freddie Jones, Heather Locklear, Martin Sheen, George C. Scott, Art Carney, Louise Fletcher; directed by Mark L. Lester; screenplay by Stanley Mann. (Grade: C.)

Number 20

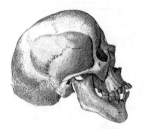

Carrie
(1974)

Nobody was really surprised when it happened, not really,
not at the subconscious level where savage things grow.

Why it made the top 100:

The story has oft been told that King originally wrote *Carrie* as a short story. He based the tale on a girl that he knew from the school where he taught but found himself stalled and threw the pages away. King's wife Tabitha came home from work, fished the pages out of the trash, read them, and insisted that Big Steve finish the story. King decided to lengthen the story by making up and inserting fictitious articles and other materials. This creative "trick" worked beautifully and *Carrie* was King's first published novel. He received a $2,500 advance for the book, but ultimately scored a $400,000 movie deal, of which he kept half. Thus, *Carrie* was the book that allowed Stephen King to quit teaching and write full-time.

Carrie White is a teenage girl with psychokinetic powers. Her mother, Margaret, is a fanatical religious fundamentalist who rants the Bible and preaches that sexual activity is the ultimate human act of abomination. Margaret also makes Carrie wear homemade clothes and forbids her to use makeup. As might be expected, Carrie is constantly tormented and ridiculed at her high school. Partly as a joke, Carrie is invited to the prom where she is subjected to the brutal humiliation of being crowned Queen of the Prom—and then having a bucket of pig's blood dumped on her as she stands on stage, smiling and wearing her crown. This is the ultimate betrayal ("you tricked me you all tricked me") and Carrie mercilessly unleashes her mighty powers. Over 400 kids end up dead and the school is burned to the ground. Carrie meets an equally tragic fate and "The Black Prom" becomes part of Maine's history.

King's ability to communicate the mindset of the typical teenager in a high school environment is amazing. His years as a teacher were well spent observing the cruelties and rigid and unforgiving caste structure so prevalent during the high school years.

The scenes at the prom when Carrie has the aforementioned bucket of blood dumped on her are riveting—as is the subsequent devastation and grisly dispatching by Carrie of her enemies.

I especially like the way Carrie kills her mother: She mentally slows Margaret White's heart until momma's dead ("Full stop"). The final segment of the novel—"Wreckage"—is also extremely well done. King neatly sums up the aftermath of Prom Night, and we also read a letter from Amelia Jenks in which she tells her sister Sandra that her 2-year-old niece Annie can make marbles fly up into the air just by looking at them ("they were mooving around all by themselfs."). Carrie's legacy lives on—but so far, we have not had the pleasure of a *Carrie* sequel by King, although the 1999 movie *The Rage: Carrie 2* (which actually isn't too bad) does pick up where the novel leaves off.

Also worth mentioning is the mature narrative tone present in the novel, and King's interjection of articles, book excerpts, court transcripts, news reports, and even a death certificate. In terms of technique, these faux documents lend an air of veracity to the novel that has since become commonplace, but which was extremely rare when King wrote *Carrie* in the 1970s.

☠ **C. V.** ☠

Main Characters

Carrie White, Chris Hargensen, Billy Nolan, Tommy Ross, Margaret White, Sue Snell.

Did You Know?

Continuing a beloved tradition in his writing, Stephen King himself makes two cameo appearances in *Carrie*, his first published novel. (Well, two *personas* of Stephen King.) One of Carrie's teachers was "Edwin King," and Stephen King's middle name is Edwin (see Chapter 1); and the folk singer who performed at the Ewen High School prom (the

Black Prom) was John Swithen. "John Swithen" was the pseudonym Stephen King used in 1972 to publish (in *Cavalier* magazine) his crime short story "The Fifth Quarter."

 ## What I Really Liked About It

The feeling throughout of one's high school years being a "place" as well as a time, and the meticulous recreation of the horrific caste system everyone who went to high school lived through.

 ## Film Adaptations

Carrie (1976), starring Sissy Spacek, Piper Laurie, Amy Irving, William Katt, Nancy Allen, John Travolta; directed by Brian DePalma; screenplay by Lawrence D. Cohen. (Grade: A.)

 ## Stage Adaptations

Carrie: The Musical (1988), starring Betty Buckley, Linzi Hateley, Charlotte d'Amboise, Paul Gyngell, Darlene Love, Gene Anthony Ray, Sally Ann Triplett; directed by Terry Hands; book by Lawrence D. Cohen; music by Michael Gore; lyrics by Dean Pitchford. *Carrie: The Musical* closed after five performances and is now known as one of the biggest failures in the history of the Great White Way.

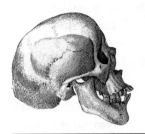

Danse Macabre
(1981)

This book is intended to be an informal overview of where the horror genre has been over the last thirty years, and not an autobiography of yours truly. The autobiography of a father, writer, and ex-high school teacher would make dull reading indeed. I am a writer by trade, which means that the most interesting things that have happened to me have happened in my dreams.

☠☠☠

Silas, bewildered by the changes thirty years had brought over his native place, had stopped several persons in succession to ask them the name of this town, that he might be sure he was not under a mistake about it.

—From Silas Marner *by George Eliot*

Why it made the top 100:

Danse Macabre holds the unique distinction of being the original source for what might be the most oft-repeated Stephen King quote to date.

That said, I will repeat it here yet again:

> I recognize terror as the finest emotion and so I will try to terrorize the reader. But if I find that I cannot terrify, I will try to horrify, and if I find that I cannot horrify, I'll go for the gross-out. I'm not proud.

King reiterated this "game plan" in a June 1983 interview with *Playboy* magazine in which he stated, "The genre exists on three basic levels, separate but interdependent and each one a little bit cruder than the one before. There's terror on top, the finest emotion any writer can induce; then horror, and, on the very lowest level of all, the gag instinct of revulsion. Naturally, I'll try to terrify you first, and if that doesn't work, I'll try to horrify you, and if I can't make it there, I'll try to gross you out. I'm not proud; I'll give you a sandwich squirming with bugs or shove your hand into the maggot-churning innards of a long-dead woodchuck." The woodchuck King is referring to appears in 1979's *The Dead Zone* in the scene where Johnny Smith touches Dr. Brown's hand:

> He found himself remembering a picnic in the country when he had been seven or eight, sitting down and putting his hand in something warm and slippery. He had looked around and seen that he had put his hands into the maggoty remains of a woodchuck that had lain under the laurel bush all that hot August. He had screamed then, and he felt a little bit like screaming now...

Stephen King has written a great deal of nonfiction during his career, but only two nonfiction books, *Danse Macabre* and his latest, 2000's *On Writing*. Compare that with the number of his nonfiction essays, articles, and other works, currently numbering more than 300 individual pieces.

King explains the genesis of *Danse Macabre* in the book's Foreword. This insightful volume came about thanks to a phone call from Bill Thompson, his editor at the time. Thompson was the visionary who happened to see a certain talent in a young writer when he first read the manuscript of a novel called *Carrie*. Thompson, fully aware of King's wide-ranging knowledge of the horror genre (a field with which, King tells us, he is "mortally involved"), suggested he write *Danse Macabre*, and also suggested that King concentrate on the 30-year span from 1950 through 1980.

The result is a "horror textbook," for want of a better term; a guided tour and analysis of the primary horror art forms—books, movies, TV shows, radio programs, and comic books—from the early 1950s through the late 1970s.

But *Danse Macabre* is more than that. It is also an astute sociocultural commentary; a discerning look at what these tales of grue and dread *mean* to the body politic, and why enjoying being frightened has been a constant throughout sentient civilization.

Some of the more interesting chapters in the book are "Horror Fiction" (which King reprinted in 2000 in *Secret Windows*), "The Last Waltz," and, what might be the fans' favorite, "An Annoying Autobiographical Pause." In that chapter, King begins telling the tale of his life, a project he would continue 20 years later in the opening sections of *On Writing*.

Danse Macabre is out of date, but King has never mentioned updating it. One wonders what he would have to say about the past 20 years of the horror genre— years that brought us Hannibal Lecter and the real-world horror of Jeffrey Dahmer. We can only imagine.

☠ **C. V.** ☠

The King Speaks

"If you want to know what I think about horror, there's this book I wrote in the subject. Read that. It's my Final Statement on the clockwork of the horror tale."

—From the Forenote to *Danse Macabre*

Main Characters

Stephen King, and a "horrific" cast of thousands from TV, the movies, radio, and books!

Did You Know?

"Danse Macabre" is Old French for "Dance of Death."

What I Really Liked About It

Three specific things (out of a thousand others):

1. Stephen King taking the horror genre seriously enough to write a book about it.
2. Stephen King knowing enough about the horror genre to write a book about it.
3. Coming away from a reading of *Danse Macabre* knowing a whole lot more about horror TV, movies, and fiction (and Stephen King) than I did before I read it.

Film Adaptations

None.

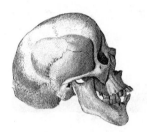

The Dark Half
(1989)

He faced himself in the mirror, touched the arc of skin under his left eye with his left finger, than ran it down his cheek to the corner of his mouth. "Losing cohesion," he muttered, and oh boy, that certainly was the truth.

Why it made the top 100:

In as many as two out of 10 births in which a single child is born, that widdle baby started out as *a twin*.

This I did not know.

And now that I know it, I'm not sure I *want* to know it. It seems that the weaker twin, the nonviable one, is *absorbed* into the developing body of the stronger twin and may end up in any number of the survivor's body organs, including the brain. These malformed parts are usually never a problem and are never discovered until an autopsy is performed. I guess this is Darwinism at its most basic level and also one of medicine's unbearably freakish secrets that you wouldn't be told unless you *had* to be told or *wanted* to be told.

This bizarre biology lesson is how Stephen King begins *The Dark Half*. It is one of his stranger tales, and one that had as its inspiration King's own experiences living with an alter ego—the nasty boy Richard Bachman—who died around the time *Thinner* came out and, thankfully, has so far agreed to stay dead.

The nightmarish premise of *The Dark Half* is, on the other hand, the "What if?" question, What if a writer's pseudonym *refused* to stay dead?

Thad Beaumont is a successful writer under his own name who has also had even greater success writing novels under the pseudonym of George Stark. After 12 years, Beaumont decides to kill off Stark, which he does in the pages of *People* magazine (where else?). Shortly thereafter, Homer Gamache is found dead in his truck ... with Thad's fingerprints all over the crime scene. The fingerprints are not Thad's, though; they are George Stark's. But Beaumont is—was—Stark. Or is he? Is Beaumont a homicidal schizophrenic? Or is George Stark a ghost from the land of the dead come back to seek revenge for Beaumont killing him?

The battle between Beaumont and Stark gets bloodier and more intense as their story progresses and it concludes with a final confrontation scene that will never allow you to look at sparrows the same way again.

Thad Beaumont, Stephen King, George Stark, Richard Bachman.

Who is real and who is the pseudonym?

The Dark Half confronts these questions and answers them ...sort of ... in a way that makes us wonder just what powers are being unleashed when writers "give birth" to a person who doesn't exist, yet who has a name, writes books, and may not like being told what to do.

The Dark Half is not only a killer suspense/horror novel; it is also a look inside the writing process and what might happen if writers take the creations of characters to the next, inevitable, possibly irreversible step.

☠ **C. V.** ☠

Main Characters

Thad Beaumont, George Stark, Liz Beaumont, William Beaumont, Wendy Beaumont, Sheriff Alan Pangborn, Danforth "Buster" Keeton, Dr, Hugh Pritchard, Shayla Beaumont, Glen Beaumont, Rawlie DeLessep, Wilhemina Burks.

Did You Know?

The Dark Half's character of Wilhemina Burks (Rawlie DeLesseps' girlfriend) seems to be an *hommage* to an earlier character of King's named Wilma Northrup. Wilma Northrup first appears in July 1979 (in *Gallery* magazine) in Stephen King's short story "The Crate." Wilma later appeared in King's 1982 animated film *Creepshow*, which included a King-scripted adaptation of "The Crate." In both versions of the story, Wilma

The King Speaks

"I started to play with the idea of multiple personalities and then I read somewhere, probably in the case of the twin doctors that the film *Dead Ringers* was based on, that sometimes twins are imperfectly absorbed in the womb and I thought, 'Now wait a minute. What if this guy is the ghost of a twin that never existed?' After that, I was able to wrap the whole book around that spine and it made everything a lot more coherent."

—From an interview in the November/December 1989
issue of Waldenbooks' magazine *W•B*

Northrup tells people, "Just call me Billie. Everyone does." The first time Wilhemina Burks is mentioned in *The Dark Half*, she is described as "The one who goes around blaring, 'Just call me Billie, everyone does.'"

What I Really Liked About It

I like this entire novel a lot, but especially the Prologue, the harrowing scenes in which the young Thad Beaumont has brain surgery and an eye is found peering out of his gray matter (causing nurse Hilary to flee from the operating room screaming). I also liked Dr. Pritchard's nonchalant coda to his surgical wizardry: "I want that silly cunt that ran out of here fired. Make a note, please." The nurse's response to this edict? The only one possible: "Yes, Doctor."

Film Adaptations

The Dark Half (1993); starring Timothy Hutton, Amy Madigan, Michael Rooker, Julie Harris, Robert Joy, Kent Broadhurst, Beth Grant, Rutanya Alda, Tom Mardirosian, Glenn Colerider, Chelsea Field, Royal Dano; directed by George A. Romero; screenplay by George A. Romero. (Grade: B-.)

23

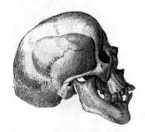

On Writing (2000)

My earliest memory is of imagining I was someone else—imagining that I was, in fact, the Ringling Brothers Circus Strongboy.

Why it made the top 100:

On Writing is probably the closest thing to a full-blown autobiography we are going to get from Stephen King. Begun before his crippling encounter with the late Bryan Smith, and completed after his painful recovery, *On Writing* is an eclectic fusion of autobiography, writing instruction manual, memoir, and popular culture appraisal. In other words, it is Stephen King *speaking his mind* on a range of subjects that are important to him. Unlike his only other book-length nonfiction work, *Danse Macabre*, which focused only on the horror genre, *On Writing* is more personal, more useful, and, to many fans thrilled with such a detailed and elegant peek into Stephen King's psyche, more entertaining.

On Writing consists of 10 individual sections:

☠ First Foreword

☠ Second Foreword

☠ Third Foreword

☠ C. V.

- ☠ What Writing Is
- ☠ Toolbox
- ☠ On Writing
- ☠ On Living: A Postscript
- ☠ And Furthermore, Part I: Door Shut, Door Open
- ☠ And Furthermore, Part II: A Booklist

GEORGE BEAHM

Stephen King fields questions from the audience during the question and answer period at a benefit for the Bangor Public Library.

All art is a fragile thing, an ethereal gesture from the artist's soul. And there is often a moment in the creation of a book, a song, a poem, a painting, or a script when something *clicks*, almost audibly, and the artist knows that the essence of the piece has been discovered, identified, and permanently etched onto the artist's consciousness. John Lennon once described this moment when talking about the writing of The Beatles' seminal hit, "I Want To Hold Your Hand." For him and Paul, it was an E minor chord. "I remember when we got the chord that made the song," he told an interviewer. "We had, 'Oh, you-u-u, got that something' and Paul hits this chord, and I turn to him and say, 'That's it! ... do that again!'" That chord was an E minor and that simple three-note combination suddenly crystallized Messrs. Lennon and McCartney's vision of the song.

In the case of Stephen King and *On Writing*, it is quite possible that the "E minor" for him was his June 1999 accident in which he was hit by the aforementioned Bryan Smith's Dodge van. Until then, *On Writing* was intended to be a book about, well, writing. The accident changed King and thus, changed this book. The result is a powerful statement about not only writing and art, but also about survival and faith.

One wonders if King would have been so forthcoming about his multiple addictions (now conquered) if he had not stood on the threshold of the door we call death.

Regardless of how the final book came into being, though, it is unquestionably an extremely important book in King's canon, as well as being a brilliant look at the inside workings of the artistic sensibility of a unique American voice.

☠ **C. V.** ☠

The King Speaks

"It's about the day job; it's about the language."

—From "First Foreword" in *On Writing*

Main Characters

Stephen King ... and a cast of thousands, ranging from writers that have influenced him and that he admires, family members, The Rock Bottom Remainders, and, yes, the Ringling Brothers Circus Strongboy.

Did You Know?

The first Advance Reader's Copy (ARC) of *On Writing* offered for sale on eBay went for over $500. This was an unsigned trade paperback sent to the media for review purposes. Following official publication of the book, ARC prices dropped drastically, down to the $30 - $200 range, although a signed copy of an *On Writing* ARC recently sold for $300 on the Internet auction site. No doubt about it: King works are collectible in *all* their incarnations.

What I Really Liked About It

As a writer, I found especial value in the "Toolbox" section, but there is a great deal more to like in *On Writing* that just the instruction. (Although when King does don his teacher's cap, the results are meritorious. His section on "perfect sentences" (noun, verb; noun, verb)—"Mountains float"; "Plums deify"—alone is worth the price of the book.) King's list of recommended books is invaluable, and the "On Living" section, written after his near-fatal accident, is quite compelling. (I also like the section about his desk.)

Film Adaptations

None.

NUMBER **24**

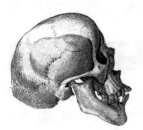

Needful Things
(1991)

You've been here before. Sure you have.

Why it made the top 100:

The small, serene town of Castle Rock is—*was*—in southwestern Maine, about 80 miles from Derry, 90 miles from Haven, and about 100 miles from Stephen King's hometown of Bangor—a mere couple of hours drive.

I say "was" because, as of the conclusion of *Needful Things*, Castle Rock was no more. *Needful Things* is subtitled "The Last Castle Rock Story" and Stephen King wasn't kidding.

The story opens with a stranger coming to town, one Leland Gaunt, an old gentleman who seemed to 11-year-old Brian Rusk to be "an *impossibly* tall figure," but with a very kind face.

Gaunt opens a store in Castle Rock called Needful Things and proceeds to fulfill the townfolks' most secret fantasies. An uncirculated, *signed*, 1956 Sandy Koufax baseball card is worth in excess of $100 becomes Brian's for the ludicrous sum of 85 cents. A photo of Elvis gives Myra Evans an earth-shattering orgasm, the likes of which she had never even imagined possible. A silver pendant (with *something* crawling around inside) takes away Polly Chalmers intractable arthritis pain.

But these delights come with a price and that price is, of course, their eternal soul. In addition to his selling price, Gaunt also insists that his customers perform an evil act on a fellow Castle Rock denizen, thereby sewing seeds of hatred and paranoia, and turning the town on itself. The result is complete mayhem, and ultimate devastation.

Who is Leland Gaunt? Is he Randall Flagg? Andre Linoge? Pennywise? No to all, and yet he is definitely a member of the same fraternity as these other evil beings, all of whom serve some dark power and all of whom thrive on fear and chaos.

Needful Things is an amazing melange of vividly drawn characters, exciting scenes of violence and terror, and a powerful narrative pull that takes us to a finale that forces us to bid adieu to one of the most beloved locales in all of Stephen King's writings.

☠ **C. V.** ☠

Characters

Main characters: Leland Gaunt, Brian Rusk, Polly Chalmers, Alan Pangborn, Wilma Jerzyck, Norris Ridgewick.

Crossover characters: Thad Beaumont (*The Dark Half*), Joe and Charity Camber (*Cujo*), Cujo (*Cujo*), Frank Dodd (*The Dead Zone*), Teddy Duchamp (*The Body*), Danforth "Buster" Keeton (*The Dark Half, The Sun Dog*), the Sparrows (*The Dark Half*), George Stark (*The Dark Half*), Homer Gamache (*The Dark Half*), Vern Tessio (*The Body*), Donna Trenton (*Cujo*), Tad Trenton (*Cujo*) Ace Merrill (*The Body*), Pop Merrill (*The Sun Dog*), Gordie Lachance (*The Body*), Chris Chambers (*The Body*), Sam Peebles (*The Library Policeman*), Naomi Sarah Higgins Peebles (*The Library Policeman*).

Did You Know?

According to the national business database on the search engine *Switchboard.com*, at the end of 2000, there were 69 businesses in the United States called "Needful Things." Of these 69, none were in Maine. In addition, there were no businesses in America by the names of "Answered Prayers," "The Mellow Tiger," "You Sew and Sew," "Nan's Luncheonette," or "The Emporium Galorium" (although there were over a hundred businesses known simply as "The Emporium"). There were three businesses named "Sonny's Sunoco" (two of which were in Vermont, nearby to King's home state of Bangor); one "Hemphill's Market" (in Tennessee); and even a "Homeland Cemetery" (in equally close-by New Hampshire). (There are also, apparently, many people in this great land of ours named "Leland Gaunt," but I did not pursue that line of research. Call me a chicken, but why tempt fate? Mrs. Spignesi sure didn't raise no dummies.)

The King Speaks

"Everything's for sale, and the only price is your immortal soul. I thought [*Needful Things*] was fucking hilarious!"

—From an August 9, 1998 UK interview with Peter Conrad

What I Really Liked About It

I was especially intrigued by the idea of Gaunt collecting the souls of his victims in a satchel and carrying them around with him. The final destruction of Castle Rock is also particularly exciting. And the coda, in which Gaunt opens a new store, Answered Prayers in Junction City, Iowa (home of Ardelia Lortz and the Library Policeman), is the perfect, ironic "to be continued" for a story that wrote the final chapter of our favorite Maine town.

Film Adaptations

Needful Things (1993); starring Max Von Sydow, Ed Harris, Bonnie Bedelia, Amanda Plummer, J. T. Walsh, Ray McKinnon, Duncan Fraser, Valri Bromfield; directed by Fraser C. Heston; screenplay by W. D. Richter. (Grade: C+.)

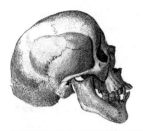

Gerald's Game
(1992)

Gerald, are you all right?

Why it made the top 100:

A half-naked woman is handcuffed to a bed for sex games with her husband. The husband has a heart attack and dies ... before he can remove the handcuffs. The woman is now shackled to a bed in a remote lake house ... it's getting dark ... and the back door of the house is unlocked.

The story told in *Gerald's Game* is one of the most palpably horrifying scenarios Stephen King has ever contrived. King flawlessly communicates Jessie Burlingame's terror. The captive wife begins to realize that she may *not* get out of her handcuffs any time soon, she may *die* in her bed in her little house on the lake, and also, that there is someone (or some*thing*) standing in the corner of the rapidly darkening room. (This is after, of course, a stray dog has eaten part of her husband's corpse.) At this point there isn't a set of fingers that can turn the pages fast enough, as the tension and terror level goes through the roof.

Does Jessie escape? Is the figure in the corner of the room real? Will the distant Ruth be Jessie's salvation?

Gerald's Game is psychological terror at its finest; razor-sharp, deeply insightful, and, as King notes below (see "The King Speaks") all the more frightening because what happens to Jessie could really happen. Whether you believe in the supernatural or not, the odds of running into Barlow, or Pennywise, or Christine as you go about your day, are pretty slim. An Annie Wilkes or a kinky husband, though ... well, those elements of our society are probably a little more prevalent than we would like to admit.

And therein lies the strength and power of *Gerald's Game*. Is it horror? Not strictly speaking. Is it horrifying? Absolutely. And adding to Jessie's (and our) nightmare is the surfacing of a long-buried childhood trauma: her molestation by her father during a 1963 eclipse. (See "Did You Know?")

In conclusion, a word of caution to all you playful, experimenting lovers out there: Don't use cop handcuffs. Stick with the padded ones with the secret escape lever. They're in the adult store right next to the whips, another item you should probably avoid. But that's a story for another time.

C. V.

Main Characters

Jessie Burlingame, Gerald Burlingame (briefly), Raymond Andrew Joubert, Prince the Dog, Ruth Neary (offstage only).

Did You Know?

King's masterful first-person novel *Dolores Claiborne* (1993) was originally intended to be the companion book to *Gerald's Game* as part of a set called *In the Path of the Eclipse*.

What I Really Liked About It

The stark and tangible sense of Jessie's reality when she is handcuffed to the bed and alone with her thoughts ... and her husband's corpse. King takes us inside Jessie's head and it's one scary place.

The King Speaks

"When I write, I want to scare people, but there is a certain comfort level for the reader because you are aware all the time that it's make-believe. Vampires, the supernatural and all that. In that way, it's safe. But these last two books [*Dolores Claiborne* and *Gerald's Game*] take people out of the safety zone and that, in a way, is even scarier. Maybe it could happen."

—From a 1992 interview in *USA Today*

Film Adaptations

None so far, although there has been talk of a *Gerald's Game* movie for years now. One topic of discussion regarding the adaptation of this novel has been the question of nudity. A significant portion of the book has Jessie Burlingame handcuffed to a bed clad only in panties. King fans have wondered how many A-list actresses would agree to a role that required them to be topless for the length of time Jessie is bound to her bed, on display for such a long period of the movie. An extremely well-known and extremely well-paid actress once said the reason she hated doing topless scenes was not because of shyness, but because her breasts always stole the scene. She remarked that she felt like (I'm paraphrasing), "I'm competing with my tits." Her point is well taken. In most cases, a topless scene distracts from the story and draws attention to the topless actress. How the makers of *Gerald's Game* will get around that remains to be seen, yet a fair guess is that the script will have Jessie in panties and bra instead of topless.

Number 26

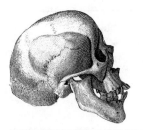

Dreamcatcher (2001)

No bounce, no play.

Why it made the top 100:

    Dreamcatcher is an interesting milestone for King. It was the first new, novel-length work King wrote after his near-fatal 1999 accident, and the violence and intensely graphic scenes in the novel obviously served as a catharsis for King. He began writing the book in longhand five months after he was hit by a van and almost killed. A colleague of mine opined that the book—which is by far the grossest thing King has ever written—was a means for the author to purge himself of the festering emotional and psychic poison caused by the accident.

    King's accident unquestionably influenced this book. In his "Author's Note" at the end of the book, he writes, "I was never so grateful to be writing as during my time of work (November 16, 1999-May 29, 2000) on *Dreamcatcher*. I was in a lot of physical discomfort during those six and a half months, and the book took me away. The reader will see that pieces of that physical discomfort followed me into the story..." King also reveals that (for ergonomic reasons to lessen his pain) he wrote the first draft of *Dreamcatcher* by hand, using a Waterman cartridge fountain pen. In *On Writing*, he writes about sitting at a desk for the first time after the accident and admits that after an hour and 40 minutes, the pain in his hip was "near apocalyptic." Thus, it makes sense that he would be more comfortable in a bed or a recliner, and either are perfect for writing by hand.

Dreamcatcher is, as described by Tabitha King, "the one about the shit-weasels." My sound-bite description of *Dreamcatcher* is "*Rain Man* and *The Body* meet *The Thing* and *Invasion of the Body Snatchers*."

Dreamcatcher is set in Derry, Maine, a town familiar to King's readers as the setting for *It*, *Insomnia*, *Bag of Bones* and other works. Derry is a Stephen King hotspot...*It* wreaked havoc for decades in the town; it played a role in the *Dark Tower* saga in *Insomnia*, and in *Dreamcatcher*, aliens land in the woods, bringing with them a byrus, a deadly, infectious fungus-like growth that could spell doom for mankind.

Prophetically, authors Stanley Wiater and Christopher Golden said in *The Stephen King Universe*, months before *Dreamcatcher* was published:

"Given that the author has spent so much time establishing Derry as one of the battlefields in the war between the Random and the Purpose, between chaos and order, and that such cosmic servants of the Random as the Crimson King and It have been drawn there, it seems virtually guaranteed that readers have not seen Derry for the last time. Stephen King is bound to return there, as he moves ever closer to the final battle that so many of his works lead toward."

Since *The Essential Stephen King* is being published within a couple of months of the hardcover release of *Dreamcatcher*, there is a strong likelihood that many of King's fans have not yet read the book. A lot goes on in the novel that I would not want to spoil by discussing here so I will defer to the official Scribner's press release for *Dreamcatcher*, which provides *just enough* information without giving away any of the book's secrets:

Once upon a time, in the haunted city of Derry (site of the classics It *and* Insomnia*), four boys stood together and did a brave thing. Certainly a good thing; perhaps even a great thing. Something that changed them in ways they could never begin to understand.*

Twenty-five years later, the boys are now men with separate lives and separate troubles. But the ties endure. Each hunting season the foursome reunites in the woods of Maine. This year, a stranger stumbles into their camp, disoriented, mumbling something about lights in the sky. His incoherent ravings prove to be disturbingly prescient. Before long, these men will be plunged into a horrifying struggle with a creature from another world. Their only chance of survival is locked in their shared past—and the Dreamcatcher.

The King Speaks

"Dreamcatcher [has] got a little bit of that *Stand* vibe. ... My accident changed everything. Not all those changes are bad. But it's a little easier to see the small shit in life for what it is after you've almost gotten the gate."

—From a live AOL chat on September 19, 2000

Stephen King's first full-length novel since Bag of Bones *is, more than any-thing, a story of how men remember—and how they find their courage. Not since* The Stand *has King crafted a story of such astonishing range—and never before has he contended so frankly with the heart of darkness.*

Also, a Castle Rock press release stated that *Dreamcatcher* combined "the bond-ing elements of *Stand By Me* with the mysticism and supernatural elements of *The Green Mile."* Not to mention a couple of surprises at the end that changes our views of certain characters. Although, interestingly, King does leave some questions unresolved and up to the reader, much the way he does with his first official 2001 publication, the short story "All That You Love Will Be Carried Away" which ends similarly inconclu-sive and arguable.

One interesting point that can be discussed without giving anything away is that, in the book, a victim of an automobile accident reveals that he learned *after* his recovery that he had died in the ambulance and had needed to be shocked with cardiac paddles to resuscitate his heartbeat. This begs the question "is this fictional incident a way for Stephen King to reveal something none of his fans had known until now?" Only King can answer that question.

Dreamcatcher is structured as a three-part epic, *Cancer*, *Grayboys*, and *Quabbin*.

King visited the Quabbin Reservoir in Massachusetts while writing the book and both the Reservoir and its Shaft 12 play an important role in the climax of the story.

Is *Dreamcatcher* connected to *It*, and is it a coincidence that there is a character named "Mr. Gray?" Is *Dreamcatcher*'s Mr. Gray the same character as "Bob Gray" in *It*? Interesting questions, with several answers, as readers learn upon finishing the novel.

Dreamcatcher will not be to every King fan's taste. As mentioned earlier, it is, in both a figurative *and* literal sense, *visceral*. (And if you look up the dictionary definition of "visceral," you will see how perfect a word it is to describe this novel.) Nonetheless, it is an important book, but like *Insomnia*, it demands effort, but it pays off at the end.

Plus *Dreamcatcher* is probably one of the few contemporary novels in which the undeniable hero is a young boy with both Down's syndrome and leukemia.

Main Characters

Jonesy, Beaver, Pete, Henry, Duddits, Roberta, Mr. Gray, Kurtz, Archie Perlmutter, Deke, Cambry.

Did You Know?

King originally titled this novel *Cancer* but changed it on the urging of his wife, novelist Tabitha King, who refused to refer to it by that title.

What I Really Liked About It

I greatly enjoyed being back in Derry again and the way King referenced the terrible events of 1985, which occurred, of course, in *It*. (See Chapter 1.) This narrative continuity serves, in a sense, to position *Dreamcatcher* as a "spin-off" of *It*, since it is another story of the town, thereby once again buttressing the argument that Stephen King has been writing one massive book his entire life and just breaking it up into individual volumes.

Film Adaptations

Film rights to *Dreamcatcher* were sold to Castle Rock before the book's publication.

Bev Vincent on Stephen King

Bev Vincent is a friend, and a terrific writer who happens to know *a lot* about the life and work of Stephen King.

You may recognize his name (yes, Bev's a guy) from the Acknowledgments section of my *Lost Work of Stephen King*.

Bev Vincent has been reading Stephen King since 1979, when he fortuitously purchased a used copy of *'Salem's Lot* in a second-hand bookstore. Bev is a software engineer, Web site designer, part-time book reviewer, and freelance writer. Over 60 of his book reviews have been published in a Texas newspaper.

Here, Bev contributes an astute review of King's latest novel, accurately discussing the book, without giving too much away. My appreciation goes to Bev for this essay, but also for his ongoing help and, yes, for *still* being every Stephen King fan's "eyes and ears!"

Stephen King's *Dreamcatcher*

by Bev Vincent

As alien invasions go, the one that precipitates the action in *Dreamcatcher* is less than a blazing success. The aliens crash their spacecraft in a remote section of western Maine and quickly discover that they cannot survive this climate and atmosphere. Nor are they a match for the paramilitary force dispatched to contain them.

Their appearance, though, has far-reaching implications. Four men who have known each other all their lives happen to be in those very woods on their annual hunting expedition. Though their paths rarely cross the rest of the year, they have repeated this ritual faithfully for over two decades. They have a powerful bond of friendship ... and something else. Each one has a subtle extrasensory power, acquired when they grew up in Derry (*It*, *Insomnia*), a city with a strange history.

As children, the foursome rescued a mentally handicapped boy called Duddits, who was being tortured by a group of high school bullies. They look on this heroic act, and their subsequent friendship with Duddits, as their finest hour. Life has not been kind to these men. Pete Moore is a raging alcoholic who had fantasies of working for NASA but ended up selling cars. Therapist Henry Devlin has recently been haunted by thoughts of suicide. Beaver Clarendon, whose dialog is peppered with an endlessly original string of profanity, has a failed marriage and an unfulfilling life. Jonesy, who teaches history at a small college, is recovering from an auto-pedestrian accident that nearly took his life—an accident that mirrors King's own near-fatal encounter with a motor vehicle in 1999. Jonesy saw death come knocking and managed to hide from it to live another day.

The friends only think that life has been bad. What happens in the wintry woods of Jefferson Tract comes at them straight out of *The X-Files*. While Henry and Peter are on a grocery expedition, Jonesy encounters Richard McCarthy wandering through the woods. Jonesy, nursing his aching hip atop a deer blind, almost shoots the man by accident. He will have cause to regret that he didn't.

From his rambling story, it appears that McCarthy may have been lost for days. He is suffering unusual ailments and has a debilitating case of flatulence. While they wait for Henry and Peter to return through an early winter blizzard, Jonesy and Beav must deal with the terrifying results of McCarthy's quickly degenerating condition.

The friends discover that the whispers of an alien invasion are more than rumor. Though the aliens cannot thrive on earth, they bring with them an infection. A cancer. As they decay, their infection spreads into human hosts. The lucky ones come down with a bad case of red fungus and telepathic powers. The unlucky ones become host to a parasite that runs amok in earth's climate. The result is *Invasion of the Body Snatchers* meets *Aliens*.

While the friends are conducting their personal battle against the alien invasion, the military sets up a covert camp to contain and eradicate the looming threat. Kurtz, a maniacal career military problem solver who rules his troops with an iron fist and believes that there is no such thing as a cost too high to attain his objective, leads them. The final third of the novel is an all-out chase through a perilous blizzard as Kurtz attempts to complete his mission.

To say more about the story would be unfair, as this is a book filled with surprises, both pleasant and unpleasant. It is also a book filled with more visceral violence and raw terror than any previous King novel. There are scenes of unflinching gore that will unsettle some readers. It is a story written by a man who has heard death come knocking and lived to tell another tale.

King originally planned to call the book *Cancer* (his wife convinced him that this would be an invitation to bad luck and trouble) and this working title is a multileveled metaphor for the different types of invasion explored in *Dreamcatcher*.

At its heart, though, as with all King stories, *Dreamcatcher* is about the characters, who live, breathe, suffer, and die as realistically as the people we know in our own lives.

King pulls out all the stops. He is unflinchingly willing to tell the story as he sees it. The tension and terror are heart stopping at times, as intense and gripping as any horror film could ever aspire to be. The prolonged chase across the snow-blind roads of New England is powerful and immediate. The reader is constantly aware that the clock is ticking toward the finale, where the ultimate surprises are laid bare and the true nature of the dreamcatcher is revealed to all.

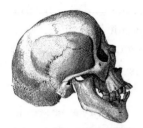

The Body
(1982)

In the years between then and the writing of this memoir, I've thought remarkably little about those two days in September, at least consciously. The associations the memories bring to the surface are as unpleasant as week-old river-corpses brought to the surface by cannonfire.

Why it made the top 100:

The Body is another of Stephen King's works that shuts people up when they attempt to dismiss him as "just a horror writer." (*Rita Hayworth and Shawshank Redemption* and "The Last Rung on the Ladder" do the same thing, in equally as effective a manner.) But as is often the case when a movie adaptation of a King work becomes an enormous hit, sometimes the original work is overshadowed. In the case of the novella *The Body*, Rob Reiner's enormously popular 1986 movie version *Stand By Me* has effectively usurped the text version in the annals of popular culture and is the work that has the higher-profile presence. In fact, I have heard people refer to the novella itself as *Stand By Me*. (I'll bet King grits his teeth when he hears people casually changing the (somewhat macabre) title of his work and then oftentimes probably shrugging off the correction.)

The Body is one of King's most autobiographical works. In fact, in the novella's final pages, the story's narrator Gordie Lachance, remembering the days of his youth, sums up his present life with a laundry list of details that could describe Stephen King himself. Grown-up Gordie is a writer who admits that "A lot of critics think what I write is shit." He sold his first book, it was made into a movie, and it was a huge hit. The same thing happened with his second book, and his third. He has three children. He gets "stressaches" (a word King himself has used to describe his own headaches); and he does not know how to interpret a world where "a man can get rich playing 'let's pretend.'"

The Body is set in Castle Rock, Maine. Maine landmarks and characters abound, including Cujo, "Constable" Bannerman (see Chapter 4), Harrison State Park, The Mellow Tiger (see Chapter 16 and Chapter 22), The Castle Rock *Call* (where Gary from "The Man in the Black Suit" (Chapter 36) published a weekly column for years), Lewiston, Motton, Pownal, and more.

The story told in *The Body* is a hybrid of coming-of-age story and quest tale. Four friends—Gordie, Chris, Vern, and Teddy—embark on a journey to find a dead body. When they do find the late Ray Brower's corpse, Ace Merrill and his crew are there to steal Gordie and company's claim, by any means necessary, and it becomes time for the four friends to, yes, make a stand.

And they do.

King's writing in *The Body* is confident, personal, and dead-on nostalgic. He recreates a time and place and, in so doing, tells us one hell of a story. *The Body* is undoubtedly (just ask Rob Reiner) one of Stephen King's classics.

 C. V.

Main Characters

Gordie Lachance, Chris Chambers, Vern Tessio, Teddy Duchamp, Ray Brower, Ace Merrill, assorted Mainefolk and lowlifes.

Did You Know?

There are two brothers mentioned in *The Body* with the last name of Darabont: Stevie and Royce. *The Body* was published in 1982. Stephen King had known *Shawshank Redemption* director Frank Darabont since 1980 when he sold Frank the rights (for $1.00) to make a short film of King's *Night Shift* story "The Woman in the Room." As a result, it seems likely that these two characters' moniker is a nod to the esteemed director.

What I Really Liked About It

This novella is Stephen King in his "let me tell you a story" mode and his authorial tone throughout is perfect for the subject of the piece.

The King Speaks

"According to Mom, I had gone off to play at a neighbor's house—a house that was near a railroad line. About an hour after I left I came back (she said), as white as a ghost. I would not speak for the rest of that day; I would not tell her why I'd not waited to be picked up or phoned that I wanted to come home; I would not tell her why my chum's mom hadn't walked me back but had allowed me to come alone. It turned out that the kid I had been playing with had been run over by a freight train while playing on or crossing the tracks...My mom never knew if I had been near him when it happened..."

–From *Danse Macabre*

Film Adaptations

Stand By Me (1986); starring Wil Wheaton, Richard Dreyfuss, River Phoenix, Corey Feldman, Jerry O'Connell, Keifer Sutherland, Casey Sziemasko; directed by Rob Reiner; screenplay by Raynold Gideon and Bruce A. Evans. (One of the all-time best adaptations of a Stephen King story to date.) (Grade: A+.)

NUMBER 28

The Long Walk
(written as Richard Bachman)
(1979)

They gave you three warnings. The fourth time you fell below four miles an hour you were...well, you were out of the Walk.

Why it made the top 100:

Stephen King has always been a seer, as well as being someone who is consistently ahead of the learning curve.

When King was in his late teens/early 20s, the crude, tasteless, mercenary TV game shows being broadcast were only a fraction of what's out there today. He was already envisioning a media-dominated future when cameras saw everything and death was the ultimate penalty for losing on a game show. We haven't gotten that far (yet) but considering the popularity of often repellent shows like *Survivor* (ritual banishment), the Internet-based *RealityRun* (civilian capture), and *Big Brother* (public humiliation and banishment) is the day far away when a losing contestant is killed, live on the air? Farfetched, you say? Perhaps, but who could have foretold the shows *Who Wants To Marry A Millionaire* or *Temptation Island*? *The Long Walk* (and *The Running Man* - see Chapter 41) was one of King's literary extrapolations of the possibility that technology, combined with the public's ever-increasing appetite for salacious voyeurism,

The King Speaks

"*The Long Walk* was written in the fall of 1966 and the spring of 1967, when I was a freshman at college....I submitted *Walk* to the Bennett Cerf/ Random house first-novel competition...in the fall of 1967 and it was promptly rejected with a form note...no comment of any kind. Hurt and depressed...I stuck it in the fabled TRUNK...but...it never escaped my mind."

—From "Why I Was Bachman"

would ultimately result in a competition like The Long Walk.

Strictly volunteer, the King-conceived, government-sanctioned Long Walk endurance competition was an appealing option for young men whose future looked to be less than rosy.

One hundred Walkers begin a non-stop, to-the-death Walk from northern Maine to Boston. The Walkers must maintain a pace of four miles per hour and if they do not, they are given a Warning. After three Warnings, soldiers following the troupe in radar-equipped jeeps execute the Walker on the spot. The winner is the last Walker left alive. The prize? The winner can have anything he wants for the rest of his life.

As those of you who have been with me since *The Complete Stephen King Encyclopedia* know, *The Long Walk* is one of my favorite Stephen King novels. In 1990, in my *Encyclopedia*, I defined The Long Walk competition as "the annual ritualized bloodlust torture of one hundred young boys" and that definition still works today, a decade later.

King himself has criticized the novel as being full of "windy psychological preachments," but for many readers, the psychology of the many characters in the story contributed to its drama and power.

In this time of ubiquitous Webcams and voyeur Web sites, *The Long Walk* still resonates, and it is still influencing readers and artists. Case in point: Jay Holben (see his essay in this volume), the director of *Paranoid* (the 2000 short film adaptation of King's chilling poem, "Paranoid: A Chant") concluded his film with the following onscreen quotation: "And when the hand touched his shoulder again, he somehow found the strength to run." That quote is the final line of *The Long Walk*.

☠ **C. V.** ☠

Main Characters

The Major,.Ray Garraty, Peter McVries, James Barker, Gribble, Hank Olson, Scramm, Stebbins,

Did You Know?

The Long Walk contains many clues that it was actually written by Stephen King instead of Richard Bachman. These include references to Pownal and Bangor, Maine, mention in the text of a "gunslinger," dedications to long-time King associates Burt Hatlen, Jim Bishop, and Ted Holmes, and a mention of King favorites Edgar Allan Poe and Ray Bradbury. Additionally there is a foreshadowing of the "playing elevator" scene in *The Shining* when Ray Garraty remembers his father picking up and swinging him wildly, and even an "RF" character, Roger Fenum, who was the 50th boy to go down.

What I Really Liked About It

The Long Walk is one of King's most psychologically dense novels and it is one of his tales which most compellingly communicates the individual terrors, insecurities, and weaknesses of its characters. To this day, my thoughts often turn to the Long Walk requirement that Walkers maintain a four-mile an hour pace, or receive a Warning. Sometimes when I'm stuck in traffic, and cars are moving at a rate of only four or five miles an hour, I imagine having to walk at that pace consistently, under fear of death. Four miles an hour may be slow in a car, but it's a fairly demanding pace when you're walking. King effectively puts us inside the minds of the Walkers.

Film Adaptations

None.

NUMBER 29

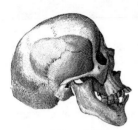

Rita Hayworth and Shawshank Redemption (1982)

I hope the Pacific is as blue as it has been in my dreams.

Why it made the top 100:

The only ghouls in *Rita Hayworth and Shawshank Redemption* are of the human ilk, typified by sadistic guards, violent rapists, corrupt beauracrats, and adulterous wives. And yet this novella, something of a departure for King, is now hailed as one of his finest works, justifiably perceived as King writing in an "anti-Bachman" mode, such is the power of its hopeful and optimistic ending. (The novella's foretitle is, appropriately, "Hope Springs Eternal.")

King fans have always loved this novella. Only *The Mist* and *The Body* topped it in a survey of hundreds of King fans conducted for this book. It is one of the four exemplary works in *Different Seasons*, perhaps King's finest novella collection. But as is often the case, Frank Darabont's *The Shawshank Redemption*, the 1994 movie version of the novella, brought a much larger audience to the source story and surprised a great many critics and readers who had fit Stephen King neatly into a "Horror Only" box. This happened on a smaller scale with Rob Reiner's *Stand By Me*, but the film garnered nowhere near the response that greeted *The Shawshank Redemption* after the movie came out in 1994.

In 1948, mild-mannered banker Andy Dufresne is sentenced to life in prison for the murder of his wife and her lover (even though he didn't do it) and sent to Maine's brutal Shawshank State Prison. Soon after his arrival, he meets the story's narrator, Red, a "regular Neiman-Marcus" who can get things smuggled in for inmates—for a price. The first thing Andy asks Red for is a rock hammer. Apparently, Andy was something of a rock hound on the outside and Red assumed he was interested in continuing his hobby, as best he could, at Shawshank. Red gets Andy his rock hammer and time passes as it inevitably does in prison: hard and slow. Andy is targeted by the vicious homosexual rapists, The Sisters, and survives. Red is turned down for parole again and again, and, following an incident on the prison roof (which almost results in Andy having an unfortunate "accident"—being thrown off the roof), the former banker ends up doing tax returns for Shawshank's guards.

Andy's second request of Red is a poster of Rita Hayworth. Red again complies and this poster plays an enormous role in the implementation of a well-thought-out escape plan that revolves around a distant Mexican town called Zihautanejo, a hidden box of money, and the reuniting of two friends, one named Andy and one named Red—outside the walls of Shawshank.

A masterful achievement, this novella (which King wrote immediately after completing *The Dead Zone*) is King at his best. The intimate first-person narrative form; the well-defined characters; the implicit tension and terror of the prison setting all combine to make this one of King's most engaging and beloved tales.

☠ **C. V.** ☠

Main Characters

Andy Dufresne, Red, Warden Samuel Norton, Captain Byron Hadley, Tommy Williams, Bogs Diamond, Brooks Hatlen, Rory Tremont, Elwood Blatch, Sherwood Bolton.

Did You Know?

Shawshank's character Brooks Hatlen was named in honor of King's former University of Maine English professor Burton Hatlen. Hatlen has written many papers and articles about King's work and King has acknowledged Hatlen's encouragement of his

The King Speaks

"I like a lot of the Castle Rock films, like *Stand By Me*, *The Shawshank Redemption*, and *The Green Mile*, because they see past the horror to the human beings. I'm a lot more interested in the people than the monsters."

—From a September 20, 2000 live AOL chat

writing when he was attending UMO. One of Hatlen's most recent articles about Stephen King's work is "Why Stephen King is a Maine Writer," published in the online journal *Joshua Maine*. It can be found online at the Web site for *Joshua Maine*:

Joshuamaine.com/JoshuaMaine.cfm?PageId=16

What I Really Liked About It

Everything.

Film Adaptations

The Shawshank Redemption (1994); starring Tim Robbins, Morgan Freeman, Bob Gunton, William Sadler, Clancy Brown, Gil Bellows, Mark Rolston, James Whitmore, Jeffrey DeMunn, Larry Brandenburg, Neil Giuntoli, Brian Libby, David Proval, Joseph Ragno, Jude Ciccolella, Paul McCrane, Renee Blaine, Scott Mann, John Horton, Gordon Greene, Alfonso Freeman, V. J. Foster, John E. Summers, Frank Medrano, Mack Miles, Alan R. Kessier, Morgan Lund, Cornell Wallace, Gary Lee Davis, Neil Summers, Ned Bellamy; directed by Frank Darabont; screenplay by Frank Darabont. (Grade: A+.)

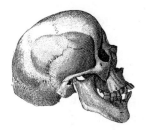

Apt Pupil
(1982)

*"Don't forget your paper, Mr. Dussander," Todd said,
holding the* Times *out politely.*

Why it made the top 100:

Evil wears many masks and one of its darkest visages has to have been Nazism and its mutant spawn, The Holocaust.

We ask, how could the Nazis have done what they did?

How could thousands of men—Nazi "soldiers"—report for duty every day and methodically and cold-bloodedly exterminate human beings—including women and young children—as though they were nothing more than cattle slated for slaughtering that particular "workday"?

Like countless others, Stephen King has asked these dark questions and, when Stephen King ponders such subjects, the end result is usually a story.

The compelling novella *Apt Pupil* is that tale.

Todd Bowden, a 13-year-old "all-American kid" discovers a horrible truth about one of his neighbors, an old man named Arthur Denker. Denker is really Kurt Dussander, a

Nazi death camp commandant now known around the world as the "Blood-Fiend of Patin." Todd has been obsessed with the Holocaust—especially the Nazi atrocities, sexual tortures, medical experiments, and the mechanics of execution—for quite some time when he eventually learns of Denker's true identity. Aptly described by King authority Stanley Wiater as the "dark heart" of the *Different Seasons* collection, *Apt Pupil* tells the story of an ordinary boy in an extraordinary situation. He is a teenager who has to make a choice as to what to do with newfound, *dangerous* information, and who ultimately takes the wrong path. The road he chooses leads to death—and not just for him and Dussander.

In the wake of the Columbine massacre, *Apt Pupil* now resonates with an eerie prescience and, like King's novel *Rage*, gives us a psychopathic teenage boy who turns to violence and who seems to exist on the fringe of normal society—a loose cannon.

Todd and Dussander's relationship quickly (and inevitably) devolves into one of mutual parasitism—"gooshy stuff" junkie Todd needs Dussander to feed his macabre need for the true details about the Holocaust; Dussander needs Todd to protect his identity.

The resolution of this sick and twisted alliance is grim, indeed, and there is probably no better indication of just *how* grim the novella's ending is than the fact that the movie adaptation completely eliminated two major plot points, one involving Todd's guidance counselor, the other involving Todd himself.

Apt Pupil is a superb character study of two fully-realized and completely honest characters, both of whom have terrible secrets, and both of whom pay the ultimate price for their deeds.

It makes you wonder if Stephen King embraces the concept of karma.

☠ **C. V.** ☠

 Main Characters

Todd Bowden, Arthur Denker (Kurt Dussander), Monica Bowden, Richard Bowden, Edward French, Morris Heisel, Andy Dufresne, Harold Pegler, Weiskopf.

 Did You Know?

Stephen King wrote *Apt Pupil* in two weeks after finishing writing *The Shining* (Chapter 3). These two incredibly intense works so wiped out King that he did not write another word for three whole months. "I was pooped," he has admitted.

The King Speaks

(When asked if he had an obsession with Charles Starkweather and the nature of evil): "Obsession is too strong a word. It was more like trying to figure out a puzzle, because I wanted to know why somebody could do the things Starkweather did. I suppose I wanted to decipher the unspeakable, just as people try to make sense out of Auschwitz or Jonestown. I certainly didn't find evil seductive in any sick way—that would be pathological—but I did find it compelling. And I think most people do, or the bookstores wouldn't still be filled with biographies of Adolf Hitler more than 35 years after World War Two. The fascination of the abomination, as Conrad called it."

—From a June 1983 interview with *Playboy* magazine

What I Really Liked About It

Apt Pupil is a page-turner of the highest order. Once you begin reading Todd and Dussander's story, it is almost impossible to stop until the final tragic scene.

Film Adaptations

Apt Pupil (1998); starring Brad Renfro, Ian McKellen, David Schwimmer, Joshua Jackson, Mickey Cottrell, Michael Reid MacKay, Ann Dowd, Bruce Davison, James Karen, Marjorie Lovett, David Cooley Blake, Anthony Tibbetts, Heather McComb, Katherine Malone, Grace Sinden; directed by Bryan Singer; screenplay by Brandon Boyce. (Grade: A-.)

NUMBER **31**

Rage
(Written as Richard Bachman)
(1977)

Two years ago. To the best of my recollection,
that was about the time I started to lose my mind.

Why it made the top 100:

Rage's notoriety now overshadows its literary merits (and flaws), and if the book is mentioned in the media at all, it is usually within the context of school shootings, the negative influences of violent popular culture, and King's deliberate decision to declare the book out of print.

There was a rash of school shootings at the end of the 20th century (the Columbine massacre is one of the most recent and the worst so far). The discovery of a copy of *Rage* in one of the shooter's locker prompted Stephen King to subsequently render *Rage* out of print, forbidding new printings and/or editions of the book. Used copies of *Rage* are still available, and also in omnibus editions of King's four "Richard Bachman" novels (*The Long Walk*, *Roadwork*, and *The Running Man* are the other three in the omnibus editions) although these will eventually become more and more difficult to find. There is the real long-term possibility that copies of the novel, in any form, may ultimately not be available at all, although existing copies will remain in the possession of King collectors (and on eBay) for decades. It is too early to determine whether or not public libraries that own a copy of *Rage* will pull it off the shelves.

The King Speaks

I've written a lot of books about teenagers who are pushed to violent acts. But with *Rage*, it's almost a blueprint in terms of saying, "This is how it could be done." And when it started to happen...particularly, there was a shooting thing in Paducah, Kansas, where three kids were killed in a prayer group...and the kid who did it, that book was in his locker. And I said, that's it for me; that book's off the market. Not that they won't find something else...I don't think that any kid was driven to an act of violence by a Metallica record, or by a Marilyn Manson CD, or by a Stephen King novel, but I do think those things can act as accelerants.

—From a BBC documentary on Stephen King that aired in the United States on December 19, 1999 on The Learning Channel

That said, how is *Rage* as a novel? As a story?

In a word (or two), gripping—and glum.

Rage is an incredibly pessimistic and depressing story and, yet, it is also a razor-sharp depiction and assessment of the alienation and anger felt by many high schoolers. In an example of bleak irony, the word "rage" is now used to describe the red-hot, boiling-over anger many people feel in mundane, everyday situations. We now speak of road rage, store rage, work rage, parking rage, phone rage, etc., and a recent *USA Today* front page article asked the question, "Why are we so angry?"

In *Rage*, which King began writing in 1966 when he was only 19, he presents a "school rage" scenario. One student, Charlie Decker, takes over a classroom, executes two teachers, and then "gets it on"—he forces his fellow students to confront each other in a vicious, often sexual, often violent psychodrama until he, like Todd Bowden in *Apt Pupil*, is "taken down" by the authorities. Unlike Todd, though, Charlie ends up in a mental institution instead of the cemetery.

King's decision to pull *Rage* from publication begs the question, will he (or *has* he) censored himself regarding story lines that could possibly act as "accelerants" (his word) to a deranged individual? After learning that his book may have given a crazed student a "blueprint" (again, his word) for a violent outburst, how can he not hesitate before penning an especially violent scene? Or a scenario that could serve as a *mise en scène* for a situation that might end up on CNN?

Tough questions; tough decisions; but ultimately ones that only Stephen King can make.

☠ **C. V.** ☠

Main Characters

Charlie (Charles Everett) Decker, Ted Jones, Mrs. Jean Underwood, Frank Philbrick, John Vance, Carol Granger, Sandra Cross, John "Pig Pen" Dano.

 Did You Know?

The "Cherokee Nose Job," vividly described by Charlie in the novel actually was used by the Plains Indians, including the Cherokees, Choctaws, Chickasaws, Creeks, and Seminoles. In Chapter 13 of his book *Commerce of the Prairies*, Josiah Gregg writes, "Adultery is punished by cutting off both the nose and ears of the adulteress, but the husband has a right to say if the law shall be executed. In fact, he is generally the executioner, and that often without trial."

 What I Really Liked About It

Even though King believes that *Rage* is full of "windy psychological preachments (both textual and subtextual)," there is no denying that the story *flies* and is a superb thriller and an exciting reading experience.

 Film Adaptations

None.

 Stage Adaptations

Rage (stage play) written by Robert B. Parker and starring Parker's son Daniel as Charlie Decker. The Blackburn Theater Company debuted *Rage* at the Blackburn Theater in Gloucester, Massachusetts on March 30, 1989.

The Girl Who Loved Tom Gordon (1999)

The world is a worst-case scenario...

Why it made the top 100:

Stephen King's monumental *Dark Tower* series was directly inspired by Robert Browning's poem "Childe Roland to the Dark Tower Came." Could *The Girl Who Loved Tom Gordon* have similarly been inspired by classic poetry, specifically William Blake's two connected poems, "The Little Girl Lost" and "The Little Girl Found"?

In his letter to reviewers of *Tom Gordon*, King admits that he wanted to write "'Hansel and Gretel' without Hansel." But there are also similarities between King's novel and Blake's two poems, (irrespective of the two works' blatant differences).

In "The Little Girl Lost," the young girl (the Trish McFarland character in *Tom Gordon*) is named Lyca. She is 7 years old, and ends up lost in a "desert wild." Like Trish, though, Lyca "wander'd long," slept under a tree, "while the beasts of prey,/Come from caverns deep,/View'd the maid asleep." Also, there is a scene in the poem where Lyca watches the moon rise, echoing a similar scene in *Tom Gordon*.

Blake's companion poem to "Little Girl Lost" is "The Little Girl Found." It contains a scene in which Lyca is found and carried in the arms of her rescuer ("In his arms he bore/Her, arm'd with sorrow sore"). This scene is similar to the scene in *Tom Gordon* in which Travis Herrick carries Trisha out of the woods ("She wanted to tell him she was glad to be carried, glad to be rescued...").

King may or may not have intended to write an *hommage* to Blake's two poems, but the literary lineage of his novel once again dramatically illustrates the literary significance of Stephen King's writings. If he did intend a tribute, the execution of the idea is masterful. If he did not and the themes are simply a reflection of the vast awareness of classic literature in his writer's subconscious, then his timeless talents are quite apparent and easily understood. Either way, *The Girl Who Loved Tom Gordon* is a well-told tale, made all the more richer for its literary heritage.

The story is archetypal: a little girl gets lost in the woods and has to depend on her wits, stamina, and some luck to survive. But Stephen King injects his own brand of narrative inventiveness and quirkiness by having Trisha receive helpful and encouraging messages from her favorite baseball player, Red Sox pitcher Tom Gordon. After a few days, however, we (and Trisha) begin to wonder if she is actually hearing the voice of Gordon, or the voice of God.

The Girl Who Loved Tom Gordon was a surprise publication; something King wrote because he had to tell the story, and something Scribner's, his new publisher, was delighted to receive, and to publish. Its quick genesis notwithstanding, *The Girl Who Loved Tom Gordon* is one of Stephen King's most gripping and emotionally powerful tales to date.

☠ **C. V.** ☠

Main Characters

Trisha McFarland, Pete McFarland, Quilla Andersen, Tom Gordon, the God of the Lost, Larry McFarland, Travis Herrick.

Did You Know?

In the "Author's Postscript" to this novel, King tells us that even though Tom Gordon the baseball player is real, the Tom Gordon in the novel is fictional. King then makes a revealing comment about the nature of fame and his *own* celebrity: "The impression fans have of people who have achieved some degree of celebrity are *always* fictional, as I can attest of my own personal experience."

The King Speaks

"My heroine (Trisha) would be a child of divorce living with her mother and maintaining a meaningful connection with her father mostly through their mutual love of baseball and the Boston Red Sox. Lost in the woods, she'd find herself imagining that her favorite Red Sox player was with her, keeping her company and guiding her through the terrible situation in which she found herself. Tom Gordon, #36, would be that player. Gordon is a real pitcher for the Red Sox; without his consent I wouldn't have wanted to publish the book. He did give it, for which I am deeply grateful....*The Girl Who Loved Tom Gordon* isn't about Tom Gordon or baseball, and not really about love, either. It's about survival, and God, and it's about God's opposite as well. Because Trisha isn't alone in her wanderings. There is something else in the woods— the God of the Lost is how she comes to think of it—and in time she'll have to face it."

—From a March 5, 1999 letter to reviewers
included with review copies of the novel

What I Really Liked About It

The dynamic pace, the "nine innings" structure, and especially one of the book's final scenes in which Trish comes face to face with the God of the Lost...or does she?

Film Adaptations

The Girl Who Loved Tom Gordon (2001?); directed by George A. Romero; screenplay by George A. Romero.

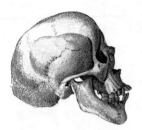

The Mist
(1980, 1985)

This is what happened.

Why it made the top 100:

After massive thunderstorms finally break "the worst heat wave in northern New England history," an enormous mist covers Long Lake, Maine and environs...and there are *creatures* in the mist. Big, hungry, apparently prehistoric creatures that were transported to our time somehow, possibly due to a secret government project known only as The Arrowhead Project.

The Mist tells the story of Dave Drayton and his trip to the supermarket following the storm.

Dave, his son Billy, his neighbor Brent Norton, and a bunch of other area folks are trapped in the market when the Mist completely covers the parking lot and anyone who ventures out into it is never seen or heard from again.

Will Dave and company escape the market and successfully make it through the Mist to safety? Will the survivors be able to elude the giant monsters from the past?

We ultimately don't know what happens to Dave and son (giving us what Dave describes in the story as an "Alfred Hitchcock ending"), but the last word of the tale *is*, after all, "hope."

Stephen King originally wrote this gripping story for an anthology called *Dark Forces* that was being put together by his then-agent Kirby McCauley. Originally, King came up dry in the "short story" department when trying to find something to write about, and then *The Mist* came to him exactly as he described it in the "Notes" section of *Skeleton Crew*. King being King, however, he described the flash of inspiration by telling us, "In the market, my muse suddenly shat on my head." At a lecture in Truth or Consequences, New Mexico (cited in George Beahm's *The Stephen King Story*), King expanded on his *Skeleton Crew* notes by remembering that he specifically thought to himself, "Wouldn't it be funny if a pterodactyl just came flapping up this aisle and started knocking over Ragu and Hunts and all this other stuff?"

Kirby McCauley remembers expecting a short story of a few thousand words from King for the *Dark Forces* anthology and being stunned when King ultimately turned in a 40,000-word novella.

In George Beahm's aforementioned *The Stephen King Story*, King authority Dr. Michael Collings makes a convincing case for comparing *The Mist* to *Beowulf*. I won't perfunctorily butcher Dr. Collings analysis here by trying to paraphrase it: Get George's book and read Collings' Intro, "The Persistence of Darkness—Shadows Behind the Life Behind the Story" yourself.

There are all kinds of "real world" references in *The Mist*. King and his family have a house on Long Lake in Bridgton, Maine where *The Mist* takes place. Dave Drayton's wife's name is Stephanie, which is the name of Tabitha King's sister (Stephanie Leonard, the founder and editor of the King newsletter, *Castle Rock*). Like Dave Drayton, King attended the University of Maine. The character of Selectman Mike Hatlen is named after King's University of Maine professor Burton Hatlen; and the next-door neighbor character Brent Norton is really King's Long Lake neighbor Ralph Drews, although King makes it clear that, unlike Brent, Ralph is a nice guy.

☠ **C. V.** ☠

Main Characters

David Drayton, Billy Drayton, Steffy Drayton, Brent Norton, Amanda Dumfries, Mrs. Carmody.

Did You Know?

In a 1997 interview with the *World of Fandom*, King spoke about the eventual hoped-for film adaptation of *The Mist*: "As far as *The Mist*, it's very much alive. Frank [Darabont]

The King Speaks

"I was halfway down the middle aisle, looking for hot-dog buns, when I imagined a big prehistoric bird flapping its way toward the meat counter at the back, knocking over cans of pineapple chunks and tomato sauce. By the time my son Joe and I were in the checkout lane, I was amusing myself with a story about all these people trapped in a supermarket surrounded by prehistoric animals."

—Stephen King, in the "Notes" to *Skeleton Crew*

and I have talked a lot about it. Right now I think, and he thinks, that there has to be an ending that works in terms of the story, but that will also please people in Hollywood, who are really uncomfortable with the way the story ends. It just sought of trails off into the mist. No one is necessarily looking for a sugary ending, but what I think they're looking for is some real closure, which the story doesn't provide."

What I Really Liked About It

There's a lot of pure story in *The Mist* and, as readers, we are caught up in it from word one.

Film Adaptations

Currently (2001) in development.

Audio Adaptations

The Mist (1986), a four and a half hour unabridged reading; *The Mist* (1987), a 90-minute, 3-D audio dramatization.

Game Adaptations

Software game (Mindscape Software, 1985).

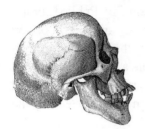

The Library Policeman
(1990)

"You have two books which belong to uth," the Library Policeman said.

Why it made the top 100:

We know from King's Forenote to *The Library Policeman* (in his collection *Four Past Midnight*) that the idea for this novella was a gift from King's son Owen (around 10 at the time). Owen was a young lad afraid to return overdue books to the Bangor Public Library because of the terrifying and ominous "Library Police."

King's storytelling eyebrows (and maybe his real ones?) shot up upon hearing the phrase "library police" (he had heard similar stories as a youth) and within days, he had mentally conceived the tale—probably pretty close to how it now appears in *Four Past Midnight*.

This novella is powerful. King, always superb when working with the shorter formats of the novella and short story, really hits home with this tale of a library from a dark place and its equally sinister librarian. Kevin Quigley, Webmaster of what might be the single best Stephen King fan site on the Web, (*members.tripod.com/charnelhouse/index.html*) once told me, "*The Library Policeman* scared me so much that it's the only King work I've read only once." Also, in 2001, The Book of the Month Club published a hardcover *Reader's Calendar* that contained all kinds of info about writers and books. The BOMC reprinted part of the "How King Kills" section from my *Complete Stephen King Encyclopedia*, and they made sure to include my entry for *The Library Policeman*, which read, "Killed by a funnel-snouted, eye-sucking, shape-changing alien librarian."

The power of *The Library Policeman*, even more than 10 years after its initial publication, still resonates.

Realtor and Insurance Agent Sam Peebles, seeking books of quotations to spice up a speech, happens to meet librarian Ardelia Lortz at the Junction City Public Library. Ardelia is an imperious figure and Sam assures her he will return his borrowed books on time. He doesn't return the books, however, and is soon visited by the library policeman who is a walking "wedge of winter." He is seven feet tall, wears a trenchcoat and felt hat that terrifies Sam and dredges up memories of his own "library policeman," a child molester from his past who is a monster that we learn has been "resurrected" by the demonic Ardelia Lortz to terrorize Sam.

Ardelia is a...what? A shapeshifter? A ghost? An alien? A demon? A being from another dimension? A glamour? An evil manitou? All of the above?

Sam must discover the truth about Ardelia. During his trial, Sam's secretary and future wife (Naomi Higgins) helps Sam by providing the clues he needs to send Ardelia back where she came from—the past, another realm, Hell, or wherever "funnel-snouted, eye-sucking, shape-changing alien librarians" reside when they're not commanding ghoulish hellhound library policeman with "collecting past due books."

My friend Kevin Quigley is right: *The Library Policeman* is frightening enough on its first read to make a Constant Reader think twice about rereading it. Thankfully, though, the *third* time most of us think about rereading it, the hesitation vanishes like a dent on Christine after Arnie gets his hands on her.

And then it's back to Junction City...and another rendezvous with Ardelia, one of the most chilling villains in Stephen King's teeming League of the Damned.

 C. V.

 ## Main Characters

Sam Peebles, Ardelia Lortz, Naomi Higgins, Dirty Dave Duncan, The Library Policeman.

 ## Did You Know?

The Library Policeman is one of those occasional works of King in which he refers to himself in the third person. (Others include *Thinner*, "The Blue Air Compressor," and

The King Speaks

"About thirty pages in, the humor began to go out of the situation. And about fifty pages in, the whole story took a screaming left turn into the dark places I have traveled so often and which I still know so little about. Eventually I found the guy I was looking for, and managed to raise my head enough to look into his merciless silver eyes. I have tried to bring back a sketch of him for you, Constant Reader, but it may not be very good.

My hands were trembling quite badly when I made it, you see."

—From "Three Past Midnight,"
the Forenote to *The Library Policeman*

"The Night Flier.") In the story, Junction City librarian Ardelia Lortz makes it quite plain to Sam Peebles that she is no fan of King's books. Ardelia tells Sam, "[I] have no desire...to read a novel by Robert McCammon, Stephen King, or V. C. Andrews." (Ardelia also tells Sam that Robert McCammon's novel *Swan Song* is the favorite novel of her children patrons. She even had a copy put in Vinabind.)

What I Really Liked About It

The frisson of terror I felt the moment I realized that the Junction City Public Library that Sam Peebles had originally visited—and the resident librarian he had dealt with—didn't really exist in Sam's present reality.

Film Adaptations

None.

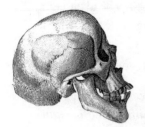

"The Reach"
(1981, 1985 [retitled only])

Who'll turn the earth this April?

Why it made the top 100:

"The Reach" is the kind of short story that ends up being dissected in high school and college English literature classes.

Why? Because this poignant story functions equally well at both the literal and the blatantly symbolic level. In addition to being a true Maine slice-of-life story with vivid characters and realistic settings, its images are also easily interpreted as metaphors for the journey towards transcendence and the curse/blessing duality of death.

Stella Flanders, a 95-year-old Maine widow with terminal cancer, has never been off Goat Island. She has never crossed the Reach, a body of water between two bodies of land that is open at both ends, separating Goat Island from the mainland. As way of explanation, Stella tells her grandchildren, "Your blood is in the stones of this island, and I stay here because the mainland is too far to reach."

The King Speaks

"There are lots of islands out there, and lots of tightly knit island communities."

—From "Notes" in *Skeleton Crew*

One day Stella begins seeing ghosts, starting with the specter of her late husband Bill, who is, we soon learn, a harbinger of her own oncoming death. She also sees her deceased friend Annabelle Frane's face in the coals of her wood stove. These visitations coincide with a worsening of her stomach pain and a calm realization that she will not see the spring that will inevitably follow the winter of 1978 when the Reach freezes for the first time since 1938. That winter Stella sees Bill standing on the frozen Reach like "Jesus-out-of-the-boat" and she begins to walk across the ice, heading for the mainland. Stella is found dead the next day—with her late husband's cap on her head. The dead of Goat Island had welcomed Stella and helped her cross over—both the Reach *and* this mortal coil.

King's writing is superb in this story. For instance, he writes of old Richard walking up a path, "his arthritis riding him like an invisible passenger." And the scenes of Stella's death contain some of King's most lyrical images to date.

The original title of this story was "Do the Dead Sing?" and the story asks that question and also the question, "Do they love?" According to the story, the answer is, yes, the dead do sing, and, yes, they love the living.

Elizabeth Hand, in a September 1999 review of *Hearts in Atlantis* in the *Village Voice Literary Supplement*, specifically singled out "The Reach" as one of King's works that achieves "genuine power and resonance." (Hand also praised *Bag of Bones* and "The Man in the Black Suit" for the same reasons.)

"The Reach" deservedly won the 1981 World Fantasy Award for best short fiction.

☠ **C. V.** ☠

Main Characters

Stella Flanders, David Perrault, Hal Perrault, Lois Perrault, Lona Perrault, Tommy Perrault, Hattie Stoddard, Vera Spruce, Alden Flanders, Bill Flanders.

Did You Know?

There is a scene in "The Reach" in which Stella recalls keeping a pot of lobster stew going on the stove at all times. Lobsters were plentiful and cheap back then, and, thus, what we know as an expensive delicacy today, was considered "pour man's soup" in Maine in 1978. Stella remembers hiding the pot when the minister came calling because of her embarrassment. This anecdote is based on King's childhood and he has told this story in interviews, remembering his mother keeping lobster stew on the stove and hiding the pot when company came.

What I Really Liked About It

"The Reach" is a well-told tale that can bring tears to your eyes and also make you think about the nature of death, the meaning of life, and why we may not need to fear either.

Film Adaptations

None (and that, my friends, is a crime).

"The Man in the Black Suit" (1994)

It's not belief I'm interested in but freedom.

Why it made the top 100:

Even seven years after its initial publication, this is the short story I like to tell people about in detail. (Mostly to introduce them to a great work and to indulge in a little bit of gloating.) My opening gambit usually goes something like this: "I read this great short story in *The New Yorker*...it's about an old man remembering back to a time when he was a young boy and met the Devil and survived to tell about it. It reminded me a lot of some of Nathaniel Hawthorne's stuff. It's a terrific story and I heard later that it won the O. Henry Award in 1994 for Best American Short Story." By now, my listener is intrigued and invariably asks who wrote this gem. "What's the name of this story? Is it an Updike? DeLillo? Is it by Saul Bellow? Joyce Carol Oates?" And then I spring it on them: "It's called 'The Man in the Black Suit' and, actually, it's by Stephen King."

Then comes the part I like best: the expression on my mark's face. Puzzlement, followed by disbelief, followed by surprise, followed (usually) by delight. "You're kidding!" is often the first thing they exclaim after processing this amazing fact, and from then on, it's just me tidying things up by telling them the date of the *New Yorker* issue (October 31—Halloween—1994) and suggesting other superior King works that may likewise surprise them.

The reason I do this is because of the (mis)perception of King by casual readers or people who only know of his work through the many movies adapted from his novels and short stories. It all comes down to one simple fact—Stephen King is a far better writer than many believe him to be. His finest work can stand with the best of 20th century American literature and, yes, be published in *The New Yorker* and win an O. Henry Award, which brings us full circle to our discussion of this remarkable short story.

The narrator—diarist, actually—of this story is an old man in his 80s named Gary, writing from his final residence—a room in a nursing home.

When he was nine, Gary met the Devil—"live" and in person—on the banks of the Castle Stream in Maine. The Dark Man told Gary that his mother was dead and that he was now going to eat Gary alive. Gary manages to flee the riverbank and make it home, but throughout his life, he is traumatized by one stark reality: he escaped the Devil through sheer luck, and not by the "intercession of the God I have worshipped and sung hymns to all my life." This cold dark fact now terrorizes the old man because if God was not there for him that day, will he be waiting for him when he crosses over into the realm where He and the man in the black suit both hold offices? Will God be waiting for him when he dies? Or will the man in the black suit be the one Gary comes face to face with—one, final, *eternal* time?

"The Man in the Black Suit" won a World Fantasy Award in 1994 as well as the aforementioned O. Henry Award. It still stands as one of Stephen King's finest short stories.

☠ **C. V.** ☠

Main Characters

Gary, his parents, Candy Bill (the dog), the man in the black suit.

Did You Know?

"The Man in the Black Suit" foreshadowed one specific narrative element of Stephen King's 1996's serial novel *The Green Mile*. In *The Green Mile* (as in "Man"), the story is told to the reader by an old man (Paul Edgecombe) writing in his diary while living in a nursing home. King has used the diary/epistolary format in other works, most notably in "The End of the Whole Mess," "Survivor Type," and *The Plant*.

The King Speaks

"['The Man in the Black Suit' comes from] a long New England tradition of stories which dealt with meeting the devil in the woods...he always comes out of the woods—the uncharted regions—to test the human soul."

—From King's introduction in *Six Stories*

What I Really Liked About It

I especially like how effective King is at subtly communicating the terror Gary feels as he nears death and wonders if the man in the black suit will be waiting for him. Where is God? He asks himself, and the fact that he will not know the answer until he dies adds an element of existential terror to the tale that elevates it to more than just a good yarn. It elevates it to a contemplation on the horrifying possibility of an indifferent—or even nonexistent—deity.

Film Adaptations

None.

Stage Adaptations

The Man in the Black Suit (Opera, 2001, American Opera Projects); music by Eve Beglarian; libretto cowritten by Beglarian and Grethe Barrett Holby.

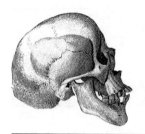

NUMBER 37

The Sun Dog
(1990)

What the picture showed was a large black dog in front of a white picket fence.

Why it made the top 100:

I'm guessing that Stephen King was elated when the idea for this novella occurred to him. No doubt about it: the premise for *The Sun Dog* is a great idea...in fact, it really should be referred to in caps, as in, "A Great Idea."

Kevin Delevan, a teenage Castle Rock, Maine resident, receives a self-developing Polaroid Sun camera for his 15th birthday. He is thrilled with his gift, except that after he snaps his first picture, he realizes that his Sun is no ordinary Sun. No matter what Kevin looks at through the viewfinder, what develops is a photo of a black dog in front of a white fence. What is most perplexing to both Kevin and his dad, though, is that with each snapshot Kevin takes, the Sun dog appears to be getting closer and closer to the viewer.

Like I said, A Great Idea.

Kevin and his dad bring the camera to Pop Merrill, Castle Rock's resident fix-it-man, curmudgeon, and usurious loan shark, for Pop to examine and, hopefully, fix. A significant part of Pop's business is selling phony occult items to a group of customers he calls his "Mad Hatters." Seeing dollar signs, Pop connives Kevin out of his camera with the intention of selling it for big money to one of his gullible clients.

But the Sun works its seductive magic on Pop and, instead of selling it, he snaps picture after picture of the black dog, moving it closer and closer to our world.

Ultimately, Pop frees the dog, but Kevin manages to "kill" it by snapping its picture at the precise moment it emerges into Castle Rock. Pop does not survive the resulting fiery conflagration, though, and the story ends with Kevin thinking the Sun dog is gone forever.

A year later, Kevin receives a word processor for his 16th birthday, and it seems as though his belief in the Sun dog's demise was a little premature. When Kevin types an innocuous sentence, what the computer actually prints out is:

> The dog is loose again.
>
> It is not sleeping.
>
> It is not lazy.
>
> It's coming for you, Kevin.
>
> It's very hungry
>
> And it's very angry.
>
> Now that's the way to end a story, wouldn't you say?

 C. V.

Main Characters

Kevin Delevan, John Delevan, Meg Delevan, Mary Delevan, Reginald "Pop" Merrill, Eleusippus Deere, Meleusippus Deere Verrill, Cedric McCarty, The Sun Dog, various denizens of Castle Rock, Maine (including characters and locales from *The Dark Half*, *Needful Things*, *The Dead Zone*, *Rita Hayworth and Shawshank Redemption*, and elsewhere).

Did You Know?

Stephen King's longtime editor, Chuck Verrill, has been honored several times in King's works by King naming characters after him. The most prominent mention would be the *Creepshow* segment "The Lonesome Death of Jordy Verrill." There is also a character named "Verrill" (a literary agent) in "Umney's Last Case," and the Verrill name pops up again, here, in *The Sun Dog* as well. In this *Four Past Midnight* novella, Eleusippus Deere's sister Meleusippus was once married to a gentleman named Verrill. Mr. Verrill was killed in the Battle of Leyte Gulf in 1944.

The King Speaks

"This story came almost all at once one night in the summer of 1987, but the thinking which made it possible went on for almost a year."

—From the Forenote to *The Sun Dog*

What I Really Liked About It

I find the idea of a photo (or a painting, for that matter) serving as a doorway to another realm, another dimension, especially intriguing. This appeal is enhanced greatly when this idea is executed as well as it is in *The Sun Dog*. Add to that the kicker that the Sun dog survives to occupy Kevin's word processor and you've got an undeniably "essential" Stephen King tale!

Film Adaptations

A short, student film adaptation (a "dollar baby"), that Stephen King liked. In his Introduction to Frank Darabont's *Shawshank Redemption* shooting script, King describes *The Sun Dog* as a "fairly impressive...adaptation." Also, as of this writing, an I-Max adaptation of the novella was scheduled for release sometime in 2001.

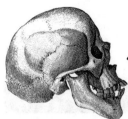

Secret Window, Secret Garden
(1990)

"You stole my story," the man on the doorstep said.

Why it made the top 100:

Catastrophic guilt, murderous psychosis and insanity, heartless revenge, adultery, arson, deception, plagiarism, and, of course, *fear—Secret Window, Secret Garden* has all this and more.

John Shooter shows up on Mort Rainey's doorstep one day accusing him of plagiarizing one of his stories, specifically a tale called "Secret Window, Secret Garden." Rainey insists that Shooter is mistaken, but Shooter is adamant that he's lying and refuses to leave him alone unless Rainey can prove that he did not plagiarize "Secret Window, Secret Garden" for his own story "Sowing Season."

Rainey then embarks on a desperate quest to find tangible, physical evidence that he wrote and published "Sowing Season" before Shooter wrote "Secret Window, Secret Garden." Rainey is sent very clear signals that Shooter is not fooling around: shortly after Shooter's visit, Rainey finds his beloved cat Bump dead from a broken neck, his body nailed to the roof of the garbage cabinet with one of Rainey's own screwdrivers.

King keeps the tension levels in the red zone as he shows us Rainey's increasingly panicked and ultimately hopeless efforts to find proof that he didn't steal Shooter's story. The truth, finally revealed after a string of deaths and tragedies, is more horrible than any typical stalker story could offer.

Secret Window, Secret Garden is a powerful and scary story that, like the equally effective *The Dark Half*, *Misery*, and *Bag of Bones*, takes us inside the mind of a best-selling author and makes us realize that sometimes that's a pretty spooky place. King is often very good when writing about writers and the writing process. *Secret Window, Secret Garden* is no exception to that rule.

☠ **C. V.** ☠

 ## Main Characters

Morton Rainey, John Shooter, Herb Creekmore, Amy Rainey, Ted Milner, Greg Carstairs.

 ## Did You Know?

King's 1989 novel *The Dark Half* and this 1990 novella are both about writers and the power that fiction can have over both the writer and the reader. Written around the same time, they are evocative and probing looks into the psyche of the writer/artist, but they also share something else in common. They are both works in which King mentions assassinated Beatle John Lennon by name. In *The Dark Half*, Liz Beaumont hopes that the people now paying attention to her newly-famous husband are not like the "mad crocodile-hunter who...killed John Lennon." In *Secret Window, Secret Garden*, Mort Rainey describes John Shooter as wearing "round wire-framed 'John Lennon' glasses." In 1980, a few days after Lennon was killed, King published a eulogy for the slain Beatle called "Remembering John." (See the chapter "In a Class by Itself.")

 ## What I Really Liked About It

I consider this one of King's most psychologically astute tales, and the final revelation of who John Shooter actually was and how he was connected to Mort Rainey is, in my mind, one of the most satisfying (and terrifying) denouements in a King story. (And who was John Kintner, and how did he figure into all this?)

 ## Film Adaptations

None.

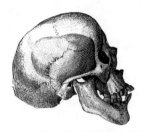

Christine
(1983)

"She was a bad joke, and what Arnie saw in her that day I'll never know."

Why it made the top 100:

As a novel, *Christine* has an awkward construction. It starts off as a first person narrative ("Dennis—Teenage Car-Songs"), switches to third person when Dennis is in the hospital ("Arnie—Teenage Love-Songs"), and then reverts back to first person for the final section, "Christine—Teenage Death-Songs."

This shift in perspective is essentially irrelevant, however, and does not take away from the enjoyment of the story (although King has admitted the shift caused him concern. King authority Dr. Michael Collings, writing in *The Stephen King Companion* about the different narrative voices in the novel concluded, "While the interruption of narrative flow may contribute to a sense that the story is somehow flawed, the fact remains that *Christine* can still offer a good read."

It is 1979 and Arnie Cunningham, a classic teenage loser, is seduced (possessed?) into buying a beat-up, 1958, red-and-white Plymouth Fury with 97,432 miles on her. Christine is her name; she is haunted and apparently pissed-off, and it isn't long before she begins to wield her power over Arnie, much to the dismay of Arnie's best friend

The King Speaks

"*Christine* [is] the first horror novel I've done, I think, since *The Shining*. That's all I'm going to say about it. Except it's scary. It's fun, too. It's maybe not my best book—it's kind of like a high school confidential. It's great from that angle."

- From "Has Success Spoiled Stephen King? Naaah," by Pat Cadigan, Marty Ketchum, and Arnie Fenner in the Winter 1982 issue of *Shayol* magazine

Dennis Guilder. The car's previous owner, the putrefactive Roland LeBay, is one of the vividest characters King has ever summoned from the character drawer of his imagination filing cabinet. (LeBay no doubt resided in one of the bottom drawers.) The way King describes LeBay paints a repulsive picture and foreshadows the crotch-grabbing, urine-reeking old man who gives Alan Parker his first ride in *Riding the Bullet* (Chapter 77). (Actor Roberts Blossom does an excellent job of capturing LeBay in the movie version of the novel.)

Point of view issues aside, though, *Christine* is one of King's most accessible novels, a page-turner of the highest caliber, and a truly enjoyable reading experience. The "lover's triangle" King introduces on the first page of the book—Arnie, his hapless girlfriend Leigh Cabot, and Christine—becomes a compelling lynchpin hook on which the book's narrator, Dennis Guilder, can hang their dark story.

Also, *Christine* is perhaps King's definitive statement on why technology should at least be watched carefully, if not actually feared. In his short story "Trucks," King brings tractor-trailers to life; in "The Monkey," it's a mechanical toy; in "Word Processor of the Gods," it's a computer. But on the American cultural landscape, there is nothing as ubiquitous as the car and, thus, *Christine* posits an even more horrifying scenario than all the cited stories combined. What if cars had a soul? And what if that soul was black?

In *Christine*, we find out the answer. And it ain't "See the USA in your Chevrolet."

☠ **C. V.** ☠

Main Characters

Arnie Cunningham, Dennis Guilder, Leigh Cabot, Will Darnell, Rudy Junkins, Regina Cunningham, Roland LeBay, Buddy Repperton, Moochie Welch, Don Vandenberg, Michael Cunningham, Sandy Galton, Christine.

The King Speaks

Randy Lofficier: Why was *Christine* written using two different narrative styles?

SK: Because I got in a box. That's really the only reason. It almost killed the book....Dennis was supposed to tell the whole story. But then he got in a football accident and was in the hospital while things were going on that he couldn't see. For a long time I tried to narrate the second part in terms of what he was hearing hearsay evidence, almost like depositions—but that didn't work. I tried to do it a number of ways, and finally I said, "Let's cut through it. The only way to do this is to do it in the third person."

—From an interview in the February 1984 issue of *Twlight Zone* magazine

Did You Know?

In the novel, it is said that Christine the car was a four-door model. The first mention of this is in the chapter "First Views" when King writes, "He tried the back door on the passenger side, and it came open with a scream." However, Plymouth never made a 4-door 1958 Plymouth Fury. They were all 2-door. (They changed the car to a 2-door model for the John Carpenter movie version.) Also, although all 1958 Plymouth Furys were manufactured in ivory color, in *Christine*, King states that Christine was custom ordered in Ford red.

What I Really Liked About It

Reading *Christine* is like eating potato chips: Once you start, it's difficult to stop!

Film Adaptations

Christine (1983); starring Keith Gordon, John Stockwell, Alexandra Paul, Robert Prosky, Harry Dean Stanton, Christine Belford, Roberts Blossom, William Ostrander, David Spielberg, Malcolm Danare, Steven Tash, Stuart Charno, Kelly Preston, Marc Poppel, Robert Darnell; directed by John Carpenter; screenplay by Bill Phillips. (This film is also known as *John Carpenter's Christine*). (Grade: B+.)

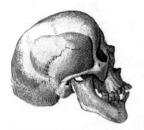

"My Pretty Pony"
(1988, 1993)

"The instruction took place in the West Orchard."

Why it made the top 100:

The short story "My Pretty Pony" is a chapter from an aborted Richard Bachman novel called *My Pretty Pony*. The novel died; the story survived.

"My Pretty Pony" is a tender story of the relationship between a grandfather and his grandson, and how one day shortly before his death, the grandfather gives "instruction" (never advice) to his rapt grandson. Stanley Wiater, author of *The Stephen King Universe* once told me that this story suggested to him what would result if "Ernest Hemingway and Ray Bradbury collaborated on a story."

Richard Bachman may ostensibly have a harder edge and present a nastier face to his reading public, but he is also capable of some incredibly gentle and lyrical writing. As many of my readers know, I have always been especially fond of the opening paragraph of Richard Bachman's novel *The Regulators*.

That paragraph (see Chapter 52) is wonderful expository writing and in "My Pretty Pony," we are treated to more of this style of "Bachman" lyricism and its attendant evocative images.

Since the moment I first read "My Pretty Pony" back in 1988, I have never forgotten the passage where King evocatively and poignantly describes the grandfather's death: "...Grandpa's pony had kicked down Grandpa's fences and gone over all the hills of the world. Wicked heart, wicked heart. Pretty, but with a wicked heart."

According to King, the grandson in "My Pretty Pony," Clive Banning, grows up to be a cold-blooded contract hitman. He remembers the episode told in "Pony" during a flashback as he prepares to slaughter rival crime bosses at a wedding reception. This fact (which we only learn from King's post-story "Notes") adds a tragic element of genuine sadness to the story. Especially since there is not even a hint that the heartless killer Clive Banning would grow up to be is the eager-to-learn young boy who is taught about the three kinds of time by his beloved Grandpa.

Since "My Pretty Pony" was originally written in the voice of Richard Bachman and because this was a Bachman tale, the elegiac tone and warmth that permeates this character study suggests to me that old Dicky Bachman might be schizophrenic...or at least harbor multiple personalities. The Bachman writings are for the most part, harder-edged; in fact, *Misery* and *Cujo*—two of the master's grimmer tales—were both originally intended to be Bachman novels. But we find that there are passages in all of the Bachman writings that hint at perhaps a *third* voice in the trinity that is Stephen King: A hybrid of the King that wrote *The Body* and "The Reach," and the Bachman that wrote *Thinner* and *The Regulators*. Echoes of both voices can be recognized in this third manifestation of King's talent. But it always surprises me to come up on a passage like the opening passage from *The Regulators* or almost anything from "My Pretty Pony" and realize that this is the same guy (Bachman, that is) who came up with the "walk until you're executed" scenario in *The Long Walk*.

"My Pretty Pony" is yet one more of those stories you can point to with glee when people tell you that Stephen King is "only" a horror writer.

☠ **C. V.** ☠

Main Characters

Clive Banning, George Banning (Grandpa), Gramma Sarah Banning, Patty Banning, Arthur Osgood, Mr. Banning (Clive's father), Mrs. Banning (Clive's mother).

Did You Know?

The Whitney Museum of Modern Art originally published the short story "My Pretty Pony" in a limited edition. The story was bound in stainless steel and its initial selling

The King Speaks

"*My Pretty Pony* [the novel] I junked...except for a brief flashback in which Banning, while waiting to begin his assault on the wedding party, remembers how his grandfather instructed him on the plastic nature of time. Finding that flashback—marvelously complete, almost a short story as it stood—was like finding a rose growing in a junkheap. I plucked it, and I did so with great gratitude."

—From "Notes" in *Nightmares & Dreamscapes*

price was $2,200. King has said that he felt that this edition was "overpriced" and "overdesigned."

What I Really Liked About It

The nostalgic tone; the Proustian rendering of an upstate New York farm in the fall; George Banning's no-nonsense, old-school attitude. (I have known good men like George, as I am sure many of you have as well.)

Film Adaptations

None.

The Running Man
(Written as Richard Bachman)
(1982)

"You a hardass, sonny?
"Hard enough," Richards said, and smiled.

Why it made the top 100:

As "The King Speaks" on page 149 indicates, Stephen King considers *The Running Man* to be probably the best of the five Richard Bachman novels he published before his ruse was discovered in 1984. (The other four were *Rage*, *The Long Walk*, *Roadwork*, and *Thinner*.)

Ben Richards, the protagonist of *The Running Man*, is mad at the world. As well he should be.

In his "dark and broken time," Ben cannot find work, his daughter is sick, and his wife has to turn tricks just to be able to buy their child her much-needed medicine. This unacceptable status quo prompts Ben to apply for a spot on the hottest show on Free Vee, *The Running Man*. All the contestant has to do is survive uncaptured for 30 days and he will win one billion New Dollars. The contestant's pursuit is televised and both the public and armed Hunters hunt him. They will kill him on first sight. He, however, is allowed to kill them first, if he can, and for every hour he is on the loose, he will earn one hundred New Dollars. This is the main reason Ben decides to play the game: to earn steady money for his wife and daughter until he is either killed or the 30 days goes by.

But like I said, Ben is pissed off at the way the world has conspired to destroy him and his family and, thus, revenge is also on his mind as he plays. Ben ultimately wins his prize at the end of the novel—but it is certainly not money and freedom.

Like most of the Bachman tales, *The Running Man* paints a bleak picture of our future and ends on a defiantly pessimistic note. This dark sensibility is why Ace Books initially rejected the novel, telling King they were not interested in science fiction that dealt with "negative utopias."

That aside, though, *The Running Man* is precisely what Stephen King says it is: pure story. King wrote it in a weekend: I read it even quicker than that. It is tightly written, exciting and scary, and is one of his most powerful statements about big government and the power of the media. In this day of the omnipresent Webcam and the millions of digital voyeur photos on the Internet, *The Running Man* has astonishing prescience.

☠ **C. V.** ☠

Main Characters

Ben Richards, Sheila Richards, Cathy Richards, Dan Killian, Bradley Throckmorton, Elton Parrakis, Evan McCone, Molie Jernigan, Amelia Williams.

Did You Know?

In August 2000, a Berlin-based company inaugurated a game called RealityRun, which the creators acknowledged was based on Stephen King's novel *The Running Man*. The main difference, of course, was that the contestant only lost the *game*, not his *life*, if he was not able to remain on the run for 24 days. The first contestant was "captured" in seven days by a German woman. She won the $10,000 grand prize that the contestant would have garnered had he been able to elude recognition and identification for the entire 24 days. The other difference between the book and the game is that viewers monitored the runner on *realityrun.com*—instead of on television. As of this writing, a San Franciso run was being planned and a September 2001 final round was scheduled.

King mentions both Harding and Derry in *The Running Man*. Harding is the setting for King's unpublished "race riot" novel *Sword in the Darkness*; Derry is the setting for *It, Insomnia, Dreamcatcher*, and other King works.

The King Speaks

"The Running Man...may be the best of them all because it's nothing but story—it moves with the goofy speed of a silent movie, and anything which is not story is cheerfully thrown over the side."

—From "Why I Was Bachman," the Introduction to the October, 1985 New American Library omnibus edition of *The Bachman Books*

What I Really Liked About It

The Running Man is one of King's "can't stop 'till you're finished" stories. Its pull is irresistible.

Film Adaptations

The Running Man (1987), starring Arnold Schwarzenegger, Maria Conchita Alonso, Yaphet Kotto, Jim Brown, Jesse Ventura, Erland Van Lindth, Marvin J. McIntyre, Gus Rethwisch, Professor Toru Tanaka, Mick Fleetwood, Dweezil Zappa, Richard Dawson; directed by Paul Michael Glaser, screenplay by Steven E. De Souza.

This is a lame-o (and unfaithful) adaptation but still notable for its interesting casting, including: former pro wrestler Jesse Ventura, Mick Fleetwood of Fleetwood Mac, Frank Zappa's son Dweezil, and *Family Feud* host Richard Dawson. Also worth mentioning is director Paul Michael Glaser, one of the original stars of *Starsky & Hutch* (he was either Starsky or Hutch); and writer Steven De Souza, also known for *48 Hrs.*, *Die Hard 1* and *2*, and *The Flintstones*. Considering the talent involved, this film should have been better than it is. King spoke out about this film in the January 2001 issue of the magazine *Writers' Journal*: "I didn't care for the way they made *The Running Man* very much. It was not very much like my book, and I liked that book a lot. I relate it to a period of my life that I enjoyed, and I remember the writing of it with great affection. I didn't like the movie, but I kept my mouth shut. Now the movie's gone, but the book rules." (Grade: C.)

NUMBER 42

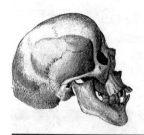

"Dolan's Cadillac"
(1985, 1989)

For the love of God, Montresor!
—"The Cask of Amontillado"

☠☠☠

For the love of God, Robinson!
—"Dolan's Cadillac"

Why it made the top 100:

If the serial novel *The Green Mile* suggests that Stephen King is the Charles Dickens of our time, then the short story "Dolan's Cadillac" likewise implies that he may also be the Edgar Allan Poe of the 20th and 21st century.

"Dolan's Cadillac" is King's modern update of Poe's 1846 short story "The Cask of Amontillado." In Poe's tale, the aristocrat Montressor exacts exquisite revenge on Fortunato, whose "thousand injuries" he had borne for too long, by entombing him alive in a wine cellar.

In "Dolan's Cadillac," the widower Robinson assesses a similar retribution by entombing the organized crime figure Dolan in his gray Cadillac beneath a Las Vegas desert highway. Robinson's wife, Elizabeth, had been in the wrong place at the wrong time and inadvertently witnessed Dolan committing a crime. After Elizabeth agrees to testify, Dolan has her killed by wiring dynamite to the ignition of her car. No witness, no trial. From that moment on, Robinson was committed to making Dolan pay for killing his beloved wife.

Robinson waits patiently for the right time and the perfect confluence of factors to execute his plan—and Dolan. Battling exhaustion, injury, and almost fatal heat, Robinson manages to dig a Cadillac-sized grave in the Las Vegas highway and trick Dolan's driver into speeding right into it. Appropriately, Robinson carries out his plan on a long July Fourth weekend and when it is over, Robinson—and Elizabeth's spirit—are both freed from the torment of knowing that Dolan walked the earth at liberty while Elizabeth lay in her grave.

After Dolan is made to pay for his crime, Robinson no longer hears Elizabeth's voice whispering to him. She—and her husband—are now both at peace.

"Dolan's Cadillac" is a well-told tale of revenge and is as gripping and horrifying as its inspirational fountainhead, and a fitting tribute to one of the fathers of the suspense tale, Edgar Allan Poe.

☠ **C. V.** ☠

Main Characters

Robinson, Dolan, Harvey Blocker, Elizabeth (voice only).

Did You Know?

Stephen King loves relevant epigraphs for his works and in the original five-part serialization of "Dolan's Cadillac" in the *Castle Rock* newsletter (February-June 1985), he used one "revenge-themed" epigraph for each segment:

1. "Revenge is a dish best eaten cold"(Spanish proverb).
2. "God says, 'Take what you want, and pay for it'" (Spanish proverb).
3. "Vengeance is mine, saith the Lord" (Old Testament).
4. "Meet revenge is proper and just" (The Koran).
5. "Vengeance and pity do not meet" (Sheridan).

In the revised version of the story that appeared in *Nightmares & Dreamscapes*, King eliminated all the epigraphs except the first.

What I Really Liked About It

The way King convinces us of Robinson's dogged, relentless commitment to making Dolan pay for murdering Elizabeth, and with the only thing of comparable value: his own life.

Film Adaptations

In production in 2001, with Sylvester Stallone as Dolan and Kevin Bacon as Robinson.

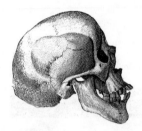

The Little Sisters of Eluria
(1998)

Time belongs to the Dark Tower.

Why it made the top 100:

This novella debuted in 1998 in *Legends*, Robert Silverberg's superb collection of fantasy short novels by authors such as King, Terry Goodkind, Orson Scott Card, Ursula K. LeGuin, Anne McCaffrey, Robert Jordan, and others.

*Little Sister*s runs approximately 30,000 words and is divided into six multi-titled "chapters":

I.   Full Earth. The Empty Town. The Bells. The Dead Boy. The Overturned Wagon. The Green Folk.
II. Rising. Hanging Suspended. White Beauty. Two Others. The Medallion.
III. Five Sisters. Jenna. The Doctors of Eluria. The Medallion. A Promise of Silence.
IV. A Bowl of Soup. The Boy in the Next Bed. The Night-Nurses.

The story begins when Roland, riding his dying horse Topsy and continuing his search for Walter the Man in Black, comes upon a seemingly deserted and dead town called Eluria. He discovers the body of a dead boy whom he expected to be wearing a "Jesus-man sigul" (again linking the *Dark Tower* tales to our world, one in which Christianity is widespread), but instead finds a gold pendant around the boy's neck revealing his name to be James.

As Roland is pondering whether or not to bury James, Topsy keels over dead and Roland suddenly sees eight Slow Mutants (this is their first appearance in the *Dark Tower* saga) advancing on him. Roland ends up almost beaten to death, and awakens in a "hospital" where he is shocked to find himself suspended in mid-air. This hospital is no hospice of respite for the sick, though, even though healing of a sort does go on here. It is actually an "incubator" in which the Doctors of Eluria—hordes of black bugs that attach themselves to the sick and wounded—heal the patients so that the "Sisters"—reminiscent of kindhearted nuns—can feed on them. The Little Sisters of Eluria are an odd breed of vampire and Roland is, apparently, their next target.

Roland is, however, protected by the pendant he took off the dead boy, and also by one of the sisters, Sister Jenna, who is the one who ultimately helps him escape. Jenna pays for her betrayal, however, in a horrible manner, leaving Roland alone to continue his pursuit of the Man in Black.

The Little Sisters of Eluria is one more contribution to the story of Roland, the last gunslinger, and of his quest for the Dark Tower. King's writing and narrative voice in this tale is as polished and assured as it is in the *Dark Tower* novels. Plus it is a genuinely entertaining and intriguing tale. In *Little Sisters*, King again reinforces the connection between the *Dark Tower* stories and the world depicted in *The Eyes of the Dragon*. In fact, he reveals that the witch Rhea of the Coos is likely the sister of the witch Rhiannon of the Coos mentioned in *The Eyes of the Dragon*.

Jake may have been correct when he told Roland "There are other worlds than these," but in the end, the truth may be that all those other worlds are all part of *one* world in which the Dark Tower stands tall and exerts its hallowed sway.

☠ **C. V.** ☠

Main Characters

Roland of Gilead, Topsy, dead James, The Slow Mutants, Sister Mary, John Norman, Sister Jenna, Sister Louise, Sister Michela, Sister Coquina, Sister Tamra, Rhea of the Coos, the Doctors of Eluria.

Did You Know?

John Norman (brother of James, the dead boy that Roland found in Eluria) is a patient in the Little Sisters' hospital, and Roland meets him during his stay there. The name "John Norman" may be King's *hommage* to the science fiction and fantasy author John Norman (real name John Frederick Lange, Jr.), author of the wildly popular series of sci-fi/fantasy novels set on the planet Gor. This is pure speculation, of course, but it makes sense that King may be a fan of Norman's and chose this way of paying tribute. Or I may be completely wrong and the name was picked purely at random. In any case, the Gor novels are fun and you might want to check them out if you're a sci-fi/fantasy fiction fan.

 What I Really Liked About It

I love the idea that there are all these stories of Roland floating about and that he had incredible and important adventures and revelations before we meet him in the first book of the series, *The Gunslinger*. Granted, the novels themselves have revealed a great deal of Roland's past, but a free-standing story like *Little Sisters* is a real treat.

 Film Adaptations

None.

NUMBER 44

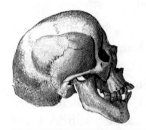

"Survivor Type"
(1982)

"How badly does the patient want to survive?"

Why it made the top 100:

Only Stephen King could have written the short story "Survivor Type."

I'm sure you can probably easily name a dozen talented writers who could have written a similarly-themed tale but, sweet fancy Moses, has there ever been a short story that was more "classic Stephen King" than "Survivor Type"?

A guy is stranded on a desert island and is forced to cannibalize himself to survive—until he is rescued, goes utterly insane, or there's nothing left to eat.

Even that one-sentence "log line" description literally shrieks *"Stephen King story!"* Even before and/or after "Survivor Type" was written, King had been thinking (and apparently still is thinking) about the "stranded on an island/survivor" storyline for quite some time.

In a September 2000 interview published in the UK newspaper *The Observer* (and online: *www.observer.co.uk/stephenking/story/0,7763,368455,00.html*) Stephen King added fuel to the (rattan) fire:

Have you seen that program *Survivor*? Pretty close to *Lord of the Flies*. They kick one guy off the island every week. They don't actually chase him with sharpened sticks, but you get the feeling they'd kind of like to. I started a book like that about fifteen years ago. It was called *On the Island*, and it was about rich people who talked these street kids into going to an island and being hunted, with paintballs. And they get there and they find these guys are actually shooting live rounds, and in my story there were two or three who escaped and waited for these rich guys to come back. I've got it on the shelf somewhere. *Survivor* is a sort of a Stephen King idea, and it's a huge hit.

Like *Survivor* the TV show, "Survivor Type" the short story is the quintessential example of a "can't stop once you start" reading experience, and King demonstrates with verve the grislier aspects of his macabre sense of humor. And that is the key to our enjoyment of the story. You just *know* King had a ball writing "Survivor Type." Like his later, equally gore-glorious nonfiction essay "My Little Serrated Security Blanket"(see Chapter 82), it is easy to imagine King hunched over his keyboard, cackling with demented glee as he decides which body parts Richard Pine should eat first or, in the case of "Serrated Security Blanket," what shape holes an ice ax would make in a human skull.

Are there problems with the story? A couple, especially the device of making Pine a med student and conveniently having him stranded on the island with heroin that can be used as an anesthetic and tools to perform his makeshift surgery. But, hey, without these plot elements, there was no story, right?

Do these minor distractions detract from our enjoyment of the tale? Not in the least.

"Survivor Type" is fast-paced and told entirely as an interior monologue by way of diary entries that become increasingly irrational as Pine consumes himself and goes irrevocably mad. What is fascinating about being inside Pine's mind as he first rationalizes his self-cannibalization, and then begins to enjoy it a little too much, is wondering what will happen first. Will Pine die from his self-butchering, or will he go completely insane. Will he just lie down on the beach (the world's grisliest multiple amputee), and die blathering about "lady fingers"?

Great story. I think I'll go watch my *Survivor* tapes again.

☠ **C. V.** ☠

 Main Characters

Richard Pine and his scrumptious body parts.

 Did You Know?

Self-cannibalism is real. It is called "autophagy," which is the term used scientifically to describe the process of self-digestion by a cell through the action of enzymes originating

The King Speaks

"We were living in Bridgton at the time, and I spent an hour or so talking with Ralph Drews, the retired doctor next door. Although he looked doubtful at first (the year before, in pursuit of another story, I had asked him if he thought it was possible for a man to swallow a cat), he finally agreed that a guy could subsist on himself for quite a while — like everything else which is material, he pointed out, the human body is just stored energy. Ah, I asked him, but what about the repeated shock of the amputations? The answer he gave me is, with very few changes, the first paragraph of the story."

—From "Notes," *Skeleton Crew*

within the same cell. The wonderful world of psychology has appropriated the term to describe people who cut off and eat pieces of their own skin.

What I Really Liked About It

King's matter-of-fact delineation of what, for most people, would be unthinkable.

Film Adaptations

None (yet). It would seem inevitable, though, that this story will someday be filmed. Let's just hope they don't chicken out when doing so. (If George Romero isn't busy...)

NUMBER 45

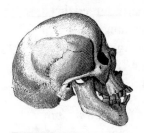

Thinner
(1984)

Billy Halleck, you're skinnier!

Why it made the top 100:

A November 2000 story in *USA Today* bore the headline "The youth of America: fat and getting fatter." Amidst the plethora of suggestions in the article for ways that overweight young people could prevent becoming overweight adults, having a gypsy curse put on them was not one of the tips.

Thinner is the Richard Bachman novel that bears the notoriety of being published first as "by Richard Bachman," and then, in February 1985, after King acknowledged that he was, indeed, Richard Bachman, as "Stephen King writing as Richard Bachman." The novel sold 28,000 copies when it was published as a Bachman novel; it immediately sold 280,000 copies when the true identity of its author was revealed, and today there are over 3,000,000 hardcover and paperback copies of the book in print. *Thinner*, which spent 41 weeks on the best-seller lists, is also the novel that prompted a Literary Guild Book Club member to write in to the Club that the novel was "what Stephen King would write like if Stephen King could write."

That snide Literary Guild member—blatant insult to King's pre-*Thinner* work aside—was right: *Thinner* is pretty close to what might be described as a quintessential Stephen King novel. In fact, on page 111 of the New American Library hardcover edition, Dr. Houston says to an increasingly worried Billy Halleck, "You were starting to sound a little like a Stephen King novel for a while there ..." Halleck then responds, "But if you add Cary Rossington with his alligator skin and William J. Halleck with his case of involuntary anorexia nervosa into the equation, it starts to sound a little like Stephen King again, wouldn't you say?"

Why is Billy worried? He is worried because by this point in the novel, he has lost 67 pounds in far too short a time for such a weight loss to be anything but Bad News. Is it the Big C? he wants to know. Why am I losing so much weight so quickly?

As is often the case with modern medicine, though, things like "Gypsy Curses: Their Etiology and Pathology" are not taught in medical school.

Billy has been cursed for accidentally killing an old Gypsy woman with his car. Billy hit her because he was distracted by his wife's spur-of-the-moment decision to manually pleasure Billy while he was driving. When Billy is let off with a slap on the wrist by his judge friend, the woman's father, Taduz Lemke, scratches Billy's cheek and whispers, "Thinner."

Ah, let the wild rumpus start.

Billy begins wasting away and ultimately learns the truth about his weight loss. He then does what any American raised on Martin Scorsese movies and *The Godfather* series might likewise consider: Billy hires a mob guy to "take care" of getting his curse lifted.

Things do not work out as Billy hoped they would and the novel ends with the innocent doomed, and Billy reluctantly accepting that he—and his loved ones—must pay a lethal price for his deeds. Taduz Lemke had succeeded in exacting from Billy the revenge he so bitterly sought.

☠ **C. V.** ☠

Main Characters

Billy Halleck, Richard Ginelli, Heidi Halleck, Taduz Lemke, Gina Lemke, Linda Halleck, Judge Cary Rossington, Frank Spurton.

Did You Know?

In *Thinner*, Richard Ginelli, an Italian organized crime boss, owns a restaurant called The Three Brothers. In King's serial novel, *The Plant*, a character named Richard

The King Speaks

"After I started really losing weight, I couldn't help but feel attached to it. There's a line in the book about how our version of reality depends a lot on how we see out physical size. I began to think about just what would happen if someone who began to lose weight found he couldn't stop."

—From an interview with Douglas E. Winter
in *Stephen King: The Art of Darkness*

Ginelli owns a restaurant called The Four Fathers. This is yet another clue that *Thinner* was written by Stephen King—but the only readers who would have noticed it were the lucky few who were receiving King's *Plant* Christmas mailings when *Thinner* was published. When King began offering the individual chapters of *The Plant* for sale on his Web site in 2000, King fans instantly noticed the Ginelli connection the day Chapter 3 (the first time Ginelli is mentioned in *The Plant*) was posted on King's site.

What I Really Liked About It

As has been the case with most of the Bachman books, *Thinner* is *pure story*. It moves along like a house afire and it has that patented pessimistic, depressing, inevitable, utterly irresistible Richard Bachman ending. (Somebody *has* to eat the pie, right?)

Film Adaptations

Thinner (also known as *Stephen King's Thinner*, 1996); starring Robert John Burke, Joe Mantegna, Lucinda Jenney, Michael Constantine, Kari Wuhrer, Joie Lenz, Time Winters, Howard Erskine, Terrence Garmey, Randy Jurgensen, Jeff Ware, Antonette Schwartzberg, Terence Kava, Adriana Delphine, Ruth Miller, Sam Freed, John Horton, Daniel Von Bargen; Stephen King; directed by Tom Holland; screenplay by Tom Holland, Michael McDowell. (Grade: C-.)

"The Woman in the Room"
(1978)

The question is: Can he do it?

Why it made the top 100:

"The Woman in the Room" is one of the saddest short stories Stephen King has ever written. Along with his classic story "Gramma," it provides an intimate look at what King and his brother David must have experienced as they lived through, first, the death of their grandmother, and then, the passing of their mother, Ruth.

"The Woman in the Room," the story that closes *Night Shift*, is painful to read, especially so for someone who has lost a parent. King was so attuned to the details of his mother's final days that the story has a remarkable specificity that is amplified by images that are at once both icily stark and richly textured. King describes the walls in the hospital as "two-tone: brown on the bottom and white on top" and writes that "He thinks that the only two-tone combination in the whole world that might be more depressing than brown and white would be pink and black. Hospital corridors like giant Good 'n' Plentys."

He describes the equipment in the hospital halls as looking like "strange playground toys" including a "large circular object...[that] looks like the wheels you sometimes see in squirrel cages. And in what might be one of the best similes I have ever read, "There is a rolling IV tray with two bottles hung from it, like a Salvador Dali dream of tits." Perfect, right?

John, the woman in the room's son, is so tormented by the dying of his mother that he has to get drunk before he can visit her. The pain from her stomach cancer has gotten so bad that the doctors had to do a cortotomy on her, an operation during which they stuck a needle into her brain and shorted out her pain center. Partial paralysis was one of the unavoidable side effects of this procedure and John knows intuitively that the operation was the beginning of the end. And this realization is what brings him to ask—and answer—the question posed in the opening line of the story: "Can he do it?" Can John help his mother commit suicide?

The answer is yes. And the story ends with John wiping his fingerprints off the bottle of Darvon Complex after feeding his mother enough to kill her.

In real life, Stephen King and his brother David were both by their mother's bedside the morning she died. King wrote about that morning in *On Writing* and an image leaps off the page at us as we read the poignant account of his mother's final moments:

In *On Writing*, King writes:

When I got into the master bedroom he was sitting beside her on the bed and holding a Kool for her to smoke. She was only semiconscious, her eyes going from Dave to me and then back to Dave again. I sat next to Dave, took the cigarette and held it to her mouth. Her lips stretched out to clamp on the filter.

In "The Woman in the Room," King writes:

He shakes a Kool out of one of the packages scattered on the table by her bed and lights it. He holds it between the first and second fingers of his right hand, and she puffs it, her lips stretching to grasp the filter. Her inhale is weak. The smoke drifts from her lips.

"The Woman in the Room" is written in a disjointed style in which dialogue has no quotation marks, paragraphs end in mid-sentence, and the point of view is first person when people are speaking, and omniscient third person all other times. These stylistic devices impart a dreamlike affect (and effect, for that matter) in which we *become* John as we read, even though we only know him and his thoughts and feelings through what we are *told*, rather than what John tells us. This narrative sophistication bespeaks a profound talent and that is why this story is universally considered one of Stephen King's best.

When an artist lives through events with his or her eyes open the result is often superb art. "The Woman in the Room" is a classic example of this.

☠ **C. V.** ☠

The King Speaks

"[W]hat really scared me most about the prospect of my mother's death was not being shipped off to some institution, rough as that would have been, but I was afraid it would drive me crazy."

—From a June 1983 interview with *Playboy* magazine

 Main Characters

John, John's mother (the "woman in the room"), Kevin; also mentioned are authors Michael Crichton and Ray Bradbury, and filmmaker George Romero (indirectly: he refers to Romero's *The Night of the Living Dead* in the story).

 Did You Know?

Stephen King once described this story in two words: "healing fiction."

 What I Really Liked About It

The immediate immersion into John's psyche and our complete understanding of everything he is thinking and feeling. The fact that King lived through the experience of watching his mother die informs this story and gives it a sharp edge and a flawlessly (appropriate, too) funereal tune.

 Film Adaptations

The Woman in the Room (1986), starring Michael Cornelison, Dee Croxton, Brian Libby, Bob Brunson, George Russell; directed by Frank Darabont, screenplay by Frank Darabont. (Note: The original version of Darabont's adaptation was completed and presented to Stephen King in 1983. The short film was released on videotape in 1986. To this day, King considers Darabont's *The Woman in the Room* a wonderful accomplishment and states that it "remains on my short list of favorite film adaptations.") (Grade: A.)

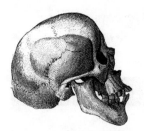

"Strawberry Spring" (1968, 1975)

In New England they call it strawberry spring.
No one knows why; it's just a phrase the old-timers use.

Why it made the top 100:

"Strawberry Spring" is a small gem of a tale; an evocative slice of 60s college life that flawlessly captures the tenor of the times, but also digs deeper and reveals a hidden darkness no amount of pot or beers can eliminate.

A serial killer is murdering women on the campus of New Sharon Teachers' College. The story of the terrible "strawberry spring" (a false spring) of 1968 is told seven or so years later by a narrator who we later learn may have been the one responsible for the murders.

The atmosphere and tone of this story perfectly evoke not only the weird, otherworldy feel of the fog-laden strawberry spring itself, but also that of the sociocultural climate of a college campus in the late 1960s: "The jukebox played 'Love is Blue' that year," King writes. "It played 'Hey Jude' endlessly. It played 'Scarborough Fair.'"

The murderer, eventually christened by the media "Springheel Jack" in honor of a serial killer from the early 19th century, is especially vicious. He decapitated one victim and took her head with him; another he propped up behind the wheel of her car, but put parts of her in the back seat and the trunk as well. At the end of the story we believe (it is, by now, unavoidable) that the narrator is without a doubt Springheel Jack, especially when he tells us "I've been thinking about the trunk of my car—such an ugly word, *trunk*—and wondering why in the world I should be afraid to open it."

One especially nice touch in the story is King's use of a *Lord of the Rings* metaphor. After the narrator exits the campus eatery called The Grinder and walks into the damp and all-encompassing fog, he muses that "You half expected to see Gollum or Frodo and Sam go hurrying past." With this simple image, King evokes all the magic and dark wonder of J. R. R. Tolkien's Middle Earth and places us squarely in the ambiance of its environs.

"Strawberry Spring" first appeared in the University of Maine literary magazine *Ubris* in 1968 when King was a 22-year-old student at the school. A substantially revised version was later published in the men's magazines *Cavalier* and *Gent* and ultimately collected in *Night Shift* and elsewhere. (If you're interested in the differences between the *Ubris* version and the later *Night Shift* version, see my *Complete Stephen King Encyclopedia*. For my "Strawberry Spring" concordance I provide complete details on the people, places, and things of the story, with separate entries for the *Ubris* version of the story when it differed from the later revised version.)

☠ **C. V.** ☠

Main Characters

Springheel Jack, assorted female victims.

Did You Know?

"Strawberry Spring" powerfully evokes the Jack the Ripper mythology (even mentioning Jack in the text) with King effectively creating his own homegrown version of the elusive serial killer.

What I Really Liked About It

I have always liked this story a lot and consider it one of King's grimmest tales. Adding to its appeal are the little touches, such as when the narrator is stopped by the State Police on campus and asked to show an ID. "I was clever," he tells us. "I showed him the one without the fangs." As the story progresses, we realize he wasn't joking. "Strawberry

Spring" is one of King's more stylistic stories and hints at the voice he would resurrect for *Hearts in Atlantis*.

 Film Adaptations

None.

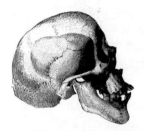

"Nona"
(1978)

Her arms reached around my neck and I pulled her against me.
That was when she began to change, to ripple and run like wax.

Why it made the top 100:

"Nona" is a chilling, atmospheric tale in which King blends the supernatural with a realistic setting and leaves it to the reader to determine if The Prisoner is insane and has completely created Nona from his delusions, or if he was actually visited, possessed, and controlled by a demonic being.

A man known only as The Prisoner meets a woman named Nona in Joe's Good Eats one night and goes on a bloody murderous rampage with her. Nona—a gorgeous creature who nonetheless transforms into a giant rat while embracing The Prisoner—may or may not have been real and the whole story of the killing spree is told by The Prisoner from his jail cell—just before he plans on killing himself.

"Nona" is one of King's "Castle Rock" stories. The Prisoner's mother came from Castle Rock and The Prisoner grew up in Harlow, a town we are told is across the river from Castle Rock.

In "Nona," The Prisoner mentions seeing the GS&WM railroad trestle off in the distance. In what might be the quintessential "Castle Rock" story, *The Body* (which appears in the collection *Different Seasons*) this railroad trestle plays a very important role.

The King Speaks

In my 1998 book, *The Lost Work of Stephen King*, I discuss King's college *Garbage Truck* columns. In one of these columns, King reviewed the movie *Easy Rider* and discussed the diner scene in the movie in which blue-collar workers taunt and bait the long-haired (for the time) Dennis Hopper and Jack Nicholson, calling them the "purtiest girls" they ever saw. King talks about the "tension and impending violence" in this scene and how this kind of hassle is familiar to any young person with long hair who hazards entering any place where he is clearly the outsider. In "Nona," King gave us *this* scene:

> The third thing that struck me was The Eye. You know about The Eye once you let your hair get down below the lobes of your ears. Right then people know you don't belong to the Lions, Elks, or the VFW. You know about The Eye, but you never get used to it.

> Right now the people giving me The Eye were four truckers in one booth, two more at the counter, a pair of old ladies wearing cheap fur coats and blue rinses, the short-order cook, and a gawky kid with soap-suds on his hands.

In "Nona," it isn't long before one of the truckers makes a crack about Christ coming back, another one plays "A Boy Named Sue" on the jukebox, and, finally, The Prisoner is confronted by a Neanderthal who asks him if he actually is "a fella." The scene in *Easy Rider*, plus King's *own* experiences as a "longhair" in the Sixties, seems to have influenced this gripping scene in "Nona." As I suggested in *Lost Work*, it seems that King was editorially commenting on his own experiences and using the character of The Prisoner to express his own feelings about being an outsider.

Another interesting reference in "Nona" is when The Prisoner tells us, "One of my 'brothers,' Curt, ran away." In King's short story "Cain Rose Up" (also in *Skeleton Crew*), the main character is a college student named Curt Garrish, obviously inspired by the Texas Tower sniper Charles Whitman. In "Cain Rose Up," Curt begins killing people from his college dorm window. If this is the "Curt" The Prisoner is referring to, it is interesting that he uses the phrase "ran away," since "Cain Rose Up" ends with Garrish continuing to shoot people from his college dorm window.

☠ **C. V.** ☠

Main Characters

The Prisoner, Nona, assorted Castle Rock denizens.

Did You Know?

"Nona" marked King's first use of his haunting (haunted?) "Do you love?" leitmotif. In the story, Nona the rat thing asks The Prisoner this question in the Castle Rock grave-yard. Four years later, in the *Skeleton Crew* story, "The Raft" (which was first published in *Gallery* magazine in 1982), Randy asks the malevolent, devouring thing in the water the same question.

What I Really Liked About It

The mood, the tone, the sense of impending doom. King revisited this sensibility in his 2000 e-novella *Riding the Bullet* over 20 years later (when Alan accepts a ride from a guy who just might be dead).

Film Adaptations

None.

Number **49**

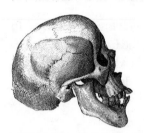

"All That You Love Will Be Carried Away" (2001)

He knew the room; it was the room of his dreams.

Why it made the top 100:

Writing for *The New Yorker* seems to bring out the best in Stephen King and this story, his most recent to appear in the esteemed magazine as of this writing, is poignant evidence of that assertion.

"All That You Love Will Be Carried Away" can be added to the short list of King's saddest stories, a list that includes "The Last Rung on the Ladder" (Chapter 65); "The Reach" (Chapter 35); "The Woman in the Room" (Chapter 46); and "My Pretty Pony" (Chapter 40).

And even though one of the earthier elements King touches on throughout the story is Alfie Zimmer's fascination with restroom graffiti, "All That You Love" is of exceptional literary merit. It is also, however, a story that does not disappoint those who greatly enjoy King's unique narrative voice. That voice is here in this tale and yet it does not shout, nor does it whisper. It speaks calmly as it tells us the story of a traveling salesman who will kill himself one evening in a motel room in Nebraska during a snowstorm. Or will he?

Alfie Zimmer is, like Arthur Miller's Willy Loman in *Death of a Salesman*, a traveling salesman. He has a wife and daughter and he makes a living by selling gourmet frozen dinners throughout the Midwest. Alfie is depressed and has stopped taking his medication. Alfie plans to kill himself in a Motel 6 on I-80 just west of Lincoln, Nebraska.

Like a good husband and father, though, Alfie calls home before he puts the barrel in his mouth and pulls the trigger. He reminds his soon-to-be-devastated wife to bring that casserole to his mother like she promised, to tell Carlene Daddy loves her, not to forget to take the dog to the vet, and to make sure she gives him the sea-jerky strips at night because they really help his hips.

This is crushingly sad, because we know that soon Alfie's body will be in a box being flown home.

But just as Alfie is ready to check out, something stops him.

Alfie suddenly realizes that when his body is found, they will also find the spiral notebook he has had for seven years in which he has been writing graffiti he has collected on the road. Devoid of commentary, Alfie knows that the notebook will make him look crazy and he does not want to put his daughter through the torment she would undoubtedly be subjected to when word got out that her dead father had been crazier than a shithouse rat.

After some thought, he decides to throw the notebook into the snowy field across the street from the motel where it will be plowed under in the spring. Then he will return to his room and kill himself. But in the distance across the field, he can see the house of the farmer who owns the land, and at the last minute, he decides to, essentially, leave his fate to fate, specifically the ebb and rush of the wind. Will he see the lights? Will he hurl the notebook? Will he eat his gun? Will he live to write the book about his collection?

"All That You Love Will Be Carried Away" echoes Joyce Carole Oates and J. D. Salinger and is King in top form. Hopefully it will be included in his forthcoming, still-untitled short story collection so that it can reach a wider audience than just those who read it when it appeared in *The New Yorker*.

 C. V.

 Main Characters

Alfie Zimmer, Maura Zimmer, Carlene Zimmer, the farmer and his family.

Did You Know?

There may be some literary linkage between this story and King's 1994 nonfiction essay "The Neighborhood of the Beast." "All That You Love Will Be Carried Away" is about a man on the road; "Neighborhood of the Beast" is about a band on the road. In "Neighborhood," King talks about seeing "Save Russian Jews, Collect Valuable Prizes" in the men's room of The Hungry Bear restaurant in Portland, Maine. In "All That You Love," the main character Alfie Zimmer imagines knocking on a farmhouse door and advising the farmer's wife to "save Russian Jews, collect valuable prizes," which was the first graffiti he mentioned in the story. Since part of King's "Neighborhood" essay is about being sick while on tour and visiting a great many restrooms on the road, the fact that Alfie Zimmer collects restroom graffiti while traveling his route seems more than coincidental. Being on the road with the Rock Bottom Remainders seems to have been a memorable influence for King.

 What I Really Liked About It

The idea of a man who is still alive and thinking ahead to what will happen after he is gone strikes me as a sad and powerful manifestation of a depression that has crossed over into the red zone. King does an amazing job of taking us inside the mind of a man caught in this kind of emotional nightmare.

 Film Adaptations

None.

NUMBER 50

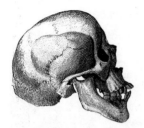

"Autopsy Room Four"
(1997)

Dear God, I'm in a bodybag.

Why it made the top 100:

Is there any greater nightmare than being buried alive? Not according to Edgar Allan Poe who, in his short story "The Premature Burial" describes the horror of living inhumation and relates several accounts of people being taken for dead, buried, and then waking up inside their own coffin.

All due respect to Mr. Poe, there is, however, a more profound horror than coming awake under the ground, inside a casket, and leave it to Stephen King to figure out what it is.

It is being *autopsied* alive, and that is precisely what Stephen King gives us in this terrifying short story.

Stock broker Howard Cottrell, zipped into a bodybag, comes to some indefinable form of consciousness while being wheeled on a gurney into an autopsy room—autopsy room four, to be specific. Howard is dead—according to Dr. Frank Jennings, the (ancient)

☠ 173 ☠

doctor who pronounced him so after finding him seemingly lifeless on the Derry Municipal Golf Course. (Figures this would happen in Derry, eh?)

But Howard can see, hear, and most horrifyingly, *feel* everything going on around him and being done to him. How can this be, he asks himself? Am I dead? And if I am dead, does this mean that all dead people are able to continue experiencing things as though they were still alive? Does this mean that every person who dies has to experience being autopsied, and embalmed, and buried, or, God help us, cremated?

Howard's body is completely paralyzed. Even his pupils do not dilate when the painfully bright overhead lights are turned on. Howard watches and listens as the pathology team, nervous Peter, Rusty the jerk, and all-business Dr. Arlen, prepare their instruments (mostly scissors and saws), and strip him naked on the cold table. He is handled and examined like a piece of dead flesh (which is, of course, precisely what he is to Dr. Arlen and company). It is Dr. Arlen's need to move Howard's penis out of the way, combined with Rusty putting two and two together, that resolves Howard's fate once and for all.

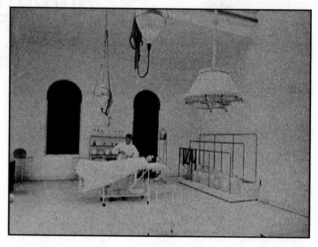

Some of you have not yet read this story because it has only appeared in the extremely rare *Six Stories* and the horror anthology *Robert Bloch's Psychos*. It will probably be included in King's next short story collection (2003?), but as of right now, it has not appeared in a trade edition of a Stephen King book. Thus, I will say no more about the conclusion of "Autopsy Room Four," nor of Howard Cottrell's ultimate destiny. Suffice to say that if we come away with anything in the way of a lesson from this tale, it is this: never wear Bermuda shorts on a golf course.

☠ **C. V.** ☠

Main Characters

Howard Cottrell, Rusty, Peter, Dr. Katie Arlen, Dr. Frank Jennings, Mike Hopper.

The King Speaks

"This story is pretty gross ... so, if anyone wants to leave, I'll just say, are you sure you locked your cars?"

—King speaking to an audience on October 29, 1998 in Sydney, Australia before reading aloud "Autopsy Room Four"

Did You Know?

During an autopsy, the coroner (in this story, Peter was playing that role) makes a huge, full-body-length "Y" incision that opens up the entire front of the body. The incision can start at either shoulder and proceed on an angle down to the mid-chest, or it can begin at the pubis and extend up to the mid-chest, connecting to the two shoulder incisions (the top of the "Y"). Thus, the corpse is split wide open by a deep cut, allowing access to the organs of the upper abdominal cavity—lungs, heart, esophagus, and trachea—as well as to the lower abdominal organs, which include the liver, spleen, kidneys, adrenals, stomach, and intestines. Once witnessed, an autopsy is never forgotten.

What I Really Liked About It

This story is so realistically told and Howard's terror is so effectively communicated, that it never fails to hit a nerve—with a 50-pound sledgehammer—for those King fans who have read it. For me, this is one of Stephen King's most frightening stories.

Film Adaptations

None. (But I would love to see what *Paranoid* director Jay Holben would do with *this* story!)

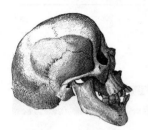

The Plant
(1982, 1983,
1985, 2000, 200?)

Do you think I should offer this book:
- Yes
- No

Can I trust people to pay:
- Yes
- No

• • •

"In this book there is some 'scary s**t!'"

Why it made the top 100:

I will be discussing here an unfinished novel, normally something I would not do. But (the unfinished) *The Plant* is a terrific piece of work and even though, at this writing, it is on hiatus, I felt that enough of it existed to talk about at this time. Also, the story *of* King's *Plant* itself (as opposed to the story *in* his *Plant*) is interesting and curious enough to warrant inclusion in this book and a ranking in *The Essential Stephen King*.

The Plant has a convoluted history and has had one of the oddest, most circuitous routes to publication of anything published in the 20th century. Add to that the fact that the hype surrounding this novel-in-progress has overshadowed the actual story itself and you've got a tale like ... well, like something out of a Stephen King story!

As many King fans know, *The Plant* bloomed to life in 1982 when Stephen King decided to do something special for his family and friends for Christmas. He wrote the first chapter of on ongoing work, self-published it under his Philtrum Press imprint, and sent it out to a select (lucky) few. It was hoped that future chapters would come each year around Christmas time.

Chapter 2 came in 1983; he took 1984 off (that year people on his Christmas card list got the limited edition of *The Eyes of the Dragon*) and then Chapter 3 came in 1985. Shortly after installment 3 was sent out, King happened to see the movie *Little Shop of Horrors* and immediately made the decision to pull the plug on *The Plant*. He believed its storyline was too close to the movie for him to be able to continue to write it with any enthusiasm or creativity.

Time passed. Fifteen years, to be precise. Then, in 1996 and 2000 respectively, Stephen King published two works in unconventional forms. In 1996, he published an entire novel—*The Green Mile*—in six monthly installments; in 2000, he published a novella called *Riding the Bullet* on the Internet, only available as a downloadable file.

All six installments of *The Green Mile* made it to the *New York Times* best-seller list. In fact, when the sixth volume was published, *all six books* were on the list at the same time—a publishing record if there ever was one. This prompted a change in policy— a title is now allowed a single slot no matter how many installments are published. *Riding the Bullet* was downloaded 500,000 times in the first few days of its appearance on Web sites.

Since Stephen King is a creative kind of guy, the wheels in that mind of his started turning and he came up with the idea of combining Internet publication with serial publication and, voila, *The Plant* began to bloom once again.

On June 7, 2000, King posted a letter on his official Web site soliciting opinions from his "Constant Readers" as to whether or not he should publish *The Plant* and whether or not he could trust people to pay on the honor system. He wrote:

> Being something of an optimist about my fellow creatures, I have the idea that most people are honest and will pay for what they get. I'm therefore willing to try selling *The Plant* on an honor system. Episodes would not be encoded. If you wanted to download the stuff to your printer, you could do that. But you gotta kick a buck; a dollar an episode seems fair enough to me. If it seems fair to you, e-mail the Web site and say so. If it seems heavy, say that. My purpose here isn't to skin anybody but to have some fun and try out a concept so old it may seem new; call it "honesty is the best policy."

On June 14, 2000, he posted the following regarding his solicitation:

> The response to my query about *The Plant* was small but enthusiastic. You seem to want it, so I am going to put it up. ... Don't send any money until the story goes up. But when it does come time to pay, remember the Philtrum Press motto: "It takes a really bad guy to steal from a blind newsboy."

The first installment was posted in early July and monthly installments continued through December, at which point King declared that the six installments published comprised the first part of the novel and that that section was called "Zenith Rising."

Much to the fans' consternation (and his critics' glee) King also declared that he was putting the novel on hiatus (uprooting it, you might say ... sorry) in order to conclude work on other more pressing projects, including the *Talisman* sequel *Black House*, *Dreamcatcher* and the *Dark Tower* series. Critics saw this as King admitting defeat, and also read it as a failure of not only the honor payment system, but of "original content" e-publishing in general. King responded by posting a letter on his site in which he declared that he considered *The Plant* a success and that he had every intention of completing it ... eventually.

The story told in *The Plant* is of a struggling paperback publishing house called Zenith House and its beleaguered, yet stalwart editors and staff. One day a query letter arrives from a young writer named Carlos Detweiller offering Zenith House an exclusive look at a book called *True Tales of Demon Infestation*. Editor John Kenton, always hungry for a saleable project, asks to see a few sample chapters and an outline, but Detweiller sends the complete manuscript, which includes photos of a Black Mass in which a human sacrifice occurs—and the photos look *real*.

Kenton freaks and sics the police on Detweiller, an action which sets in motion a psychotic revenge plot against Kenton and Zenith House, which begins with the arrival of a seemingly innocuous little ivy plant named Zenith. From the day Zenith arrives, the Zenith House mavens are hurled into a world of the living dead, sentient, talking plants, psychic communication, and all manner of untimely and bizarre death.

Is *The Plant* worth reading in its current truncated, "paused" form?

Absolutely. As King has said, the first part of the novel ("Zenith Rising" runs a hefty 270 pages) is an exciting read on its own and concludes by wrapping up several storylines, offering some closure, and leaving us with anticipation for the next installment, whenever it comes.

The complete six-part first section is now available (with a nifty cover) for download for seven dollars on Stephen King's Web site: *Stephenking.com*. If you have not read it, now is a good time to buy the whole thing and read it in its entirety. Then put it aside and look forward to other King works, as well as the eventual completion of *The Plant*.

I look at it this way: We *Dark Tower* fans are used to waiting five years between installments of that epic, so why should there be an uproar over waiting a length of time for the next sections of *The Plant*?

☠ **C. V.** ☠

 Main Characters

John Kenton, Roger Wade, Herb Porter, Riddley Walker, Carlos Detweiller, Bill Gelb, Sandra Jackson, Norville Keen, Tina Barfield, General Iron-Guts Hecksler, Harlow Enders, Anthony LaScorbia, Ruth Tanaka.

The King Speaks

"There's a lot of available barn space on the Internet, and a lot of people are going to put on shows. I was delighted to be one of the first, and I'm not done yet. Goodness, why would I be? I'm having a hell of a good time."

—From "*The Plant*: Getting a Little Goofy," King's online-only response to a *New York Times* editorial about *The Plant*

Did You Know?

In the story, editor John Kenton is offered a novel that he immediately believes could be a potential best-seller for Zenith House. The book is called *Last Survivor* and is about a TV network that comes up with a game show idea that involves stranding 26 people on a desert island for six months and testing whether or not they can survive. Sound familiar?

What I Really Liked About It

I especially like the way the story took a nasty turn during the visit to the nursery and also the way King killed off characters (or did he?) that we expected to be with us for the duration of the story.

Film Adaptations

None.

Number **52**

The Regulators
(Written as Richard Bachman)
(1996)

Scared tonight. So scared.

Why it made the top 100:

Fictional characters taking on different roles in different works the way actors take on different fictional roles in different movies. Now *there's* an intriguing structural premise that is probably beyond only the most skilled and imaginative of fiction writers.

With the dual publication of *Desperation* and *The Regulators*, we are given concrete evidence that it is most assuredly *not* beyond Stephen King. Characters from *Desperation* also appear in *The Regulators* in wildly different scenarios, even to the point of certain dead folks from *Desperation* showing up alive and (not so?) well in *The Regulators*.

The narrative premise of the tale is ingenious: the psychic vampire Tak from *Desperation* invades the mind and spirit of an autistic boy named Seth Garin and makes real the violent scenarios from Seth's most popular TV shows and movies.

Set in the good old American Hometown of Wentworth, Ohio (think a modern-day Mayberry ... *briefly*), the action begins immediately when mysterious brightly-colored

The King Speaks

"The most interesting thing about *The Regulators* is that Bachman and I must have been on the same psychic wavelength. It's almost as if we were twins, in a funny way."

—From the publicity materials that accompanied the release of *Desperation* and *The Regulators*.

vans begin moving down Wentworth's streets and inexplicably start killing miscellaneous residents. These are the MotoKops, a Power Rangers-like squad created from Seth's subconscious.

Too involved to summarize here in the limited space available, *The Regulators* is, at its core, the story of Tak's possession of Seth and his Aunt Audrey's and other Wentworthians' battle to rid the boy (and the town) of the malevolent demon. And since this is a Bachman book, it is dark, graphically violent, often pessimistic, and the body count is high. But that's Dicky Bachman for you, right?

Oh, and one more thing: There's a hero writer in the story, too. Go figure.

C. V.

Main Characters

Tak, Seth Garin, Ellen Carver, Raphie Carver, Cynthia Smith, Brad Josephson, Belinda Josephson, Cary Ripton, Johnny Marinville, Gary Soderson, Marielle Soderson, Kirsten Carver, David Carver, Audrey Wyler, Herb Wyler, Peter Jackson, Jim Reed, David Reed, Susi Geller, Tom Billingsley, Collier Entragian, Steve Ames, Mary Jackson, Kim Geller, Debbie Ross, Cammie Reed, Allen Symes, Colonel Henry, Major Pike, Snake Hunter, Bounty, Rooty, Cassie Styles, No Face, Countess Lili.

Did You Know?

It is possible (actually, it's quite likely) that the names of the writers of the (fictitious) *Regulators* screenplay excerpted in *The Regulators*—Craig Goodis and Quentin Woolrich—are King's specific *hommage* to two popular mystery and suspense writers, David Goodis and Cornell Woolrich. Goodis, who died in 1967, was the author of many

Chuck Verrill Speaks

"The former Mrs. Bachman says that, to the best of her knowledge, Bachman never travelled to Ohio, 'although he might have flown over it once or twice.' She also has no idea when this novel was written, although she suspects it must have been late at night. Richard Bachman suffered from chronic insomnia."

—From the Editor's Note leading off *The Regulators*.

popular mysteries, including *Dark Passage* (1946), *The Moon in the Gutter* (1953), *Shoot the Piano Player* (1956), and his final novel, *Somebody's Done For* (1967). Woolrich, who died in 1968, wrote *Rear Window*, the *Black* novels, innumerable pulp mysteries, and is credited with creating the genre now known as "noir."

What I Really Liked About It

The Regulators is an acid trip between covers; a violent, gory, Oliver Stone acid trip in words that is an unusual and irresistible hybrid of supernatural suspense and science fiction. Weird? Yes. Fun? Indubitably.

Film Adaptations

None (unless, of course, you count the fictitious film *The Regulators*, which is mentioned in *The Regulators* and in *Hearts in Atlantis*).

Number 53

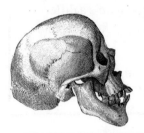

"The Neighborhood of the Beast" (1994)

Above all, this gospel of mine went, you have to be clear-headed (and clear-minded) enough to accept three evaluative facts about yourself all at the same time: The things you know you can do, the things you think you can do, and the things you know in your heart you will never be able to do.

Why it made the top 100:

This lengthy nonfiction essay was King's contribution to an anthology called *Mid-Life Confidential: The Rock Bottom Remainders Tour America with Three Chords and an Attitude.*

Mid-Life Confidential chronicled the 1993 nine-city tour by The Rock Bottom Remainders, a zealous, old-time rock 'n' roll band made up of really great writers who are not-that-great musicians, plus a couple of truly great "ringers" like Al Kooper. (Remainder member Dave Barry is on record as admitting, "The band plays music as well as Metallica writes novels.")

King's conversational offering for the book begins, "In the summer of 1971, when I was 23 and had been married less than a year, something unpleasant happened to me in Sebec Lake."

Tabitha King Speaks

"No doubt there are morons out there demanding to know if I don't have enough money. Well, would you work for diddly-shit? No. You wouldn't. Just what I thought. Probably if you had enough money, you wouldn't work at all. So who's got the work ethic here? I *have* enough money. There's a difference between having enough money and *getting paid* enough to compensate for the work. I knew you'd understand."

—From tour photographer Tabitha King's essay
"I Didn't Get Paid Enough"

Yes, as only King can do, he begins his essay about touring with a one-step-above-a-garage-band motley crew of writers with a gripping personal anecdote that could easily have come from one of his novels or short stories.

Because Stephen King is who he is, after he tells us how he almost drowned that day and reveals that the only thing that saved him was realizing that if he panicked, he would die; he then relates the story of an especially nasty diarrhea attack that kept him trapped in a grimy Nashville barroom toilet stall minutes before he had to go onstage and play.

As is typical for a Stephen King nonfiction piece, his consistently engaging and appealing narrative voice booms through to the reader and we feel as though we're sitting somewhere listening to King talk about whatever's on his mind.

King is a chronicler of the contemporary American landscape, and he is very good at it. Writer J. N. Williamson once defined King as a "noticer," an extremely apt description of King's sensibility. In "The Neighborhood of the Beast," King "notices" the graffiti on the toilet stall walls wherein he sits and also recounts pithy Graffiti of the Past he couldn't help but remember, such as "Dogs Fuck the Pope (No Fault of Mine)" and "Save Russian Jews, Collect Valuable Prizes." (See Chapter 49.)

Speaking of graffiti, the title, "The Neighborhood of the Beast" refers to something King saw written on the back of the bathroom door precisely at his eye level: "664/668: THE NEIGHBORHOOD OF THE BEAST." What number sits precisely between "664" and "668" ? The ominous numbers 666, of course, the Biblical sign of The Beast, a.k.a. Satan.

In his essay, King tells the story of how the band got together and how their first gig was at a bookseller's convention. He does a terrific job of communicating the sheer euphoria the band members felt after their performance.

King also tells the story of meeting a bouncer in a bathroom who asked him if he was the guy who wrote *The Shining* and *The Dead Zone*. When King acknowledged that he was, indeed, that guy, the bouncer replied, "Man, I love all your movies." This bouncer's reaction is a constant in the World of King. When people ask me what I've written and I mention King as one of the subjects I've published books about, they invariably say either, "I love his movies," or "I can't stand his movies." King is a writer first but this frequent reaction to King's name indicates that an awful lot of people know King through the film adaptations of his work instead of his books. This is understandable when you consider that, at best, maybe two or three million people will buy and read an edition of a King book while anywhere from double that number to five times that number may see a Stephen King movie. (This says something scary about American culture, don't you think?)

"The Neighborhood of the Beast" is one of Stephen King's most entertaining nonfiction essays, made all the more special because, for the most part, we are usually only treated to King's nonfiction when he is talking about his stories, in Introductions, Notes, and Afterwords. Here he gets to play journalist and write about something completely unrelated to his fiction ... and yet the magic is still there.

☠ **C. V.** ☠

Main Characters

Stephen King, Tabitha King, and the Rock Bottom Remainders, which at the time consisted of Dave Barry, Tad Bartimus, Roy Blount Jr., Michael Dorris, Robert Fulghum, Kathi Kamen Goldmark, Matt Groenig, Josh Kelly, Barbara Kingsolver, Al Kooper, Greil Marcus, Dave Marsh, Ridley Pearson, Jerry Peterson, Joel Selvin, Amy Tan, and Jimmy Vivino.

Did You Know?

Musical director Al Kooper considered the Rock Bottom Remainders tour "the nadir of western civilization."

What I Really Liked About It

Stephen King's chatty voice throughout the essay; his insider's backstage look at the tour, and his "I almost drowned" opening story.

Film Adaptations

None, although there are videos available of performances by the Rock Bottom Remainders.

Number 54

"In the Deathroom" (2000)

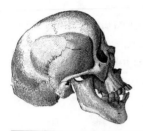

Crazy was a hard state to define.

Why it made the top 100:

This chilling story (which originally made its debut in an audio-only version) made me think of the title of the essay director Jay Holben contributed to this book: "Stephen King is NOT a Horror Writer."

Is "In the Deathroom" horrific?

Since it's almost a given that a story set in a third-world torture chamber would, by definition, be horrific, then "In the Deathroom" qualifies. But "In the Deathroom" offers nary a whiff of the "Ghosties, ghoulies and things that go bump in the night" that Jay Holben acknowledges are the trappings of the work of "Stephen King, the horror writer."

This story is *real-world* horror—which can often be far more terrifying than otherworldly horror. Case in point: is there anything more frightening than a doctor's waiting room? Or, for that matter, a basement room in the Ministry of Information where a machine with dials and an ominous looking steel probe attached to it by a wire is hooked to a Delco car battery? ("In the Deathroom" does have plenty of *gore*, especially during Fletcher's attempted escape scene, but vampires, demons, or ghosts? This story boasts only the human kind.)

Fletcher is a *New York Times* reporter stationed in an unnamed country in Central America where the language spoken is Spanish and where Escobar, the Minister of Information, sometimes does the weather report on local television.

As the story begins, Fletcher is being interrogated for allegedly providing information to the now-dead Tomás who, in turn, apparently funneled it to a Communist insurgent set on taking over the government in a bloody coup. It is made perfectly clear to Fletcher that the people in the room were responsible for Tomás's death and that he will probably be next if he lies to them. His means of death will be excruciating electric shock, administered by a smiling demon named Heinz.

Will Fletcher be tortured? Will he escape? Will his captors survive to torture another day?

King takes us inside Fletcher's mind and makes us understand what being in a Central American deathroom *feels like* and, it ain't, Constant Readers, a day at Disneyworld.

So far, this story is only available on audiotape and in the hard-to-find Book of the Month Club anthology detailed below. There is hope that it will appear in King's forthcoming short story collection (2003?) for it is one of his more visceral dark visions and one that does not need a haunted *anything* to work its terrifying magic on the reader.

☠ **C. V.** ☠

Main Characters

Fletcher, Escobar, the Bride of Frankenstein, Ramón, Heinz, Tomás, Núñez, Carlo Arcuzzi.

Did You Know?

The character of Escobar in this story, identified as the "Minister of Information" for a Central American country, may have been named after real-life Columbian billionaire cocaine trafficker Pablo Escobar, who was killed by Columbian security forces on Thursday, December 2, 1993. After Escobar's death, Andres Pastrana, a Colombian legislator said, "Escobar ended up being a symbol of violence and narco-terrorism. Now the country can begin to live more peacefully."

What I Really Liked About It

This story offers high-test tension and is King at the top of his game when writing in the suspense genre.

 Film Adaptations

None.

 Audio Adaptations

This story is one of three that were released on audiotape as part of King's collection *Blood and Smoke* in 2000. The other two stories on the tapes were "Lunch at the Gotham Café" (which had appeared previously in King's privately-published collection *Six Stories*) and "1408," which, like "In the Deathroom," made its debut on *Blood and Smoke*. "In the Deathroom" was later reprinted in a text version in King's 2000 collection *Secret Windows: Essays and Fiction on the Craft of Writing*, published by the Book of the Month Club in conjunction with the release of King's 2000 nonfiction book, *On Writing*.

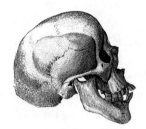

"Leaf-Peepers"
(1998)

The season tilts. Everything creaks. One can hear it—the sound is the bony skitter of small animals moving through the trees, doing the last of their pre-winter shopping. In these weeks, the woods give up their secrets.

Why it made the top 100:

"Leaf-Peepers" is an exquisitely crafted meditation that, on the surface, is about the change of seasons in Maine and the arrival of the leaf-peepers, but which is actually a deeper, more contemplative reflection on the cycles of life.

The essay is about change, in all its myriad manifestations, from the way Downeasters talk and the different types of vehicles on the roads as the seasons turn; to the new visibility of the lake when the leaves are down, and how the shadows suddenly fall straight.

In a mere 677 words, Stephen King is able to transport his readers to Maine, first in the autumn, then in the winter, and all while making some poignant and astute observations about getting older.

This is a remarkable essay that ranks with some of the best passages from King's fiction, and that could easily be plugged into something like *The Body* or *The Dead Zone*.

Main Characters

Stephen King, the leaf-peepers (foliage-worshiping tourists), and a few Maine residents.

 Did You Know?

"Leaf-Peepers" is yet another work by Stephen King that was originally published in the tony magazine *The New Yorker*, which is considered a prestigious and sought-after publication for any writer. King's nonfiction essay "Head Down" (Chapter 81); his short story "The Man in the Black Suit" (Chapter 36), for which King won an O. Henry Award for Best American Short Story; "All That You Love Will Be Carried Away" (Chapter 49); and his story "That Feeling, You Can Only Say What It Is In French" (Chapter 76) also made their debut appearances in *The New Yorker*.

 What I Really Liked About It

The way Stephen King can use his narrative magic to transform a seemingly innocuous subject like tourists on the hunt for bright colors into what my agent John White described as "a lovely piece, filled with sharp perceptions of local life and with image-filled meditations on the deeper meaning of the cycle of seasons."

 Film Adaptations

None.

NUMBER 56

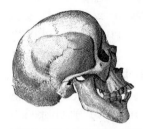

"Gray Matter"
(1973)

"They had been predicting a norther all week and along about Thursday we got it, a real screamer that piled up eight inches by four in the afternoon and showed no signs of slowing down."

Why it made the top 100:

"Gray Matter" can justifiably be called a classic, and not just a *Stephen King* classic, but a *horror* classic as well.

The basic plot is quintessential horror: A guy drinks a bad can of beer and transforms into a giant, oozing slime-slug that eats dead cats and doubles in size on a regular basis. (I see horror fans everywhere nodding thoughtfully, as if to say, "Yes, and then what?")

One bitter January night, Timmy Grenadine comes into Henry's Nite-Owl in Bangor, Maine during one of the worst blizzards in years. Timmy has a horrible story to tell about his father Richie. It seems that Richie polished off a case of bad beer a few months back and has now changed into something terrible—a huge mass of putrid gray "jelly" (the gray matter of the story's title) that eats dead cats and lately has taken to killing and eating people too. Richie has sent Timmy to Henry's for a case of beer but young Timmy can't keep this dark secret anymore and confides in Henry what has happened to his father.

Henry, Bertie, and the story's (unnamed) narrator leave Timmy at the store with Henry's wife and take the case of beer to Richie themselves. On the way, Henry tells the others what Timmy told him and by the time they arrive at Richie's house, they are all glad that Henry brought his .45 caliber with him.

Richie's house reeks of rotted flesh and the hall floor is covered with gray slime. Henry talks to Richie through the door and demands that he admit that he is responsible for the dead wino and the two young girls who had all recently disappeared in town.

Richie tells Henry to leave the beer or he will come out and get it himself. Henry calls his bluff and Richie bursts through the door, a huge, putrescent monstrosity with four eyes. The men are horrified to see that Richie is now in the process of splitting himself into two right down his rank middle.

Bertie and the narrator flee, but Henry stays and fires three shots.

"Gray Matter" ends with Bertie and the story's narrator back at the store waiting to see who followed them. ("32,768 times two is the end of the human race.") "I hope it's Henry," the narrator thinks. "I surely do."

"Gray Matter" is another story set in King's hometown of Bangor. A character named George Kelso is mentioned in the story but it isn't said if he is related to the voted-out-of-office Sheriff Carl Kelso from *The Dead Zone*.

King was in his early 20s when he wrote "Gray Matter" and yet the narrative tone in the piece is that of a much older, much more mature writer. It was clear even at this early stage in King's career that here was a writer of exceptional talents.

"Gray Matter" was one of King's "skin mag" stories, those wonderfully gruesome tales that King churned out by the dozen during the 1970s for very little money. The checks for these stories, however, often arrived just when King and Tabitha needed money for an antibiotic for one of their kids' ear infections or to pay the phone bill.

☠ **C. V.** ☠

Main Characters

Richie Grenadine, Timmy Grenadine, Henry Parmalee, The Narrator, Carl Littlefield, Bill Pelham.

Did You Know?

"Gray Matter" was first published in 1973 when King was 26, and contains one of King's first uses of a giant spider as a monster figure. (*It* would come in 1986, 13 years later). In "Gray Matter," the story is told of a Bangor Public Works Department worker named George Kelso who quit his job after descending into a sewer pipe and coming upon a "spider as big as a good-sized dog setting in a web full of kittens..." Henry Parmalee, proprietor of the Nite-Owl, summed up this tale trenchantly: "I'm not saying there's any truth in it, but I am saying that there's things in the corners of the world that would drive a man insane to look 'em right in the face." (Well put, Henry.)

What I Really Liked About It

The slow, stately pace of the narrative and the absence of hyperbolic, verbal pyrotechnics. King just calmly relates a tale that slowly builds until its supremely horrifying finale. The story is more than enough and King wisely steps aside and lets Richie Grenadine's grim reality swallow the reader (figuratively, of course, although in Richie's case, "swallow" might also be literal).

Film Adaptations

None.

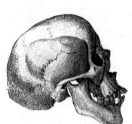

Stephen King's Golden Years
[series teleplays]
(1991)

"Wish upon wish upon day upon day
I believe, O Lord
I believe all the way."
—David Bowie, from his song "Golden Years," the theme to this series

Why it made the top 100:

Stephen King's Golden Years is the exciting story of a mild-mannered janitor named Harlan Williams who one day is caught in an explosion at the agricultural testing facility where he works. This "agricultural facility" is actually a front for government Shop-sponsored experiments in tissue regeneration for military use on the battlefield. These experiments are doing more than exploring the possibilities of mice regrowing limbs, however. The crazy scientist in charge, Dr. Todhunter (King describes him as "that maddest of mad scientists"), has been working with experiments to actually turn back time, and when one of his labs explodes, our hero Harlan is bathed in the mysterious green stuff and this begins his age regression.

From the explosion on, Harlan begins to grow younger... and the Shop wants to keep him under lock and key (or possibly do away with him altogether). Thus, the chase begins.

That is the basic premise for King's series and yet there are two storylines to discuss here.

The King Speaks

"I envisioned this as a 14- or 15-hour series—something that would run for one entire season, with a two-hour opening episode and a bang-up two-hour finale. I began to discuss the idea and actually show some of the work after I had written four hours' worth of script. No one was very interested."

—From "How I Created *Golden Years*...And Spooked Dozens of TV Executives" in the August 2, 1991 issue of *Entertainment Weekly*

Golden Years had been something King had been thinking about writing as a novel when the idea for an original TV series presented itself. King especially liked the idea of telling Harlan Williams's story, the suspenseful tale of an innocent janitor caught up in a secret government experiment, pursued across the country by a Shop agent determined to eliminate him with extreme prejudice. In an interview, King described Jude Andrews, his amoral Shop agent, as "an insane version of *The Fugitive*'s Lieutenant Gerard," an apt comparison since earlier, King had written "As a kid, the only TV series I really liked was *The Fugitive*."

Golden Years gave us Terry Spann, an especially comely government agent (played by Felicity Huffman, who would go on to the series *Sports Night*) who decides to help Harl and his wife, and an especially mean Shop agent who wants to erase *all* evidence of the accident. The series also introduced us to a gen-yoo-wyne mad scientist, a blind female activist, a reference to Shop agent John Rainbird from *Firestarter*, a character who took the name of Cap'n Trips from *The Stand*, and a cameo by Stephen King himself as a surly bus driver who Terry shuts up with a warning and a glare.

After seven episodes aired during the summer of 1991, the series ended with Harlan tied to a bed in captivity under Jude Andrews (and, it is assumed, evil scientist Dr. Todhunter's) control. Harlan's devoted and loving wife, Gina, was dead, Jude Andrews' flunky Major Moreland was dead, Shop Agent Burton was still possessing his ear (and his other twistable body parts), hippie Shop informant Cap'n Trips was dead, and Terry Spann and General Crewes were on the run. This cliffhanger ending left several questions unanswered, including:

- How young would Harlan get?
- Why did Harlan cause earthquakes and make the sun fly across the sky at midnight?
- How did time travel figure into Dr. Todhunter's experiments?
- How did Terry get so tough?
- Would Jude Andrews get his due one day?

Stephen King's Golden Years was not renewed for CBS's fall 1991 schedule and, thus, some decisions had to be made about what to do about all these loose ends for the videotape release of the series.

I liked *Golden Years* a lot and would have loved to have seen it continue as a regular series, with Terry Spann as the continuing character (a la Fox and Mulder in *The X-Files*), but that was not to be. It was an enthralling show. I was not thrilled with a few of the performances, but it was definitely an enjoyable summer series. King's writing is very good in this series, and he inserts fun references to his own work and even to the Kennedy assassination, thereby reinforcing the subtext of paranoia running throughout his teleplay. If you did not see it when it originally aired, it's definitely worth a rental and four hours of your time.

☠ **C. V.** ☠

Main Characters

Harlan Williams, Gina Williams, Terrilyn Spann, general Louis Crewes, Jude Andrews, Major Moreland

Did You Know?

Prior to *Golden Years*, actress Frances Sternhagen ("Gina Williams") appeared in the 1990 film adaptation of King's novel *Misery*, opposite James Caan, Kathy Bates, and Richard Farnsworth. Also, Brad Greenquist ("Steve Dent") starred in King's *Pet Sematary* (1989) as the dead (but ubiquitous) Victor Pascow.

What I Really Liked About It

Golden Years is an honest-to-goodness spy thriller containing elements of science fiction and the paranormal, combined in a way that Stephen King does especially well.

Film Adaptations

None.

TV Adaptations

Stephen King's Golden Years (July 16, 1991 - August 22, 1991 - seven episodes); starring Keith Szarabajka, Felicity Huffman, Ed Lauter, R.D. Call, Bill Raymond, Frances Sternhagen, Stephen Root, Matt Malloy, Adam Redfield, Jeff Williams, Peter McRobbie, Sarah Melici, Lili Bernard, Graham Paul, J.R. Horne, Brad Greenquist, Alberto Vázquez, Susan King, Don Bland, Todd Brenner, Tim Parati, Randell Haynes, D. Garen Tolkin, Stephen King; directed by Allen Coulter, Kenneth Fink, Michael Gornick, Stephen Tolkin; four teleplays by Stephen King; three by Josef Anderson based on Stephen King's story. (Grade: A.)

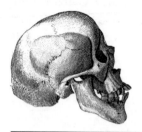

Number 58

"The Jaunt"
(1981)

"Longer than you think, Dad!" it cackled. "Longer than you think! Held my breath when they gave me the gas! Wanted to see! I saw! I saw! Longer than you think!"

Why it made the top 100:

"The Jaunt" is one of King's finest short stories, one that is exciting, scary, thought-provoking, and one of these rare stories that starts out as hard science fiction (one of King's infrequent forays into the genre) and then takes a hard turn and veers off into horror. (See "The End of the Whole Mess" (Chapter 62) for another example of King doing sci-fi.)

The year is 2307 and teleportation is commonplace. Man has colonized the planets and now uses Mars and Venus as a source of oil so bountiful that it now sells for four cents a gallon on Earth. The big dilemma now is potable water and humans have likewise turned to the other planets in our solar system for answers to that problem, especially Mars. The first waterlift from the Red Plant—"Operation Straw"—took place in 2045 and Texaco Oil is now Texaco Oil/Water.

Mark Oates, a Texaco executive, has agreed to take a two-year assignment on Mars and, after much thought, has decided to move his family to Mars with him. They will use The Jaunt to get there. The Jaunt is an instantaneous teleportation process invented by Victor Carune in 1987. You lay on a couch, inhale from a mask that puts you to sleep, and 0.000000000067 of a second later, you're on Mars, or Venus, or anywhere else you want to be.

There is only one problem with Jaunting, however: If it's done while fully awake, the results are disastrous. The travelers either come out the portal at the other end incredibly aged and completely insane ... or dead.

In order to assuage their apprehension before *their* trip to Mars, Mark Oates tells his kids the fascinating story of The Jaunt and the always-curious 12-year-old Ricky Oates decides to hold his breath during *his* Jaunt and see what it's like.

The dreadful climax of "The Jaunt" is horrifying and I, for one, would love to see this story adapted as a short film. It is probably one of the best *Twilight Zone* episodes that was never on *The Twilight Zone*, if you know what I mean.

Here, King is very good at fleshing out and fully realizing his ideas: The mechanics of the Jaunt, complete with the Nil button to erase all of the emergence portals, are completely believable and realistic. (And I know what the editors of *Omni* originally said about this aspect of the story, but as a reader, I was caught up.)

I also like the inclusion of details from a book written about The Jaunt called *The Politics of The Jaunt*. This device gives King the opportunity to go even deeper into the story and give readers a lot of exciting background of the discovery of teleportation and the sometimes-tragic events surrounding its early use.

"The Jaunt" is not that long, yet King creates an entire history for the story, complete with a wide array of characters and an enormous time span. "The Jaunt" is a virtuoso performance by the Man from Maine.

☠ **C. V.** ☠

Main Characters

Ricky Oates, Mark Oates, Patty Oates, Marilys Oates, Victor Carune, Lester Michaelson, Mrs. Michaelson, Rudy Foggia.

Did You Know?

It's always fascinating when authors postulate what the future will be like and the reality that ensues doesn't even come close to their vision. In the "Energy Crisis" years of the late 1970s and early 1980s, ("The Jaunt" was written around 1980), 1987 seemed like a long way off and King decided to set the discovery of Jaunting during that year. We should have been so lucky, eh?

The King Speaks

"This was originally for *Omni*, which quite rightly rejected it because the science is so wonky. It was Ben Bova's idea to have the colonists in the story mining for water, and I have incorporated that in this version."

—From "Notes" in *Skeleton Crew*

What I Really Liked About It

Everything. This is one of my favorites.

Film Adaptations

None.

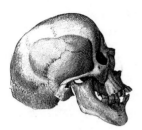

Stephen King's
Storm of the Century
(1999)

"If we get in trouble ... we're in trouble."

Why it made the top 100:

I am not reviewing the TV-miniseries *Storm of the Century* here. Although Stephen King wrote the three-night drama, there are too many other elements involved to consider the broadcast version of the story an independent King work. The acting (good and bad), production (very good), editing (excellent), etc. all contributed to the end result that aired on ABC; yet none of these have anything to do, really, with what Stephen King originally wrote, other than his screenplay serving as the source for these visual components.

So, that said, let me say that the published *Storm* screenplay *reads* better than it plays on TV, and offers a historical connection that adds a great deal to the power of the tale.

"*Historical* connection?" But it's just a horror movie, right?

Wrong. And here's why.

The King Speaks

"I wrote *Storm of the Century* exactly as I would a novel, keeping a list of characters but no other notes, working a set schedule of three or four hours every day, hauling along my Mac PowerBook and working in hotel rooms when my wife and I went on our regular expeditions to watch the Maine's women's basketball team play their away games in Boston, New York, and Philadelphia."

—From the Introduction to the published
Storm of the Century screenplay

The first person born of English parents in America was Virginia Dare. She was born in 1587 on Roanoke Island, off the coast of present-day North Carolina. Nine days after Virginia was born, on August 27, 1587, Roanoke's Governor John White was forced to return to England for supplies. Before he left, he worked out a secret code system for the colonists to use if they were forced to leave the island. They were to carve the name of their new destination on a clearly visible tree or post. As part of the code, Governor White instructed them to carve a Maltese cross over the name of the place if they were being forced to leave because of Indian attack or because of an assault by the Spaniards. Four years to the month after he left, Governor White returned to Roanoke Island to find it completely deserted. Carved into a tree was the lone word "Croatoan," and there was no Maltese cross above the word.

To this day (until *Storm of the Century*, that is), no one knows where the colonists went or what was the nature of their fate. Virginia Dare and everyone else that was part of the Roanoke Island New World contingent are now known as the Lost Colony.

Stephen King has an idea about what happened to the Roanoke Island colonists. And it has a lot to do with *Storm of the Century*'s Andre Linoge (whose name is an acronym for "legion").

In his published *Storm* screenplay, Roanoke and "Croatoan" (inexplicably spelled "Croaton") are mentioned several times. By the end of the script, when we learn what Andre Linoge wanted when he kept repeating "Give me what I want and I'll go away," the fate of the Roanoke Island colonists is clear. They were presented with the same horrific ultimatum as were the residents of Little Tall Island, yet they refused to acquiesce to Linoge's demands, thereby condemning themselves to group annihilation. These people are now referred to as the Lost Colony and King indicates that the townsfolk of Little Tall are in for the same fate if they do not give Linoge what he wants.

This element of the story seems to have been overlooked, or at least, dismissed as secondary by many reviewers and fans. Personally, I think an emphasis on this subtext adds historical veracity to the story and elevates it to another level. When we finally understand that Linoge is not only pure evil, but that he also may be *eternal*, the story becomes even more terrifying.

In an especially chilling scene, everyone shares the identical dream:

> They're all here. And tattooed on each foreh]ead is that strange and ominous word: CROATON. They march toward the camera—and their death in the frigid ocean—like lemmings. We don't believe it ... and yet we do, don't we? After Jonestown and Heaven's gate, we do.

Linoge is showing the Little Tall residents what will happen to them if they do not oblige him ... and the word CROATON on their forehead makes the direct connection to Roanoke Island and the fate of the Lost Colony. Linoge gleefully takes full credit for the death of the colonists ... as he will gleefully take credit for the death of everyone on Little Tall if they do not turn over to him their children.

Although King wrote *Storm* as an original screenplay, he conceived it as a novel and has admitted that if ABC passed on producing it, he would have adapted his unpublished screenplay into a full-blown novel. King's narratives have always been tough to squeeze through the funnel of visual adaptation. *Storm* doesn't suffer from this debilitating compression *too* much, but there is more in the text than in the broadcast version.

Truth be told, it is one hell of a story. A stranger named Andre Linoge comes to Little Tall Island during the biggest blizzard in recent memory and the first thing he does to get the islanders' attention is viciously murder a little old lady. While in custody he is able to manipulate people into heinous acts and, on top of this, he knows everybody's darkest secrets—and is not hesitant to reveal them.

Linoge wants an heir and the bottom line is that the townsfolk must agree to give him what he wants—one of their children—or they all die, just like the colonists on Roanoke Island in 1591.

Do yourself a favor: Read the screenplay. If you're reading *The Essential Stephen King*, I'd bet you've already seen the miniseries. You now need to experience the full vision of King's nightmare.

☠ **C. V.** ☠

 ## Main Characters

Mike Anderson, Andre Linoge, Molly Anderson, Alton "Hatch" Hatcher, Robbie Beals, Cat Withers, Ralph Anderson, Ursula Godsoe, Donny Beals, Sandra Beals, Ms. Stanhope, Billy Soames, Jack Carver.

Did You Know?

The setting for *Storm of the Century*, Little Tall Island, is where Maddie Pace from King's short story "Home Delivery" was born, and also where King's novel *Dolores Claiborne* takes place.

 What I Really Liked About It

The Roanoke Island connection to the story.

 Film Adaptations

Stephen King's Storm of the Century (ABC-TV miniseries, 1999); starring Timothy Daly, Colm Feore, Debrah Farentino, Casey Siemaszko, Jeffrey DeMunn, Julianne Nicholson, Dyllan Christopher, Becky Ann Baker, Spencer Breslin, Myra Carter, Nada Despotovich, Kathleen Chalfant, Jeremy Jordan, Ron Perkins, Steve Rankin; directed by Craig R. Baxley; original screenplay by Stephen King. (Grade: A.)

60

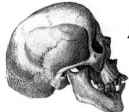 *"The Man Who Loved Flowers"*
(1977)

"He had that look about him."

Why it made the top 100:

"The Man Who Loved Flowers" is utterly masterful, and one more example of just how good a short story writer Stephen King is.

The story begins idyllically. A young man obviously in love (even passersby can tell) walks the early evening, springtime streets of New York in May. He is dressed for a date, and we soon learn that the name of his love is Norma. He stops at a flower vendor and buys tea roses for Norma and then heads off for their rendezvous. As he walks, we are told that the radio "poured out bad news that no one listened to." The bad news includes updates on the Vietnam "situation," the fact that the Russians had exploded a nuclear device, the grisly news that a woman's body had been pulled from the East River and, most ominously, the news that a hammer killer was still on the loose. Bubbling under the surface of springtime in New York is a darkness suggesting secrets and misery.

The young man turns onto a street that was "a little darker" and waits for Norma. When he sees her ("...it was always a sweet shock—she looked so young") he calls out her name and we believe we will now witness a lovers' reunion.

But "Norma's" smile fades when she sees him ... and that is when he pulls the hammer out of his pocket and her mouth transforms into "an opening black O of terror."

This young lady is not Norma. Norma has been dead for 10 years and this man who loves flowers is a serial killer who has been searching for his dead love for a decade, having killed five previous times when he discovers that the beautiful young girls he sees are not Norma.

The bloodstains will not show on his suit, and the man who loved flowers leaves the "dark shadow sprawled on the cobblestones" and jauntily makes his way down 73rd Street. Again, passersby notice his smile and demeanor and the story concludes with a middle-aged married woman thinking that if there is anything more beautiful than springtime, it was young love.

Chilling.

☠ **C. V.** ☠

Main Characters

The man who loved flowers (King tells us his name was "Love"), the old lady, the flower vendor, Norma, the girl in the sailor blouse.

Did You Know?

"The Man Who Loved Flowers" was originally published in the men's magazine *Gallery* in 1977. The story's only appearance beyond that initial magazine publication has been in King's *Night Shift* collection in 1978.

What I Really Liked About It

Flowers look pretty and smell lovely; but they have dark, moldering roots and when they rot they give off a terrible stench, like the smell of a funeral that has gone on too long. King captures the essence of this reality brilliantly in this story.

Film Adaptations

None.

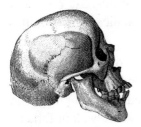

Cycle of the Werewolf
(1983, 1985)

He knows. He knows who the werewolf is.

Why it made the top 100:

Cycle of the Werewolf was originally conceived as a calendar.

Land of Enchantment publisher Chris Zavisa pitched King on the idea of a "story calendar" at a World Fantasy Convention in 1979. King liked the idea and agreed to participate but ultimately found the 500-word maximum-per-month too limiting. Thus, the proposed 6,000 word calendar blossomed into a 40,000 word or so novella.

The tale is divided into 12 chapters, one for each month of the year, and it tells the story of a small Maine town under siege by a werewolf. Each month, on the night of the full moon, the Beast claims a victim. The victims ultimately include five men from town, one unnamed drifter, one woman, one child, nine sow, two boar, four deer, and the Reverend Lester Lowe.

King's novellas are some of his finest work and *Cycle of the Werewolf* is no exception. (Stanley Wiater and Christopher Golden, writing in *The Stephen King Universe*, describe *Cycle* as "classic King.") King's writing is tight and the story flows smoothly from one month to the next, with King effectively bringing to life the terrified residents of Tarker's Mills, and powerfully depicting their battle against an enemy hidden in their midst. He shows us how mob mentality can take over a town and also gives us an unlikely villain who is revealed by a child.

The hero of *Cycle of the Werewolf* is Marty Coslaw, a 10-year-old boy who is paralyzed and confined to a wheelchair. King has often created heroic characters who are physically disabled in one way or another, from stuttering Bill Denbrough in *It* to mentally retarded (from Down's syndrome) Duddits in *Dreamcatcher*. *Cycle*'s Marty Coslaw is part of that fraternity and he admirably ignores his handicap and triumphs over the werewolf.

Interestingly, in the "May" chapter of the story, Reverend Lowe has a dream in which his congregation all turn into werewolves during a sermon in which he tells them that "The Beast is everywhere," emphasizing that he could be your next door neighbor. The Beast is the Great Satan and, considering the true identity of the werewolf in Tarker's Mills, this could be interpreted as King suggesting that all our monsters—vampires, werewolves, witches, etc.—may all be manifestations of the Dark Man himself, Satan. And if this is a valid reading of Lowe's sermon, then there might be some connection between the werewolf in *Cycle of the Werewolf* and the other manifestations of ultimate evil in King's works. Namely Randall Flagg (*The Stand, The Dark Tower*), the Crimson King (*Insomnia*), It, Tak (*Desperation*), and Andre Linoge (*Storm of the Century*), etc. Just a thought.

 C. V.

 Main Characters

Marty Coslaw, Kate Coslaw, Uncle Al, Grandfather Coslaw, Mrs. Coslaw, Elise Fournier, Kenny Franklin, Elbert Freeman, Brady Kincaid, Mr. Kincaid, Alfie Knopfler, Reverend Lester Lowe, Arnie Westrum, Stella Randolph, Clyde Corliss, Constable Lander Neary, Milt Sturmfuller, Donna Sturmfuller, Ollie Parker, Elbert Freeman.

 Did You Know?

In *Cycle of the Werewolf, Today* show weatherman Willard Scott tells his viewers that a foot of snow fell in the Canadian Rockies on September 21st (Stephen King's birthday).

The King Speaks

"My wife, Tabby, reminded me that a year where all the full moons fell on holidays would be a mad year indeed. I agreed, but invoked creative license. 'I think your license should be revoked for speeding, dear,' she said, and wandered off to make us all something to eat."

—From the "Foreword" to *Silver Bullet*, the volume containing the original *Cycle of the Werewolf* novella and King's *Silver Bullet* screenplay

 What I Really Liked About It

I particularly like the "February" chapter of this novella. This section tells the story of overweight virgin Stella Randolph who is paid a Valentine's night visit by the werewolf. The tone of this segment is reminiscent of one of King's most powerful stories, "Nona," (See Chapter 48) and it is tight, evocative, and ultimately terrifying. Especially its last line: "Love is like dying."

 Film Adaptations

Silver Bullet (1985, aka *Stephen King's Silver Bullet*), starring Gary Busey, Everett McGill, Corey Haim, Megan Follows, Robin Groves, Leon Russom, Terry O'Quinn, Bill Smitrovich, Joe Wright, Kent Broadhurst, Heather Simmons, James A. Baffico, Rebecca Fleming, Lawrence Tierney, William Newman; directed by Daniel Attias, screenplay by Stephen King. (Grade: C.)

NUMBER 62

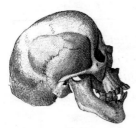

"The End of the Whole Mess"
(1986)

The direct injection works very fast. I figure I've got somewhere between forty-five minutes and two hours, depending on my blood type.

Why it made the top 100:

"The End of the Whole Mess" is one of Stephen King's most interesting short stories. The story told is terribly sad, yet the way King tells it makes it one of his most fascinating tales.

Bobby Fornoy, the savant brother of the story's narrator Howard "Bow-Wow" Fornoy (modeled on King's brother Dave—see "The King Speaks"), discovers that the water in a small Texas town called La Plata contains a chemical that removes aggressiveness from the human temperament. (Violent crime does not exist in La Plata and this is what made Bobby curious.) The only problem (which is discovered far too late) is that the La Plata water causes premature senility in the form of widespread Alzheimer's disease. By the time the world learns of this side effect—this tragically ironic consequence of global peace—Bobby and Howard have already synthesized 60,000 gallons of the La Plata water, airlifted it to a ready-to-erupt volcano on an island near Borneo, and blasted it into the Earth's atmosphere. Giving everyone on the planet a "peace shower." (They gave peace a chance, you might say.)

The story itself consists of the final journal entries of Howard, who has decided to kill himself with a direct injection of the La Plata water. He, like Charlie in the equally sad story "Flowers for Algernon" (filmed in 1968 as *Charly*), rapidly loses his mental faculties as the water takes effect. His final entry begins, "I have a Bobby his nayme is bruther and I theen I an dun riding..."

But before he is that far gone, Howard tells us the story of Bobby and his peace water, and in so doing, we learn about bees, wasps, avionics, broadcasting, palmism, art forgery, the Krakatoa volcano eruption, nuclear winter, and the specific component found in beans that make you fart. (It's sulfur.)

"The End of the Whole Mess" is a bit of a departure for Stephen King, since it is a blatant science fiction story and King does not write much science fiction. But when he does, he almost always hits a home run. Proof of the pudding: This story originally appeared in *Omni* magazine, a periodical known for its impeccable standards for science fiction. (They rejected King's "The Jaunt" because the science was too "wonky.") "The End of the Whole Mess" is a Kafkaesque look at one possible future—and how the end of mankind may not come about due to a devastating, apocalyptic war, but from a much more benign catalyst: good intentions. Congresswoman and *Vanity Fair* writer Clare Booth Luce might have said it best: "No good deed goes unpunished."

☠ **C. V.** ☠

Main Characters

Howard Fornoy, Bobby Fornoy, their parents, assorted researchers, and the degenerating citizens of Earth.

Did You Know?

In one of the most entertaining scenes in the story, young Bobby the genius builds a glider with forward-facing wings and Howard launches him (successfully) into the air off his American Flyer red wagon. In the story King notes that plans for forward-wing fighter planes were on the drawing boards of both the American and Russian air forces. He was right. In 1986, NASA was working on the Grumman X-29, a fighter plane with forward wings. In *Orders of Magnitude: A History of the NACA and NASA, 1915-1990*, Roger E. Bilstein wrote, "The Grumman X-29 [was] a plane whose dramatic configuration matched that of the HiMAT [a plane built with Highly Maneuverable Aircraft Technology]. The X-29 had a single, vertical tail fin and canard surfaces—not unique in the 1980s. What made the X-29 so fascinating was its sharply forward-swept wings."

The King Speaks

"Dave King is what we New Englanders call 'a piece of work.' A child prodigy with a tested IQ of over 150 (you will find reflections of Dave in Bow-Wow Fornoy's genius brother in 'The End of the Whole Mess') who went through school as if on a rocket-sled, finishing college at eighteen and going right to work as a high-school math teacher at Brunswick High. Many of his remedial algebra students were older than he was. Dave was the youngest ever to be elected Town Selectman in the state of Maine, and was a Town Manager at the age of twenty-five or so. He is a genuine polymath, a man who knows something about just about everything."

—From "Notes" in *Nightmares & Dreamscapes*

 What I Really Liked About It

King's deft touch (and playfulness) with his imagining of one possible future—and his fully realized execution of his hypothesis.

 Film Adaptations

None.

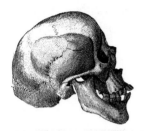

"One for the Road"
(1977)

I've never seen a man who looked that scared.

Why it made the top 100:

Gerard Lumley from New Jersey, with his $300 coat and little sissy boots not worth spit, takes a wrong turn during a ferocious Maine blizzard and ends up in Jerusalem's Lot.

After the town burned down.

Yes, "One for the Road" is about the haunted (and vampire-infected) town of 'Salem's Lot, and the story takes place after the final incendiary events of the novel *'Salem's Lot*.

After driving his Mercedes into a snowdrift, Gerard Lumley walks six miles in the snow to Tookey's Bar, half-frozen to death and near hysterical about leaving his wife and daughter while he went for help. The bar's proprietor, Herb Tooklander, and the story's narrator, Booth, decide they must go after Lumley's wife and daughter, but they both know that not only might the two never be found, but that they themselves are taking a grave risk.

The Lot is filled with vampires, you see, and Booth and Tookey both know that the odds favor Janine and Francie having already been "inducted" into that dark society.

"One for the Road" is vividly told - we hear the wind, feel the spit of the snow, and we are in Herb Tooklander's four-wheel drive Scout with the three men as they determinedly drive to where Lumley left his car. What they find when they arrive haunts Booth for years, gives Herb a heart attack, and seals Gerard Lumley's fate for all time.

"One for the Road"—the epilogue to *'Salem's Lot*—closes *Night Shift* (except for the poignant encore story "The Woman in the Room") while the story "Jerusalem's Lot"—a prologue to the novel—opened the collection. Both enrich the mythology of the town of Jerusalem's Lot, Maine and add both a backstory and coda to the superb fountainhead novel.

☒ **C. V.** ☒

Main Characters

Booth, Herb Tooklander, Gerard Lumley, Francie Lumley, Janie Lumley, Billy Larribee.

Did You Know?

The locales mentioned in this story—Falmouth and Cumberland, Maine—are real towns in Maine. They are approximately seven miles north of Portland and, based on the directions given in the story, the town of 'Salem's Lot is west of Falmouth, south of Cumberland, and somewhere between I-95 and I-295 in southern Maine. It's probably a good idea to avoid that part of Maine if you happen to be traveling through the area.

What I Really Liked About It

"One for the Road" is sheer *story* - it moves along powerfully, until the climactic confrontation scenes that are some of the most chilling (no pun intended) King has ever written. I especially liked the appearance of Lumley's wife and daughter as the vampires they have become. These two scenes are breathtaking. ("She was standing there, you see, but she was standing *on top* of the snow..." Yikes.)

Film Adaptations

None.

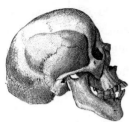

"The Road Virus Heads North"
(1999)

I'm going outside, I think.

Why it made the top 100:

A good friend of mine—a man who is extremely well versed in all things King—has always told anyone who would listen that Stephen King is at his absolute best with the short form, i.e., novellas and short stories. If my friend were pleading this argument in court, he would unquestionably offer "The Road Virus Heads North" as evidence. The plot is simple: A famous writer buys a painting at a tag sale that begins to change. Terror ensues. But there is much more to this story than that.

> "You think I'm crazy, don't you,
>
> pretty girl? ... You and half the
>
> fiction reading population of America, I guess."

Aside from being a gripping, fast-paced, terrifying tale, "Road Virus" also serves as a forum for Stephen King's wry (and quite trenchant) commentary on his own fame and career. The main character of the story is a horror writer named Richard Kinnell, a blatant Stephen King doppelganger.

Like King, Kinnell is enormously popular (he aptly describes his novels as "numbingly successful") and also like King, he is critically maligned. We learn that a reviewer for *Esquire* magazine began a review of Kinnell's latest novel with this little bouquet: "Richard Kinnell, who writes like Jeffrey Dahmer cooks, has suffered a fresh bout of projectile vomiting. He has titled this most recent mass of ejecta *Nightmare City*." (Ouch.)

But King uses this story (and Kinnell's character) to get in a couple of good-natured jabs at both his critics and his fans. Regarding literary elitists, he muses, "He knew what most of the audience at the PEN panel discussion would have thought:

> Oh, yes, great picture for Rich Kinnell; he probably wants it for inspiration, a feather to tickle his tired old gorge into one more fit of projectile vomiting.

> But most of these folks were ignoramuses, at least as far as his work went, and what was more, they treasured their ignorance, cosseted it the way some people inexplicably treasured and cosseted those stupid, mean-spirited little dogs that yapped at visitors and sometimes bit the paperboy's ankle."

His commentary on his fans is gentler and funnier. "He'd spent the ride down working out what he'd say on the panel if certain tough questions were tossed at him, but none had been. Once they'd found out he didn't *know* where he got his ideas, and yes, he *did* sometimes scare himself, they'd only wanted to know how you got an agent."

On his way home to Derry, Maine from a literary panel discussion in Boston, Kinnell stops at a tag sale and buys the aforementioned painting; a dark creation called "The Road Virus Heads North." This watercolor is the last surviving work by Bobby Hastings, a brilliant young artist who had hung himself during a psychotic (or demonic?) break. (We are told Bobby wore the same T-shirt every day—"It had a picture of the Led Zeppelins on it.")

The painting is of a young man with fangs instead of teeth driving a Grand Am convertible. Each time Kinnell looks at it on his way home, however, this scene—and the driver — have changed ... the Road Virus really is heading north ... and north is where Rich Kinnell lives.

"The Road Virus Heads North" is a terrific short story and it is King at the peak of his game. It originally appeared in *999*, a horror anthology edited by Al Sarrantonio, who introduced this tale by describing it as "one hell of a story." He was right.

This story has not been reprinted elsewhere as of this writing, but since King has a short story collection coming out sometime in 2003, we can hope that he decides to include "Road Virus" in that still-untitled omnibus.

☠ **C. V.** ☠

"Richard Kinnell" Speaks

(on being asked where he gets his ideas) "I don't know. ... They just come to me. Isn't that amazing?"

 Main Characters

Richard Kinnell, Judy Diment, Aunt Trudy, Bobby Hastings (the dead artist), the Road Virus guy (he looked like "a Metallica fan who had escaped from a mental asylum for the criminally insane.").

 Did You Know?

The narrative element of a painting that inexplicably changes is a plot point that has interested King for some time, and with this story, he has used this device in a novel (*Rose Madder*); a novella (*The Sun Dog*); and a short story. A possible inspiration for these works is Oscar Wilde's classic of English literature, *The Picture of Dorian Gray*, in which a derelict slacker retains his youth (irrespective of his desultory ways) as his portrait visibly ages following each of his decadent deeds.

 What I Really Liked About It

The relentless pace of the narrative, a technique that gradually provides us with a clear understanding of Kinnell's inevitable fate. When we realize what is happening with the picture, we know Kinnell is doomed and this adds to the story's ever-increasing air of terror, culminating in a final paragraph that is one of the most chilling King has ever written.

 Film Adaptations

None.

"The Last Rung on the Ladder"
(1978)

When I close my eyes and start to drift off, I see her coming down from the third loft, her eyes wide and dark blue, her body arched, her arms swept up behind her.

Why it made the top 100:

"The Last Rung on the Ladder" is a unique story in Stephen King's canon. It is perhaps one of his most poignant stories; it contains nary a whiff of the darkness beyond our ken; and it has *never* been reprinted beyond its original *Night Shift* appearance.

"Last Rung" is heart wrenching; its final line—"She was the one who always knew the hay would be there."—is one of King's saddest. And "Last Rung"—like *Rita Hayworth and Shawshank Redemption*, *The Body*, and the nonfiction essay "Leaf-Peepers"—is the kind of story that surprises *non*-Constant Readers who have a pre-conceived notion of Stephen King *only* as America's Horrormeister.

Kitty and Larry are brother and sister, and they shared what many would consider an idyllic childhood. They grew up on a farm (in *The Stand*'s Mother Abagail's home-town of Hemingford Home, Nebraska), had loving parents, and did well in school. Kitty won a beauty contest the summer after high school (and married the judge); Larry won a football scholarship and became a wealthy corporation lawyer.

"Last Rung" tells the story of one particular incident in Larry and Kitty's childhood. The two kids liked to climb a ladder in their barn that was nailed to a crossbeam in the third loft. This ladder was 70 feet off the ground and Larry and Kitty liked to scale it and then jump off into a pile of hay on the barn floor. One day, as Kitty was climbing for her turn to jump, the ladder pulled away from the crossbeam and left Kitty hanging from its last rung, 60 feet off the barn floor. Larry told Kitty to keep her eyes shut as he frantically piled hay up on the floor beneath where she was dangling. When he felt there was enough to cushion her fall, he told her to let go and, such was the trust in her brother, Kitty did, and ultimately survived the fall.

Larry, as the older sibling, was punished for Kitty's broken ankle, and the two of them never climbed the ladder again.

Larry and Kitty drifted apart, both emotionally and geographically, and after a time, Kitty stopped writing to Larry. He did receive one final letter, though, written before she committed suicide by jumping off the roof of an insurance building in Los Angeles:

> Dear Larry,
>
> I've been thinking about it a lot lately ... and what I've decided is that it would have been better for me if that last rung had broken before you could put the hay down.
>
> > Your,
> > Kitty

This final letter got to Larry, who had recently moved a couple of times, too late, and he was not able to "put the hay down" one more time for his sister.

"The Last Rung on the Ladder" is evocative, beautifully written, and a literary tone poem of sadness and loss.

☠ **C. V.** ☠

Main Characters

Larry, Kitty, their parents, Dr. Pedersen.

Did You Know?

Joseph Reino, Ph.D., writing in *Stephen King: The First Decade*, described "The Last Rung on the Ladder" as "one of the subtlest psychological studies King has ever devised."

The King Speaks

"I have made the dollar-deal, as I call it, over my accountant's moans and head-clutching protests sixteen or seventeen times as of this writing. Stories filmed include..."Last Rung on the Ladder" from *Night Shift*."

—From King's Introduction to
The Shawshank Redemption: The Shooting Script

What I Really Liked About It

As I said, this might be King's most poignant story to date and its emotional power gets me every time I reread it.

Film Adaptations

1. *The Last Rung on the Ladder* (student film adaptation, 1987); starring Adam Houhoulis, Melissa Whellden, Nat Wordell, Adam Howes; directed by James Cole; screenplay by James Cole and Dan Thron. (Grade: B+.)
2. *The Last Rung on the Ladder* (Maine Public Television production, 2001?); Lucas Knight, director, and screenwriter.

NUMBER 66

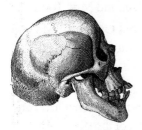

"Mrs. Todd's Shortcut" (1984)

*Summer people are trotters; us others
that don't put on ties to do our week's work are just pacers.*

Why it made the top 100:

"Mrs. Todd's Shortcut" reads like a fable, and is something of a departure for King. He has said that he is especially fond of this story, mainly because he loves the sound of Homer Buckland's voice in the tale.

Homer (named after the poet Homer) is the caretaker for the Todd's Maine home.

Worth Todd and his second wife are "summer people"; those visitors to Maine who arrive on Friday and leave on Sunday and who are never really as interesting to the locals as are their own.

To Homer, though, the *first* Mrs. Todd—Ophelia was her name—was something right special. She drove a champagne-colored, two-seater Mercedes sportster and was absolutely rabid about finding shortcuts—especially to Bangor and back.

One day Homer took 'Phelia up on her offer and rode with her to Bangor. This trip was to change Homer's life. Mrs. Todd, you see, had found a shortcut that took her to

Bangor all right, but via "Motorway B," a bizarre otherworldly road that Homer had never even heard of. It seemed as though the trees tried to reach out for them as they sped past them on this strange highway. Even stranger, Mrs. Todd seemed to transform into a goddess, like the beautiful and legendary Diana, as she drove her weird route.

'Phelia Todd had somehow found the road to the mythical land of Olympus. It wasn't much later that Mrs. Todd invited Homer to travel with her to Olympus in her Mercedes go-devil ... and 70-year-old Homer happily went with her.

Worth Todd waited a good seven years—and then one more year for good measure—before he had Ophelia declared dead and he married the second Mrs. Todd.

But as we learn at the conclusion of the story, the truth is that Ophelia Todd and Homer are not dead—they are instead somewhere magical ... although everyone thinks Homer just went to Vermont.

In "Mrs. Todd's Shortcut," the cadence of Homer's narrative takes a little getting used to, but the payoff is worth it. The ending of the story elevates it to another level and it becomes transcendent. King takes his time building to the climax of the story—Homer and Ophelia's departure for Olympus—and leaves us with a palpable sense of what it feels like to be left behind. While not as powerful as "The Reach," this story nonetheless proves that King has a sensitive side that he can use to tell a story that does not require darkness to engage its readers.

C. V.

Main Characters

Ophelia Todd, Mrs. Todd (the new one), Homer Buckland, Dave Owens.

Did You Know?

Tabitha King is the real Mrs. Todd, although so far she has not traveled to Olympus. (Or if she has, she has not yet talked about it.) It seems that Mrs. King is always looking for a shortcut and that's where King got the idea for the story.

What I Really Liked About It

The feeling that this story tells us not only what real Downeasters are like, but also what they think of we "outlanders."

The King Speaks

In the "Notes" to *Skeleton Crew*, King revealed that this story was repeatedly rejected by women's magazines specifically because of the line, "a woman, who will pee down her own leg if she does not squat!" Philistines.

Film Adaptations

None.

Number **67**

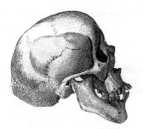

"Umney's Last Case" (1993)

Peoria Smith, the blind paperboy, was standing in his accustomed place on the corner of Sunset and Laurel, and if that didn't mean God was in His heaven and all was jake with the world, I didn't know what did.

Why it made the top 100:

Of all the stories in *Nightmares & Dreamscapes*, "Umney's Last Case" is Stephen King's personal favorite, and it's easy to understand why.

Part Raymond Chandler pastiche, part time travel tale, and part contemplation on the nature of writing and the creation of characters and other places and times, this story flows effortlessly towards its inevitable conclusion, and neatly takes a final U-turn into a chilling cliffhanger. Its final line, "This time nobody goes home" resonates on several levels, even though it literally refers to Clyde Umney's determination to get even with his creator, Sam Landry.

Los Angeles gumshoe Clyde Umney awakens one morning to an L. A. day that, at first glance, seems perfect. But then things start to go wrong. His noisy neighbors (and their perpetually annoying dog) are now silent. The blind 12-year-old newsboy Peoria Smith suddenly turns on Umney after years of pretending to like him. One of Clyde's favorite hangouts, Blondie's, is suddenly closed, the elevator operator in his building has lung cancer and is retiring; painters are brightening up his floor, and his cherished secretary Candy Kane ups and quits after writing him a stinging—and totally unexpected—goodbye letter.

Things are not right, and Umney is at a loss to explain how everything can suddenly go so bad, so quickly.

His explanation comes in the form of a visit from his final client, one Samuel Landry, the landlord of his building and, as Umney soon learns, Umney's personal Creator.

Umney learns that he is a character in a series of novels that Landry has been writing for years. Because of personal tragedy in his own life, Landry has decided to take Umney's place in the 1930s and live out a perfect, peaceful life in a world of his own making.

Does Landry succeed in eventually killing off Umney? Is Umney's "life exchange" with Landry permanent? Can Landry's godlike powers forestall any attempts by Umney to save himself from literary oblivion?

King juggles these ideas and questions deftly and entertainingly, resulting in one of his most accomplished and fully-realized tales.

"Umney's Last Case" is an important story in the Stephen King canon and the one that Penguin Books chose to celebrate in 1995 with a special single-volume edition (a "Penguin Single") commemorating the publishing company's 60th anniversary. These 88-page mini-books are now collector's items.

☠ **C. V.** ☠

Main Characters

Clyde Umney, Peoria Smith, The Painters, Samuel Landry.

Did You Know?

Samuel Landry's New York agent in the modern world is named Verrill, an *hommage* to Stephen King's longtime editor and friend, Chuck Verrill.

What I Really Liked About It

In a way, "Umney's Last Case" reminded me of *The Dark Half* and *Secret Window, Secret Garden*, two of King's works of which I am very fond of and two works which concern a writer's characters interacting with the writer, their "God." King is especially

The King Speaks

"For a long time I steered clear of that Chandlerian voice, because I had nothing to use it for...nothing to say in the tones of Philip Marlowe that was *mine*....Then one day I did."

—From "Notes" in *Nightmares & Dreamscapes*

good at this dynamic, easily shuffling two distinct personas and making the reader relate to each of them individually.

Film Adaptations

None, although this story would make a great Raymond Chandler movie—or *Twilight Zone* episode! (Don't you miss that show? Rod Serling and Stephen King working together ... now *that's* something I'd pay to see!)

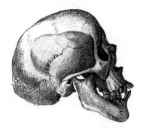

"The Doctor's Case" (1987)

*I doubt that I shall ever forget this particular case no matter how murky
my thoughts and memories may become, and I thought I might as well
set it down before God caps my pen forever.*

Why it made the top 100:

"The Doctor's Case" and "Umney's Last Case" (both from *Nightmares &
Dreamscapes*) made it onto the list of the top 100 works in *The Essential Stephen
King*. Partly because these two terrific short stories resonate off each other: "Umney's"
is a Raymond Chandler *pastiche*, written in the style of the legendary "hard-boiled"
crime writer; "Doctor's" is a true Sherlock Holmes story, an *hommage* to the great Sir
Arthur Conan Doyle.

"Umney's Last Case" is Stephen King's favorite of the two but, personally, I like
this Sherlock Holmes "locked room" story a little more.

The premise is classic: Narrated by Dr. Watson (Sherlock Holmes is 40 years in his
grave), "The Doctor's Case" is about the one time Watson solved a crime before the
great detective.

Sherlock Holmes is called upon by Inspector Lestrade to investigate the scene of a perplexing death. The wealthy and contemptible Lord Hull (his son William describes him as "the lowest creature to crawl upon the face of the earth since the serpent tempted Eve") is found dead. This is shortly after gloating to his wife and three sons about his new will, a document that bequeaths the four of them nothing, instead leaving his entire fortune to, ahem, Mrs. Hemphill's Home for Abandoned Pussies.

Lord Hull is found dead in his locked—from the inside—study, with his *old* will (the one leaving his estate to his family) in his hand, and a dagger buried deep in his back. Although Holmes is initially called upon to solve this mysterious murder, it is his stalwart associate Dr. Watson who ultimately solves the crime.

To say more would be to ruin a carefully crafted solution, well-thought-out and logically presented by King; thus, I refer you to the story (if you have not already read it) for more.

Suffice to say that the answer to the riddle is artistically concocted by King and leaves the reader with a feeling of satisfaction. Nope, nothing wrong here: All unresolved loose ends are resolved and Watson, nearing his 100th birthday, can rest knowing he has set the record straight.

King has always been a fan of British mystery writers (see the chapter *Wimsey* in my *The Lost Work of Stephen King* for details on a "Lord Peter Wimsey" novel King began writing) and in "The Doctor's Case," he proves himself an apt pupil.

☠ **C. V.** ☠

Main Characters

Dr. Watson, Sherlock Holmes, Inspector Lestrade, Lord Albert Hull, Lady Rebecca Hull, Stephen Hull, William Hull, Jory Hull.

Did You Know?

The address King uses in the story for Sherlock Holmes's residence, 221B Baker Street, London, is, of course, the same used by Arthur Conan Doyle for his complete Sherlock Holmes series. This address does not actually exist, yet to this day, mail is still sent there on a regular basis by Arthur Conan Doyle/Sherlock Holmes fans.

What I Really Liked About It

"The Doctor's Case" is an artfully unfeigned Sherlock Holmes story; the handiwork of an authentic Arthur Conan Doyle fan.

The King Speaks

"When he was a kid, King remembers much the same books as many of his contemporaries: Tom Swift, the Hardy Boys and Nancy Drew series, and the works of Jack London and Mark Twain. 'Nobody told us that *Huckleberry Finn* was a classic, we just read it because we liked it.' When the bookmobile came to town, he'd grab books from McBain's 87th Precinct series. 'I liked the continuity from book to book,' he said. There was also Sherlock Holmes, of course, and C. S. Lewis' adventures in Narnia, which was, King said, one of the ways he developed his taste for fantasy. Fantasy, mysteries, a little bit of wry humor. With those books in his head one wonders what Stephen King will be when he grows up."

—From an interview with Catherine Russell in the May 11, 2000 issue of *Maine Times*

Film Adaptations

None (although this story would make a great Sherlock Holmes movie).

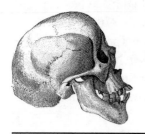

NUMBER 69

"Gramma" (1984)

PleaseGoddon'tletherwakeupuntilMomcomeshomeforJesus'sakeAmen.

Why it made the top 100:

King has always been terrific at chronicling childhood and in "Gramma," he goes one step further by taking us inside the mind of an 11-year-old who not only is terrified for most of the story, but who ends up crossing over to the dark side by the tale's conclusion.

When we learn that "Gramma" is based on real-life events from Stephen King's childhood, the terror becomes even more palpable. (See Chris Chesley's comments below.)

The 11-year-old George Bruckner has to stay home alone with his 83-year-old invalid grandmother while his mother goes to visit his injured brother in the hospital. Gramma is obese, blind, and bedridden, and it is Georgie's job to make her her tea and attend to any of her other needs—*if* she wakes up when his mother is gone.

George is afraid of Gramma, and although he isn't sure exactly *why* she terrifies him, we learn that his fear is for good reason. Gramma practiced black magic before she

The King Speaks

"Then there was my father's mother, Granny Spansky, whom David and I got to know when we were living in the Middle West. She was a big, heavyset woman who alternately fascinated and repelled me. I can still see her cackling like an old witch through toothless gums while she'd fry an entire loaf of bread in bacon drippings on an antique range and then gobble it down, chortling, 'My, that's crisp!'" In *Danse Macabre*, King also refers to Granny Spansky, writing "my paternal grandmother enjoyed frying half a loaf of bread in bacon fat for breakfast..." (Guess it depended on how hungry she was.)

—From a June 1983 interview with *Playboy* magazine

became ill and her family knows the dark secrets of her powers: One buried tragedy was the death of Gramma's son Franklin from peritonitis from a burst appendix. George's mother and George's Aunt Flo know, though, that Gramma cast the spell that killed Frank.

As George is nervously watching the clock and waiting for his mother's return, he hears "[f]rom the other room...a choking, rattling, gargling noise."

George realizes that the noise he heard was Gramma's death rattle (his tormenting older brother Buddy had taught him the term) and that he was now alone in an empty house with the corpse of a dead witch.

The real terror begins when George goes in to pull the covers over Gramma's head and her dead hand grabs his wrist. George flees to the kitchen, and to his horror, Gramma gets out of bed and follows him, calling him to her.

At this precise moment, George's Aunt Flo calls and when she realizes what happened—and what is presently *happening*—she tells George to tell Gramma to "lie down in the name of Hastur."

The occult command works and when George's mother finally arrives home, Gramma is back in bed—but her powers have now passed on to little George, whose first demonic act is to kill Aunt Flo with a massive, long-distance brain hemorrhage.

"Gramma" ends with George lying naked in bed eagerly awaiting the return of his nasty older brother, and malevolently plotting just what he will now be able to do to him, thanks to Gramma's dark gift.

☠ **C. V.** ☠

Chris Chesley Speaks

"Gramma" is based on Stephen King's years living in Durham, Maine when his mother Ruth(!) took care of her aged parents. In an interview I did with King's childhood friend and collaborator (*People, Places, and Things*) Chris Chesley for my *Complete Stephen King Encyclopedia*, Chris talked about the roots of this tale:

> When I first knew Steve, his mother was...taking care of his grandparents. They lived in the house with Steve and his mother, and Steve's story "Gramma" from *Skeleton Crew* came out of that.
>
> In that story, the grandmother has been transformed into a supernatural thing about which a child has to make a decision. Should I give this...what seems to be a monster...should I give this creature the tea? Well, that giving of the tea is based directly upon his life at that time, when he was a boy between ten and twelve. The grandparents lived in the downstairs front room. The grandmother was invalided. She was not able to talk. And for kids that age, someone who is invalided and very old is kind of a horrifying presence.
>
> And so Steve had that experience, and it was borne home on him, and you can see the connection between that experience, and how affected he must have been by that situation to be motivated to later turn it into such a powerful story.
>
> When I read the story—sitting there by myself in the night—it raised the hackles on my neck, even though I knew from whence the story was derived. And I thought to myself at the time, think of how much he took in. Think of how affected he was by that in order to have the psychological motivation to spit it back out by writing this hair-raising story.

Main Characters

George Bruckner, Ruth Bruckner, Gramma, Aunt Flo, Buddy Bruckner.

Did You Know?

"Gramma" (from *Night Shift*) is one of King's "Castle Rock" stories. The Castle Rock Strangler's mother Henrietta Dodd (from *The Dead Zone*) makes a cameo appearance, as does Joe Camber from *Cujo* (his hill is mentioned) and Cora Simard from *The Tommyknockers* (she gossips with Henrietta on George's party line).

What I Really Liked About It

The sense of claustrophobic terror that King captures so well; he remembers the kind of childhood fear that made us hide under beds during a thunderstorm or an eclipse.

Film Adaptations

None.

TV Adaptations

The New Twilight Zone (CBS series, "Gramma" episode broadcast February 14, 1986), starring Barret Oliver, Darlanne Fluegel, Frederick Long, teleplay by Harlan Ellison, directed by Bradford May. (Grade: A.)

Audio Adaptations

Skeleton Crew: Book Two (Recorded Books, Inc.), read by Frank Muller; *Stories from Skeleton Crew* (Warner Audio Publishing), read by Gale Garnett.

70

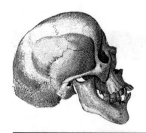

"The Raft"
(1982)

*"I'll tell you what," Randy said, "let's go on out to Cascade Lake.
We'll swim out to the raft, say good-bye to summer, and then swim back."*

Why it made the top 100:

"The Raft" is a classic horror story that echoes Joseph Payne Brennan's legendary early-1950s short story "Slime," and is one of King's simplest, yet scariest narratives.

The set-up takes place in the beginning passages of the story and is utterly straight-forward: Four college kids (two couples) drunkenly decide to drive 40 miles to Cascade Lake in October. They strip to their underwear and swim in 45 degree ("fifty at most") water, out to a raft still anchored in the middle of the lake. Their ritual farewell to summer accomplished, they will then swim back to shore, get dressed, return to the dorm, get undressed again, and rut like ruminants in heat.

The four—Deke, Randy, Rachel, and LaVerne—all make it to the raft, but halfway there, Randy notices something unusual in the water to the left and behind the float. At first he thinks it's an oil spill, but who ever heard of an oil spill in a lake and also, aren't oil spills ill-formed and shapeless? This thing looked like a big checker floating on the surface of the lake. And, Randy noticed, it seemed to be moving towards the raft.

It isn't long before tragedy befalls three of the four formerly carefree youths, and King's descriptions of their deaths are gruesome and horrifying.

"The Raft" is compelling evidence that Stephen King did a great deal of reading in his early, formative years, and vivid proof that even a Master Storyteller can learn from the Master Storytellers.

☠ **C. V.** ☠

Main Characters

Deke, Randy, Rachel, LaVerne, the thing in the water.

Did You Know?

King wrote a short story in 1968 called "The Float" which he submitted to the men's magazine *Adam*. The story was accepted and payment—$250—was promised on publication. King eventually received a $250 check from *Adam*, but it seems as though the story was never published. In the "Notes" section of *Skeleton Crew*, King asked anyone who had seen the original version of the story to contact him, but so far, it seems as though "The Float" exists only in the dead zone.

What I Really Liked About It

"The Raft" is genuinely frightening and King is a master at taking us inside the fear of his characters. We can completely relate to the terror of the three survivors who watch as Rachel is eaten by the blob. The story's conclusion is perhaps the scariest moment of all.

Film Adaptations

Creepshow 2 (1987, the segment "The Raft"); starring Daniel Beer, Jeremy Green, Page Hannah (Daryl's sister), Paul Satterfield, Shirley Sonderegger (King's secretary at the time, she appeared in the "Old Chief Wood'nhead" segment); Stephen King (he played a truck driver in "The Hitchhiker" segment); directed by Michael Gornick; screenplay by George A. Romero. (Grade: B-.)

NUMBER 71

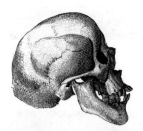

"The Boogeyman" (1973)

"All I did was kill my kids. One at a time. Killed them all."

Why it made the top 100:

One of the dictionary definitions for "boogeyman" is "a terrifying specter; an object or a source of fear, dread, or harassment" and in "The Boogeyman," that is precisely what terrorizes Lester Billings, the main character of this chilling and iconic *Night Shift* short story.

The story begins with Lester Billings's first visit to Dr. Harper, a psychiatrist. Lester is convinced that a boogeyman has killed his three children, but that he himself, their own father, was the one ultimately responsible for their deaths. Why? Because he always knew his children were being stalked by the boogeyman, but never did anything to protect them.

Lester Billings is not a very nice person. He is arrogant, a sexist, a racist, a potential abuser, and a snob. Billings is not someone you could easily warm up to. Yet King uses our repulsion towards Billings to paint a complex portrait of the character, so that we

The King Speaks

"The melodies of the horror tale are simple and repetitive, and they are melodies of disestablishment and disintegration...but another paradox is that the ritual outletting of these emotions seems to bring things back to a more stable and constructive state again. Ask any psychiatrist what his patient is doing when he lies there on the couch and talks about what keeps him awake and what he sees in his dreams. What do you see when you turn out the light? the Beatles asked; their answer: I can't tell you, but I know that it's mine."

—From *Danse Macabre*

begin to wonder whether or not he *has* murdered his kids and is now trying to absolve himself of his guilt by making up the story of the boogeyman. Or if there really is a boogeyman

At the very end of the story, we learn the dark truth.

"The Boogeyman" is one of King's most important short stories and in it, he first proffers two of his most resonant themes—fear of the dark, and the possibility that if you fear something long enough, it will become real.

Interestingly, "The Boogeyman" foreshadows other King works, most notably "Something To Tide You Over" (1982) and *It* (1986).

At one point in the story, Billings relates a dream in which he talks about an old *Tales From the Crypt* comic book story in which a woman drowns her husband in a quarry, but he comes back "all rotted and black-green." This *Crypt* story inspired King's *Creepshow* tale "Something To Tide You Over" (except that Leslie Nielsen (the jilted husband in the story) buries Ted Danson up to his neck on a beach and lets the tide do his dirty work. Ted comes back later, "all rotted and black-green" to exact a watery revenge.

Later in "The Boogeyman," Billings tells Harper that he started to think "that it lost us for a while when we moved. It had to hunt around, slinking through the streets at night and maybe creeping in the sewers." The sewers are a malevolent presence, as well as being an evil sanctuary for Pennywise the Clown in all his guises, in *It*.

☠ C. V. ☠

Main Characters

Lester Billings, Dr. Harper, The Boogeyman, Nurse Vickers, three dead Billings children: Denny, Shirl, and Andy.

Did You Know?

Stephen King has twice described *himself* as a boogeyman. In a 1991 article he wrote for *Entertainment Weekly* magazine called "How I Created *Golden Years*," King wrote, "At some point between *'Salem's Lot*, my second book, and *The Dead Zone*, my sixth, I became America's Best-Loved Bogeyman." King authority George Beahm later paid homage to King's remark in the title of his own 1998 book, *Stephen King: America's Best-Loved Boogeyman*. Earlier, in "Straight Up Midnight: An Introductory Note" from his novella collection *Four Past Midnight*, King wrote, "When this book is published in 1990, I will have been sixteen years in the business of make-believe. Halfway through those years, long after I had become, by some process I still do not fully understand, America's literary boogeyman, I published a book called *Different Seasons*." One other interesting item regarding "The Boogeyman": In the story, King mentions Frankenstein, The Wolfman, and The Mummy, all of whom make cameo appearances in *It*.

What I Really Liked About It

No question: the surprise ending. I also like the ultracool *Twilight Zone* reference, one that adds a welcome tinge of weirdness. In the opening segment of the story, King is describing how Billings is lying ramrod straight on the psychiatrist's couch and then uses this blatantly Rod Serlingesque image: "Picture of a man enduring necessary humiliation."

Film Adaptations

The Boogeyman (1983, Granite Entertainment, video only), starring Michael Reid, Bert Linder, Terence Brady, Mindy Silverman, Jerome Bynder, Bobby Persiceth, Michael D'Agostino, Nancy Lindberg; directed by Jeffrey C. Schiro, teleplay by Jeffrey C. Schiro. (Grade: A-.)

NUMBER 72

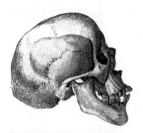

The Tommyknockers (1987)

It's either all an accident...or all fate.

Why it made the top 100:

The Tommyknockers hit the number one spot on the *New York Times* best-seller list and was adapted as a successful TV miniseries. Yet the novel did not receive a single vote for "Favorite Novel" in the poll I conducted among hundreds of Stephen King fans for *The Essential Stephen King*.

Part of the problem with *The Tommyknockers* is that the novel was written when King—by his own admission—was in the throes of a serious cocaine addiction. In *On Writing*, he tells us, "In the spring and summer of 1986 I wrote *The Tommyknockers*, often working until midnight with my heart running at a hundred and thirty beats a minute and cotton swabs stuck up my nose to stem the coke-induced bleeding." The result is a bloated novel that is still an exciting read, but which, in the opinions of many fans and critics, should have been edited severely before publication. Many feel that the novel would have been more effective if it was a third shorter, and that some of the tangential chapters (the history of Haven, etc.) act as intrusive speed-bumps on what could had been a seamless, smoothly-moving narrative freeway.

That said, though, there is still a great deal to admire and enjoy in this science fiction/ horror novel, not the least of which is its premise. An alien spaceship crashes into Maine and its occupants are in stasis for millions of years. Then one day, the Tommyknockers (the name the Havenites assign to the beings in the ship) "wake up" and begin exerting an "influence" on the residents of Haven, improving them and giving them powerful capabilities which they use to improve their lives. This influence, however, also seems to slowly destroy them as they progress through "The Becoming," the process by which they become Tommyknockers—at the cost of their humanity.

The heroine of the story is Bobbi Anderson, a writer of popular westerns, and one-time lover of alcoholic poet Jim "Gard" Gardener. Bobbi is the one who discovers the ship and is the first to feel the effects of the aliens as they put forth their toxic sway. (2001's *Dreamcatcher* (Chapter 26) revisits some of these story elements.)

The Tommyknockers is another of King's works in which he blatantly indulges his paranoia concerning ever-increasing technological advancements. In *The Tommyknockers*, it is nuclear power that wears the mask of the boogeyman, and the physical effects of "becoming" (tooth and hair loss, etc.) mimic the effects of radiation poisoning. At one point in the story King even refers to the October 5, 1966 partial nuclear meltdown of the Enrico Fermi breeder reactor in Michigan, citing the engineer who took one look and said, "You guys almost lost Detroit," and then fainted.

The Tommyknockers has its problems, granted, but by the conclusion of the book, as we watch the doomed and dying Jim Gardener fly off into space on the transparent floor of the resurrected spaceship, we cannot help but be moved. This one scene makes us forget some of the more leaden passages in the novel.

☠ C. V. ☠

 ## Main Characters

Roberta "Bobbi" Anderson, Jim "Gard" Gardener, Peter the dog, Ruth McCausland, Hilly Brown, David Brown, Ev Hillman.

 ## Did You Know?

In *The Dark Tower III: The Waste Lands*, we learn that Roland's archenemy, Richard Fannin, is also Maerlyn and, most importantly, Randall Flagg. Interestingly, in *The Tommyknockers*, Ruth McCausland's next-door-neighbor is Wendy Fannin, and she has a son named Billy. There is no mention of a Mr. Fannin. In the story, Wendy seems

The King Speaks

"Writers of fantasy and make-believe are born, not made...it's like a chunk of metal buried inside the earth of your mind and when the needle that should turn to something nice and sweet, more conscientiously constructive, should point to that sort of 'true north'...but instead it swings toward the thing that's buried in the earth."

—From an April 10, 1984 interview in *The Paper,*
Fordham University's Student Journal
of News, Analysis, Comment and Review

to embrace the "becoming" perpetrated by the tommyknockers and tells Ruth, "We'll 'become' a little more and that part will end." Is Wendy Fannin another manifestation of Richard Fannin and, therefore, a manifestation of Flagg? Or are the identical surnames a coincidence?

What I Really Liked About It

I greatly enjoyed King's depiction of the wish-fulfillment improvements to the Haven residents' lives. A hovering tractor? A typewriter that reads your subconscious mind and writes for you while you're sleeping? A water heater that operates at dozens of times the efficiency of a normal water heater? Almost makes you want to move to Haven. Almost.

Film Adaptations

Stephen King's The Tommyknockers (1993); starring Jimmy Smits, Marg Helgenberger, John Ashton, Allyce Beasley, Robert Carradine, Joanna Cassidy, Traci Lords, Cliff DeYoung, E. G. Marshall; directed by John Power; screenplay by Lawrence D. Cohen. (Grade: C.)

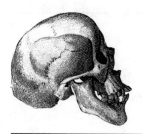

The Langoliers
(1990)

My God, my dear God, they are eating the world.

Why it made the top 100:

Flying is de facto frightening, and no one is more attuned to the heightened particulars of the myriad manifestations of fear than Stephen King. Thus, we have *The Langoliers*, a "what if?" tale that should not be read by anyone even *thinking* about boarding a plane in the foreseeable future.

Exhausted American Pride pilot Captain Brian Engle lands his plane in Los Angeles to learn that his ex-wife Anne has died tragically in a condo fire in Boston. He decides to hitch a ride back to the East Coast on an American Pride plane to tend to Anne's burial, etc. He immediately falls asleep and when he is awakened by a fellow passenger's screams, he discovers that almost everyone on the plan has vanished, leaving behind on their seats anything non-organic that was on their person - including surgical pins, a pacemaker, and even a dildo. The pilot and co-pilot are also gone and it isn't long before Engle is piloting the possibly doomed aircraft.

The few people left behind had all been sleeping and they soon discover that American Pride Flight 29 has gone through some kind of time portal and is now flying over a deserted America, and will soon be landing at an empty airport in Bangor, Maine.

Now that's a set-up for one hell of a story, and King does not let us down.

The survivors are a motley crew, and one of them, Craig Toomy, is certifiably psychotic, a classic "bad guy" in a tale of survival such as *The Langoliers*.

Toomy plays a role in explaining what the langoliers actually are. Using as a metaphor a deep-sea fish that will explode if it nears the surface, King reveals that the langoliers are the creatures that eat the past. (You always wondered where all our yesterdays went, didn't you?) Now usually, we are not privy to the langoliers' work. In the case of Flight 29 and its hapless survivors, though, traveling through the rip in time, has trapped them in the in-between realm where the langoliers ply their trade.

Will Captain Engle, the blind psychic Dinah, the British spy Nick, Jewish violinist Albert, psycho Craig, and the others be able to escape their entrapment in the twilight zone? And if so, will they all manage to survive the ordeal?

The Langoliers is one of King's most exciting and scary novellas (he really does shine in the novella format), one that is a comfortable hybrid of psychological terror, science fiction, and horror. It is a tale that works much better on the page than it did on the screen in the 1995 TV miniseries adaptation.

☠ **C. V.** ☠

Main Characters

Captain Brian Engle, Dinah Bellman, Albert Klausner, Laurel Stevenson, Nick Hopewell, Don Gaffney, Craig Toomy, Robert Jenkins, Bethany Sims, Rudy Warwick, The Langoliers.

Did You Know?

In *The Langoliers*, Albert Kaussner plays a Gretch violin. An extensive Internet search resulted in no violin manufactured under the name Gretch. But there is a guitar called a Gretch and a musician by the name of Ron Gretch played the violin on a 7" single ("Farewell"/"Bring It On Home To Me") recorded by Rod Stewart on September 27, 1974. (You can be sure that I *do know* that this is a ridiculously obscure and esoteric reference but King is such a huge rock fan that it would not surprise me if the Gretch guitar and/or Ron Gretch was, indeed, the source(s) for the name of Albert's violin.) (Steve?) And if it isn't, well, then it just suggests that the theory of synchronicity might be more than just a theory.)

The King Speaks

"I kept thinking that it would be great if you could knock yourself out while you where flying. That would be the ideal....So I was flying with some guys who had a small jet and I said, 'This would be really great if only you didn't have to be aware through the whole thing. If you could just get on and there'd be a black place in your mind.' And the guy says to me, 'Well we can lower the oxygen back there and you'd go right out.' And I said, 'Do it.' And they wouldn't do it, but...but I got a story out of it."

— From an April 3, 1998 interview with Dennis Miller on HBO

What I Really Liked About It

I really like the premise of this novella, the idea that all our yesterdays need to be eaten by transdimensional cleanup guys—the Langoliers—beings who serve no purpose but to keep the time/space continuum running smoothly. Very Serlingesque.

Film Adaptations

Stephen King's The Langoliers (TV miniseries, 1995); starring Patricia Wettig, Bronson Pinchot, Dean Stockwell, Kate Maberly, David Morse, Mark Lindsay Chapman, Chris Collet, Kimber Riddle, Frankie Faison; directed by Tom Holland; screenplay by Tom Holland. (Grade: B-.)

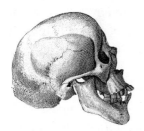

Everything's Eventual
(1997)

I've always had something, some kind of deal, and I sort of knew it,
but not how to use it or what its name was or what it meant.

Why it made the top 100:

Stephen King's voice in this intriguing science fiction novella is that of the master at his most engaging.

As soon as the main character, Dinky Earnshaw, starts "speaking" to us, we're pulled *in* and pulled *through* the story, almost (as, again, many have described the experience) as though we're not actually reading the words.

Dinky is one of the few, one of the special, one of the one in eight million who is a *tranny*. A person with the paranormal ability to willfully kill by sending to selected targets personalized e-mails (or letters) containing odd, toxic shapes called japps, mirks, bews, smims, sankofites, and fouders.

People who are able to recognize these gifted types identify Dinky, and he is then hired by the mysterious Trans Corporation. He is put through a period of training (which is akin, he tells us, to programming a hard drive), and then set up with his own house, a 70-dollar-a-week allowance, and the wondrous DINKY'S DAYBOARD, a kitchen chalkboard on which he writes down whatever he wants (from a not-yet-released CD to a homemade apple pie or Rembrandt fake) and voila!, it's there when he returns home from the movies or a walk.

Dinky is told that he is working for the betterment of mankind and at first, he accepts this. He then begins to learn more about the people he sends DINKYMAIL to (specifically, three high profile suicides that end up in the newspaper). He also wonders about the motives of the clandestine organization that takes care of all of his needs—as long as he sits at his computer and performs his e-mail executions.

One day, Dinky receives a clandestine message from a fellow tranny, a missive that may possibly offer an escape from the life he has been ensnared in, setting in motion events that may result in even *more* deaths—but not the kind that Dinky was being paid to do.

Everything's Eventual is science fiction with a touch of the fantastic. Once again, King looks at "wild talents," those human beings gifted (some would say cursed) with wondrous abilities that can be used for good or evil. (*Carrie*, *Firestarter*, *The Shining*, *The Dead Zone*, and "The End of the Whole Mess" are other examples of King writing about such "gifted" individuals.)

King is especially good with short fiction and this novella is an exceptionally entertaining story as well as being an important contribution to not only King's *Dark Tower* saga, but also to his growing body of science fiction works.

It was reported to me by an unimpeachable source that Stephen King told Peter Straub that the character of Dinky is a "Breaker," like Ted in the novel *Low Men in Yellow Coats* (in *Hearts in Atlantis*), thereby connecting this tale to the world of *The Dark Tower*, *The Stand*, and other King *Dark Tower* works.

In *Low Men in Yellow Coats*, it is explained that the Dark Tower "holds everything together." There are Beams protecting the Tower and "Breakers," working for the Crimson King, endeavor to destroy the Beams. The Breakers, it is made clear, do *not* do this work voluntarily. If Dinky is, indeed, a Breaker, then it is quite possible that Mr. Sharpton and his Trans Corporation may figure into future events in the story of Roland the Last Gunslinger and his quest to find the Dark Tower.

☠ **C. V.** ☠

 Main Characters

Dinky (Richard Ellery) Earnshaw, Ma, Mr. Sharpton, Pug, Charles "Skipper" Brannigan, Mrs. Bukowski, Mrs. Bukowski's dog, Mr. Shermerhorn, Dr. Wentworth, Muffin, Mr. Columbus, Ann Tevitch, Andrew Neff, General William Unger, Pete Hamil, Liz Smith, The Cleaners.

Did You Know?

Everything's Eventual is one of those occasional King works in which the author refer-ences himself. In Part 17 of the novella, Dinky tells us, "There was this show me and Pug used to watch one summer back when we were little kids. *Golden Years*, it was called. You probably don't remember it."

What I Really Liked About It

I have always greatly enjoyed Stephen King's science fiction and this novella is no exception. Augmenting the story's appeal is the fact that it is also a *Dark Tower* story, but unlike "The Little Sisters of Eluria," which features Roland and other *Dark Tower*-specific characters, events, and locales, *Everything's Eventual* is in orbit somewhat outside the *DT* saga's narrative sun.

Film Adaptations

None.

Number **75**

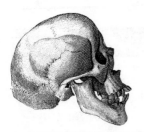

The Breathing Method
(1982)

Here, sir, there are always more tales.

Why it made the top 100:

The four novellas in Stephen King's *Different Seasons* collection are some of King's finest work (they all made *The Essential Stephen King*'s Top 100) and *The Breathing Method* (foretitled "A Winter's Tale") is no exception.

In addition to being a compelling and horrifying Christmas tale having nothing to do with Christmas (except that a birth takes place on Christmas Eve), *The Breathing Method* is also notable for being the first time King used the phrase which has become almost totemic to him: *"It Is The Tale, Not He Who Tells It."* Many King fans and scholars interpreted this as a not so thinly veiled comment by King on his burgeoning celebrity and the ever-increasing interest in him as a person. By 1982, the year in which *Different Seasons* was published, Stephen King had become a brand name for horror. He had published seven enormously successful novels (*Carrie, 'Salem's Lot, The Shining, The Stand, The Dead Zone, Firestarter,* and *Cujo*) as well as the *Night Shift* collection, and the acclaimed nonfiction book, *Danse Macabre*. He had

The King Speaks

"In my novella *The Breathing Method* in *Different Seasons*, I've created a mysterious private club in an old brownstone on East 35th Street in Manhattan, in which an oddly matched group of men gathers periodically to trade tales of the uncanny....That men's club really is a metaphor for the entire storytelling process. There are as many stories in me as there are rooms in that house, and I can easily lose myself in them.

　　　　—From an interview in the June 1983 issue of *Playboy* magazine

become, at the age of 35, a world-famous, instantly recognizable, literary star of the brightest magnitude.

And, apparently, it was getting on his nerves.

I am not suggesting that King wrote *The Breathing Method* as a way of telling his fans to lighten up with the obsessive attention. I think he wrote it for the same reason that he has written all his other works—the story demanded to be told.

But the novella's narrative underpinnings—a stately gentleman's club where unusual tales are told—provided King with the perfect vehicle to make a statement on the relationship between a writer and his readers.

That said, it must also be acknowledged that *The Breathing Method* is never preachy or demagogic. It is first and foremost a chilling tale of a mother who was determined to give birth to her child, even after she is decapitated during the delivery process. Yes, for those of you who haven't read the novella (although by now, 18 years after the novella's initial publication, this plot point is common knowledge among King fans), Sharon Stansfield's headless body continues to breathe and deliver her baby as her still-sentient noggin locomotive-pants to assist the process.

Sandra Stansfield's story is told by her doctor, Emlyn McCarron, in a gentlemen's club where there are many rooms, many corridors, many entrances and exits, and where Stevens the butler (the name is not an accident) is the "host" of the periodic gatherings.

The Breathing Method is dedicated to Peter and Susan Straub and seems to have been directly inspired by Straub's "Chowder Society" Men's Club in *Ghost Story*. Regardless of its genesis, though, for all its horror and its gruesome conclusion, this is one of King's more literary works, told in a leisurely tone, yet not lacking punch or pleasure.

For an interesting spin on the subtext of *The Breathing Method*, read the insightful essay "The Fear That Fame Will Fail: Stephen King's Canonical Anxiety" by Emily Hegarty. The complete text can be found online at: *members.aol.com/eahegarty/king.htm*.

Main Characters

David Adley, Dr. Emlyn McCarron, Sandra Stansfield, Stevens, assorted club members.

Did You Know?

One of the most interesting bits of (true) cultural trivia King inserts into this story is his recounting of the accepted practice in 1935 of encouraging overweight expectant mothers to, incredibly, *take up smoking*. A popular advertising slogan of the time was "Have a Lucky instead of a sweet."

What I Really Liked About It

The consistent reinforcement throughout the novella that David Adley is in a place not of this world.

Film Adaptations

None. In *The Stephen King Universe*, authors Stanley Wiater, Christopher Golden, and Hank Wagner wrote, "It is telling to note that thus far [*The Breathing Method*] is the one piece in this collection that has not been filmed. Nor is it likely to be, given the hideousness of the conclusion...." I'd like to add that when one considers the anthology in which this novella appears, the continued reluctance of filmmakers to adapt *The Breathing Method* for the silver screen is a powerful statement about its genuinely horrific ending. After all, *Different Seasons* has already provided filmmakers with source material for three exceptional films: Rob Reiner's *Stand By Me* (*The Body*); Frank Darabont's *The Shawshank Redemption* (*Rita Hayworth and Shawshank Redemption*); and Bryan Singer's *Apt Pupil* (*Apt Pupil*).

NUMBER 76

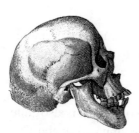

"That Feeling, You Can Only Say What It Is In French"
(1998)

"Oh-oh, I'm getting that feeling," Carol said.

Why it made the top 100:

This is one of Stephen King's *New Yorker* pieces; those occasional stories or essays King offers to the magazine, and which are of such a high caliber, they are snapped up and billboarded on the cover. Other King works initially published in *The New Yorker* include "Head Down," "The Man in the Black Suit," "Leaf-Peepers," "All That You Love Will Be Carried Away," and excerpts from *On Writing*. (Although I do admit that I have never been a fan of "Head Down," it is an exceptionally well-written piece and it does appear in the *Essential Stephen King*'s top 100.)

"That Feeling" mostly takes place in the mind of Carol Shelton, on her way to a second honeymoon vacation with her husband Bill to celebrate their 25th anniversary. As they are driving to their hotel, Carol begins getting "those feelings"...flashes of vivid recall known as *deja vu*, a weird biological short circuit in the brain that makes the experiencer interpret new events as memory.

We eventually learn that the initial events of the story are a dream Carol is having while on the plane to the resort airport.

We then move on to the second segment, where she wakes up, deplanes, and heads off to their hotel. Soon, we begin to get a sense of unease about what is actually happening to Carol because she is again having frequent spells of *deja vu*. Some of her visions are horrific, and a subtle sense of dread seeps into the narrative. Once again we learn that this car ride, too, is a chimera, and Carol and Bill have been on their chartered plane the whole time. A chartered plane flown by Floyd the pilot, someone Carol has been seeing and hearing the whole time she has been dreaming.

Is their plane headed for a mid-air collision? Have Carol's dreams been premonitions? King gives us the answer—sort of— but it is ultimately up to the reader to come to his or her own conclusions. I know what *I* think happened…you will have to make up your own mind.

In addition to the suspense and terror of this story, the subtext of the tale is also quite interesting. We learn that Carol has been lying for years about having had an abortion early in her marriage, and her guilt has obviously been crushing. Questions become apparent: If you believe that Carol dies in a fiery plane crash, is King saying that she is paying the ultimate price—her own life—for snuffing out a potential life? Or if all of Carol's harbingers of doom are dark, delusional fantasies, is King instead suggesting that these kind of psychotic episodes are her mind (or the universe; or God) punishing her for her decision to end her pregnancy?

As in the best fictions, much of the interpretation lies in the sensibility of the reader. This story is an excellent example of the layers of meaning that can be found in a well-crafted narrative.

 C. V.

 ## Main Characters

Carol Shelton, Bill Shelton, Floyd, Carol's Mom and Dad, Carol's Gram, Sister Annunciata, Sister Dormatilla, the Blessed Mother, Mother Teresa.

 ## Did You Know?

This is one of King's few stories set outside of Maine. "That Feeling" takes place in Florida, where, not so coincidentally, Stephen and Tabitha King now have a home where they spend most winters, and where Stephen went to recuperate following his 1999 accident. (During King's recovery, his wife Tabitha took some photos of him on a Florida beach that were to be used as publicity materials and by the media.)

What I Really Liked About It

The increasingly worrisome sense we get that something really bad is going to happen to Carol, a foreboding that becomes a reality (or does it?) when we read the word "Delta."

Film Adaptations

None.

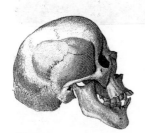

Riding the Bullet
(2000)

Fun is fun and done is done.

Why it made the top 100:

The Internet-only publication of *Riding the Bullet* unquestionably overshadowed the story itself. After the e-dust settled, the story itself is what survived...and it's a corker. Stephen King himself aptly described *Riding the Bullet* as "a ghost story in the grand manner" and it's got everything you'd expect in such a tale: a graveyard, a terrifying visitor from the other side, a spooky moonlit night, and more.

Simon & Schuster published this 16,000-word story on the Internet on March 14, 2000 in conjunction with King's publishing company, Philtrum Press. The story was initially only available to eBook and PC users (King, a Mac user, could not download his own story) and, for the first few days, the story was given away by such big book e-tailers as Amazon and Barnes & Noble.

Riding the Bullet was published in an allegedly secure format that prevented it from being printed. As should have been expected, hackers cracked this feature within hours of the story's release and many purchasers did ultimately print it out. Hackers also

The King Speaks

"I was intrigued by the success of *Riding the Bullet* (stunned would probably be a more accurate word), and since then have been anxious to try something similar, but I've also been puzzling over issues of ownership when it comes to creative work. On one hand I applaud Metallica's decision to try and put a few spikes into the big, cushy radial tire that is Napster, because creative people should be paid for their work just as plumbers and carpenters and accountants are paid for theirs. On the other hand, I think that the current technology is rapidly turning the whole idea of copyright into a risky proposition...not quite a joke, but something close to it. It took hackers only forty-eight to seventy-two hours to bust the encryption on *Bullet* (as Tabitha says, spending invaluable hours to obtain an item that sold for $2.50 and was at many sites given away).

—From a June 7, 2000 letter by King posted on *Stephenking.com*

figured out a way to make a Mac version available as an Acrobat Reader document and that, too, was uploaded to many unofficial Web sites and downloaded for free by fans all over the world. These problems and oversights aside, though, *Riding the Bullet* was an extremely successful publication.

Close to 500,000 *official* copies of *Riding the Bullet* were downloaded within the first few days of its availability, and King later revealed that he earned approximately $450,000 for the story. Compared with the $10,000 he would have received if he had published it in *The New Yorker*, the e-publication of the story proved that offering a literary work solely on the Internet could work if, there was a ready audience for the product.

Several months later, King and his Philtrum Press expanded his electronic publishing "division" by offering individual chapters of his serial novel *The Plant* on his Web site, relying on the honor system to collect the $1 it cost to purchase each chapter. Payment has been greater than the 75% cut-off King mandated, and publication continued until King put it on hiatus.

Riding the Bullet provided a model for electronic publication and is, thus, a groundbreaking literary work, but how is it *as a story?*

It is fast-paced and scary, and, considering that it's the first thing King wrote after his near-fatal accident, it is even more remarkable than the sum of its words and history.

Alan Parker hitchhikes to the hospital where his mother lies following a stroke. He is picked up by a repulsive old man, and then by a guy named George, who just so happens to be dead. To reveal more would be criminal, but I can tell you that Alan goes through a dark night of the soul, an experience so unbelievable that he waited until now (he narrates *Bullet*) to tell it.

If you do not have a computer, you will be happy to learn that King has confirmed that a text version of *Riding the Bullet* will appear in his still-untitled short story collection sometime in 2003. Until then, don't hitchhike. You'll find out why after you read the story.

Those of you who *have* read *Riding the Bullet* already know why.

☠ **C. V.** ☠

Main Characters

Alan Parker, Jean Parker, Mrs. McCurdy, George Staub, Hector Passmore, the Morose Insurance Man, Ralph, Bram Stoker, Sigmund Freud, the Tobacco Chewing Farmer, Yvonne Ederle the Information Lady, Muriel, Anne Corrigan, Dr. Farquahr, Dr. Nunnally, Foreigner, Led Zeppelin, AC/DC, Bob Dylan, Hattie Carrol, Tom Paxton, Dave Van Ronk, Bill Clinton.

Did You Know?

The dog that distracted Maine driver Bryan Smith, causing him to hit and almost kill Stephen King with his Dodge van in June of 1999, was named Bullet.

What I Really Liked About It

"Riding the Bullet" is an old-fashioned horror story that reminded me of another King favorite, *The Road Virus Heads North*. It's pure, scary escapism.

Film Adaptations

Riding the Bullet (2002?) directed by Mick Garris; screenplay by Mick Garris.

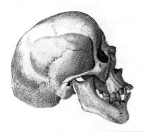

"Graveyard Shift"
(1970)

*We're going to clean the whole basement level. Nobody's touched it
for twelve years. Helluva mess. We're going to use hoses.*

Why it made the top 100:

"Graveyard Shift" is a very early story by King (his third published; he was in his early 20s when he wrote it) and it is one of his all-time best. The narrative is succinct and controlled in the way it unfolds and the resolute "Then this happened, then this happened" pace adds to the impact of the truly horrific scenarios depicted in the story. (King has always admired—and practiced—this "story rules all" touchstone of storytelling. In *The Mist*, he uses what is probably the single best opening of all time: "This is what happened"; although in *Secret Windows*, King admits that he "borrowed" that from Douglas Fairbairn's novel *Shoot*. I prefer to consider it an *hommage*.)

Hall, the protagonist of "Graveyard Shift," is an on-and-off drifter. His on-the-road jobs before landing the "graveyard shift" job at the Gates Falls textile mill included busboy, stevedore, short-order cook, taxi driver, dishwasher, as well as briefly attending college.

The King Speaks

"Rats are nasty little buggers, aren't they? I wrote and published a rat story called "Graveyard Shift" in *Cavalier* magazine four years prior to *'Salem's Lot*—it was, in fact, the third story I ever published—and I was uneasy about the similarity between the rats under the old mill in "Graveyard Shift" and those in the basement of the boarding house in *'Salem's Lot*. As writers near the end of a book, I suspect they cope with weariness in all sorts of ways—and my response as I neared the end of *'Salem's Lot* was to indulge in this bit of self-plagiarism."

—From *Danse Macabre*

King was unsuccessful in using the rats scene twice, however. In his June 1983 *Playboy* interview, King revealed the following:

"In the first draft of *'Salem's Lot*, I had a scene in which Jimmy Cody, the local doctor, is devoured in a boardinghouse basement by a horde of rats summoned from the town dump by the leader of the vampires. They swarm all over him like a writhing, furry carpet, biting and clawing, and when he tries to scream a warning to his companion upstairs, one of them scurries into his open mouth and squirms there as it gnaws out his tongue. I loved the scene, but my editor made it clear that no way would Doubleday publish something like that, and I came around eventually and impaled poor Jimmy on knives. But, shit, it just wasn't the same."

The mill is a horribly nasty place and King paints a bleak picture of the working environment for the millworkers. Oppressive heat, rats (*big* rats), and unrelenting filth are just a few of the daily ordeals the crew faces.

After three months at the mill, the hated boss Warwick asks Hall if he wants to work the Fourth of July week cleaning the mill's basement. It's more money ($2.00 an hour instead of the usual minimum $1.78, plus double time on the Fourth) and Hall reluctantly accepts. As the epigraph reveals, the plan was "to use hoses." That subliminally ominous remark hints at what the crew could expect to find in the basement and King fulfills this suggestion with a sublime, almost Elysian subtlety as he shows us the huge, antique looms, the moldy ledgers, "smashed rolltop desks," wet floors and, of course, the rats.

It's bad enough when the men are in the mill's basement. The story takes a dark turn into hell when Hall finds a trapdoor leading to a sub-basement beneath the mill's lower level. By now, Hall's hatred for Warwick has reached toxic levels and he makes the ultimately fatal decision to blackmail Warwick into descending into the nether regions...and Hall accompanies him down in a move that will guarantee Warwick's doom, but will also seal Hall's fate as well.

What do Warwick and Hall find down below? In addition to "a skull, green with mold" (a chilling image that speaks volumes about the place's history) they also find a mutant, legless, blind queen rat (the *magna mater*) the size of a Holstein calf. And the Queen has many children. Warwick's and Hall's fate is sealed.

"Graveyard Shift" is a classic.

☠ **C. V.** ☠

Main Characters

Hall, Warwick, Harry Wisconsky, Charlie Brochu, Brogan, Carmichael, Dangerfield, Cy Ippeston, Nedeau, Tony, Ray Upson, Stevenson.

Did You Know?

The name of the main character in this story, Hall (no first name is given), has the same surname as King's longtime childhood friends, the Hall brothers, Douglas, and the twins Dean and Dana.

What I Really Liked About It

The slow build to unrelenting terror; the calm, cool narrative tone that parallels Hall's deliberateness as he plans to do away with the loathsome Warwick; the restrained, yet vividly evocative description of the mutant rats and the magna matter.

Film Adaptations

Stephen King's Graveyard Shift (1990); starring David Andrews, Kelly Wolf, Stephen Macht, Brad Dourif, Andrew Divoff, Vic Polizos; directed by Ralph S. Singleton; screenplay by John Esposito. (Grade: C.)

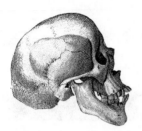

"The Mangler"
(1972)

There was a bad one today…The worst.

Why it made the top 100:

The Hadley-Watson Model-6 Speed Ironer and Folder is possessed by a demon that was summoned when a virgin's blood accidentally splashed into its workings. (Of course.) It is up to Officer John Hunton to stop the machine's grisly attacks (which involves pulling humans into its rollers and gears) and make the Blue Ribbon Laundry safe again for wet sheets (and people).

"The Mangler" is very early King (it originally appeared in *Cavalier* magazine in 1972) and yet it most assuredly has literary legs. It has been reprinted regularly over the past three decades, its most recent appearance being in the 1999 Lowell House trade paperback *Technohorror: Inventions in Terror*.

This is a very well crafted story. There are several characters, a fully realized plot, and an internal logic that adheres to the traditional rules for demonic possession and the banishing thereof. (Holy Water, The Bible, and the communion host are the primary anti-demon weapons...but you knew that.)

This story also contains one of the most, uh, "compelling" (and funny) lines King has ever written. Officer John Hunton is discussing with his partner Roger Martin the plan of attack against the demonic ironer. Roger suggests talking to a female laundry worker who may have provided the virgin's blood necessary to summon the possessing demon. Officer Hunton is less than thrilled with this tactic:

> "I'll run right over to her house," Hunton said with a small smile. "I can see it. 'Miss Oulette, I'm Officer John Hunton. I'm investigating an ironer with a bad case of demon possession and would like to know if you're a virgin.'"

I never worked in a laundry but I did work in a dry cleaners. Let me tell you, some of those washers and pressing machines were scary. We used one machine called The Puffer, which was a headless and armless human torso that spurted steam when you stepped on a pedal. The Puffer was used to eliminate wrinkles on jackets and blouses that didn't have a crease. When the torso was "dressed" with a blouse and then the pedal was stepped on, the blouse filled up with steam in a second, and its arms waved around like some kind of possessed headless demon shuddering in agony. If you were standing nearby, you would get whacked in the head by a flapping, steam-filled arm.

Thinking back to those days in the cleaners, I cannot help but wonder if King was on to something.

☠ **C. V.** ☠

Main Characters

Officer John Hunton, George Stanner, Adelle Frawley, Mark Jackson, Bill Gartley, Roger Martin, Annette Gillian, Alberta Keene, Herb Diment, Sherry Ouelette, and, of course, The Mangler.

Did You Know?

When Stephen King graduated from the University of Maine in 1970, he discovered to his dismay that his "B.A. was worth absolutely nothing." Unable to find work as a teacher, King took a job in an industrial laundry (the New Franklin Laundry in Bangor). His experiences working there—coupled with a dynamic and inventive imagination—inspired and informed this terrifying short story. As King said in a 1999 BBC profile, "The first thing I am is a husband; the second thing I am is a father; the third thing that I am is, I'm a man of my place and my time and my community. And I have to be all those things first because if I want to be a writer, everything trickles down." "The Mangler" is stark evidence of this: Everything trickles down.

The King Speaks

SK: I worked in a laundry while I was writing for men's magazines.

Q: Was working in the laundry weird?

SK: There was a guy who worked there who fell into the pressing machine, or "mangler," as you call it. He was over the machine dusting off the beams when he just lost his balance and fell.

Q: And the machine ate his hands?

SK: Yeah, it swallowed his arms. So he had two hooks where his hands used to be.

Q: Must have been tricky doing up his laces...

SK: True. And he always wore a white shirt and a tie. We used to wonder how he got that tie knotted so perfectly. He used to go to the bathroom and run one hook under the hot tap and one under the cold, then he'd creep up behind you and put the hooks on your neck. That was his little joke.

—From a 1998 interview with journalist Ben Rawortit

What I Really Liked About It

Honestly now, is there anything more terrifying than getting pulled into—wide-awake and without warning—an industrial ironing machine? 'Nuff said.

Film Adaptations

The Mangler (1995); starring Robert Englund, Ted Levine, Daniel Matmor, Jeremy Crutchley, Vanessa Pike; directed by Tobe Hooper; screenplay by Tobe Hooper, Stephen Brooks, Peter Welbeck. (Grade: C.)

NUMBER 80

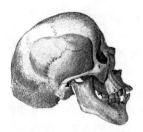

"Uncle Otto's Truck"
(1983)

Any tale of grue should have a provenance or a secret.

Why it made the top 100:

"Uncle Otto's Truck" is a scary short story about a haunted, malevolent, sentient truck. It was published (originally in *Yankee* magazine) the same year as *Christine*, King's novel about a haunted, malevolent, sentient car. (Guess 1983 was an "I'm terrified of (or at least paranoid about) vehicles" year for King, eh?)

"Uncle Otto's Truck," even though it is a "Castle Rock" story, contains one of the earliest (if not the earliest) mentions of the town of Derry, Maine, the setting for *It, Insomnia, Dreamcatcher,* and an important place in the King universe. (Derry is also referred to in passing in a great many of King's other novels and short stories.) In "Uncle Otto's Truck," Quentin Schenck tells us that his grandfather settled in Derry when he emigrated here from Germany because of the town's lumber industry.

The story told here, though, is not of Quentin's grandfather; it is of his uncle Otto. Otto and his partner George McCutcheon founded a successful chain of hardware

The King Speaks

"The truck is real, and so is the house..."

—From "Notes" in *Skeleton Crew*

stores and lumberyards. One day while out driving in Otto's Cresswell truck (both of them "shithouse drunk"), Otto overheated the engine and it exploded. They left the truck by the side of the road. Some time later, Otto and George came to loggerheads over whether or not to sell the company. George wanted to sell; Otto didn't. This stalemate was resolved, so Quentin tells us, when Otto killed his partner by crushing him beneath the Cresswell.

Otto then built a house across the road from the truck and began to go slowly insane. He began to see the truck moving towards him and one night, he tells his nephew, he awakened to find the truck right outside his window.

As Otto ages and gets crazier and crazier, good nephew Quentin continues to bring him his groceries. But then one night, he finds his uncle dead, and with a huge sparkplug in his mouth (which Quentin kept). An autopsy finds over three quarts of oil in Otto's body and the official ruling is suicide by drinking motor oil.

But Quentin knows the truth: McCutcheon killed Otto by using the Cresswell. How does Quentin know for sure that this is what happened? As he was examining his uncle's dead body, he looked up to see the Cresswell staring at him from outside the window of his uncle's one-room house. Spooky, eh?

"Uncle Otto's Truck" was included in the DAW Books anthology *The Year's Best Horror Stories Series XII* in 1984, and deservedly so. It is one of King's scariest tales. (The story was later collected in King's own *Skeleton Crew*.)

☠ **C. V.** ☠

Main Characters

Otto Schenck, Quentin Schenck, George McCutcheon, Billy Dodd, The Selectman, Baker, Carl Durkin.

Did You Know?

In "Uncle Otto's Truck," Quentin Schenck tells us that his Uncle's Cresswell truck "gave up in spectacular fashion. It went like the wonderful one-hoss shay in the Holmes poem." King is referring here to the poem "The Deacon's Masterpiece" by Oliver Wendell Holmes. The 120-line poem's first stanza is:

> Have you heard of the wonderful one-hoss shay,
> That was built in such a logical way
> It ran a hundred years to a day,
> And then, of a sudden, it—ah, but stay,
> I'll tell you what happened without delay,
> Scaring the parson into fits,
> Frightening people out of their wits, —
> Have you ever heard of that, I say?

> For those interested, the complete poem is available on line at:
> *www.library.utoronto.ca/utel/rp/poems/holmes9.html*

What I Really Liked About It

The moment when Quentin looks up and sees the Cresswell outside the window of his uncle's house. That scene can actually make you *jump*.

Film Adaptations

None.

81

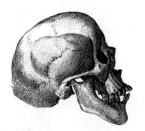

"Head Down"
(1990)

"What are they going to take with them?" I ask Dave.

Why it made the top 100:

In this nonfiction essay, "Head Down," Stephen King does what he does best in his finest fiction: he paints a portrait of vividly drawn characters engulfed in high drama and faced with crises of will and tests of faith unlike any they have ever faced before.

This essay (which King describes as being more like a diary) tells the story of the Bangor West All-Star Little League Team's quest for the 1989 Maine State Championship. (They won.)

King's son Owen played on the team and King was there at practices and away games, watching everything that went on. He was taking voluminous notes on not only the games, but on the kids and the coaches and the parents involved in what, for many 12-and 13-year-old kids, is an adolescent rite of passage.

The sky-high and rock-bottom-low emotions of being on a Little League team are of enormous interest to King. Reading "Head Down," it is starkly obvious that he *paid attention* during the many weeks it took for his son's team to rise to the top of the Maine Little League and earn that year's championship.

The King Speaks

"My method of working when I feel out of my depth is brutally simple: I lower my own head and run as fast as I can, as long as I can. That was what I did here, gathering documentation like a mad packrat and simply trying to keep up with the team. .... Hard or not, 'Head Down' was the opportunity of a lifetime, and before I was done, Chip McGrath of *The New Yorker* had coaxed the best nonfiction writing of my life out of me."

—From "Notes" in *Nightmares & Dreamscapes*

The little things that make King's fictional characters so true to life are also here in this piece. King notices how the best batters stand; he notices the horrified expression on the face of a pitcher terribly shaken by accidentally hitting two batters in a row; he notices the palpable excitement a bunch of 12-year-old boys exude as they study a breast-examination ad in the latest *People Magazine*. ("You can't see everything," one of them explains, "but you can see quite a lot.")

As indicated in "The King Speaks," a decade ago, King considered this essay the finest nonfiction writing he had done to date. No doubt about it, "Head Down" is a superior piece of nonfiction writing, but it would be very interesting to know if King now still considers this his best nonfiction writing, 10 years after it was written.

If yes, then it is clearly one of the best things he has ever written. If it has been usurped by something new in King's mind, then that, too, would be fascinating to know.

☙ **C. V.** ☙

Main Characters

The Bangor West All-Star Little League Team, Ron St. Pierre, Dave Mansfield, Neil Waterman, the Bangor All-Star's opponent teams.

Did You Know?

"Head Down," which originally appeared as a "Sporting Life" article in *The New Yorker* on April 16, 1990, was reprinted in *The Best American Sports Writing, 1991* (which was edited by the esteemed David Halberstam), as well as in King's own *Nightmares & Dreamscapes*.

 ## What I Really Liked About It

Even though I am most definitely not a sports fan, "Head Down" reads so much like a short story that even a non-fan like myself could get caught up in the drama. (Interestingly, it seems that even King himself realized how much the piece read like a fictional narrative. In his "Author's Note" leading off the piece, King writes, "I am breaking in here, Constant Reader, to make you aware that this is *not* a story but an essay—almost a diary.")

 ## Film Adaptations

None.

NUMBER 82

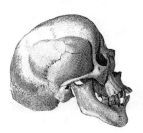

"My Little Serrated Security Blanket" (1995)

Boy, I think, you are one sick American.

Why it made the top 100:

This brief nonfiction essay (around 500 words) is Stephen King having a great deal of fun in a very well-written piece. He is imagining the kind of damage an ice ax could do to the human body, even though he admits that he "tries not" to think of murder when he looks at the DMM Predator. (We have come to accept that this kind of contemplation is, after all, part and parcel of Stephen King's official job description, right?)

I especially like King's realization that the holes the business end of the ax could make in a human body would be "lozenge-shaped." In fact, he even pinpoints the specific areas he would "apply" the ax to: the gut, throat, forehead, nape of the neck, and orbit of the eyeball. And he even knows how far he would put it in: to the "11th serration." It is after this macabre musing that King metaphorically shakes his head, laughs, and pronounces himself "one sick American."

"My Little Serrated Security Blanket" was written for *Outside* magazine and appeared in their December 1995 issue. The introductory tag line to the article read, "The blacksmith of horror rejoices in the potentialities of an ice ax" and the piece has never been reprinted. ("Blacksmith of horror"...that's a new one, eh? Also, on the Index page of *Outside Online*, King was also described as the "laureate of gore.") This essay is online and can be read in its entirety at the following URL:

Outsidemag.com/magazine/1295/12f_king.html

☠ **C. V.** ☠

Main Characters

Stephen King...and a rather nasty ice ax.

Did You Know?

In a hilarious instance of truly bizarre synchronicity, the same issue of *Outside* that published King's grisly ode to wood-chopping mayhem also included a jaw-droppingly perky tribute to top-of-the-line *First Aid kits* by none other than our national Doyenne of Perkiness, Neat Kitchen Cabinets, and the Glue Gun, Martha Stewart. (In *her* tagline, *Outside* described Stewart as "Homemaking's High Priestess." That works, eh?)

What I Really Liked About It

King's macabre sense of humor throughout the piece.

Film Adaptations

None (although the possibilities are endless, wouldn't you agree?)

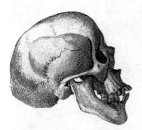

*"You Know They Got
a Hell of a Band"
(1992)*

When does the show start?

Why it made the top 100:

(Poppa-oo-mow-mow.)

On a sightseeing trip through Oregon, Clark and Mary Willingham start out lost, and end up...trapped.

Driving through the state in their Mercedes, Clark and Mary ultimately arrive in what they perceive to be a quaint, northwestern town with the prosaic name of Rock and Roll Heaven. King describes the burg as "a perfect jewel of a town nestled in a small, shallow valley like a dimple" and, at first, they are delighted to have found an oasis of comfort and civilization out in the boonies.

As is often the case with King's female characters (many of whom are far more intuitive than his male characters); Mary Willingham immediately gets a bad vibe about Rock and Roll Heaven. At first, Mary teases Clark, reciting to him Rod Serling's classic "There's a signpost up ahead..." line as they approach the town. And upon arriving in town, the small, clean Rock-a-Boogie Restaurant "went a fair distance toward allaying Mary's fears."

This feeling is short-lived, however, as Mary begins to sense that the people in town are in some way known to her. "They look familiar to me," she tells her husband, referring to two guys she sees who are actually Ronnie Van Zant and Duane Allman, both of whom, Mary knew, were rock stars who also happened to be dead.

Alarm bells go off in Mary's head, but it's too late. Refusing to heed a warning scribbled on a napkin by a waitress/rock hostage ("GET OUT WHILE YOU STILL CAN"), Clark seals their fate. He and his wife are doomed to remain in Rock and Roll Heaven forever, as part of a captive audience for dead rockers, who put on a concert every night and who carry out *literally* the rock motto and rallying cry, "Rock and roll will never die."

GEORGE BEAHM

Stephen King at a Rock Bottom Remainders concert in Bangor, Maine; the concert benefited a local charity

And neither will their audience, a hapless group of unfortunate souls who are lost to the world and who will never age. Just like rock and roll.

Party on, Clark. Party on, Mary.

I guess there's always a signpost up ahead somewhere.

☠ **C. V.** ☠

 Main Characters

Clark Willingham, Mary Willingham, Steve Earle and the Dukes, Wilson Pickett, Al Green, Pop Staples, Lou Reed, Terry Brooks, Stephen Donaldson, J. R. R. Tolkien, Ralph Ginzberg, Norman Rockwell, Currier & Ives, Ray Bradbury, The Moonglows, The Five Satins, Shep and the Limelites, La Vern Baker, Chubby Checker, The Big Bopper, Sam Cooke, Janis Joplin, Rick Nelson, Roy Orbison, Buddy Holly, Gary Busey, Lynyrd Skynyrd, Ronnie Van Zant, Duane Allman, John Lennon, Jim Morrison, Jimi Hendrix, Otis Redding, Elvis Presley, Sissy Thomas, Frankie Lymon, Crystal, Alan Freed, Freddie Mercury, Johnny Ace, Keith Moon, Brian Jones, Florence Ballard, Mary Wells, Cass Elliot, King Curtis, Johnny Burnette, Slim Harpo, Bob "Bear" Hite, Stevie Ray Vaughn, Steve Gaines, Marvin Gaye.

The King Speaks

"What I felt here—the impetus for the story—was how authentically creepy it is that so many rockers have died young, or under nasty circumstances; it's an actuarial expert's nightmare."

—From "Notes" in *Nightmares & Dreamscapes*

Did You Know?

The title of this story comes from an old Righteous Brothers song called "Rock and Roll Heaven," which includes the lyric, "If there's a rock and roll heaven, you know they got a hell of a band."

What I Really Liked About It

The fully-realized gestalt of a town populated by dead rock stars. King makes us see Roy Orbison and Janis Joplin in the diner and Jim Morrison hanging out on a corner. Great fun.

Film Adaptations

None, although this story could make one hell of a movie—if they can get past the awkwardness often associated with an actor playing someone iconic; someone known around the world, like Elvis or Jim Morrison or Roy Orbison. This was the problem (for me anyway) with the 1999 VH1 movie *Two of Us*, about a meeting between John Lennon and Paul McCartney in 1978. I just could not get past the fact that two actors were *pretending* to be John and Paul. A movie version of "Hell of a Band" would present the same kinds of problems, but if done right (maybe with digital recreations?) this could be one kick-ass flick.

84

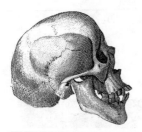

"The Bogeyboys"
(May 26, 1999)

This is a violent society.

Why it made the top 100:

The Columbine High School shootings took place on Tuesday, April 20, 1999.

King delivered "The Bogeyboys"—his 1999 Keynote Address to the Vermont Library Conference—about a month after the Columbine massacre, when the images of a gravely wounded student being dropped out a window and the term "Trenchcoat Mafia" were still fresh in America's collective consciousness.

Now, two years later, does King's trenchant analysis of not only what went wrong with Dylan Klebold and Eric Harris, but what is wrong with American society, still hold up?

Yes, and King's thoughts about what transforms previously "good kids" into "bogeyboys" is even more insightful now that the smoke has cleared and a renovated Columbine is home to students who are desperately trying not to let what happened in their school frighten them too much. As King tells us, "Our fear spawns a creature with no face, one I know very well: it's the bogeyman. When kids die on the highway, it's sad but not nationwide news. When the bogeyman strikes, however...that's different. Then everyone, even the politicians, take notice."

"The Bogeyboys" is an important American writer thinking through an American tragedy, and trying to make some sense of it. Stephen King is uniquely qualified to comment on what happened at Columbine. Following a Kentucky school shooting in which Michael Carneal killed three of his classmates, a copy of Stephen King's novel *Rage* was found in the killer's locker. *Rage* is about a high school student who brings a gun to school, shoots a teacher, and then holds his classmates hostage. Because of the Kentucky shooting and other reasons, King has asked his publishers to render *Rage* out of print.

Stephen King used his forum of a keynote address to discuss, and try to understand, *why* the shooters did what they did. Was it mental instability? Toxic cultural poisoning? Easy access to guns? All of the above?

King assigns primary blame for the creation of Klebold and Harris to two things: the easy availability of guns and America's violent culture.

"Isn't it fair to say," King says, "that in America, one of the great religions is The Holy Church of the Nine-Millimeter? The gun people don't like to hear it, but I think it has to be said."

Guns, King tells us, are too easy for bogeyboys with violent temperaments to get their hands on.

But is a restriction on guns going to solve the problem?

No, not completely, and King is honest enough to acknowledge that popular culture can influence what he describes eloquently as the "already-amplified teenage culture-politic."

"Yes," King declares, "there needs to be a re-examination of America's violent culture of the imagination. It needs to be done soberly and calmly; a witch-hunt won't help. Never mind burning Marilyn Manson's records in great fundamentalist bonfires or removing Anne Rice novels from the local library...It's time for an examination of why Americans of all ages are so drawn to armed conflict (*Rambo*), unarmed conflict (World Wrestling Federation), and images of violence."

Stephen King's "The Bogeyboys" is an important contribution to the ongoing dialogue in this country about how something like Columbine could happen; why we didn't see it coming; and how we can prevent something like it from happening again in the future.

☠ **C. V.** ☠

 Main Characters

Mark Twain, Jerry Springer, Eric Harris, Dylan Klebold, Carrie White, Charlie Decker, Todd Bowden, Thomas Solomon, the NRA, Michael Carneal, John Steinbeck, Upton

The King Speaks

"There are factors in the Carneal case which make it doubtful that *Rage* was the defining factor, but I fully recognize that it is in my own self-interest to feel just that way; that I am prejudiced in my own behalf. I also recognize the fact that a novel such as *Rage* may act as an accelerant on a troubled mind; one cannot divorce the presence of my book in that kid's locker from what he did any more than one can divorce the gruesome sex-murders committed by Ted Bundy from his extensive collection of bondage-oriented porno magazines. To argue free speech in the face of such an obvious linkage (or to suggest that others may obtain a catharsis from such material which allows them to be atrocious only in their fantasies) seems to me immoral."

—From "The Bogeyboys"

Sinclair, Jackie Chan, Walker, Texas Ranger, Metallica, Marilyn Manson, AC/DC, the ACLU, John Tomlin, Rachel Scott, Anne Rice, Rambo, the World Wrestling Federation.

Did You Know?

The complete text of Stephen King's Keynote Address "The Bogeyboys" can be read online at: *members.tripod.com/charnelhouse/index.html*.

What I Really Liked About It

King's sober-minded analysis of events, which carry even more weight because of his willingness to acknowledge that popular culture can sometimes contribute to the development of people like the Columbine shooters.

Film Adaptations

None.

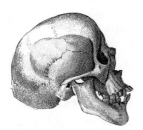

"I Am the Doorway"
(1971)

*Beneath the bandages, my new eyes stared blindly
into the darkness the bandages forced on them. They itched.*

Why it made the top 100:

Even though "I Am the Doorway" has all the trappings of science fiction—space ships, travel to other planets, malevolent aliens, etc.—King deftly uses these genre elements to write an unabashed *horror* story, brilliantly blurring the barrier between the two genres and creating the memorable hybrid genre of scifi-horror.

A deep-space astronaut named Arthur returns from a mission to Venus "infected" with creatures who burrow up through the skin of his fingers and grow eyes with which they view our world.

The crippled and wheelchair-bound Arthur (he was seriously injured during re-entry) is the "doorway" for these creatures who can control his body at will and make him kill at their command.

The eye creatures first make the astronaut kill an innocent young boy who made a living as a beachcomber. They blew up the boy's head "[a]s if someone had scooped out his brains and put a hand grenade in his skull."

After Arthur tells his friend Richard the whole story of his and his crewmate Cory's trip to Venus and his subsequent infestation, Richard agrees to dig up the murdered boy's grave. The boy's body is gone, however, and the eye creatures then eliminate Richard by making Arthur summon a lightning bolt from the sky.

After Richard's death, Arthur decides he can no longer let these eye beings live and so he douses his hands with kerosene and plunges them into the fireplace. He ends up with hooks for hands with which he can type and even tie his own shoelaces, but burning his hands off did not solve Arthur's "doorway" problem. Thus, at the conclusion of the story, Arthur is preparing to kill himself with a shotgun.

Why? "It started again three weeks ago, you see," Arthur tells us. "There is a perfect circle of twelve golden eyes on my chest."

King has Arthur fearing that the early manifestations of his "infestation" is actually leprosy, utilizing the theme of the horrors of physical "decay"—a leitmotif that he will return to again and again in his work. King will later make very effective use, for instance, of the metaphor of cancer being an alien creature eating a person up from the inside out. In "I Am the Doorway," he actually has the enemy alien creatures *living* inside Arthur and using him as a host for their murderous deeds. In 2001's *Dreamcatcher*, King revisits this theme in an even more horrific scenario.

"I Am the Doorway" was written in 1971, a year after the Russian unmanned spacecraft *Venera-7* landed on Venus and transmitted data from the surface of the planet back to Earth. NASA currently lists no planned manned missions to either Venus or Mars through at least 2010.

☠ **C. V.** ☠

Main Characters

Arthur, Cory, The Boy, Richard.

Did You Know?

"I Am the Doorway" was the story chosen as the source for the cover illustration for the Signet paperback edition of *Night Shift*. The (uncredited) cover drawing shows a right hand half wrapped (unwrapped, actually) in gauze; the top half of the hand revealing eight beautiful blue eyes scattered across the fingers and palm.

What I Really Liked About It

This is one of those stories that grow on you after you have read it and the magnitude of what has happened to the main character really begins to register with you. A sentient,

The King Speaks

"My own feeling...is that almost all horror stories mirror specific areas of free-forming anxieties. And that sounds like a mouthful, a lot of intellectual bullshit, but what I mean is, when you read a horror novel or see a horror film, you make a connection with the things you're afraid of in your own life."

—Interview with Charles Grant, April 1981

alien creature living inside a human, burrowing up through the skin, and forcing him to do their bidding. Yikes. I also especially like the resolute tone in Arthur's narration: no panic, no hysteria, just the cold, horrific facts. "I Am the Doorway" is a scifi/horror gem.

Film Adaptations

None.

86

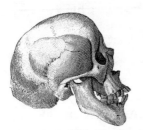

"Cain Rose Up"
(1968, 1985)

---

*Garrish put the window up and rested his elbows on the ledge,
not letting the barrel of the .352 project out into the sunlight.*

Why it made the top 100:

In "Cain Rose Up," a depressed college student named Curt Garrish succumbs to the frustration of college life by randomly shooting people with a rifle from his dorm window.

This story, originally published when King was in college, was revised somewhat for its *Skeleton Crew* appearance. The new version is more visceral and effectively communicates Garrish's completely delusional state of mind. A state of mind that actually rationalizes his brutal murders as a fulfillment of a what he perceives as a mandate from God that he believes is hidden in Genesis: "God made the world in His image, and if you don't eat the world, the world eats you." The story concludes with Garrish murmuring to himself, "Good God, let's eat."

Maine horror writer and fellow University of Maine student Rick Hautala remembers reading "Cain Rose Up" in the University of Maine student literary magazine *Ubris* in 1968 and thinking that "this story—and this King-fella—were somehow...different."

The King Speaks

[When asked "Where do you think you'd be today without your writing talent?"] "I might very well have ended up there in the Texas tower with Charlie Whitman, working out my demons with a high-powered telescopic rifle instead of a word processor. I mean, I know that guy Whitman. My writing has kept me out of that tower."

—From a June 1983 interview with *Playboy* magazine

"Cain Rose Up" was the first Stephen King story Hautala had ever read and he was instantly hooked on everything King wrote from that point on. (King and Hautala later became friends and King wrote favorable blurbs for Hautala's first two novels, *Moondeath* and *Moonbog*. For an interview with Hautala in which he talks about King, see my book, *The Complete Stephen King Encyclopedia*.)

In "Cain Rose Up," Garrish's father is a Methodist minister. This fact, combined with Garrish's twisted interpretation of the Bible, suggests some kind of subtle psychological damage caused by religion—a theme King would later re-visit in *Carrie* (remember Margaret White?), *The Dead Zone* (Vera Smith), and other works.

The locales in "Cain Rose Up" parallel real landmarks and buildings on the campus of the University of Maine, King's alma mater. In the story, "Carlton Memorial" was actually Androscoggin Hall on the UMO campus.

Some of the pop culture references in "Cain Rose Up" include Humphrey Bogart, *Playboy* magazine, Howdy Doody, Pig Pen, and a Ford station wagon. There is also a reference in the story to Rodin's classic sculpture, "The Thinker."

For possible added insight into the story of Curt Garrish, see "Nona" (Chapter 48, also in *Skeleton Crew*). It is feasible that Curt and The Prisoner (the narrator) from "Nona" were college roommates. If this is actually the case (Steve?), that sure was some school, eh?

☠ **C. V.** ☠

Main Characters

Curt Garrish, Harry the Beaver, Bailey, Pig Pen, Rollins, and, of course, Cain and Abel.

The King Speaks

"I think most men are wired up to perform acts of violence, usually defensive, but I think that we're still very primitive creatures, and that we have a real tendency toward violence. Most of us are like...well, most of us are like most airplanes. Remember TWA Flight 800, the one that exploded over Long Island Sound? That was an electrical problem, or at least they feel that it was probably an electrical problem, and a fire started in the wiring. And when you see a guy who suddenly snaps, a guy who goes nuts, a Charles Whitman, who goes to the top of the Texas tower and shoots a whole bunch of people, when a guy goes postal—that's the current slang—that's a guy with a fire in his wires, basically."

—From a September 24, 1988 interview with *Salon* magazine

Did You Know?

"Cain Rose Up" fictionalizes the real-life murderous rampage of Charles Whitman, a former Marine and academically overloaded college student who went on a shooting spree from a 27-story tower on August 1, 1966 at the University of Texas in Austin. Whitman ultimately killed 12 people and wounded 33 others. King had been fascinated by Whitman's story and decided to try his hand at putting himself into the mind of a student pushed just a tad too far. He was, as the story reveals, extremely successful at "understanding" Whitman and those like him.

What I Really Liked About It

The sense of being completely inside the mind of a guy who has "fire in his wires." As in the best fiction, in "Cain Rose Up," King does not *tell* us Curt is insane; he calmly, dispassionately, and ultimately horrifyingly, *shows* us.

Film Adaptations

None. (Interestingly, the novella *Apt Pupil* concludes with a similar sniper scene as in "Cain Rose Up," but the movie version of the novella rewrites King's ending to make it more palatable, I suppose.)

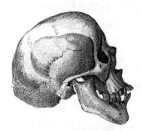

"I Know What You Need" (1976)

As the days passed it occurred to her that she had never met anyone, male or female, that seemed to understand her moods and needs so completely or so wordlessly.

Why it made the top 100:

"I Know What You Need" from *Night Shift* is one of King's "college" stories—those handful of tales with college students as the main characters and a college campus as the setting. These stories reflect King's interest in creating stories using real-world elements in an attempt to capture a time and a place with flawless accuracy. Others of this "genre" include "Strawberry Spring" and "Cain Rose Up"; as well as the novel *Hearts in Atlantis*.

Throughout his career, it is also worth noting that King has also used grammar school and high school settings (as well as teachers as main characters) for several other tales. These include *Carrie*, *The Shining*, *Rage* (especially), "Sometimes They Come Back," *The Dead Zone*, *Christine*, "Here There Be Tygers," and "Suffer the Little Children."

In "I Know What You Need," a short, skinny weirdo—Ed Hamner—who doesn't wash his hair too often and who wears mismatched socks approaches Liz Rogan one evening in the library as she's desperately cramming for her Sociology final. The first thing Edward Jackson Hamner Junior says to Liz is "I know what you need," and it turns out he's not kidding. After some hesitation on Liz's part to get involved with this guy, she eventually gives in and Ed provides her with a verbatim transcript of last year's Sociology final exam. With this kind of help, she scores a 97 on her test, guaranteeing her scholarship for next year.

Thus begins an odd relationship that will end in Liz's boyfriend Tony getting killed in a suspicious car accident; and with Liz learning that Ed Hamner has some truly dark secrets involving black magic and voodoo. To her horror, Liz will learn that Ed not only used voodoo to make her fall in love with him, but that he was also responsible for Tony's death.

Liz ultimately confronts Ed in his dark apartment where she finds a locked closet containing texts like *Haitian Voodoo* and *The Necronomicon*; as well as a little toy red Fiat with a piece of Tony's shirt attached to the front.

The story ends with Liz throwing the car off a bridge and finally managing to break free from Ed Hamner's nefarious hold.

I like this story, especially the tone and the flawless portrayal of the college student's angst over grades.

One nice touch is King having Liz's roommate Alice lying in bed reading the erotic novel *The Story of O*. That blatant acknowledgment of Alice's sexuality plus her enterprise in finding out the truth about Ed Hamner made me want to know more about the smart and confident, "comes-from-money" Alice. So far, this character has not popped up in any later King works...but there's always hope, right?

☠ **C. V.** ☠

Main Characters

Liz Rogan, Edward Jackson Hamner Junior, Tony, Alice.

Did You Know?

The demonic book *The Necronomicon* mentioned in King's story does not exist. Horror writer H. P. Lovecraft invented it in 1927 in an essay. Here is an excerpt from Lovecraft's discussion of the diabolic *Necronomicon*:

> Composed by Abdul Alhazred, a mad poet of Sanaá, in Yemen, who is said to have flourished during the period of the Ommiade caliphs, circa 700 A.D. He visited the ruins of Babylon and the subterranean secrets of Memphis and spent ten years alone in the great southern desert of Arabia—the

Roba el Khaliyeh or "Empty Space" of the ancients—and "Dahna" or "Crimson" desert of the modern Arabs, which is held to be inhabited by protective evil spirits and monsters of death. Of this desert many strange and unbelievable marvels are told by those who pretend to have penetrated it. In his last years Alhazred dwelt in Damascus, where the Necronomicon (Al Azif) was written, and of his final death or disappearance (738 A.D.) many terrible and conflicting things are told.

What I Really Liked About It

One of the scariest scenes in the story is Liz's "lying in an open grave" nightmare—this is a very eerie and extremely effective scene.

Film Adaptations

None. Although in *The Stephen King Universe* by Stanley Wiater, Christopher Golden, and Hank Wagner, the authors note the following: "The powers of Ed Hamner in 'I Know What You Need' are quite similar to those of the main character of a classic *The Twilight Zone* TV series episode which might have inspired King. Its title? 'What You Need.' "

NUMBER 88

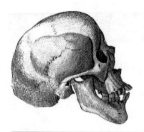

"The Monkey" (1980)

Jang-jang-jang-jang, who's dead?

Why it made the top 100:

"The Monkey" is a chilling, well-written story that struck a (simian) chord with horror fans: Including its 1985 *Skeleton Crew* appearance (after its 1980 *Gallery* debut), "The Monkey" has been reprinted almost 10 times.

When Hal Shelburn was a young boy, he found an old wind-up monkey in the back of a storage area in his Aunt Ida's house in Maine. The monkey was in a Ralston-Purina cereal box and Hal didn't think it even worked anymore. He put it on a shelf in his bedroom and forgot about it.

The monkey, however, was not really a toy: It was actually a cursed demonic murderer who could kill at will—just by banging together its worn brass cymbals.

Shortly after Hal "liberated" the monkey from its hiding place, the deaths began. First, it was Hal's best friend Johnny McCabe who fell from a treehouse and broke his neck. Then it was Aunt Ida's Manx cat. Soon Uncle Will's dog Daisy was dead; as was Hal's brother Bill's friend Charlie Silverman. And then the worst death of all occurred:

The monkey clanged its cymbals and Hal and Bill's mother dropped dead of a cerebral embolism while standing at the water cooler at work.

Hal decided to do away with the monkey once and for all and, after covering its cymbals so it couldn't bang them together and kill anyone else, he threw it down the artesian well in the backyard of Aunt Ida and Uncle Will's house.

Twenty years go by and Hal is now a software engineer recently laid off from National Aerodyne in California. The only job that he could find in his field was in Texas—for *less* money—and so he moved his family to Arnette where they all tried to make the best of it. (Arnette, Texas, the place where Charles Campion "touched down" at Hapscomb's Texaco Station after he was infected by the Project Blue virus in *The Stand*.)

During a visit home to Maine, Hal's eldest son Dennis finds the monkey—*the same monkey* Hal threw down the well those many years ago—in an old Ralston-Purina in the attic of the old home place. Thus begins Hal's *second* terrifying battle to rid the world of the demonic toy once and for all.

In "The Monkey," the newspaper that ran the story "Mystery of the Dead Fish" was *The Bridgton News*. Bridgton was the Maine town where Dave Drayton and his family lived in *The Mist* and is also the real Maine town where King and his family has a house on Long Lake.

The original manuscript of "The Monkey" is in the Stephen King Archives in the Special Collections Library at Stephen King's alma mater, the University of Maine in Orono, Maine.

☠ **C. V.** ☠

Main Characters

Hal Shelburn, Dennis Shelburn, Bill Shelburn, Colette Shelburn, Mr. and Mrs. Shelburn (Hal's mother and father), Petey Shelburn, Terry Shelburn, Uncle Will, Aunt Ida, Johnny McCabe, The Monkey.

Did You Know?

King got the idea for the monkey during a visit to New York. He passed a street merchant who had a battalion of little toy wind-up monkeys lined up on a blanket on a street corner and the sight so frightened King that he returned to his hotel room and wrote almost the whole story in longhand.

The King Speaks

"[The monkeys] looked really scary to me, and I spent the rest of my walk back to the hotel wondering why. I decided it was because they reminded me of the lady with the shear...the one who cuts everyone's thread one day." (See Chapter 11 for more on "cutting the thread.")

- From "Notes" in *Skeleton Crew*

What I Really Liked About It

The way King brilliantly communicates the ominous presence of the monkey. It is a ridiculous little toy, but King is able to make us fear it nonetheless.

Film Adaptations

None.

Audio Adaptations

"The Monkey" was once adapted by horror writer Dennis Etchison for a radio performance on Halloween night, October 31, 1985, to benefit UNICEF.

Number 89

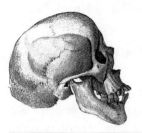

"Rainy Season" (1989)

The air was stuffed with falling shapes.

Why it made the top 100:

"Rainy Season" is a terrific horror story, but also a sly commentary on tourism and how natives feel about those seasonal visitors—"summer people"—who pack up and leave when they have exhausted their interest in a place, and need to get back to something more important. ("You come to our town and don't respect our customs? Well, we'll just see about that.")

Every seven years in Willow, Maine, it rains toads. And not just your ordinary, garden variety toads. *Killer* toads. *Carnivorous* toads. It's all part of the "ritual," a recurring event that natives expect, accept, and prepare for, but do not understand. All they know is that every seven years, when visitors come to town on June 17th, a local always warns them about the rain of predacious toads expected that evening. The visitors always scoff, the toads always come, the visitors are always eaten, the toads always melt away in the morning sun, and the town then enjoys another seven years of peace and prosperity.

In "Rainy Season," the hapless, uncooperative visitors are John and Elise Graham. John has rented the Hempstead Place in Willow for the summer to work on a book about the in-migration of the French during the 17th century. When they arrive in town, they are duly informed by old-timer Henry Eden that it would probably be wiser if they stayed out of town for the evening. In fact, Laura Stanton, Henry's significant other, has even reserved a motel room for them.

But why? The Grahams want to know. Henry and Laura then fulfill their part of the "ritual" by telling them that, because it is June 17th, killer toads will rain from the sky that evening.

As the old couple expects them to do, John and Elise beat a fast path back to their car and do stay the night in the Hempstead Place.

The toads start falling before midnight and John and Elise end up being toad food. Another seven-year cycle has ended.

"Rainy Season" is a great deal of fun, mainly because King plays it straight. There are no *Creepshow*-style histrionics, nor comic book conventions—we believe that toads fall from the sky and that the way John and Elise react is the way *normal* people would react. Unbelieving at first, but then desperate to survive when the truth is made clear.

☠ **C. V.** ☠

Main Characters

John Graham, Elise Graham, Henry Eden, Laura Stanton, a rain of killer toads.

Did You Know?

"Rainy Season" made its original appearance (it can now be found in *Nightmares & Dreamscapes*) in a horror magazine called *Midnight Graffiti* in their spring 1989 issue. According to editor Jessie Horsting, King sent the story in unsolicited to the then-new mag, allowing Horsting and company to build an entire "Stephen King Issue" around the story. King accepted scale payment for the tale and this issue is now a highly sought-after collectible.

What I Really Liked About It

Why does it rain toads every seven years in Willow, Maine? It just *does*. I especially like the way King just presents this supernatural event as a given and then thrusts ordinary people into the eye of the storm. One cannot help but wonder if he or she would have taken Henry and Laura's advice or ignored it the way the Grahams did.

The King Speaks

"Enclosed is a short story, 'Rainy Season,' which I thought might be right for *Graffiti*. It's pretty gross."

> —Stephen King's cover letter to *Midnight Graffiti*
> accompanying his submission of this story.

Film Adaptations

None (although I'll bet George Romero would have a ball with this one).

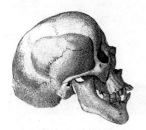

"Sneakers"
(1988, 1993)

"Weren't any dead flies in my stall."

Why it made the top 100:

"Sneakers" is Stephen King having fun with music—something he would do for real a few years later when he toured with his band The Rock Bottom Remainders. (Performing live and, lately, recording, is an ongoing avocation of King's.)

"Sneakers" is about a haunted toilet stall. King has said that he figured since he had written about haunted houses, it was now time to write about "a haunted shithouse." King acknowledges the black humor in this brainstorm by having John Tell muse to himself that "gruesome as the story had been, there was something comic in the idea of a ghost haunting a shithouse."

"Sneakers" contains some terrific music references: The three main characters of the story are John, Paul, and George. (Alas, King did not deign to work a "Ringo" into the mix.)

King made an interesting revision when he reprinted "Sneakers" in *Nightmares & Dreamscapes*. In the original appearance of the story (in the limited edition *Night Visions 5* edited by Douglas E. Winter), King has Paul Jannings describe The Dead

Beats by saying, "These guys make The Dead Kennedys sound like the Beatles." In the *Nightmares & Dreamscapes* version, King changes "Dead Kennedys" to "Butthole Surfers."

"Sneakers" seems to be King's rehearsal for his longer, more ambitious rock and roll story "You Know They Got a Hell of a Band" which was first published in the anthology *Shock Rock* in 1992. (See Chapter 83.)

John Tell first sees a pair of dirty white sneakers when he glances under the door of the first stall in the third floor bathroom in the building where he is working as a recording mixer on the new Dead Beats' album. (King tells us that The Dead Beats were "composed of four dull bastards and one dull bitch" and that they were "personally repulsive and professionally incompetent.")

John is working for legendary producer Paul Jannings. As the weeks go by, he notices

GEORGE BEAHM

Stephen King at a Rock Bottom Remainders concert in Bangor, Maine

that the cruddy sneakers are always in the same place no matter when he visits the bathroom, only as time passes, dead flies and other insects begin piling up around the crummy, mislaced shoes.

John learns that the sneakers belong to the ghost of a cocaine deliveryman who was stabbed to death with a pencil in the eye back in the 1970s. After acknowledging that he is, indeed, seeing what he is seeing, John is told by Sneakers himself who killed him, leaving John stunned to learn who the killer was.

Because he has told the truth about who murdered him, Sneakers is now in peace and disappears from the third floor stall to travel to his final resting place, wherever it may be.

John makes a personal decision (requiring an ugly confrontation with someone he thought was a friend) about how to handle the information he has been given. The story ends with John returning to a "regular" (pun intended) non-haunted life, reading *Rolling Stone* and not being afraid to enter the third floor bathroom anymore.

What starts out as a ghost story evolves into a mystery with supernatural elements that also tells the story of John Tell's redemption.

◻ **C. V.** ◻

The King Speaks

"I played briefly in a band during my senior year—organ, not guitar—but I didn't last much past the original rehearsals. My rock-and-roll aspirations (such as they were) foundered, as almost all my other extra-curricular activities did, on the fact that I lived seven miles from town, and had no car even after I had managed to get my driver's license."

—From "The Neighborhood of the Beast"

Main Characters

John Tell, Paul Jannings, Georgie Ronkler (no Ringo), Sneakers.

Did You Know?

There really is a Dead Beats band. (They're a hip hop band.) Also, it is possible that the name of the recording studio in the story—Tabori Studios—is an *hommage* to the British author and founder of the International Writers Guild, Paul Tabor, who wrote fantasy and science fiction under the pseudonym "Paul Tabori." Tabori's novels include *The Green Rain* (1961); *The Survivor* (1964); *The Invisible Eye* (1967); *The Doomsday Brain* (1968); *The Torture Machine* (1969); *The Demons of Sandora* (1970).

What I Really Liked About It

The way King shows us John Tell's dawning realization that he's not crazy and that he is seeing Sneakers for a reason.

Film Adaptations

None.

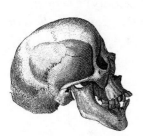

"Myth, Belief, Faith and Ripley's Believe It or Not!" (1993)

Most of all, I do believe in spooks, I do believe in spooks, I do believe in spooks.

Why it made the top 100:

A couple that once lived next door to my wife and I were of a breed found in every neighborhood: call them The Seasonal Decorators. You know the type. Cardboard turkeys and cornucopia for Thanksgiving; lights, wreaths, and a tree in the front window for Christmas and New Year's; hearts on the door for Valentine's Day; flags for Memorial Day (that stay up right through the Fourth of July); and, of course, witches and ghosts for Halloween.

One night when I pulled into our driveway, I saw a horribly dressed bum leaning against a tree on my neighbor's lawn. Let me admit to you all right up front that he scared the shit out of me. The dramatic effect of my headlights swinging over my neighbor's lawn and then suddenly spotlighting this ragged old man leaning against a tree was heart-stoppingly frightening.

And immediately following the visceral terror of the visual image of this guy coming out of the dark into my line of sight came my fervent wish that I had had my gun with me. Who knew what this guy wanted, or if he was crazy, or violent, or both? And what had he done to my neighbors? And, God forbid, had he gone near my house? All of these night terrors flew through my consciousness in a millisecond ... and then I realized it was a scarecrow.

Yes, my SD (Seasonal Decorator) neighbors had gone all out that year and built a life-sized scarecrow for their front yard. (He actually looked like the scarecrow on the cover of the hardcover edition of *Nightmares & Dreamscapes*, which contains the essay we will soon be discussing.)

For a tiny slice of time (which felt, of course, like all of eternity) I *believed*—wholeheartedly—that the scarecrow was real—and a ghoul out to get me. I *believed*.

And that kind of all-encompassing, doubt-swallowing belief is what Stephen King talks about in the essay which is the subject of this chapter, "Myth, Belief, Faith and *Ripley's Believe It or Not!*," a personal piece which serves as the Introduction to his third book of short stories, the 1993 collection, *Nightmares & Dreamscapes*. (The first two books of King's short story trilogy were *Night Shift* [1978], and *Skeleton Crew* [1985]).

In this Introduction, King talks about how the *Ripley's Believe It or Not!* paperbacks from his childhood (published by, in one of those wonderful instances of synchronicity, King's future publisher, Pocket Books, an imprint of Simon and Schuster) were *scripture* to him. Every fantastic fact, amazing natural wonder, astonishing human freak lovingly chronicled in *Ripley's* was a carved-in-stone *real fact* to the young Stephen King. He already knew the mundane stuff: a dime placed on a railroad track will derail the train; the center of a tennis ball contains poisonous gas that will kill you in a heartbeat. *Ripley's* turned King on to the *fantastic*. And he believed every word.

King uses the *Ripley's* books to make the point that every story he writes has, likewise, to be *believed* first and he tells us here that every story in *N & D* passed muster.

King is eloquent about the writing process and, even here, in 1992 and 1993; he was wondering if he had said all he wanted to say and was nearing retirement. Serious King fans know he has been wrestling with the fear of self-parody for years and that he has always said he would shut down his PowerBook when he felt that that was inevitable.

If King's publications since the writing of this essay (*Insomnia, Desperation, The Green Mile*, and *Bag of Bones*) are indicative of his ongoing narrative gifts and talents (which I think they are) then it seems that he need not worry about that particular fear for some time yet.

This is one of King's all-time best nonfiction pieces.

☠ **C. V.** ☠

Main Characters

Stephen King, at various ages ... oh, and Mr. Ripley.

Did You Know?

Nightmares & Dreamscapes is one of King's most eclectic collections, containing not only a novella and short stories, but a teleplay, a nonfiction essay, a poem, and King's rewriting of a Hindu parable.

 What I Really Liked About It

The opening paragraph, which is one of King's best, and his voice at his most personal and most conversational. It sets the stage for a wonderful essay that engages Constant Reader and prepares him or her for the joys and thrills to follow.

 Film Adaptations

None.

NUMBER **92**

"Nightmares in the Sky: Gargoyles and Grotesques" (1988)

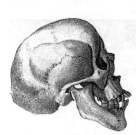

gargoyle (gär-goil) n.
1. A roof spout in the form of a grotesque or fantastic creature projecting from a gutter to carry rainwater clear of the wall.
2. A grotesque ornamental figure or projection.
[T]he act of understanding is often a kind of little death for the intuitive writer, but some things are better off dead.

Why it made the top 100:

Stephen King begins this intriguing essay (an introduction of sorts to f stop Fitzgerald's photo book) by admitting a reluctance to even tackle such an imposing project.

Asked because he was thought to be the "ideal person" to write the essay, King admits early on that his lack of training in photography and sculpture, combined with his limited knowledge of art as a discipline, made him extremely hesitant to write about architectural gargoyles. These are the stone monster-demons that peer down on us from apartments, office buildings, churches, libraries, museums, courthouses, and other stone structures.

King may have been nonplused at having such a certifiable literary identity that he would be the first one the producers of "Nightmares in the Sky" thought of ... but let's face it: *we know what they meant, don't we?*

Stephen King has metamorphosed into an adjective. When we describe something as being "Stephen King-like," almost anyone immediately knows what that suggests, right?

Much of Stephen King's nonfiction writing consists of prose that is often as entertaining and appealing as his fiction, and, his artistic insecurities aside, Stephen King delivered yet again with "Nightmares in the Sky." He came through with a wonderful essay that includes autobiographical musings; thoughts about writing and fear; reflections on TV and movies; and some genuinely intuitive ideas about morality and mythology.

King's writing in this piece, as in his best nonfiction works, is informal, conversational, and intimate, while at the same time, instructive and extraordinarily interesting. However, King is also cruelly self-effacing here, wielding his insecurity like a lash, writing in his best hairshirt, "Big-Mac-and-fries," how-can-I-be-any-good-when-I'm-this-successful? mode. Thankfully King has, for the most part, abandoned this ritualistic self-deprecation in recent years. Perhaps he realized that any writer who can create works such as *Dolores Claiborne*, *The Green Mile*, *Desperation*, and *Bag of Bones* (all published after this essay appeared) may be a tad off the mark describing his words (as King does in the essay) as "paltry things." Not to mention citing Truman Capote's blast at Jack Kerouac ("That's not writing, that's typing") when referring to his own work.

That said, though, King's (unjustified) downplaying of his own literary merit does not detract from the undeniable merits of this piece. As King muses about gargoyles and their eerie presence in cities everywhere, a question occurs to the reader. It is a question King doesn't come right out and ask, but which he inevitably leads us to with his ruminations: Why have these faces been *deliberately added* to the facades and roofs of buildings for so many centuries? Their *function* is to act as a drain for rainwater, but if form does dictate function, then all that would be necessary would be a pipe. Instead, we have grotesque *faces* serving this purpose. Granted, some gargoyles are cherubic angles; but most seem to be these leering, silently shrieking, often insane faces growing out of buildings like, as King aptly describes, "a tumor." And that leads King into a discussion of the symbolic meaning of architectural gargoyles over the ages, thereby achieving what the best art can do—provide a context that opens up the subject and, hopefully, enlightens.

"Nightmares in the Sky" is one of King's finest nonfiction efforts and is, unfortunately, out of print. There was talk recently of reissuing the book in paperback, but nothing has been published and the only way to read it is to locate it at a nearby library, or buy a used copy of the book, currently ranging in price from $25 to over $100.

☠ **C. V.** ☠

 Main Characters

Gargoyles. *Stone* gargoyles, although, as we learn in King's essay, their concreted physicality aside, these bad boys are *alive*.

The King Speaks

"Coffee-table book or not, I would suggest a coffee-table might be the worst place for this particular tome; coffee-tables, after all, are low pieces of furniture, accessible to children, and I am as serious as I can be when I say that this is no more a book for children than George Romero's *The Night of the Living Dead* is a movie for them."

—From "Nightmares in the Sky"

Did You Know?

(Note: This is one of the more obscure bits of King arcanum offered in this book. You have been warned.) In section 8 of this essay, King writes, "How is this particular effect, which changes in its specifics, but seems to maintain a constant emotional key-chord of fear, even horror, achieved?" In the January 1971 issue of *Onan*, a University of Maine student literary magazine, 24-year-old Stephen King published an untitled poem that had as its first line, "In the key-chords of dawn...." "Key-chord" as a noun is not a word in any dictionary I consulted and seems to be an original construct of Stephen King's. This essay may contain King's only other use of this word after he first used it in his untitled poem in 1971. (If any of you out there know of another time King has used the word "key-chord" in any of his works, fiction or nonfiction, would you either e-mail it to me at: *stephen@stephenspignesi.com,* or write to me in care of my publisher? Molto grazie!)

What I Really Liked About It

Once again, King very effectively makes us see the surreal in the real and the spooky in the commonplace.

Film Adaptations

None (unless you count *Ghostbusters*, ha, ha, ha).

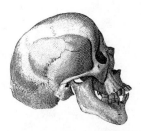

"The Ten O'Clock People"
(1993)

Welcome to the back of the bus, Pearson thought, looking at his fellow Ten O'Clock People with a species of exasperated amusement. Oh well, mustn't complain; in another ten years smokers won't even be allowed on board.

Why it made the top 100:

The truly strange premise for this terrific story is that horrible bat-like creatures (Batmen) with oozing tumors on their face and a taste for humans (especially eyeballs it seems) have infiltrated the highest levels of American business and culture (the Vice President is one).

Their determined plan is to take over the world, ultimately using the human race as their own personal All-You-Can-Eat buffet.

A few "lucky" humans—including the main character of this tale Brandon Pearson—are the only ones can see these Bat creeps in their true form. And why is it that only certain folks are gifted with the ability to see the Bats' malformed, tumor-ridden, grayish-brown, hairy visages?

Because they are all Ten O'Clock People: cigarette smokers who are in that anxious, unpleasant area between smoking like a chimney and quitting completely. The Ten O'Clock People have restricted their smoking to between five and 10 butts a day, and

The King Speaks

"The expensive buildings are now all no-smoking zones as the American people go calmly about one of the most amazing turnabouts of the twentieth century; we are purging ourselves of our bad old habit, we are doing it with hardly any fanfare, and the result has been some very odd pockets of sociological behavior. Those who refuse to give up their old habit—the Ten O'Clock People of the title—constitute one of those....I hope [the story] says something interesting about a wave of change which has, temporarily, at least, re-created some aspects of the separate-but-equal facilities of the forties and fifties."

—From "Notes" in *Nightmares & Dreamscapes*

that seems to be the intake range within which their brains develop the ability to see the Bats. The Bats, however, do not know who can, or cannot, see them.

King got the idea for "The Ten O'Clock People" while wandering around Boston one morning and noticing the groups of smokers gathered in front of their buildings having their "ten o'clock" nicotine fix.

"The Ten O'Clock People" revolves around the aforementioned Brandon Pearson, a young banker. After being stopped from screaming the first time he sees a Batman, he ends up being mentored by his savior, Duke Rhinemann. Duke is a fellow worker who can also see the Bats, and who initiates Pearson into a small society of Ten O'Clock People who meet a couple of times a week to discuss strategies for monitoring the Bats—every one of whom is a horrible monster—and to share information on what they've each recently learned about the invaders.

The conclave is helmed by a charismatic leader named Robbie Delray who the Ten O'Clock People look to for guidance and for the assurance that they will be able to survive against the Bats' murderous ways.

But at the largest meeting of the Ten O'Clock People ever—and the first one Pearson attends—they all learn that Delray has a dark secret, one that will ultimately threaten the lives of each and every one of them.

After a horrific confrontation, the story ends with Pearson traveling the country seeking out the Bats and killing as many as he and a few followers possibly can. Brand ultimately learns that, as with quitting smoking, when it came to killing Bats, you had to start somewhere.

☠ **C. V.** ☠

Main Characters

Duke Rhinemann, Brandon Pearson, Robbie Delray, assorted Ten O'Clock People, assorted Batmen.

Did You Know?

"The Ten O'Clock People" has a black hero. Duke Rhinemann is described as "good-looking young black man." When we consider King's comment about the move away from smoking creating a throwback to archaic social mores, the race of the hero can perhaps be interpreted metaphorically, as well as on a purely narrative level.

What I Really Liked About It

The fact that "The Ten O'Clock People" is a complete, full-blown, self-contained horror movie told in less than 50 book pages.

Film Adaptations

None (although this story just screams to be adapted).

Number **94**

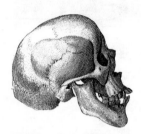

"1984, a Bad Year if You Fear Friday the 13th" (1984)

The year I'm really dreading is 1996. In that triple-whammy year I'll be 49. Can you add 4 and 9? As Mr. Rogers says, "I knew you could."

Why it made the top 100:

I have always preached (usually to the converted, I'll admit) that Stephen King boasts one of the most engaging nonfiction writing voices of today, and this informative and entertaining article for *The New York Times* once again proves that point.

King begins with a discussion of the historical origins of triskaidekaphobia, the fear of the number 13, citing the story of the 12 Norse gods invited to party at Valhalla. The uninvited Loki—the 13th god—crashed the fete, got into a beef, and Baldur, "the most popular god in the pantheon" was killed.

King then talks about the "three on a match" superstition and admits that he still refuses to light three cigarettes on one match.

The thesis of this essay, though, is that there are dreadful consequences that can befall us all in what King calls a "triple whammy" year—a year in which there are not one or two, but *three* Friday the 13ths in the span of 12 months.

☠ 304 ☠

King then looks at some of the events that took place in triple whammy years, including the terrible flooding in Indiana in 1959; a deadly military plane crash in 1956; and the fact that Jack the Ripper claimed his final victim in 1888—a three "Friday the 13th"s year. "My rational mind," King admits, "just loves information of this sort."

If Stephen King were revising this essay today, I'm betting he would add details of the tragic story of Princess Diana's fatal car accident in Paris in 1997. As you'll recall, this was probably the single biggest news story of that year and the media all reported the same details, one of which gave all triskaidekaphobics the feeling of a cold finger scraping up their spine. Diana's car crashed when her driver lost control and slammed into the *13th* support pillar of the tunnel they were driving through.

For the Stephen King fan, though, all this fascinating historical info pales when compared with the personal details King reveals in the essay. When talking about his own secret fears of the number 13 (with, as he describes it, "shamefaced honesty"), he tells us how he manages to cope with this "neurosis" (his word):

> I always take the last two steps on my back stairs as one (making 13 into 12)...When I am reading, I will not stop on page 94, page 193, page 382, et al—the digits of these numbers add up to 13.

This behavior, he rationally acknowledges, is "neurotic" (again, his word); but it is also, he believes, "safer."

King obviously did his research before writing this article. He cites historical events with surety and notes that although it might just be coincidence that bad things happen in history's triple whammy years, "veteran triskies such as myself are not convinced."

King then concludes his essay with a revealing look at Stephen King in the year 1984, a guy he describes as "doing the best he can under circumstances that would give even the hardest triskie fits." King notes that in addition to 1984 being a triple whammy year; that year he had been married 13 years; he had a daughter who was 13 years old; and he had, so far, published 13 books.

"1984, a Bad Year if You Fear Friday the 13th" is yet another example of Stephen King's talents and enviable ability to both entertain *and* educate at the same time, all within the confines of a brief, 1,000 word essay.

☠ **C. V.** ☠

 Main Characters

George Orwell, Loki, Baldur, Jesus, John Foster Dulles, Judge Irving R. Kaufman, Julius and Ethel Rosenberg, Aaron Burr, Alexander Hamilton, Arnold Schoenberg, Jack the Ripper, Rasputin, Hitler, Bela Lugosi, Dracula, The Beatles, the Loch Ness Monster, Prussian serfs, the Wright Brothers, Mr. Rogers.

The King Speaks

"I try to stay at home cowering under the covers on Friday the 13th. God, I once had to fly on Friday the 13th—I had no choice—and while the ground crew didn't exactly have to carry me onto the plane kicking and screaming, it was still no picnic. It didn't help that I'm afraid of flying, either. I guess I hate surrendering control over my life to some faceless pilot who could have been secretly boozing it up all afternoon or who has an embolism in his cranium, like an invisible time bomb. But I have a thing about the number 13 in general; it never fails to trace that old icy finger up and down my spine. When I'm writing, I'll never stop work if the page number is 13 or a multiple of 13; I'll just keep on typing until I get to a safe number."

—From "The *Playboy* Interview: Stephen King" (June, 1983)

 ## Did You Know?

This essay has only appeared in print twice. The first time was in the "triple whammy" year of 1984 in *The New York Times*; the second time was in *Castle Rock: The Stephen King Newsletter* in 1987.

 ## What I Really Liked About It

What else? The feeling that Stephen King is talking directly to each of his readers and telling them something fascinating.

 ## Film Adaptations

None.

NUMBER **95**

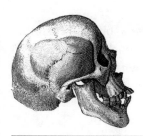

*"What Stephen King
Does for Love"*
(1990)

---

*The heart has its own mind, and its business is joy. For me, those two things—joy
and reading—have always gone together, and another of my life's pleasures was
discovering that sometimes they mature together.*

Why it made the top 100:

This is one of the most important nonfiction essays Stephen King has ever written. In this revealing essay, King discusses at length the influences on his writing, his resistance to reading what was assigned him in school, and the differences between reading for love and reading because you're *told to, which is* a paradigm King describes as consisting of two continents called "Wanna Read" and "Gotta Read."

As is common for many high schoolers, King hated many of the classics he was assigned to read.

King has a sharp recall for the reading he had to swallow like bitter medicine taken without even a speck of sugar to ease its way down. He singles out Herman Melville's *Moby Dick*, Shakespeare's *Hamlet*, George Eliot's *Silas Marner*, the poems of Emily Dickinson and Robert Frost. In addition, he mentions Charles Dickens' *The Pickwick Papers*; Mark Twain's *The Adventures of Huckleberry Finn*; John Updike's *Pigeon*

Feathers; James Fenimore Cooper's *The Deerslayer*; all of Ernest Hemingway; and, most surprisingly, the works of Edgar Allan Poe.

King takes no prisoners in his "review" of these writers and their works. What is especially fascinating (and revealing) about this essay is that King *the man* realizes that much of his resistance to these works and his animosity towards their authors was based on the immaturity of King *the high schooler*. He frankly admits that he was wrong about several of the texts assigned to him in high school and that when he re-read them as an adult, he saw new beauty, revealed talent, and, yes, he even felt excitement and got goosebumps from specific moments in the works.

Later in life, King still hates *Moby Dick* and *Pigeon Feathers*, but his sensibility has matured to the point where he now finds *Hamlet* "tremendously exciting." And *Huckleberry Finn* gave him the aforementioned goosebumps when his kids *insisted* that he read it to them after he finished reading them *Tom Sawyer*: They absolutely *demanded*, he tells us, "to know the rest of the story."

King also changed his mind about Dickens.

He writes that he re-discovered the great Victorian scribe during an illness in his mid-20s:

> I remember putting down *A Tale of Two Cities* and asking myself if this could really be the same man who had written *The Pickwick Papers*. It hardly seemed possible; *Pickwick* had been awful, *Cities* was wonderful. So, I discovered, was *Oliver Twist*...and if *Hamlet* is the greatest play ever written, then *Great Expectations* may be the greatest novel. And if you think I'm kidding, try it. I defy you not to finish it after reading the first fifty pages. That sucker kicks.

The writing legend and icon that is "Stephen King" (separate from Stephen King the *man*) exists as a manifestation of countless influences; not the least of which is a massive and ceaseless exposure to the popular culture of the 20th century.

In "What Stephen King Does for Love," King talks about the voracious reading he did willingly (even eagerly) when he was a kid, noting that if he had a dime for every book he read on his own, he could buy a car with the money.

He specifically cites as favorites John D. MacDonald's "Travis McGee" novels, Ed McBain's "87th Precinct" stories, the work of Shirley Jackson, especially *We Have Always Lived in the Castle* and *The Haunting of Hill House*, J. R. R. Tolkien's "Middle Earth" tales, the teleplays of Rod Serling; the dark horror novels of Dickens' contemporary Wilkie Collins, Ken Kesey's *One Flew Over The Cuckoo's Nest*, early essays by Tom Wolfe, "about a trillion comic books," plus the works of Robert Howard, Andre Norton, Jack London, and others. He also admits to having read three sex manuals in one week when he was a curious young lad, moving straight from *A Sex Guide For Troubled Teenagers* to the far more mature *The Kinsey Report*.

For King fans interested in who King himself believes to have influenced his writing, there is a very interesting section on the writer Thomas Hardy. King writes in the school of naturalism, a literary philosophy that revolves around the belief that fate rules man, but through free will we have the ultimate power to make moral—or immoral—choices. King's introduction to naturalism came when he was assigned to read Hardy's classic *Tess of the D'Ubervilles*. He admits that he didn't care about the underlying literary foundations that propelled *Tess* forward; he was only interested in Tess's *story*, and describes Tess as a character "so naive that she was raped without knowing it."

King tells us that *Tess* so impressed him that he went on to read other Hardy works and was also extremely moved by Hardy's final novel, the gloomy *Jude the Obscure*. (Interestingly, both *Tess of the D'Ubervilles* and *Jude the Obscure* were originally published in magazines in serial form. In 1996 King published his own novel, *The Green Mile*, in six separate monthly paperback installments, a groundbreaking publishing event that prompted the release of several serialized novels in the months to follow.)

"What Stephen King Does For Love" is Stephen King at his most engaging; it is Stephen King as Teacher. Reading this essay brought to mind something that Clive Barker, King's contemporary and fellow horror writer, once said about reading: "I forbid my mind nothing," making the same point that King has often made about censorship and forbidding kids to read certain works. King has often advised kids to go to the public library or bookstore and read what their parents and teachers most definitely do not want them to read (including some of his own books).

"You can't legislate ... [John] Steinbeck in place of [Danielle] Steel," King writes. "[K]ids are going to go right on reading for love, and God love them for it."

The whole point of "What Stephen King Does for Love," then, is not simply to dump on the classics or relate the story of how one man grew to appreciate the stuff he loathed as a kid. That's there, of course, but I think the underlying point King is making is that kids should read *everything and anything* that they want to—even comic books, sex manuals, and science fiction. It is the *reading* that counts; not necessarily *what* is being read. He is telling us that even though high school English teachers seem to some-times deliberately assign stuff guaranteed to bore their students to tears, this should *not* sour young people on reading (as it so often does). They should just go out and get their hands on what they *want* to read—even if it's something as "unliterary" (for lack of a better word) as Jack London's thrilling Alaska story, *White Fang*.

Seek literary adventure, King exhorts in this essay; and "Do more than enjoy it; swim in that heady brew, fly in that intoxicating ether. Why not?"

Why not, indeed.

☠ **C. V.** ☠

 ## Main Characters

This essay does not have "characters" but King does mention or refer to the works of the following writers: Herman Melville, Danielle Steel, Dean Koontz, William Shakespeare,

George Eliot, Emily Dickinson, John D. McDonald, Ed McBain, Shirley Jackson, J. R. R. Tolkien, Reginald Rose, Tad Mosel, Rod Serling, Charles Dickens, Wilkie Collins, Ken Kesey, Tom Wolfe, Robert Howard, Andre Norton, Jack London, Margaret Mitchell, Agatha Christie, Margaret Millar, Joseph Heller, Thomas Hardy, Theodore Dreiser, Frank Norris, Edgar Allan Poe, Robert Frost, Ernest Hemingway, John Updike, James Fenimore Cooper, John Steinbeck, and Stephen King.

 ## Did You Know?

This wonderful essay, which first appeared in *Seventeen* magazine in 1990, was out of print until Stephen King himself reprinted it in his 2000 collection *Secret Windows*, which contained essays and short stories having to do with writing. *Secret Windows* was published by the Book of the Month Club as a companion volume to King's *On Writing*.

 ## What I Really Liked About It

King's blatant enthusiasm for the sheer joy of reading. We could use more of that today.

 ## Film Adaptations

None.

96

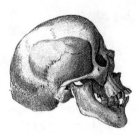

Introduction for
The Shapes of Midnight
(1980)

I killed the six-pack. I killed the evening.

Why it made the top 100:

Joseph Payne Brennan's 1980 volume *The Shapes of Midnight* was a collection of his short stories that had originally been published between 1953 and 1961—tales that so defined classic horror that none other then Stephen King himself agreed to write the Introduction.

I knew horror writer and poet Joseph Payne Brennan and had considerable contact with him in his final days. He and I share the hometown of New Haven, Connecticut and, before he died in 1990, he was very helpful to me as I was finishing up the *Complete Stephen King Encyclopedia*. That book contains Joe Brennan's final interview, as well as a reprint of his legendary short story "Canavan's Back Yard." The story is set in New Haven, which Stephen King talks about at length in this Introduction (*Encyclopedia* also includes a reminiscence of Joe Brennan by none other than Donald Grant, Stephen King's *Dark Tower* publisher, and Brennan's collaborator on the novella *Act of Providence*.)

The King Speaks

"Joseph Payne Brennan is one of the most effective writers in the horror genre, and he is certainly one of the writers I have patterned my own career upon; one of the writers whom I studied and with whom I kept school."

—From the Introduction to *The Shapes of Midnight*

Joseph Payne Brennan was a poet and short story writer who influenced a great many writers working today. A World Fantasy Award-winning writer, Brennan was born in 1918 in Bridgeport, Connecticut, but lived all his life in New Haven where he worked as a librarian at Yale University. He also was a cat lover and that especially endeared him to me personally. He wrote poems about cats, and I was proud to include a photo of Joe (courtesy of Mrs. Brennan) in my *Encyclopedia* in which he is seen playing with one of his beloved felines.

Like King, Brennan is a very accessible writer. His narrative voice is plain and direct and yet his narrative style is confident and imaginative. It is, indeed, a winning combination. Stephen King read Brennan when he was growing up and considers him to be one of the writers, along with Richard Matheson, Robert Bloch, and others, who profoundly influenced his own work.

Stephen King's Introduction sets the stage for a virtuoso performance by Brennan and it dramatically illustrates just how powerful (and important) it is for a writer to have a passion for his subject. It does show up in the final product.

☠ **C. V.** ☠

Main Characters

Joseph Payne Brennan, Stephen King, John Silbersack, Mark Twain, Bram Stoker, Harlan Ellison, Virgil Finlay, H. P. Lovecraft, Lord Dunsany, John D. MacDonald, Clark Ashton Smith, Charlie Rull, E. B. White, Charlie Grant, Russell Mellmer, Dan Mellmer, Henry Crotell, Canavan, Charlotte Parkins Gilman, William Faulkner, Charles Beaumont, Ray Bradbury, Richard Matheson, Fritz Leiber.

Did You Know?

Stephen King's 1982 short story "The Raft" seems to have been directly inspired by Joseph Payne Brennan's 1953 classic horror story "Slime." (The 1982 version of "The Raft" is a rewrite of a story King wrote in 1968 called "The Float" which was submitted to, and accepted for publication by, *Adam* magazine, but which never appeared in print. King never got the manuscript back, so he rewrote the story from memory and published it in *Gallery* magazine in 1982. "The Raft" later appeared in King's 1985 collection *Skeleton Crew*.)

What I Really Liked About It

King's unbridled passion, admiration, and respect for Brennan's work, an Argument (as in "a course of reasoning aimed at demonstrating truth") that does precisely what King intends it to do: compel you to begin reading the stories immediately. King makes you not want to delay experiencing Brennan's magic a second longer than it takes to read his Introduction.

Film Adaptations

None.

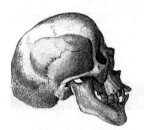

Foreword to Night Shift (1978)

"Let's talk, you and I. Let's talk about fear."

Why it made the top 100:

This Foreword has always meant a lot to me personally, because it is from this superb essay that I culled the title of my first book about Stephen King, *The Shape Under the Sheet: The Complete Stephen King Encyclopedia*. (*Shape* was the first book of my "Stephen King trilogy." *The Essential Stephen King* is the final book; *The Lost Work of Stephen King* came in between.)

I first read this Foreword when it was published in 1978 and I always remembered it as one of King's most astute nonfiction pieces. Seven years later, when I began researching and writing the book which, at that point, was known to myself and my editor simply as the "King Encyclopedia," I reread (yet again) this Foreword, and, straight away, I had my title.

King sets the stage:

The field has never been highly regarded ... It may be because the horror writer always brings bad news: you're going to die, he says; he's telling you to never mind Oral Roberts and his "something good is going to happen to you," because something bad is also going to happen to you, and it may be cancer and it may be a stroke, and it may be a car accident, but it's going to happen.

And then he hits hard (and this is where my title came from):

And he takes your hand and he enfolds it in his own, and he takes you into the room and he puts your hand on the shape under the sheet...and tells you to touch it here...and here...and here...

Yes, King crafted one of his most striking metaphors in this Foreword; the idea that the horror writer puts your hands on the shape under the sheet, and that shape is *your own* dead body.

And that sets the stage for what follows: a thoughtful, insightful, undeniably *informed* meditation on the nature of writing and the essence of fear. And although this is a Foreword to a collection of (mostly excellent) short stories, King self-effacingly does not mention—even one time—the title of any of the tales this Foreword is intended to introduce.

This essay is an important one, and one that is also an enormous amount of fun to read.

☠ **C. V.** ☠

 ## Main Characters

Stephen King, Tabitha King, Ruth King, Joe King, Owen King, Naomi King, Louis L'Amour, Dylan Thomas, Ross Lockridge, Hart Crane, Sylvia Plath, Bram Stoker, Renfield, Beowulf, Grendel, Sam Gamgee, Shelob, J. R. R. Tolkien, Henry James, Nathaniel Hawthorne, Goodman Brown, Dracula, Edgar Allan Poe, Dan Blocker, Freddie Prinze, Janis Joplin, Paul Harvey, seven blind men, an elephant, Johnny Carson, H. P. Lovecraft, Kurt Vonnegut, Oral Roberts, Fyodor Dostoyevsky, Edward Albee, Ross Macdonald, Lew Archer, a Welsh sineater, Steve McQueen, Michael Landon, Elisha Cook, Jr., Stanley Kubrick, Brian De Palma, Sauron, Adolf Hitler, Bob Dylan, John Steinbeck, Albert Camus, William Faulkner, James Joyce, T. S. Eliot, Anne Sexton, Frodo Baggins, Norman Bates (and his beloved mother, the indomitable Mrs. Bates), Pickman, a wendigo, Edgar Rice Burroughs, Bill Thompson, Robert Lowndes, Douglas Allen, Nye Willden, Elaine Geiger (Koster), Herbert Schnall, Carolyn Stromberg, Gerard Van der Leun, Harris Deinstfrey, King's constant readers.

Peter Straub Speaks

"Although most readers and a surprising number of writers cherish a literary version of free will, from early on King understood that subject matter selects the writer instead of the other way around. This determination is experiential, not pessimistic, and realistic, not fatalistic. It is grounded in deep common sense, like a sense of humor. King knows that the only sensible answer to the question as to why he wishes to squander his talent on topics like brutalized women and possessed automobiles is, as he says here, Why do you assume that I have a choice?"

—From Peter Straub's Introduction to *Secret Windows*

Did You Know?

In 2000, King published a companion volume to his second nonfiction book, *On Writing*, called *Secret Windows*. It was only available from the Book of the Month Club and it collected nonfiction and fiction related to the art and craft of writing. Tellingly, King included his Foreword to *Night Shift* in *Secret Windows*, as well as another essay that made the runners-up list for this book, "On Becoming a Brand Name." (Non-BOMC members who would like a copy of *Secret Windows* can try Bangor's Bettsbooks: *bettsbooks.com* or *bettsbooks@aol.com,* or check out eBay, although an auctioned copy will likely sell for considerably more than the list price of $19.95.)

What I Really Liked About It

The quintessential Stephen King "Sit down and let me tell you something" voice that, when done right, seems so effortless, but which is incredibly difficult to pull off without reeking of hubris.

Film Adaptations

None.

NUMBER **98**

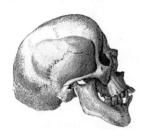

Foreword to
Stalking the Nightmare
(1982)

"You don't make it over the long haul on the basis of your personality."

Why it made the top 100:

King begins this engaging Foreword to Harlan Ellison's seminal short story collection by telling us, "It drives my wife crazy, and I'm sorry it does, but I can't really help it." What drives the esteemed Mrs. King—as King so delicately puts it—"absolutely BUGFUCK"?

Homilies, little sayings, proverbs, and adages.

Things like "There's a heartbeat in every potato." (What?)

And, "You'll never be hung for your beauty."

And, "[F]ools' names, and their faces, are often seen in public places."

Why does King tell us this seemingly irrelevant stuff in a Foreword to a book by Harlan Ellison?

Because King uses the opportunity of recounting this family anecdote to write it *like Harlan Ellison* would.

King is—correctly—making the point that Ellison's voice is so singular, so unique, and so pulsing with *energi literaria*, that after reading him for a while, you cannot *help* but start writing like him.

Balancing his thesis, though, King also talks about the art and craft of writing and how important it is for a writer to begin "sounding like himself sooner or later" at the risk of ending up being nothing more than "a ventriloquist's dummy."

While discussing this "Development of a Writer" process, King makes a couple of revealing remarks about what it's like to look back and re-read stuff written when you were young and inexperienced:

> [T]here comes a day when you look back on the stuff you wrote when you were 17...or 22...or 28... and say to yourself, Good God! If I was this bad, how did I ever get any better?

They don't call that stuff "juvenilia" for nothing, friends 'n neighbors.

King also notes some of the writers who he believes have influenced his own distinct narrative voice. They include H. P. Lovecraft, Raymond Chandler, Ross MacDonald, Robert Parker, Dorothy Sayers, Peter Straub, and, last but not least, Harlan Ellison.

King then begins his discussion of Harlan Ellison as a writer and man and uses the word "ferocious," or a form thereof, no less than six times to describe both Harlan's personality and writing style. King also bluntly admits, "There are folks in the biz who don't like Harlan much."

Those of us who write for a living and who often work in the fields of Dark Fantasy and Science Fiction know this to be true, but it is a surprise to read it in a Foreword to one of Harlan's own books. But we *are* talking about Harlan Ellison here, a man who holds the written word in such high regard that there is no chance in Hell that he would even *consider* editing out King's comment about his occasionally prickly mien. Nor would Harlan likely ever ask King to delete it so that he could look good to his *Stalking the Nightmare* readers.

King's Foreword to *Stalking the Nightmare* is a literary tour de force and an impressive display of stylistic virtuosity.

Stephen King has written a great deal of nonfiction. Much of it contains some of his finest writing. This essay made the top 100 because it is a flawless evocation of Harlan Ellison and his work—which is precisely what an effective Foreword is supposed to do. Plus it's a whole heck of a lot of fun to read.

☠ **C. V.** ☠

Main Characters

Stephen King, Tabitha King, Joe King, Owen King, Harlan Ellison, Fredric Brown, Andy Warhol, Rona Barrett, Norman Mailer, H. G. Wells, Wilkie Collins.

Did You Know?

Since the late 1970s, Harlan Ellison has held the rights to an unpublished Stephen King story called "Squad D," which King wrote specifically for Harlan Ellison's *The Last Dangerous Visions* anthology, a volume that has yet to be published. (See my chapter on "Squad D" in *The Lost Work of Stephen King* for more info about this story.)

 What I Really Liked About It

This essay is Stephen King with the volume turned up.

 Film Adaptations

None.

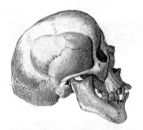

"Did I tell you I can't go out no more?"

Why it made the top 100:

This 100-line poem takes us inside the mind of a person (gender not specified, although for expediency we will refer to the narrator as a male) who is completely paranoid (*textbook*) and utterly mad.

The poem's narrator sees people watching him and knows that "Men have discussed me in back rooms." His mother has been investigated, the FBI is monitoring him, and the old woman who lives upstairs from him is radiating him with a suction cup device attached to her floor. His mail contains letter-bombs; he has seen UFOs; waitresses are poisoning his food; and "a dark man with no face" has surfaced in his toilet to listen to his phone calls. (See the "Did you know?" section for more on this "dark man.")

King effectively communicates madness with his superb use of language and disjointed free form lines; taking us inside the mind of a man who has created a bizarre, fully-realized interior reality that must, for the reader, co-exist with the mundane details of the narrator's *exterior* reality. This is a literary high-wire act and yet King pulls it off masterfully.

King uses some very powerful surrealistic images in this poem, especially that of the black crows with black umbrellas and silver dollar eyes standing at the bus stop looking at their watches. Very Magritte.

As the quote on page 322 from King's live AOL Chat in September 2000 makes clear, King publishes very little poetry. There are some University of Maine publications containing early Stephen King poems still extant; and there have been three poems published in his anthologies. (There are also poetry fragments in King works written by King characters, especially *The Tommyknockers* that has as one of its main characters a poet.) But King obviously feels that the bulk of his poetry, as he puts it, "doesn't work." This makes the appearance of a poem such as "Paranoid: A Chant" (and even the other poem from *Skeleton Crew*, "For Owen") a special event indeed. When Stephen King's poetry does work, it is evocative, insightful, and often chilling. (See my book *The Lost Work of Stephen King* for a discussion of an early King poem called "The Hardcase Speaks," which is downright horrifying.)

☠ **C. V.** ☠

Main Characters

The narrator, the man in the raincoat, the man in the subway, men in back rooms, the narrator's mother, the narrator's brother, the narrator's sister-in-law, black crows, an old woman, the dog with brown spots, tall people, the waitress, a dark man with no face, physicians.

Did You Know?

The poem "Paranoid: A Chant" seems to be connected to the world of *The Dark Tower* and *The Stand*. There is a line in the poem, "Last night a dark man with no face crawled through nine miles/of sewer to surface in my toilet…." And in *Danse Macabre*, when talking about the genesis of *The Stand*, King revealed, "I wrote 'A dark man with no face' and then glanced up and saw that grisly little motto again: 'Once in every generation a plague will fall among them.' And that was that. I spent the next two years writing an apparently endless book called *The Stand*." As King's readers know, Randall Flagg first appears in *The Stand* and then resurfaces in various manifestations in *The Dark Tower* series and in other King works. It appears Flagg may have also visited the narrator of "Paranoid: A Chant."

The King Speaks

"I have written a lot of poetry, but I show very little of it. Most of it just doesn't work. I even taught it for a semester, about a million years ago! I think some of the basic things apply: honesty and vivid language being only two of them."

—From a live AOL chat on Tuesday, September 19, 2000

What I Really Liked About It

In a word? The *tone*.

Film Adaptations

Paranoid (short film, 2000); starring Tonya Ivey, screenplay by Stephen King (the script is the complete text of "Paranoid: A Chant"), directed by Jay Holben. This film is an 8-minute interpretation of King's poem and it is an existential visual masterpiece (as the poem is likewise, except in text form). The most surprising element to me was the decision to make the narrator a woman. I had always heard a man's voice when reading the poem and the switch to a woman was interesting, to say the least. The image of the "man with no face" is mega-spooky (it literally is a man *without a face*) and Tonya Ivey does an incredible job of communicating an over-the-top paranoia that has escalated into full-blown psychosis. Tonya gives her entire performance in a motel room (and its bathroom) dressed only in panties and a sleeveless t-shirt. The room is dark, her notebooks are laid out on the bed, and all her dialogue (the text of the poem) is heard in voice-over, except for the line "Would you like some coffee, my love?" which she delivers staring straight into the camera. If I have any criticism at all, it would be the minor point that I would have preferred a slightly flatter line reading, only because I always heard this poem in my head in something of a monotonous drone-like voice. But this is a small point and the overall effect of the film is hypnotic. More information about the film is available at *paranoidthemovie.com*. This is without a doubt one of the finest "dollar babies" to date. (And the credits end with the last line of *The Long Walk*, an especially appropriate reference.) (Grade: A+.)

"The Subject This Week Is Cops"
(1969)

"Funny thing about cops—not too many people seem to like them."

Why it made the top 100:

When Stephen King was attending the University of Maine, he wrote a weekly column for the school newspaper called *King's Garbage Truck*. (He didn't give it that title, his editor did.)

King's November 13, 1969 installment of his *Garbage Truck* column may be one of the most important he ever wrote.

Why? Because it is an incredibly passionate, scathingly angry, and sublimely intelligent defense of cops.

King starts off by checking off for his readers the people who did *not* (at that time) like cops. This group includes the New Left, the Supreme Court, jaywalkers, people who can't get their tickets fixed, and taxpayers.

And who *did* like the cops? "Well, I do," King states with pride, admitting that "Mostly it's the New Left that ticks me off." King does not like the cartoons in underground newspapers that show cops as pigs in uniforms beating people up. He also doesn't like people who defend Huey Newton, "who shot one." King describes these "whiners" as "idiots who prate insane nonsense about... 'fascist pigs' and 'racist gunslingers.'"

King then details the specifics of the life of a New York City cop. A cop makes $8,500 a year, King tell us, and out of that has to come his uniforms, shoes, and accessories. "For this incredible fortune," he notes, "your average cop is faced with the garbage of humanity."

King then describes some of the scum of the earth that cops have to deal with on a daily basis, including mothers who beat their kids and dump them in the trash; blacks who loot "for the greater glory of the struggle"; and whites who loot "to show their support."

King also lists the "piggy" things cops do like: arrest heroin dealers, fire their weapons at people who are shooting at them, use Mace to break up race riots, stand all-night stakeouts, and cover up dead bodies after accidents, and for all this they have lousy insurance, lousy vacations, lousy pensions, and they have to work holidays.

"It's a dirty old world," King writes, and blasts the New Lefters who "exist with their heads in the rosy clouds of Marxism, socialism, liberalism, urban reform, racial reform, world reform, and spiritual reform."

King describes cops as "the people who stand between you and the chaos of an insane society."

This "Garbage Truck" column should be reprinted and posted on the bulletin boards of every precinct station house and public building in the United States. Back in the late 1960s when King was writing these columns, there was a strong anti-cop sentiment throughout the land. It was because the U.S. was being rocked by a tidal wave of societal and cultural upheaval and the cops often found themselves in the uncomfortable position of having to restrain and oftentimes arrest their friends and neighbors. Things are somewhat different now but there is still a faction of society that thinks any and all police presence and authority is too much.

This is, of course, nonsense and, as King reminds us in this column, cops are the only people "trying ... to make sure that the rest of us aren't robbed, raped, kidnapped, conned or killed."

This *Garbage Truck* column contains anything but. (Garbage, that is).

 C. V.

 Main Characters

Cops.

Did You Know?

As good as many of Stephen King's UMO *Garbage Truck* column's are, he has consistently refused to allow them to be reprinted. He apparently feels that his nonfiction writing as a 20-year-old does not hold up three decades later. Perhaps. But there is a great deal to admire and enjoy in these columns, and "The Subject This Week is Cops" is a prime example of just how good King was even in his college years.

What I Really Liked About It

King defiantly stating his conservative ideology in a forum that was more than likely equally defiantly liberal.

Film Adaptations

None.

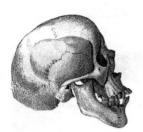

"The Thing at the Bottom of the Well" (1960)

"Come on down," said the voice. "And we'll have jolly fun."

Why it was included as number 101:

Written when Stephen King was 12 or 13, "The Thing at the Bottom of the Well" is a very important early King story and is essential to our understanding of the recurrent themes King continues to work with throughout his career. Also, the evident narrative deftness in this well-told tale—even at such a young age—hints at the writer that Stephen King was on his way to becoming.

"The Thing at the Bottom of the Well" may be King's first use of the archetypal "thing in the sewer/closet/crate/under the bed/etc." monster creature that later became Pennywise the Clown in *It*.

This one-page story begins with the reader being told that "Oglethorpe Crater was an ugly, mean little wretch." And King's not kidding about Oglethorpe. Some of the tortures this little creep inflicts upon both people and pets include: sticking pins in cats and dogs, pulling the wings from flies, pulling worms apart and watching them squirm (although his fun with the worms lost its appeal when he learned that they didn't feel any pain), and tying a rope across the top of the cellar stairs so that the cook would trip and fall.

One day when Oglethorpe was out "looking for more things to torture," he spotted a well. He yelled "Hello" down into it, and heard a voice reply, "Hello, Oglethorpe. Come on down, [a]nd we'll have jolly fun."

Oglethorpe went down into the well and wasn't found for a month. Then one day, the manhunt finally found his body in the well.

His arms and legs had been pulled out, and pins had been stuck in his eyes. As they took away his remains, they all heard laughter drifting up from the bottom of the well.

The monster under the bed, the boogeyman in the closet—this thing at the bottom of the well appears to be the ancestral grandfather of all these fiendish King bad guys.

Also, in this story, we have King using the naturalistic theme that he would re-visit later in countless other stories, the idea that fate rules man, but that we, as rational beings, have the ability to make moral choices.

It was fate that Oglethorpe stumbled upon the monster in the well, yet his decisions to act in such a morally reprehensible way were his own choices. The universe turned in such a way as to put things right. The Wheel spun and Crater paid the price for his terrible behavior.

☠ **C. V.** ☠

Main Characters

Oglethorpe Crater, Oglethorpe's mother, the cook, the thing at the bottom of the well.

Did You Know?

Stephen King has never allowed "The Thing at the Bottom of the Well" to be republished, although, interestingly, he did allow his one-page story "The Hotel at the End of the Road" (also from the *People, Places, and Things* collection) to be published in the 4th (1993) and 5th (1996) editions of *The Market Guide for Young Writers*, published by Writers Digest Books.

What I Really Liked About It

In addition to its foreshadowing of the later King, I also really like the idea of being told a complete horror story in a single page.

Film Adaptations

None. (Unless, ha, ha, you count the *It* miniseries.)

IN A CLASS BY ITSELF

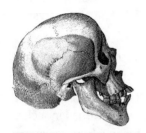

"Remembering John"
(1980)

Lennon was a cynic, a poet, a sarcastic son of a bitch, a public figure, a private man. ... And he had his fans like me, who looked at the paper on the morning of Tuesday the 9th of December and then sat down hard, unable to believe it at first ... and then, horribly, all too able to believe it.

Why this is in a class by itself:

The Fab Four's gestalt permeated the 1960s, redefining social mores, and expanding the contemporary global consciousness the way the Renaissance redefined art and culture for civilized mankind in the 16th and 17th centuries.

Like many baby boomers (those born in the post-World War II years between 1946 and 1964), Stephen King grew up with The Beatles. How could he not have? From February 7, 1964 (the day The Beatles first arrived in New York to appear on *The Ed Sullivan Show* on the 9th) through April 10, 1970 (the day Paul publicly announced the group's breakup), their engaging and enervating presence was ubiquitous.

I remember one specific incident from that period that powerfully illustrates just how big The Beatles were. When I was in my early teens, cars had AM radios. *Only* AM radios. And in my hometown of New Haven, Connecticut, there were at least four AM stations that played Top 40 music. Much to my mother's annoyance, I had pro-

grammed four of the push buttons on her white Dodge Dart's radio to these four stations. One day on the way home from school, I spent the entire trip pushing each of the
four buttons sequentially every few seconds. No, I wasn't barmy. I was excited beyond
words that every station in our area was playing a Beatles song. If I recall correctly,
they were "Please Please Me," "I Want To Hold Your Hand," "I Saw Her Standing
There," and, of course, "She Loves You."

The Beatles were bigger than Elvis.

Paul was adorable and clever; George, quiet and shy; Ringo, lovably goofy.

And then there was John.

John Lennon was one of those rare characters who dramatically emanated *gravitas*.
His words seem to carry more weight; his art was more serious and less disposable than
you would expect from a pop musician; his political and spiritual philosophies grew from
the same soil that did Gandhi's, Martin Luther King's, and Christ's. John preached love,
equality, and peace.

Paul and George and Ringo also wrote and sang about love, but it was often within
the context of romantic love and the girl they wanted to hold hands with or dance with.

John, on the other hand, was known to write and sing that love was all you need, and
he boldly demanded that the world give peace a chance. John told us tomorrow never
knows; Paul told us about yesterday. Paul was willing to let it be; John wanted a revolution.

No doubt about it, John Lennon was a groundbreaking artistic figure on the landscape of 20th century art.

And then, in December of 1980 at the age of 40, and on the verge of an artistic,
social, and personal rebirth, John Lennon was murdered in New York City, mere steps
from the front door of his fortress-like home, The Dakota Arms.

Like many of us, Stephen King was moved to write about all this after hearing of
John's death, and King's essay, "Remembering John"—a moving eulogy for Lennon,
written within days after Lennon's assassination on December 8, 1980 and published
five days later—is the result.

King begins this memorial with a slurry of no-nonsense facts about what John was
not. He was not the first ex-Beatle to have a critical success. (George's *All Things
Must Pass* album won that race.) He was also not the *handsome* former Beatle: We all
know that award goes to Paul. And John wasn't a movie star, like Ringo was.

"But somehow, for me," King writes, "he was the only ex-Beatle who really seemed
to matter."

Exactly.

In 1988, HBO aired a miniseries written by Gary Trudeau and directed by Robert
Altman called *Tanner*, which was about a fictional Presidential candidate, which was
sort of like HBO's *The Larry Sanders Show* or Showtime's *Beggars and Choosers*
for politics.

In one memorable episode, Tanner and his staff are hanging out in a hotel suite between political rallies and someone asks the always-popular question, "Who's your favorite Beatle?" Each gives an answer, and then Tanner, played by Michael Murphy, delivers a spontaneous, impassioned speech about the purpose of politics and the nobility of wanting to serve and work for a greater cause. His staff listens dumbfounded because this speech proves even more powerfully to them that this guy is obviously the real thing. Tanner then gets up to leave, but stops at the door turns, and says, "And by the way, the right answer is John Lennon."

Exactly.

In "Remembering John," King talks about John's persona and his charm, touching on some of the landmark moments in John's life, including his "we're more popular than Jesus" remark. King also discusses his own initiation into the world of rock-and-roll (it was getting a 78-rpm single of Elvis singing "Don't Be Cruel" that did it for King).

King then astutely coalesces the enormous *difference* The Beatles made and the lines of demarcation that were drawn between parents and kids following The Beatles' arrival on American shores.

King repeats a story told to him by his friend Phil Thompson. Thompson and his girlfriend were sitting on Phil's living room floor watching the Beatles' aforementioned first *Ed Sullivan Show* appearance. Phil's parents were sitting on the sofa behind them. Phil remembered that "when The Beatles started to play, I felt something snap between the people that were sitting on the floor and the people who were sitting on the couch."

Exactly.

About halfway through "Remembering John," King makes some biting remarks about what it feels like to be a celebrity in America (and he oughta know):

> We make a business here, apparently, of dining upon the bodies of those who have given us the most pleasure and some of our fondest memories; first we lionize them, and then we eat them.

Ironically, though, King then writes about feeling "a little bit like a ghoul" when he went out and bought a $200 collection of Beatles records the day after John died—something that millions of other Beatles fans around the world did, too. King can clearly recognize the hunger on the part of fans for more and more and more of their icons; but he, too, cannot help but feed that hunger when it comes to himself.

It's a strange paradigm we're talking about here. If Stephen King were to slip the bonds of this earth someday. If, say, he had died after being struck by a van, while walking on the side of the road in Maine in June of 1999, his fans would undoubtedly go out and buy all of his books they didn't have and possibly new copies of ones they did have in a fervid attempt to be closer to their idol. It happened with Princess Diana, it happened with Tupac Shakur, it happened with Frank Sinatra.

And it happened with John Lennon.

"Remembering John" is a tribute and a tirade, and an important essay by one of the world's most important living literary figures.

But "Remembering John" is also more than that: It is a nostalgic look back by just one more John Lennon fan, except that *this* fan—a world-famous writer with a household name—knows what it is like to be on *both* sides of that strange fan/celebrity coin.

King more fully explored the specifics of that strange place in American history known as the 1960s in 1999's *Hearts in Atlantis*, but he mourned its *spiritual* demise almost 20 years earlier when he noted the passing of John.

"Remembering John" has only appeared in print once, in the December 13/14 issue of *The Bangor Daily News*. Those of you who would like to read it can write or e-mail *The Bangor Daily News* and inquire as to whether or not specific articles from back issues of the paper are available for sale to the public.

Perhaps King will one day decide to reprint the piece (perhaps in his planned 2003 collection?) but for now, it is a Stephen King rarity not easily accessible.

It is our hope that this summary and discussion provides you with a sense of the mood and style of King's eloquent eulogy.

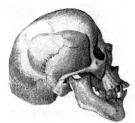

Mick Garris on Stephen King

Mick Garris

Mick Garris holds the distinction of being one of those few directors who have helmed more than one Stephen King film project. (George A. Romero and Frank Darabont are two others.) Through the spring of 2001, Mick has directed four cinematic versions of Stephen King's stories: King's original screenplay *Sleepwalkers* (1992); King's miniseries *The Stand* (1994) and *The Shining* (1997); and King's short story, "Chattery Teeth" for *Quicksilver Highway* (1997). It is expected that Mick will soon direct his fifth and sixth King films, *Desperation* and *Riding the Bullet*.

I asked Mick to participate in *The Essential Stephen King* by asking him to complete the sentence "Stephen King is..." Thus, this touching tribute.

Stephen King is...

Stephen King is still alive.

I don't think most of us realize how close that statement came to no longer being true. When King was hit by a van in June of 1999, he came perilously near meeting his maker, and all of us would have been far poorer for it. Though he has shown incredible tenacity in mending—quicker and better than any of the medical masters could have predicted—we came too damned close to losing the master of a genre that has become his own.

I first met King as a fan at a bookstore signing back in the 70s. Who knew I would be lucky enough to direct the man's own screenplays of his finest works? Not me. Neither did I ever guess then that we'd become friends. But we have, and my life (and I'm not speaking professionally now, though that is true as well) is all the richer for it.

Few would guess what a happy, childlike, loyal and generous man the Big Guy is. I call him El Queso Grande, or La Grande Fromage, for he is, in many matters, the Big Cheese. He is hilariously funny, a great guy to spend time with, and his towering size belies the sweetness of his heart. When I first had a meeting with him on *Sleepwalkers*, it was at a diner in New York, not the Russian Tea Room. He showed up in busted out sneakers, and his knees were peeking out of the smiles of his jeans. He's the least affected rich guy you could know. Maybe it's because he still lives in Maine, not in mediacentric LA or NY. But I've a feeling that no matter where he resides, he'd still just be Steve.

Stephen King is a loving husband and father, a true family man, as well as a great writer. And he's still alive, and we're all richer for it.

—Mick Garris
Toronto, Canada
December 2000

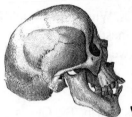

James Cole on Stephen King

James Cole

Jim Cole is a very close friend of mine. I first met Jim in the late 1980s when I was working on the *Complete Stephen King Encyclopedia* and he contacted me to ask if I would be interested in reviewing his "dollar baby" short film adaptation of Stephen King's short story "The Last Rung on the Laddder." We have been *compadres* ever since (I have christened him an honorary Italian) and, with this essay, he has contributed to all three of the books of my Stephen King trilogy.

Jim is a writer, of course, but that does not fully define the depth of his talent. He is a superior short story and non-fiction essay writer, but his true artistic strengths lie in screenwriting. Jim directed the "Last Rung" short film (which Stephen King mentioned by name in his introduction to Frank

Darabont's *Shawshank Redemption* script) and Jim has also penned several other terrific original screenplays, including one called *Stereopticon*. I have had the privilege of reading this script in various drafts and I consider *Stereopticon* one of the great unproduced scripts of our time. The day will come when it is produced, however, and you will understand my passion for it when you see it for yourself.

Jim loves and lives movies and is one of the few friends of mine who can usually identify the deliberately obscure movie quotes I use to sign off my e-mails. (Although he is definitely getting tired of "Go Trig Boy, it's your birthday" *(American Pie)* and "So where's your hose, Mr. Lombardo" *(Wild Things)*; he still doesn't seem to mind, "This is Ripley, last survivor of the Nostromo, signing off" *(Alien)*.)

Currently Jim lives in Los Angeles and is working on a new script. If you want a glimpse of Jim, check out the final party scene in the movie *Free Enterprise*. At the very beginning of the scene, Jim can be seen standing directly beneath a green spotlight, looking like he is on the verge of being "beam-napped" to a UFO. (Jim is also seen later in the scene "dancing" but we won't talk about that.)

The following essay by Jim is evocative and personal and bespeaks the powerful influence the work of Stephen King has had on him personally and, by extension, on all of us who love to read, and consider Stephen King's work one of the great pleasures of the act.

Stephen King is ...

Stephen King is the writer who made me love to read.

I was always a good reader, blessed with parents who read to me as a youngster and teachers that helped me to read on my own. In school I couldn't wait for those Scholastic books to arrive—books about monster makeup or life in Colonial times. Yet they always had illustrations. It wasn't until 3rd grade that I first tackled books without pictures. These included James Blish's *Star Trek* adaptations and a cheesy mystery series, *Alfred Hitchcock and the Three Investigators*. Though I enjoyed them, it was always a struggle to finish.

Any book longer than one hundred pages intimidated me. And novels? They were for grownups. How could I get through three to five hundred pages of tiny typeface, let alone have the courage to start? By 7th grade I had to. My English teacher assigned Dickens' *Great Expectations*, a book that almost made me *hate* reading. I was convinced that all novels must be boring, so why bother?

Stephen King changed all that ... with a little help from my dad.

My father is a voracious reader. His bookshelf was lined with dog-eared paperbacks, their spines bowed from being broken in so many places. One day a freshly read paperback with a black cover appeared on the shelf: *The Dead Zone*. Intrigued by the title, I read the back cover summary. A guy comes out of a coma with second sight? Cool! Yet as I fanned the pages, the sheer volume of words was frightening. Still, I sat down and read the first page. Then the second, then the third.

William Shakespeare Was...

Dr. Michael Collings is the most erudite scholar writing about Stephen King today. His several books about King's work are insightful, intelligent, and have taught me almost everything I know about the "literature" adroitly interwoven within the skeins of King's astonishingly entertaining writing.

Like the finest writers and speakers, Michael can elucidate a maelstrom of meaning with the fewest of words ... and he proves it here, on this very page, with the following one-liner, a statement which, as Michael notes, "conceals as much (or, with luck, more) than it reveals ..."

William Shakespeare was the Stephen King of his generation.

I couldn't stop. King's writing was the most descriptive, most *visual* style I had ever encountered. I could see what was happening in my head. Most important: I cared about the characters, felt like I knew them. I wanted to know what was going to happen to them even as I didn't want the story to end.

I later realized *The Dead Zone* was not my first encounter with King (I had read *The Shining* on vacation the previous summer), yet it was the first time reading felt *easy*. I was no longer conscious of the number of words or how many pages there were to go. The process of reading itself had changed, and I began to devour other books on the shelf: Clive Cussler. John Gardener. John D. McDonald. Some were good reads, some great, some dull. Some I didn't even finish. But that didn't matter.

Thanks to Stephen King, I was no longer afraid to start.

—James Cole
Los Angeles
December, 2000

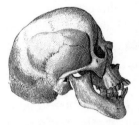

Jay Holben on Stephen King

Jay Holben

Jay Holben is the director of the film *Paranoid*, a short adaptation of Stephen King's brilliant *Skeleton Crew* poem, "Paranoid: A Chant." (See my review of Jay's film in my chapter about the poem.)

Jay has been in the movie business since 1994, and has worked as everything from a gaffer and chief lighting technician to second unit camera operator, producer, and director. Some of the films he has worked on include *Wag the Dog*, *Free Enterprise*, *Jack Frost*, *Deep Cover*, and *Mothman*.

Here, he talks about Stephen King who, he tells us, may not be the kind of writer many people think he is.

Stephen King is ...

Stephen King is *not* a Horror Writer.

Ghosties, ghoulies and things that go bump in the night—to the casual observer, these are the trappings of Stephen King.

If it makes you break out in gooseflesh, or leap like an Olympian pole-vaulter from the bathroom threshold into your bed in the dark of the night—it must be the work of Stephen King.

But these declarations are superficial and made without examination into the works of a writer whom I feel is one of the greatest observers of human behavior, and one of the most astute social-commentators of our time.

To the unlucky masses that only know King's work from a casual impulse-buy at the supermarket checkout counter, or the latest weak film adaptation airing at 2 a.m. on their local super station, King is synonymous with horror—but, in reality, his pen scratches so much deeper into the very nature of the human soul. King's true gift is not in conjuring up werewolves and vampires, but in capturing the essence of real people; complicated, honest characters who often find themselves in extraordinary—and yes—horrifying situations.

Many of King's greatest works don't even live in the neighborhood of horror—*The Long Walk* and *The Gunslinger* series are just two examples of unblemished non-horror writing. If we look deeper within the pages of King's prose, we find real people struggling with real problems and trying their desperate best to make their worlds right again. We find people who mirror our siblings, friends, and even ourselves. King manages to terrify his readers not so much with snarling beasts (although he's got his share) but more often by immersing the reader into the pages of the book and into their worse fears and insecurities about themselves. In his most potent tales, we find men like Jack Torrance and Louis Creed—men who are fighting tooth-and-nail to keep their families together. King brings us Ray Garraty (*The Long Walk*), Paul Sheldon (*Misery*), Jessie Burlingame (*Gerald's Game*), and Dolores Claiborne (*Dolores Claiborne*)—all very real people who are merely trying to make it through the day. They are all fighting against powers well beyond their comprehension, but we have all faced those moments. If you've ever spent a long night in a sterile hospital waiting room measuring breath after breath in anticipation of news of a loved one—you've lived a Stephen King story.

King's true mastery is capturing the essence of one person's tribulations and leading the reader on an often heart-wrenching journey to the eventual success - or demise - of that character. From time to time, King outdoes himself and will plunge readers not just into the mind of a tortured human, but descend them deeply—and with extraordinary believability—into the tortured mind of a dying dog.

Although the proclaimed Master of Horror has openly embraced this title—such a simplistic label stops short of describing the true depth of Stephen King's work. More often than not the humble scribe from Maine transcends the horror genre, and today's narrow-minded, pedestrian-pedagogues will find their jaws agape as King's words live easily well beyond his years to be the greatly studied tomes of tomorrow's tortured souls.

—Jay Holben

Los Angeles

January 2001

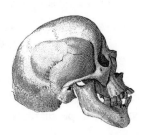

10 Questions with
Stephen King Supercollector
Charlie Fried

I shouldn't even try to write an introduction to this interview, mainly because my dear friend Charlie Fried probably would prefer there not even be one (an Introduction, that is. He doesn't mind the interview itself.)

Charlie—who is profiled in *Who's Who in America*—is the definition of the term "low profile." He has one of the five most important Stephen King collections in the world (I think the term "supercollector" was coined specifically for him) and yet he is almost completely unknown to Stephen King fans, many of whom are unaware of the complex (and often expensive) world of collecting.

Charlie approaches collecting Stephen King the way he does everything else: with commitment, passion, and above all, integrity.

Do not misunderstand: Charlie *has* talked to the media in the past and has been featured on CBS and elsewhere in short interview segments, usually conducted at a Stephen King book-signing or speech, many of which Charlie tries to attend. This, however, is one of the first fullblown interviews Charlie has granted in which he talks openly about his legendary collection, and I want to express my appreciation for his confidence in me and for his participation in *The Essential Stephen King*. I first met Charlie back in the late 1980s when I was teaching a seminar on Stephen King and writing the *Complete Stephen King Encyclopedia*. I still have a letter he wrote me shortly after the seminar and, over the years, he has been an invaluable help to me. He has generously made available to me for research extremely rare and valuable one-of-a-kind King pieces and I was able to write the *Lost Work of Stephen King* in large part due to Charlie's assistance. In fact, he was so integral in the completion of that volume that I dedicated it to him. And that meager gesture does not even come near to expressing my appreciation for Charlie's friendship and help over the years.

Here is my talk with Charlie Fried:

1. How did you get started collecting Stephen King?

First I started as a reader. I read *The Stand* when it first came out in 1978 and loved it. That book will always be a favorite because, like first love, it occupies a special place in your heart. I then went back and read *Carrie*, *'Salem's Lot*, and *The Shining*, although I don't remember if I read them in that order. I stayed away from the short stories because I was into reading novels. I remember reading *Thinner* before it was admitted that King was Bachman and telling people, "If you like King, read this." I continued on reading each King novel as it came out, although I had trouble finishing *The Tommyknockers*, which remains, to this day, my least favorite King work.

Then, sometime around 1990, I saw a "short course" (a half-day seminar-type event) advertised on the works of Stephen King. It was being offered in New Haven, the town where I work, so I decided to take it.

It was at this course that I met a wonderful person named Stephen (Spignesi, not King) and, as they say, the rest is history.

GEORGE BEAHM

Stephen King and Charlie Fried

Actually a little more background is required to fully understand why I got started collecting. First, you need to know that at heart *I am a collector.* I have long collected stamps, owls (not real ones), videos, and other things that interest me. Some might say I am anal-retentive (after all I am a CPA), but that's too easy a label and, after all, why blame my mother? I am just a collector by nature. After the short course, I *really* got into King and started collecting King hardcover first editions. Fortunately, I have had the means, as well as the inclination, and have built up a sizable collection in less than a decade.

Also, applying a little layman's psychology, it was probably the right time in my life to get back into books.

My father, who passed away many years before, was a lexicographer and editor by trade. In my teen years he was an editor of trade fiction for World Publishing Company and our house had a room lined with wall-to-wall bookshelves. Books were always *his* thing, so I may have had a reaction formation and deliberately shied away from collecting books.

But it seems as though enough time had passed and I decided (perhaps subconsciously) that it was time to pay a tribute to him and build a book collection I think he would have appreciated. He was a big fan of science fiction and even liked horror; and he was a close friend of Fritz Leiber (who I once met at my younger brother's wedding).

So, in a way I would never have predicted 20 years ago, with my book collecting I am carrying on a tradition of my father.

2. How would you describe the current state of your collection, or in general terms, what is it comprised of?

It is relatively complete, but there are still plenty of items I don't have.

It is probably one of the top five collections in the world that I am aware of. The hundreds of pictures in George Beahm's book *Stephen King Collectibles: An Illustrated Price Guide* are of my collection. I would characterize what I have now as fairly comprehensive, and it is, consequently, overflowing my house. My wife keeps worrying that one day the second floor of our house may collapse into the first.

I collect U.S. and UK first editions, advance reading copies or proofs, anthologies with King stories, limited editions, signed (inscribed and flat signed) copies, books about King and his works, books with introductions or afterwords by King, artist portfolios, large print books, proof dust jackets, movie press kits, assorted publicity and promo materials (many signed), screenplays, movie props, newsletters, magazines, calendars, photos, playbills, audio tapes, video tapes, DVDs, manuscripts, correspondence ... the list goes on.

3. What are your collecting criteria; i.e., what determines what you seek out and eventually buy, and do you have any tips and/or suggestions for fans who want to get started in collecting Stephen King?

My first criteria is to determine if a particular piece is related to King and, if so, do I have it?

Then I determine if is it related to King's writings or films based on his writings. This means it can be by him or be about him or his works.

I have no interest in purchasing things that relate solely to his personal life. For instance, I don't own his high school yearbook, his old sneakers, a used handkerchief, etc., nor would I want to!

I have been given some things that I consider peripheral and have not thrown them away, but I would not purchase them. I like to believe that I am collecting things based upon a body of work and not a personal private life, though the two obviously intertwine.

There are two ways to start collecting, start small and cheap, or buy the most expensive things you can afford. For investment purposes the latter will yield the best results, but collecting warrants some short term gratification so the former is often a requirement of getting started. I would suggest that you stick to first edition hardcovers and always strive for excellent condition. Something like a signed copy would add distinction to your beginning collection and not be priced out of sight.

Another thing I strongly urge is that you read everything you collect. Books are first for reading and if you have experienced what you are collecting—i.e., actually read the contents—it will mean so much more to you.

Also, if you want to collect, read as much about collecting as you can. Buy a price guide, use the Internet, visit dealers and their sites, auction sites, read the newsgroups and clubs, become as knowledgeable as possible. These things will make your collection more than just an accumulation of things. Knowledge will bring added life and meaning to your collecting.

4. What are the most valuable items in your collection? What is the most personally meaningful?

The most valuable items in my collection include the first state of *'Salem's Lot* with the $8.95 priced dust jacket, the asbestos *Firestarter*, three binders of correspondence from early in King's publishing career, a couple of the early oversized Doubleday ARC's, and some one-of-a-kind original manuscripts.

The most meaningful is probably a book that Mr. King signed and personally inscribed to me at a book signing.

5. What do you have no interest at all in collecting?

I collect almost everything, except foreign language editions. There are a few exceptions, though. I try to have one Stephen King book in every language, just to have a specimen of that language. I collect selected foreign editions if they have a specific meaning to me. For instance, the French edition of *Firestarter* is titled *Charlie*. Also because of the publishing controversy, I have a German *Nebel* (*The Mist*) and *Es* (*Misery*).

I also do not collect anything but first editions and I stay away from trade paperbacks.

I have not sought out newspaper articles about Mr. King, though I have some and certainly have a large number of magazine articles, and, I hope all article appearances that exist in book form.

6. What acquisition gave you the most satisfaction as a collector?

To answer this you need to understand what it means to be a collector. The hunt is as important (or more so) than having the item. So I have to first answer that the asbestos limited lettered *Firestarter* was probably the most satisfying to acquire, mainly because it was held out as "the" ultimate Stephen King collectible from the time I started collecting.

I am also very proud of three loose-leaf binders of correspondence from the early days of King's publishing career. But anything I don't have and then finally acquire has its individual moment of glory for me. To quote another supercollector from an interview I participated in for CBS TV in Bangor, "the excitement is in the hunt." Once you acquire something it goes on the shelf, not to be seen that often.

7. Can you give us some examples of what is currently on your "want list?"

There are a number of obscure magazines with King articles, whether by or about him that I still need. The most elusive items, though, are a few of the early Doubleday oversized Advanced Read Copies and some of the early British ARCs. Also, I am always looking to add more one-of-a-kind items such as correspondence and manuscripts to my collection.

8. Someone does not invest as much time and energy into collecting the work of someone who is only marginally interesting to them. Could you describe your personal feelings for the work of Stephen King?

I have read everything that he has published and many things that have not been published, and I really like at least 90% of it. That means that his writings really speak to me. Whether it is because of their literary merits, their ease of reading, or because I have identified a part of myself with his works, does the reason really matter? Rest assured I wait anxiously to read the next King written item I can get my hands on, and of course to collect same.

9. What are your Stephen King favorites, specifically novels, short stories, and movies?

Never an easy thing to do, pick favorites, so here, not in any order, and always subject to change, are a few:

- **Novels:** *The Stand, It, The Dead Zone, Hearts in Atlantis* (my college minor was Hearts and cafeteria), *'Salem's Lot, Misery,* I could go on...
- **Short Stories:** "Squad D," "The Raft," "Gray Matter."
- **Novellas:** *Apt Pupil* (really scary), *Rita Hayworth and Shawshank Redemption, The Mist.*
- **Movies:** *Misery, The Shawshank Redemption, The Green Mile, Carrie* (I know it may not be that good but I will never forget the end shot of Carrie's hand reaching out of the grave I jumped sky high), *The Stand* miniseries.

10. To conclude, why do you think Stephen King is, at the same time, an astonishingly popular writer, as well as an artist who is more and more being acknowledged as an important literary talent?

Because I am far from a literary critic, all my comments should be taken with a grain (maybe a whole shaker) of salt.

To me, Stephen King is the ultimate storyteller. He speaks in a language that is easily accessible and flows smoothly. The story does not get hung up in unnecessary words and descriptions. When you read King, most times you feel yourself a part of his stories, and maybe that is what adds to the horror and to our understanding of the human condition he portrays.

To quote King himself, his fiction is both populist *and* literary. In the beginning I liked him for bringing some of my own personal demons to the surface. Now I think I appreciate him more for pointing out the true horrors of the human condition, those that dwell in the human psyche. I believe that if we are aware of the dark side of our nature, we can better control it, and how we treat other people.

The Final Word

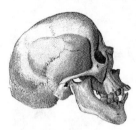

Stephen King: Survivor Type
By George Beahm

What can I say about the inestimable and gifted George Beahm that most of you don't already know?

How about that George Beahm is my Harlan Ellison?

In Stephen King's Foreword to Harlan Ellison's masterful collection *Stalking the Nightmare* (Chapter 98), King admits that if he were to have a heart attack in the middle of a strange city, the only person he would want by his side would be Harlan Ellison. Not his wife, not his agent, not anybody but Harlan. Why? Because Harlan would do whatever it took to keep him alive. King then goes off on this hilarious riff about Harlan running through hospital corridors carrying IV bottles and biting the heads off snooty doctors.

I feel the same way about George Beahm. If George were with me, I *know* I would have a fighting chance. George Beahm can fly *jets*, for heaven's sake. George is, if anything, *capable*—and to a level beyond that of mortal man.

King chronicler George Beahm curbside at the Kings' home.

All his extracurricular activities aside, though (he is a Major in the Air Force Reserve), nowhere does George's capability manifest itself more than in his writing. And "Stephen King: Survivor Type" is a quintessential example of just how good a writer George Beahm actually is.

The Major is the last voice heard in this book, and I can't think of anyone I would rather have draw the curtain on *The Essential Stephen King* than my friend, George Beahm.

☠☠☠

Stephen King is a survivor type.

For over a quarter century, King has survived the vicissitudes of everything life has thrown at him, from his early poverty as a child growing up in rural Maine to his heady success that has justifiably made him a household name.

King is proof that, as Harlan Ellison said, "...*anyone* can *become* a writer. ... The trick is not in *becoming* a writer, it is in *staying* a writer. Day after week after month after year. Staying in there for the long haul."

For King the long haul began when, at age 13, he wrote a short story that he considered publishable. After carefully studying the markets, he sent it off to *Alfred Hitchcock's Mystery Magazine*, which in due course turned it down, but it was a start. In his small bedroom that he shared with his brother Dave in Durham, Maine, Stephen King pounded a nail in the wall on which he impaled his first rejection slip; and as the years passed, when the nail couldn't support the dozens of rejection slips, he took it down and put up a spike.

The long walk. The long haul. The writer's path. King in search of his own dark tower.

☠☠☠

Since 1988 I've been to Maine on a regular basis, because my vocation required it. I've never gone up in the winter, though, because it's simply too cold. It's the one rule about traveling to Maine that I've never broken, at least until late January 2001 when I found myself in a Dodge mini-van with four other passengers who were also stranded at Boston's Logan Airport. We had to endure a four hour drive that put us into Bangor at 2 in the morning, 10 hours after we had been scheduled to arrive by plane. None of us had counted on an unexpected winter storm that shut down airports from Boston to Virginia. It wasn't the storm of the century —maybe the storm of the month—but it was bad enough to paralyze air traffic that weekend.

Later that morning, I turned the TV on to catch the local weather forecast and the weatherman cheerily reported that it was *one* degree fahrenheit. Great, I thought. Hope it warms up.

According to Stuart Tinker of Betts Bookstore, who has braved Maine winters all his life, this was one of the coldest winters on record and it hadn't gotten above freezing for at least a month.

I came to Maine because MSNBC had wanted to interview me about King, and I wanted to see them do a better job than CBS had done with the A&E biography on King, which was riddled with errors, large and small. I especially wanted to see MSNBC give due credit to Stuart Tinker as the co-owner of Betts Bookstore, instead of mislabeling him in a photo ID as "Book Collector."

During the course of several conversations with the producer, who admittedly hadn't read much of King's work, she asked me if I thought King had had it tough as a writer.

I told her that he certainly did. She, however, felt that he had enjoyed success at an early age, so, really, how tough was it?

Plenty tough.

What the producer didn't realize was that at 13, King had gotten his first rejection slip, with a handwritten note that encouraged him to continue. For the next eight years, however, there were no more personal notes on the rejection slips—nothing to tell him that he was on the right track ... or was he simply pursuing a fool's dream?

In January 1973 King submitted *Carrie* to Doubleday; the firm bought it in March but had to send a telegram to him, because the Kings had reluctantly removed their phone.

Four months later, however, King's life changed forever when *Carrie* sold to NAL. King, in due time, would earn $200,000 for his share.

At the ripe, "young" age of 27, three years shy of his 30th birthday, King was finally on the road to success. *Carrie*, published in 1974, made everyone sit up and take notice. Here's a writer to watch.

After many years of paying his dues, King was finally accepted in the club of professionally published authors. It was high time to put his career in high gear: He quit his job teaching high school English, for which he earned $6,500 annually, and soon got on with his life's work, his calling—telling stories.

☠☠☠

Considering that King began professionally submitting at 13 and finally published a book at 27, it meant that he spent 14 years to get up to the first rung on the ladder. It meant years of pulling stories out of his head, pounding away as a young teenager on a broken-down manual Underwood typewriter on days when his friends were outside having fun. It meant writing ferociously and reading ferociously, trying to find his own distinctive voice, a conscious decision to pull away from the gravitational pull of the writers who influenced him—John D. MacDonald, Don Robertson, and Richard Matheson. It meant writing what he wanted to write instead of writing what his classmates at UMO and his professors thought he should be writing: The Great American Novel, and reading Literature instead of popular trash.

It meant surviving as a *writer*.

To a non-writer, the sale of *Carrie* would seem sufficient proof that King had arrived, that his financial troubles were over. So wasn't it time to kick back and enjoy life a bit?

No.

As King knew, any such celebration would be premature. As any writer will tell you, the prospect of a *second* book is just as daunting as the first, perhaps even more so, because the bar has gone up: the publisher, booksellers, critics and readers have high expectations. Sure, King sold *Carrie*, and it was a helluva read, but could he do it again? Could he hit a home run again and knock the ball out of the park?

In my mind I see King at a baseball field. He's warming up near the plate and he picks up a bat, puts it over his shoulder, and swings it tentatively. It's a smooth, easy swing — graceful, in fact — but that bat doesn't *feel* right. He lays it down, picks up another bat. *This* one has the right heft, the right feel, and he swings it with the sure confidence of a player who had done this before countless times.

He steps up to the plate, taps his bat against his cleats to knock off the dirt, and assumes a ready position: His eyes focused on the man on the mound, his torso twisted to the left, his hands gripping the base of the wood bat, and his legs firmly planted on the ground. His muscles are tensed, ready to swing the bat with all his strength, because he wants to knock this one out of the ballpark. He balances himself on the balls of his feet, cocks the bat back as the pitcher winds up, and at the ball streaks toward him at nearly 90 miles per hour—a white blur coming straight at him — he explodes into action. He swings the bat, hitting the ball *exactly* where he had intended: the bat's sweet spot striking the ball square-on, launching it in a high arc as the spectators in the bleachers — King's publishers, booksellers, critics and fans—look up in awe at a small white object rising rapidly, out of sight, clearing the stadium walls to land in the field that surrounds the ballpark.

Grand slam!

King knew it when he connected bat to ball; he *felt* it, knew it would be a homer, and set out to round the bases. He had a crazy, lop-sided grin on his face.

That ball was *'Salem's Lot*, a deeply textured, rich novel that proved *Carrie* was no fluke. Although it was not a bestseller in hardback, *'Salem's Lot*'s success as a paperback reprint meant that King was doing what every writer *must* do: build an audience, word by word, book by book, earning a right to the reader's undivided attention.

To extend the baseball metaphor further, each book represents King getting up to bat. Sometimes, it's a bunt (a poem), or a single (a short story); sometimes, it's a double or triple (a novella), but most often, it's a home run (a novel), because that's what readers want ... and that's what King *delivers*.

☠☠☠

Norman Mailer once remarked that Truman Capote had survived the greatest shock facing a writer—critical and financial success at any early age. Mailer knew that early success can warp a writer, make him heady, seduce him. Fame, Mailer knows, can distract any writer from what's really important—the writing.

King clearly is demon driven, haunted by the years of early poverty, spurred on by the desire to simply tell stories.

Since *Carrie*—published over a quarter century ago—King realized early on that fame itself is ephemeral, and as substantial as pink cotton candy. Fame for fame's sake has never interested King, because it's fool's gold.

King derisively calls it the "cult of the celebrity," and he detests it because it focuses on the person and personality, and not the work.

For King, being famous means getting accosted in public for autographs, during meals at restaurants or at a ball game. It means getting tons of mail from a pool of millions of readers, each of whom secretly hope his letter is so unique, so special, that it will warrant a personal response. It means having to hire a secretarial staff to juggle your busy schedule —- time spent *not* in writing but in stoking the star-making machinery.

I sometimes think that no matter how difficult it was for King to write when he was living in those pre-*Carrie* days in Hermon, Maine, in a rented trailer, with kids underfoot, in that tiny furnace room and a portable Olivetti as his constant companion ... it was a more innocent time. Now, King has to worry about readers' expectations, the publisher's desire to see huge sales figures, the image of booksellers licking their chops, and the critics sharpening their knives—a universe of people and their sometimes unrealistic expectations build around one guy who sits in a room and pulls stories out of his head.

Case in point: On King's Web site, he points out that despite all the things written about *The Plant*, which he serialized online, the discussions have focused on its sales and marketing instead of discussions of the story itself. Let's get back to that, he says, because that's where the attention belongs.

That kind of diversion—distracting from the work and calling attention to the marketing of it—comes with the territory. It is no longer just the tale that his fans are interested in; they want to know about the one who tells the tale, as well.

☠☠☠

In *On Writing: A Memoir of the Craft* King discusses with his usual candor the demons that nearly did him in—his alcoholism and his drug addiction. Now that it's history, he felt comfortable in coming clean, so to speak, with his readers with whom he's always been honest. I screwed up, he says, and then I realized that the high price I was paying with the booze and the drugs was going to cost me everything that meant anything to me—my family and my writing—and I had to get back on track.

King is back on track. Even after a near death experience, a run-in with a mini-van near his summer home, King has stayed focused on family and fiction, because the former *is* life and the latter is his way of "getting up, getting well, and getting over," as he wrote in *On Writing*.

Since the accident, he's been spurred to literary activity, as if he feels his own mortality and is rushing to beat the clock, to tell the tales before the sands run out of the hourglass, so to speak: *On Writing* (Nov. 2000), *Secret Windows: Essays and Fiction on the Craft of Writing* (Nov. 2000), *Dreamcatcher* (March 2001), and new installments of *The Plant*. Currently in the works, *From a Buick Eight*, the sequel to *The Talisman*, and a collection of short fiction.

Contrary to what some people may believe—or want to believe—King is not slowing down. He is, in fact, going full steam ahead, writing at a ferocious clip, because the stories demand to be told.

It is true, however, that King is winding down the star-making machinery; he will no longer accept books in the mail for signing. Nor will he be touring to support *Dreamcatcher*. He's also spending a lot of time in the winter at his home in Florida, instead of dealing with the bitterly cold Maine winters.

It's time we as readers be thankful for what he has given us; and if he chooses to spend the rest of his life out of the public eye, he deserves it. The work has been more than enough, but King over the years has given so much of himself ... yet the fans demand more because they cannot be satiated.

☠☠☠

In an essay in *On Being a Writer*, Harlan Ellison observed that "...it is not a single book or story or play that wins or loses the day, it is the *totality* of what has been produced. Not a single hill, but a mountain range that stretches and rises and dips, and has sweep that can be judged."

That King has produced such a body of work, and in fact has inspired other writers to write about him and his work at such length, with such respect, is to King's credit:

King does not demand it, but his work does. Burton Hatlen, Douglas E. Winter, Drs. Michael R. Collings and Anthony Magistrale—all approach King's work with a sense of awe and a touch of reverence. All of these gentlemen realize that, as Harlan pointed out, the *totality* of the work is what will stand the test of time, and the critics be damned.

I think King's work will be read a hundred years from now, long after some of his contemporaries' books have faded, mercifully, into well-deserved oblivion. Either the literary work commands respect ... or it doesn't.

And King's work clearly does.

☠☠☠

Which brings me, finally, to the book you are reading, *The Essential Stephen King*, and its author, Stephen J. Spignesi.

It may seem to some to be an act of hubris for one writer to rank another writer's works, an admittedly highly personal and idiosyncratic listing that is guaranteed to stir the soup, to incite controversy, to invite discussion.

I think it's an act of courage. Let me explain.

No matter *what* order in which Stephen Spignesi has ranked the stories, fans will disagree. Reams will be written online in King discussion groups debating the merits of *this* choice or *that* choice, but I personally think that's what Steve wants his readers to do: to sit up and pay attention to King's stories, to give the stories their due respect—the same respect that he has shown in all the years that he's studied King, with an intensity that exceeds my own, with a reverence that makes me look like an acolyte, and with a pure, undiluted love that springs from his respect of fine writing, no matter the source.

When Steve published *The Shape Under the Sheet*, it instantly became a "must read" for King fans. Like Douglas E. Winter's ground-breaking book, *Stephen King: The Art of Darkness*, *The Shape* — a massive book that took shape for many years— also struck me as one long love letter to King, saying "I love your work. I respect it enough to spend years of my life studying it, chronicling it, giving it the most careful reading I can, and by publishing *this* book I'm sharing my love and enthusiasm of your work with the rest of the world. I'm *celebrating* it."

Since then Steve Spignesi has gone on to publish two meticulously detailed trivia quiz books, a book on the little-seen King (*The Lost Work of Stephen King*), and with this book — for the first time in the King field — a ranking of King's considerable canon.

Think about it: King and Spignesi share the same first name (both are Stephens), they live in the same geographical area (New England), they both are baby boomers, and they both celebrate pop culture. They also write using the same word processing program (Microsoft Word) on the same computers, Apple PowerBooks. The similarities, though, go far deeper than the obvious.

What ultimately links them together is a shared vision of what it means to be a writer. Both deeply appreciate what it means to have survived a lifetime of vicissitudes, of early rejections, of getting through life in order to write about it, and both realize that it's a privilege to have a readership that cares about the work.

I think King himself summed it up best, in *On Writing*, when he wrote: "Writing isn't about making money, getting famous, getting laid, or making friends. In the end, it's about enriching the lives of those who will read your work, and enriching your own life, as well."

Stephen King "entered" my life in 1975, when *'Salem's Lot* was published and he put his hook in me so deep that I eventually published seven books about him and his work. Stephen Spignesi entered my life in 1988, when I began writing *The Stephen King Companion* (1989)—a book that allowed me to live my dream as a full-time, freelance writer. Since that time, Stephen Spignesi has been a permanent fixture in my life.

In reading the work of both men, I have felt my life enriched almost beyond measure ... and I sincerely hope you have felt a similar enrichment, because in the end that's all that truly matters: A writer touching and enriching your life as a reader through the magic of writing.

—George Beahm
Williamsburg
January 2001

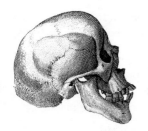

Index

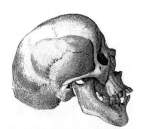

About the Author

Stephen J. Spignesi is a fulltime writer who specializes in popular culture subjects, including historical biography, television, film, American and world history, and contemporary fiction.

Spignesi—christened "the world's leading authority on Stephen King" by *Entertainment Weekly* magazine—has written many authorized entertainment books and has worked with Stephen King, Turner Entertainment, the Margaret Mitchell Estate, Andy Griffith, Viacom, and other entertainment industry personalities and entities on a wide range of projects. Mr. Spignesi has also contributed essays, chapters, articles, and introductions to a wide range of books.

Spignesi's 30 books have been translated into several languages and he has also written for *Harper's*, *Cinefantastique*, *Saturday Review*, *Mystery Scene*, *Gauntlet*, and *Midnight Graffiti* magazines; as well as the *New York Times*, the *New York Daily News*, the *New York Post*, the *New Haven Register,* the French literary journal *Tenébres* and the Italian online literary journal, *Horror.It*. Spignesi has also appeared on CNN, MSNBC, Fox News Channel, and other TV and radio outlets; and also appeared in the 1998 E! documentary, *The Kennedys: Power, Seduction, and Hollywood*, as a Kennedy family authority; and in the A & E *Biography* of Stephen King that aired in January 2000. Spignesi's 1997 book *JFK Jr.* was a *New York Times* bestseller. Mr. Spignesi's *Complete Stephen King Encyclopedia* was a 1991 Bram Stoker Award nominee.

In addition to writing, Spignesi also lectures on a variety of popular culture and historical subjects and teaches writing in the Connecticut area. He is the founder and Editor-in-Chief of the small press publishing company, **The Stephen John Press**, which recently published the acclaimed feminist autobiography *Open Windows*.

Spignesi is a graduate of the University of New Haven, and lives in New Haven, CT, with his wife, Pam, and their cat, Carter, named for their favorite character on *ER*.